RAVENWORD

AND

THE HOUSE OF THE RED DEATH

RAVENWORD

AND

THE HOUSE OF THE RED DEATH

JUSTIN MICHAEL GREENWAY

ISBN-13: 9780692896839
ISBN-10: 069289683X
Library of Congress Control Number: 2017908540
Wind Woven Pages, Portland, Oregon

This novel is dedicated to

Jodi Berg Caldwell

While I have the deepest appreciation for all my loved ones, whose faith, encouragement, and support enabled me to complete this project, the most validating endorsement a writer can have is someone who is willing to take the time to read their work. From an uncertain beginning, my dear friend, you read while I wrote, waited patiently for the next installment, and provided astute and intelligent feedback. You never treated my efforts like a pipe dream and always made me feel like an author. Your enthusiasm for the story and the characters fanned the flames of my motivation, for which I am so grateful!

Contents

Acknowledgments

Kirk Watson • William Hurtt • Will Parrish • Edward Farris • Chrisanthy Karis • Rose Roberts Bidney
There are times when even the best-laid plans and preparations are unable to meet the demands of an unpredictable reality. In those instances, I have been profoundly fortunate to have you in my life. Each of you has put your faith in me into action when life didn't go according to plan and thrown me a lifeline with no small measure of love and generosity. It is no exaggeration to say that I would have been lost without your friendship and all the fun and adventure we've shared. I hope this project validates your faith in me.

Gary Coats • Bret Finning • Eric and Neva Goodrich • Daniel Lebedies • Rand Benfiet
While it is impossible to list everyone who has touched this process, I feel that I would be neglectful if I didn't include these wonderful friends for getting me through the

challenges of a hostile world while pursuing my dreams with wine and nibblies, and humor and hospitality. Your love, kindness, and encouragement nourish my soul and sustain my faith in the future. Thank you so much for dreaming with me.

Jesse Demel • Steve and Debbie Demel
• The Demel Family

A substantial portion of this novel was written in the big, sometimes scary, home of Steve and Debbie Demel situated on six secluded acres steeped in the glorious gray of a Great Northwest winter. A writer couldn't ask for a better setting! It was no small leap of faith for you to let a room to an acquaintance claiming to want a situation in which to write a novel, despite my association with Jesse. Yet you welcomed me warmly and made me feel like a part of the family with hospitality beyond expectation, a lot of encouragement, and a healthy measure of accountability. I especially want to express my appreciation to Debbie for providing a sounding board for my writing process, sharing your wisdom, and nurturing me and my muse with a lot of tasty treats and conversation. I must also thank dear Jesse for suggesting the situation, challenging me at every turn, and enriching my life with so much joy and spontaneity!

Kirk Watson • Holly Handson

A special thanks to you, my beloved old friends. For nearly twenty-five years, neither of you have ever wavered from the belief that I would eventually be an author. Even when projects were started and never finished, you prodded me with the conviction that I am nothing if not a writer. In doing so, you reminded me of my true self, engendered a sense of attainability, and breathed life into my motivation. Thank you.

Patricia Dunley • Lottie Zorn • Dennis Fisher • Sandi Clinton • Rose Roberts Bidney • Daniel Lebedies • Eric and Neva Goodrich • Michael Timineri • Derek Byrne • Susie Jankowski • Brian Oldham • Tara Marion • Sophia Do

My dear GoFundMe contributors, thank you for believing in me enough to support my campaign with encouragement as much as with donations. It's no small gesture to be supported in such a way, and I appreciate your endorsement more than you know.

"I am liberty, neither judge nor justice. By the mercy of my right hand, suffering is ended, and by the tyranny of my left, hope is cut short. Your entire world has been created and endures by my hand, yet I am loathed by all creatures."

CHAPTER 1

The Invitation

THE MORNING DAWNS UNDER NEBULOUS battalions of dark clouds that stoop low to unleash their vindictiveness upon the waking landscape. The storm had been predicted, but the full-bodied violence of its fury had not. It is the type of disturbance that in ages past would have been considered a harbinger of some unforeseen misfortune, as if nature itself were aware of some dark blight forcing its way into the region. The oldest and strongest of trees bow beneath the dismembering onslaught of howling squalls that lash the town. Such storms are known to other regions, but in temperate California, this tempest has wrought a specter of an undefined dread. There seems something more to fear in the oppression than damage or calamity. A weight so heavy that not even the angry gales can dislodge it from looming ominously in the heavy atmosphere.

On the wings of this foreboding dawn have come eight invitations for Ravenword, a literary society associated with the local university. Braving the punishing weather, the modest fellowship has defied pernicious Poseidon to pass the morning in the distillation and cotton of their common bond. Their current volley of contentious banter surrounds a creased manuscript fragment in the hands of Vin Singh.

"That's not Poe."

From a deep slouch, a greasy-haired twentysomething casts a cold and incredulous gaze on the fragment and then on Vin.

William Jackdaw is better known as Billy by the few who acknowledge him as a friend and by more derogatory terms by most others. He is the most unlikely member of Ravenword, yet even those among his peers who look on him with disdain have come to respect his divergent insights. On this occasion, however, his tone does nothing except annoy them.

"I am aware of that," Vin rebuts. "It was written by Professor Fichtenberg."

The sound of jostling dishes leaches from beyond the shelves, crammed with mite-infested books like so many compacted teeth, to sequester them beside a quivering plate-glass window. Within the ring of musty wingbacks, the group exchanges bracing glances by a flash of lightning pressed through the creaky boughs of a sycamore.

"Cool! Where'd you get it?" Julia Nguyen trumpets, moving to examine the parchment.

"I found it in my complete works," Vin offers, passing her the parchment. "It was folded between the pages of 'Masque of the Red Death.'"

"It's from his novel!"

"His novel was crap," Billy carps as the wind splatters rain against the yawning window as if to punctuate his summation.

"That's your opinion," Vin rebuffs.

"Its sales prove me right."

Another gust rattles the glass.

The members of Ravenword rustle uneasily in the shabby chairs. The only exception is the pristine young woman with her hair pulled back so tightly that her eyebrows hover unnaturally high above her impeccably dressed eyes.

"Let's move on to this semester's club charity," Motisha interjects presumptuously.

The pair of fading goths in chairs pulled closely together look at her with the same tired expression. Well beyond the juvenile affectation of the subculture, their dark aesthetic testifies to their lingering affinity for the somber romance between eternal night and the breath of life.

"We've already chosen the Oak Park Youth Program," Agnot counters after savoring her hot chai. Known until the onset of puberty as Agnes Eleanor Roundhouse, she promptly disfigured her name in favor of her blossoming lesbian identity in the expression of gothic rebellion. *Disfigured*, by the way, was the adjective used by her mother's repugnance for the "phase" her daughter was going through. As an adult, however, it is her particular badge of honor, similar to others carried by those who have survived that struggle.

Motisha's bristle is camouflaged by a practiced smile and manicured disposition. "I was hoping we could revisit that decision."

The group grumbles in concert with the storm as Parson takes a ginger sip of his latte, looking at the imperious beauty like a nun with a mouthful of lemon. Weary of the ongoing antagonism between Motisha and Agnot, he quells the impulse to mediate. Parson has known many of the struggles endured by both women without, however, nurturing the hostility they've somehow construed as a necessity.

Motisha's hand moves from the armrest of her wingback chair to that of her boyfriend, T. J., and squeezes it firmly. "I would still prefer to pursue something that doesn't reinforce the stigma on African American youth."

"Jeezus christ, Mo!" Agnot erupts.

"Please don't call me that."

"We can't even consider it?" T. J. interjects.

Agnot's fervor is tempered by her respect for the collegiate athlete who forsook the glory of sport in deference to the words of his grandmother, which have been riveted to his soul by her love. "Terrence James Elders! The hell your family before you has gone through w' all be for nothin' if you throw away the thing that makes you equal as any white man: your brain! Education is the only equalizer, and only a fool would spit on that!"

Whereas T. J.'s fellowship in Ravenword is rooted in his grandmother's admonition, Motisha's primary motivation for participating in this small society is to offset any vulgar influences the company might impress on him. It is the influence of his gravitas, applied to her argument, that burnishes her countenance with a gratified gleam.

Charlie, Agnot's lover and best friend, issues a weary sigh. "Motisha, you agreed."

Julia sinks into her chair, hoping to avoid being drawn into another confrontation between Motisha and the lesbians. Behind her, the gusts throw the rain against the gray window angrily.

"Well, I've reconsidered," Motisha rebuffs. "And my father's firm has stated their preference for another choice as well."

"They're pulling their pledge?" Julia gasps, despite herself.

"I can't believe you!" Billy chides, lurching in his chair.

Vin leans into the circle swiftly with hands sweeping the air. "Okay, okay, this shouldn't be something we do grudgingly."

"There are a lot of other charities Ravenword can support," T. J. interjects.

"But we've already done all the legwork for the youth program!" Agnot growls through clenched teeth.

With a fleeting glance at Parson, Vin looks to Motisha. "What about the AIDS Foundation?"

"Why did you look at me when you thought of that?" Parson balks. "HIV/AIDS is not a gay disease. Twenty-eight million straight people are dying from it in Africa alone, and it's spreading through India and Russia faster than your sister on fleet week."

Julia giggles at Parson's gibe as the café lights flicker under the storm.

"And African American women are at the greatest risk in the United States," Motisha adds quickly in hopes of parlaying acquiescence.

Vin looks from Motisha and T. J. to the rest of the members. "So we've decided?"

One by one their reluctant affirmations congeal, and Billy's eyes narrow as they shift to Vin. "It's because of Fichtenberg, isn't it?"

The wind and rain continue to beat against the window as the company falls silent under the grave accusation. Beyond the exchange between glass and gale, however, a crackling yawn is chased by a stunning explosion.

Flying from the buttresses of the tiny kitchen, the bewildered proprietor is harrowed by the sight of the devastated café at the hands of the stricken sycamore. Dazed and dusted with debris, Ravenword pull themselves out from under the jagged tendrils of blitz-woven branches, shattered books and shelves, and decimated facade. As Vin finds his footing, Parson shakes the glass out of his golden hair. "I'm still in Kansas! How about you Dorothies?"

Julia steadies her trembling uncertainty against a branch and slaps the shards from her quirky ebony pigtails. Tiptoeing across the catastrophe through crunching glass and wind and rain, she makes her way along the downed limb with trepid fascination. Her face rises to the storm to gawk at the tree that has so abruptly ended their discussion.

"Wow!" she calls back to the company as she is quickly drenched. "It's like lightning struck it or something!"

Billy looks from his bloodied hands to the terrified Motisha, who is wrapped around T. J. "There was no lightning."

II

Living mere blocks from the unfortunate haven of New Halvetia, Vin bundles himself up against the battering elements, leaving the scene of sirens and surveyors to the ruins. Walking beneath the ranks of sycamores that line the streets like bullied titans, he passes with a hypervigilant awareness of their careening boughs and a visceral need for the confines of home. As he quickens his pace, the black and chrome bulk of a 1960 Matador pulls up beside him with Agnot hollering from the driver's window. "How 'bout a lift, V-spot?"

"It's not that far," he calls back without breaking his stride.

"Get in the fucking car!" Charlie yells from shotgun.

Succumbing to his want of shelter, Vin jogs into the street and around the batwing fins just as Billy lumbers up the weather-beaten sidewalk behind him.

"Oh shit," Agnot moans.

"Hey, can I get a ride?" Billy hails, his voice sailing on the gusts as he shuffles up to the rumbling embodiment of sinister affectation.

Agnot looks at Charlie and then into the rearview mirror to Vin, who leans over and unlocks the door from which Billy falls in with a gastronomic exclamation.

The lesbians grimace in disgust as Agnot puts the car in gear and pulls away.

"Goddamnit, Billy!"

III

Stalking a row of Victorian conversions, the grimacing Dodge wades into a large puddle that hugs the curb like a giant leech mottled by the elements before stopping. Vin exits on quick farewells and, rounding the back of the quavering behemoth, hurries to the sidewalk, where his eagerness to escape the day is tempered by a careful ascent up the glazed and dripping steps. Whereas the porch is usually deep enough to keep him from the weather, the aim of the relentless rain leaves him cowering as he retrieves his keys. As the front door swings open, his swift grab rescues the mail from the box before rushing into the comfort of his living room. A protestation of thunder is muted abruptly as he slams the door and, with a swift turn of the latch, locks himself against the ambiguous menace.

With a renewed appreciation for home and hearth, he crosses the room to the thermostat, rubbing his hands against the interred chill before removing his soggy coat. After placing it on the rack by the front door, he returns to the mail that he had thrown absently on the coffee table. Sorting through flyers and junk mail, he finds the only proper piece of postage is an ivory envelope postmarked from Italy.

Turning it over slowly, Vin prepares to open it when a clamor at his door startles him so abruptly that he jumps.

The ivory post slips from his grasp.

The barrage hammers the door violently and floods him with a rush of fear.

"Who's there?"

The terrible din subsides, and a low, disembodied moan prickles the hairs on the back of his neck.

The door looms in unsettling stillness.

With eyes peeled dreadfully and pores icing his skin, he leans to peer past the sheers.

"Hello?"

Despite the lingering daylight, he is unable to make out an offender.

"Is somebody there?"

The door erupts again with the terrible clamor, pushing him back, his fingers grappling for the light switch.

The anemic porch lamp sheds what light it can, but he can still see nothing beyond the curtains of the convulsive door.

The tumult subsides again, coaxing his fortitude and challenging his tolerance.

"Get the hell out of here, or I'll call the cops!"

Mustering his courage, he pulls his phone from his pocket and brings his face to the veiled glass, bracing himself for the reveal.

Nothing.

Vin waits as the reprieve swells into a disconcerting silence. He turns his phone in hand as his fingers find the latch. With senses piqued, he turns the lock slowly.

Throwing open the door with affected bravado, he is met only by a dappled porch and gushing eaves.

An uncanny gale shoves past him, yanking the door out of his grasp as it barrels into the house. Papers fly amid flailing curtains and harassed houseplants as Vin, shivering under the invisible influence, steps through the rush to examine the street. It is a desolation, as it has been all day, animated only by debris hassled by the storm to impersonate pedestrians in the wind.

Returning to the comfort of his apartment, Vin shuts the door with a bolstering sigh, locking it brusquely. Upon turning off the porch light, his blood abruptly curdles.

Past the sheers the reflection of a horrible figure stares back at him from the glass.

He spins on his heels.

His rush of fright is, again, met by nothing. His home is as empty as it should be. Glancing back to the pane, he realizes the reflection is merely that of a golden Lakshmi on her ornate throne, surveying the living room from the shelf in the corner above the lamp.

Vin indulges a nervous chuckle.

Another deep breath calms his drumming chest, and he returns to the ivory envelope waiting on the coffee table, strangely unmoved by the gust. Taking the envelope, he pauses and assesses the lamp next to the couch. He does not recall turning it on but assumes that he, like so many do, did so without thinking before being unnerved by the door.

Taking a letter opener, he slides the shiny blade under the lip of the envelope. Without warning, however, he finds himself suddenly in the blunting dim of the stormy gray dusk.

The lamp has gone out.

He surveys the room. His supposition of a power outage, however, is confounded by the clock on the DVD player glowing according to design.

Vin sits in the darkness with the shiver retracing his neck. He waits, silently applying all of his senses to his surroundings. Slowly he reaches up and turns the spindle.

The bulb bursts to life, washing the littered room with warm yellow light.

Vin grabs the remote and turns on the radio, hoping to shake the lingering ethereum. The new song from Rihanna is just beginning, comforting his nerves and filling the space with a moody, familiar air. Taking up the letter opener again, he cuts the envelope with one swift stroke, and an opulent invitation introduces itself. He draws it out and admires the beauty of its foil embossing and print. Opening it, he reads:

Kulvinder Singh
Ravenword Literary Society
California State University

You and your fellows are cordially invited to be my guests at the Castello Nel Buio in the environs of Northern Italy, wherein the elementals of Poe's famous work whisper in the marvelous ruins. Please find the invitation details included.

Your literary comrade,
Professor Thomas Fichtenberg

Fichtenberg. The name recalls the controversy that sullied the renowned professor and forced him from his tenure while Vin was still a student. Unfounded accusations, which in turn germinated vile rumors, swirled around the celebrated instructor—murmurs that could only be forgotten with his absence and the passage of time. For those who had been fortunate to earn a seat in his lectures, the injury and questions surrounding his flight have hardly abated. Now, five years later, the invitation arrives as if the tomb encasing that sullen history were yawning open.

Vin sets the invitation aside and removes the accompanying letter.

IV

"Have a nice night," Agnot says sweetly as Billy swings open the passenger door behind her. "Now get the fuck out of my car."

Billy smirks. Although tainted with genuine hostility, the sardonic jab is carried on an inclusive familiarity that makes him feel better about begging the ride. Charlie's farewell, however, is cut short by Billy's characteristically ill-timed slamming of the car door.

As if the lesbians have ceased to exist, he dashes through the downpour and into the courtyard of the small, dated, and seedy complex wherein resides his small, dated, and seedy apartment.

After using several keys in several deadbolts, Billy enters his apartment only to be halted at the threshold by a stunning waft of sour sick. His senses expand swiftly, as if his brain were keen to record every detail. The wind and rain of the deepening evening blow in behind him. The lights of the grimy apartment are all on, and Rihanna's smoky intonations weep from the radio. On the floor, a stain has been added to the multitude inflicted upon the worn and filthy carpet. Affixed to the rancid blight, his roommate lies blue-faced and rigid, surrounded by beer cans and half-eaten bags of stale ships.

The question of foul play insinuates.

Maybe he was poisoned.

Billy's fanciful imaginations are short-lived, however, as knowledge of the dead man's habits usurp any plot-worthy devices. Assessing the grim scene, he surmises that his unfortunate roommate had overdosed on something handy and choked on his own vomit. Regardless of the cause, he is most certainly dead.

Unmoved, Billy remains in the doorway, examining the scene with a morbid fascination purer than that of a rubbernecker, until his attention is drawn to an ivory envelope in the dead man's hand. He steps into the room, tossing the door shut behind him, and leans over the corpse. A draft of fetid feces slaps his nostrils, pushing him away from the body, but not before taking the letter from the lifeless hand. Flipping it over, he is surprised to find that it is a letter addressed to him from Italy.

V

The vintage Matador lumbers into a deserted parking lot with headlights sweeping the unyielding deluge to cast a stark glaze on the checkerboard of weathered postboxes beyond the plate glass. Charlie leaps out of the rumbling smog monster and dashes into the lobby.

A single ivory envelope waits inside the postbox like a spider in its hole as Charlie turns the key to open the diminutive door of number 2003. As she reaches in to withdraw the post, the wash of headlights revealing the face of the envelope is interrupted.

Italy.

Charlie turns, expecting to meet the source of the crossing shadow, only to find the lobby empty. Beyond the glare, she can see nothing.

• • •

Agnot's brow furrows as she watches Charlie stare into the light. She turns down the volume on Rihanna seducing the speakers with smoke and fire when a bludgeoning clap crashes her senses.

The world shatters.

Darkness smothers.

Just as her senses clear, the terror twisting Charlie's face freezes Agnot's blood as the Matador lunges through a curtain of exploding glass.

Charlie's screaming body tumbles over the hood.

Agnot's own howl fills her senses, only to be drowned by the bay of the building's alarm. Shoving frantically against the unyielding door, Agnot slams her elbow through the granulated glass and scrambles out the window with no thought of the jagged frame.

Raking the ruination wildly, Agnot finds Charlie crouched and sobbing behind a tumbled kiosk. Falling over her in untamed relief, Agnot's urgent cries are unintelligible even to her. As the two clutch each other madly, their dazed attentions are distracted by the groan of metal.

A fat urban cowboy slides out of the driver's side of the gnarled full-size pickup that has just launched the classic beast into the post office. His forehead is splayed grotesquely, and he falls to the asphalt with a bottle of Wild Turkey.

Meteoric raindrops dance on his back, sending blood into the rolling currents.

Again, sirens swell in the wet streets.

VI

T. J. makes his way through the dark hallway of a hospital. Every ten feet an auxiliary light pours meager illumination over his path. Ahead, Motisha sits erect on a gurney near the nurses' station. Her rigid expression does not wane with his approach.

"Did you call my parents?"

"Your mother is on her way," T. J. answers carefully. "You father is still in San Francisco."

"Is he coming?"

"Well…he asked me if you were hurt—"

"I *am* hurt! Would I be in a hospital if I weren't?"

"Minor lacerations and a bruised right femur," the physician reports as she steps out of a nearby doorway. She turns to the nurse and hands him Motisha's chart.

"Any news on when we'll get city power?" she asks as if Motisha were not stewing within striking distance.

"No, doctor," the nurse answers before returning to his duties.

"You'll be tender for a while but ambulatory," the physician states with finality.

Motisha's face blossoms with her practiced, patient, and polite smile but for her eyes, which burrow into the physician. "It doesn't feel bruised. It feels broken."

The doctor glances at T. J. with sympathetic resignation that turns to irritation when her gaze once again falls on Motisha. "Have you ever had a broken bone?"

"I needn't be a mechanic to know when my car is broken," Motisha counters defiantly.

"Maybe there's something you can give her that will help," T. J. suggests, taking Motisha's hand.

"I'm sure there is, but I think a prescription will do for now," the physician quips before retreating.

Motisha crosses her arms petulantly as the hairs on the back of T. J.'s neck prickle in concert with the cold swell in the core of his chest.

"What is that?" he hisses.

Motisha follows his strange and hawkish gaze into the dark hallway behind her.

There, in the islands of darkness between the utilitarian lighting, a stygian void slowly slides upward from the floor to the wall.

T. J. and Motisha stare wide-eyed.

Both can feel their stare returned from the inky depth of the queer blot and shiver.

The blackness seeps into the dark crook between wall and the ceiling. As if crossing a bridge, it squeezes past the light to creep closer.

"Nurse," T. J. calls hoarsely.

There is no response.

The atmosphere drains, as if there were suddenly no other living soul in the building.

The uncanny shadow creeps closer still.

"Nurse!" Motisha repeats in a chilled voice only slightly louder than T. J.'s.

The nurse arrives at their side, puzzled by their trans-fixed expressions. He waves a cautious hand in front of T. J.'s face.

T. J. starts violently and looks at him with a face drawn with horrible fascination. "Do you see it?" he whispers, his eyes leading into the darkness.

The nurse knits his brow and peers into the hallway.

Following their gaze, he moves into the corridor.

Motisha grabs T. J., pulling him close.

The nurse turns and looks at the two. "I don't see anything."

Behind him, the shadow yawns, as if unfurling black enveloping wings to devour the hapless man.

Motisha screams.

T. J. rushes him.

The auxiliary lights fail.

The nurse shouts.

Motisha presses her hands over her ears as T. J. screams.

The lights flicker to life.

Motisha forces herself to open her eyes.

T. J. is clutching the nurse and the hallway is empty.

"Jeezus christ! What the hell is the matter with you!" the nurse roars, shaking off T. J. and rushing away.

T. J. stands in a silent stupor, staring at Motisha.

"We did not imagine that!"

The physician emerges from around the corner with prescription samples in hand.

Motisha and T. J. are glazed in cold sweat.

"What the hell is going on?" the doctor snaps impatiently.

VII

Julia sits on her purple velvet sofa, engrossed in the images flashing from the television set that haunt the lush décor of her dark studio apartment with a blue cast. The two days since the incident at the café have remained tumultuous, as if the storm were reluctant to move into the Sierra Mountains to the east. Experience has taught that it is best to stay in during inclement weather, as most people forget how to drive when water is falling from the sky. Ongoing coverage of "*Storm Watch!*" on the local news only seems to aggravate the reckless tendencies of the population. This, coupled with the destruction of New Helvetia, has kept Julia settled snugly on her sofa, occupying her time with video voyeurism.

On the screen, a news reporter rambles on the shoulder of Interstate 80 at the gateway to the deep mountains, bundled in a hooded ski jacket against the elements as headlights trail past him.

The uniformity of those streaming lights breaks, and the picture is blinded by the swelling glare.

The feed becomes a jumble of chaos.

Screeching tires and shouting blast from the audio, exploding into a roar of gravel and crashing metal.

The scene quickly cuts to the stunned and ashen faces of the studio reporters.

Julia jolts on the sofa with the chiming of her cell phone, which startles her so abruptly that she can't help but giggle at the betrayal. Snatching the phone from the coffee table with one hand and the remote with the other, she turns down the TV as the opened invitation falls to the carpet in neglected abandon.

"Hey, Parson!"

She stands, fixated on the television. "I'm watching the news!

"No, no! They had what's-his-name up at Blue Canyon like they always do, and I think he just got wiped out by a car! ...I'm serious! ...Channel ten.

"Yeah, it looks like you missed the good stuff." She points the remote at the TV, a finger on mute, before stepping into her pantry-size kitchen and flipping on the light absently.

"I know!" she pipes, opening a cheery cupboard and pulling out a package of popcorn. "She loved that car more than *Warcraft*! There's a bad moon somewhere…"

As she tears the cellophane with her teeth, her eyes grow wide.

"No! Right there in the middle of the living room? Gross!"

Julia puts the popcorn in the microwave and flattens the envelope on the glass plate, riveted to her cell phone. "Okay, I'm sorry, but even Billy had to be freaked out by that!"

She taps the Popcorn button on the microwave and leans against the counter.

"Oh, spare me her drama. I don't know how T. J. puts up with her," Julia drones, rolling her eyes, as the microwave's oven light surges. "The one good thing about Charlie and Agnot is they'll have the money to go to Italy now."

She surveys the bowls smiling from the cupboards deliberately as Parson buzzes in her ear.

"I have no idea. It's not like I can ask my parents." Julia's eyes dart to the television screen, and she jumps up straight.

"Oh! I think they're going to show what happened to what's-his-name!" she squeals, rushing into the living room.

Behind her the microwave explodes, sending her to the floor and shrapnel into the walls.

CHAPTER 2

The Journey

AN UNREMARKABLE YELLOW TAXI PULLS up to the curb at San Francisco International Airport near the sidewalk check-in kiosk where a beleaguered T. J. is coordinating a gaggle of luggage with Motisha barking orders over his shoulder. The sky is a wide canvas of deep blue, which is unusual for the Bay Area, despite the fact that it is late May. Contrary to popular imagination, not all of California is perpetually washed in sunshine, even in spring, and nowhere is this truer than the sullen northern coast of the Golden State. For many, as attested by Samuel Clemens, their coldest winters were indeed summers spent in San Francisco, where the billowing fog is pulled in and out of the Golden Gate on the wings of the biting Pacific wind. But today all suggestion of gloom or calamity is vanquished in the disregard of sunlight and anticipation. Parson emerges from this taxi to the chorus of humanity's coming and going with Motisha's strident vocals taking center stage. As the cab driver moves swiftly to the trunk to transfer his luggage to the baggage cart of an approaching porter, Parson watches Motisha and T. J. with a devilish grin. After tipping the taxi driver and skycap, he strolls up to them, his eyes dancing from point to counterpoint.

"First class!" Motisha shouts over the noise of cars, public announcements, and passengers walking in all directions and chattering away in a world of their own. "First class!"

"It's world business class, honey," T. J. corrects as he and the baggage handler fumble in their haste to tag the cases.

Motisha scorns him with a glance, but he is too preoccupied with getting the luggage taken care of in the time she has allotted to notice. "World class, even better."

"No, no," the handler corrects through a burdensome accent, "all the same. Bags all the same, no class for them."

Motisha is just about to unleash on the unsuspecting attendant when Parson takes mercy on him and makes his presence known. "Jesus on a stick, the wealthy know how to travel!"

T. J. looks up with a grin, but the only offering Parson gets from Motisha is an impatient scowl. The athlete straightens and extends a hand that Parson waves back like a swarm of gnats.

"Handshakes are for business and pussies, which in this part of the city are the same thing," he chides, pulling T. J.'s tall frame into an embrace.

T. J. chuckles awkwardly, patting him on the back politely.

"Come on, Miss Bitch, you're not so mean as to scare me off," Parson levels at Motisha.

Her commanding facade drops momentarily, giving Parson his shot at a genuine exchange, but as soon as the hug is over, she's back on the handler like a spider on a fly. Parson and T. J. share a sympathetic sigh, and then Parson slips into the crowd. "See you on board or at Betty Ford!"

Inside he finds Vin, Agnot, and Charlie waiting at the gate, where panoramic windows showcase the bustling tarmac.

"Two lesbians and a straight man," he bellows, striding up to them with his arms outstretched.

Charlie smiles brightly and is the first to give him a hug.

"The perfect recipe for straight porn," he continues, moving on to Agnot, "or so they say."

Agnot's embrace is brief but sincere, while Vin braces himself for Parson's lingering squeeze. Parson, however, waves him back, feigning disinterest.

"No, I don't think you get one today, mister."

Vin's face drops with surprise as his cheeks flush with dejection.

"Oh, who am I kidding?" Parson gushes, wrapping his arms around him. Vin returns the tease with a bear hug that leaves Parson pulling away with a red face of his own. "Brute."

"We weren't sure you were gonna make it," Agnot says as Parson shoves Vin's shoulder playfully.

He composes himself and looks at the three proudly. "Well, I almost didn't. Some basher over on Hill Street didn't know who he was fucking with. I gave him one swing and then the beating of his life. While he was lying in the gutter crying like Lindsay Lohan in an orange jumpsuit, I kicked him in the ribs and asked him how it felt to get his ass kicked by a fag! Then I took his wallet and used his ATM card to supplement this little excursion to Italy."

"You did not!" Charlie gasps.

"Yes I did," Parson retorts defiantly. "The dumbass had his pin number on the back of his card, so I dragged myself up all pretty and pulled as much out of his accounts as I could. Whoever watches the surveillance camera will see Miss India Man at her most delectable."

"You kicked a gay-basher's ass?" Agnot echoes skeptically.

"I haven't gone to the gym every day for the past six years just to look gorgeous at the beach—which I do. It's a dangerous world, and we've got to take care of ourselves."

Julia suddenly appears at their side, jumping up and down giddily and convulsing with eager giggles.

Parson quickly drops his austere stance and joins her pogo.

"I wonder how many people he's got in that head," Agnot quips.

In full bounce mode, Julia grabs Parson and wraps her arms around him before bounding to Vin, whose attempt at hugging her while she bounces causes their friends to snicker. Moving to Agnot, Julia makes a genuine attempt at subduing her effervescence, but it only changes manifestation. Instead of jumping up and down, she runs in place like a child waiting outside a bathroom.

"Parson was just telling us how he got spending money for the trip," Charlie reports upon her turn.

Julia's jubilation deflates and she turns back to Parson. "I hope it didn't involve a microwave and three months of physical therapy."

The voice over the PA system announces the boarding for their flight, interrupting the exchange and pressing them to grab their carry-ons and tighten up in line.

"Where's Billy?" Julia asks, rolling one of her rings around her finger.

Vin answers quietly. "I don't think he was able to get the cash together."

II

After the customary queue and shuffle, the five settle into their own little block of coach seats near the back of the plane. Vin's first act is to put his face to the window and survey their surroundings.

"Hmm, the fog is rolling in," he observes, "and fast."

Julia sets her knees on her seat between him and Parson and leans across to replace his face at the window. "That's weird."

"Honey, it's going to be hard for me to have a conversation with your ass if you keep moving it around like that," Parson rebukes with a playful spank.

Behind them, Agnot rolls her thickly mascaraed eyes. "Yeah, fog in San Francisco—that's really fucking weird."

Julia turns to hover over the back of her seat and face her antagonist. "Agnot."

"*Julia.*"

"It's like some creepy presence is—"

"Oh shit," Charlie moans, bringing the playful vignette to a sudden close.

"There's your creepy presence," Agnot follows quickly, nodding toward the front of the plane.

Billy is driving toward them with a dangling backpack careening dangerously past the heads of the unfortunate passengers in the aisle seats.

Julia turns and catches his attention with a fanning wave, which prods him to quicken his pace, much to the dismay of those who have been watching his haphazard approach.

"Good afternoon, ladies and gentlemen," the captain's voice announces from overhead. "The tower has cleared us to get going ahead of schedule, so if you will please take your seats and buckle up, we'll get on our way."

"We're really getting socked in," Vin reports from his window as the engines wind up and the plane backs out.

Ahead of them a flight attendant takes the stage to recite the safety procedures, and Billy plops down in the seat next to Charlie.

"So…" Charlie begins, searching for the most diplomatic confirmation of her own misfortune as she can manage, "… you're sitting here?"

"Yeah. Why?" Billy replies defensively.

"No reason," Charlie says with a plastic smile.

Agnot leans forward and looks at him through narrowed eyes. "You do one disgusting thing, and I'll give you a mile-high beating. Got it?"

Billy shrinks into the back of his seat, and Julia shoots Agnot a silent rebuke.

"You can sit next to me," she chimes happily, nodding to Parson.

"Sure, the lesbians and I can be the queer line of aerial defense."

"Just don't do anything gross, okay?" Julia adds quickly in her sweetest tone.

"Thanks. Maybe I'll take you up on it later," Billy answers before reaching down into his backpack and retrieving a surprisingly well-cared-for hardbound.

Julia notices the raised eyebrow of the flight attendant at the back of the plane and rights herself, snapping the seatbelt in place with a giggle.

III

The jetliner is soon in the air with the San Francisco Bay shrinking behind and the six members of Ravenword tossing idle talk between them. In business class, T. J. is reclining with a warm hand towel over his eyes as Motisha is returning her improperly prepared cocktail to the attendant when a bout of turbulence rattles the fuselage.

The plane lurches, sending T. J.'s hand towel to the floor.

Motisha's fingers dig into his arm.

"We're okay," he assures, patting her hand and looking to the jostled attendant making her way back to the service station with Motisha's drink like a cat on a trampoline with a six-year-old.

The seats begin to tremble, prompting Motisha to release her grip in favor of her seatbelt, much to T. J.'s relief.

"This is your captain. Looks like we've come up on some unstable air. Please remain seated while we try smooth things out for you."

Overhead, the seatbelt indicators light up.

A second pitch throws the passengers forward, and the cabin lights dim.

The turbulence melts into a sluggish glide. The lights do not return, but the low setting draws a relaxed sigh from Motisha. She sits back and closes her eyes contently, savoring the ethereal ease of the carrier's momentum. She soon remembers, however, that she is due a cocktail and turns to stare down the flight attendant.

The aisle recedes darkly, yet she can make out a pale figure huddled in the back and convulsing. Annoyed at the prospect that the woman is wasting time laughing, no doubt flirting, with someone in the shadows while she waits for her drink, Motisha raises her hand and snaps her fingers. The wan attendant nods to the order and straightens. A moment later she is approaching.

Could she be any slower? Motisha gripes in the glacier of her mind.

As she draws closer, Motisha's irritation bleeds away. The woman seems horribly pale, as if her arteries have been cut at the ankles.

Motisha stares. *How can a flight attendant be airsick?*

The attendant looms, extending a dubious cocktail. Gray circles bag her eyes, and perspiration blisters her forehead and upper lip.

Motisha recoils.

The woman's thin, purple lips issue a shallow, nearly inaudible apology.

A sinister cold bites Motisha's fingers as she takes the glass absently.

A tiny bead of crimson blooms on the brow of the sallow incubus and methodically trails her ghostly face.

Motisha's eyes are wide and track the bead until it dangles on the woman's jaw.

It releases to dive and expand cloud-like in the cocktail.

Motisha throws the glass to the floor. Grappling wildly with her seatbelt, she bolts to her feet. "What is the matter with you? How can you be serving drinks? You're going to get us all sick!"

Before the rant is expelled, T. J. is checking her with the same expression of shock and confusion as the surrounding passengers.

Dumbfounded, the attendant can only gape as her crewmates rush to her side.

Motisha falls silent, blinking at the lovely attendant, who is suddenly a vision of youth and health.

The cabin is bright and permeated with the monotonous droning of the engines.

Motisha grapples for T. J.'s hand as her brain reels.

Confounded, he takes her hand with a reassuring squeeze.

Her mouth stretches into an assumed smile as her posture stiffens. "Excuse me, where is the ladies' room, please?"

Speechless, the attendant gestures toward the service station.

"Thank you." Motisha clasps her hands at her waist, turns in an about-face, and proceeds down the aisle, throwing her head and shoulders back in a rigidly dignified display of composure.

"What was that about?" the second stewardess asks the first as they make their way back to their station.

"I have no idea, but it's too early in the flight to have someone freaking out," she replies churlishly, trying to shake the incident from her nerves.

"Well, I'd better go back to coach. I doubt there's anyone on the plane who didn't hear that."

IV

"Did they let you see her?" Julia asks as Parson returns to his seat.

"Not at first, but then I told them she's my snooty older sister," he answers, taking his seat beside her sideways to face the group.

Agnot looks at the blond-haired, blue-eyed Caucasian incredulously.

"What?" he sings with a shrug. "I told them she was adopted."

"Is she okay?" Vin checks.

"What happened?" Julia interjects.

"Couldn't tell ya. She just freaked out, and now her lips are tighter than Hemsworth's abs."

"Who the hell is Hemsworth?" Billy asks, with little interest in Motisha's drama.

Parson's eyes scroll over Billy. "Never mind."

With new and rich fodder, the five dissect the intriguing vignette as the airliner carries them over the continent, leaving Billy to his book. As the plane leaves the eastern seaboard, night overtakes the flight rapidly, and they follow the cue of dimming lights in a bid to sleep in the cramped confines of coach. In business class both Motisha and T. J. slumber soundly in the cradle of sedatives provided by the very accommodating crew.

Crack!

Vin is torn from his rest by the stunning clap. His bleary eyes dart to the window as a blazing bolt ravages the wing. Fiery fractures race to the fuselage, harrowing him to the core.

Crash! Roar!

Julia wakes screaming as the ceiling is ripped away!

Debris is sucked into the thunderous black stratosphere. Corpses in the surrounding seats, bloated and purple, compound Parson's horror as they quake grotesquely in the tempest.

Shrapnel from an exploding engine blasts Agnot's window, splaying it with fractures as the plane pitches. Gasping in the hurricane of decompression, she turns to Charlie amid the clarion groan of splitting metal.

A voiceless scream taps Charlie as seatbelts snap around her like minds in a madhouse. Rising like demons, the dead tumble through the cabin to the abyss of the growing breach.

Aghast, Billy watches the last of the corpses sail by in a concert of grotesque thuds and crunches.

The front of the plane tears away, sending Ravenword strapped to their doom.

Shrill screams jar the passengers from their slumber as stricken flight attendants sweep to the heart of the primal alarm to find the six howling and convulsing in their seats as if wired to electric chairs.

"Stop it!" an attendant shouts, shaking Parson frantically. "Stop it!"

Vin's eyes fly open and spin in confusion.

"Stop it now!" the attendant shrieks as another attendant begins shaking Billy and Charlie.

Both wake with the same crazed and terrified expression.

Parson grapples with his seatbelt.

Charlie and Agnot lunge in their seats, gasping, as if breaking the surface of a pool.

All eyes, fear-riddled or vexed, are fixed upon Ravenword. The terrible ethereum of the nightmare lingering like a spell until it is broken by a barking voice ordering them out of their seats.

Under the hard and forceful glare of a rigid and imposing man, the six file to the station at the back of the plane in contrite obedience as the flight crew attends the cabin full of shaken travelers.

Barricading the aisle with his commanding form, the stern agent surveys them one by one. "A stunt like that warrants charges."

Vin looks at his companions and then to the man who, by his bearing and authority, Vin assumes to be an air marshal. "It wasn't a prank. I dreamt the plane was struck by lightning."

"Twice," Julia adds fretfully.

"Three times," Agnot corrects.

The six look at each another with faces drawn in horrible wonder, their minds wrestling against the implications.

"Were there dead bodies in yours?" Parson whispers, his voice faltering.

"Yeah, they were being sucked out of the plane," Billy answers flatly.

"This is impossible!" Charlie cries, clutching Agnot.

"And then we fell," Julia finishes. "The front of the plane broke off, and we fell."

The agent assesses Billy momentarily, his instincts insinuating that the youths are not lying. "Pull yourselves together."

"I think it's time you return to your seats," the lead flight attendant chides.

"No," the man counters, looking to the attendant gravely, "give them time to shake it off. Something to drink would help."

"You don't—" she begins, only to be interrupted.

"My treat," he interjects sharply. "I'll take one too."

V

The flight into Europe's gray morning is restless and drawn for everyone on the plane but happily uneventful. The arrival of Ravenword in Paris is equally subdued, save for the scornful glares and murmurs from their fellow passengers. The disdain of those traveling on to Milan, however, is palpable but tempered by the compulsory mad dash en masse to the gate of their connecting flight.

Motisha and T. J., kempt but not fresh, are already boarding while their six cohorts wait in a line headed by a flock of
nuns in classic black-and-white habits. Their Italian banter
and jovial laughter gives Vin a sense of relief, while Agnot
wonders how many of them are lesbian. Parson, travel-weary
as he may be, is not so beleaguered to allow any of the attrac-
tive Frenchmen to escape his attention. His bleary eyes smile
with every unspoken salutation from a handsome passerby.
Most of this is lost on Charlie, whose head is propped on
Agnot's shoulder while Julia sits wilted on the floor behind
them, holding her head in her hands. Trailing, as usual, Billy
continues to bury his oily face in a black-bound hardback.

To everyone's relief, the wait is brief, and they are soon
boarding. The six coach-class members of Ravenword sink
into their seats without speaking, sharing the hope of more
and peaceful sleep. In business class, Motisha shoos away the
attendant with a wave of her hand as she reclines and closes
her eyes to enjoy the music feeding through her headphones.
But this particular attendant is French and has little patience
for spoiled Americans.

"Mademoiselle will upright her seat, s'il vous plaît," she
orders with icy professionalism. "We must all be in order for
takeoff."

T. J., seeing the sharp seriousness behind the attendant's
polished smile, pats Motisha's hand earnestly.

She opens her eyes and glares at the attendant as she
pulls the headphones from her head.

"Mademoiselle will upright her seat, s'il vous plaît," she
repeats, returning Motisha's glare without flinching or sac-
rificing her smile.

Surprised by the attendant's fortitude, Motisha offers the flight attendant her most dour smile and uprights her seat. "I've traveled all the way from *California* and am quite tired."

"Then you would not want to do anything to prolong the flight, oui?" the attendant replies before turning away. "Merci."

"Je voudrias le mimosa, s'il vous *plaît*," Motisha volleys before the stewardess can get away. "*Merci!*"

T. J. sinks in his seat, well aware of how this stretch of the flight is going to unfold. As the engines roar to life, he offers Motisha a weak smile.

VI

Unlike Paris, Milan hits their senses like a chorus of opera singers. Whether due to fatigue or distraction, de Gaulle seemed harried and stifling, whereas Linate is animated, colorful, and laced with a mixture of elusive aromas. To everyone's surprise, Motisha is waiting for them at the gate.

"None of us stole anything from you, Miss Sis, so you can go on ahead and get your bags," Parson quips as the manicured masses sweep past them.

"Actually, my *luggage* is being forwarded to my hotel."

Motisha's deflection is answered with raised brows and a variety of exasperations.

"So you're not coming with us to the castle?" Agnot surmises in the driest tone she can conjure.

Motisha looks at the disheveled group of collegiate pedestrians, struggling to suppress her blithe smile.

"No," she answers bluntly. "I have no interest in a bus and donkey ride into the back hills of Italy when Milan awaits."

Parson crosses his arms, looking at her like a mother catching her child after curfew. Charlie's weary countenance, however, brightens at the prospect of a Motisha-free holiday. Julia simply stands staring at Motisha in disbelief, while Billy continues to read his book, camouflaged in apathy.

"You came all this way to shop?" Vin stammers, stunned by her decadence.

Motisha's smile is just about to crescendo when she notices a small, dark figure beside her. With the rest of Ravenword, her attention is drawn to the shriveled old woman standing with dark, wild eyes transfixed on them as if she were witnessing the horrors of her history.

"Excuse me," Motisha says with gelid politeness. "Can I help you?"

The old woman lifts her tortured eyes from the company as a whole to meet Motisha's, and her freckled hand rises to meet her wrinkled gasp.

"La clemenza," she whimpers in an old-grain Italian dialect.

A blanketing darkness falls upon them with the utterance, vanquishing the cheerful greeting of Italy and leaving only the old woman's anguished face. Her stare descends on them one by one, like a cold draft. Motisha takes T. J.'s hand, and the rest of Ravenword tighten their ranks.

A sun-beaten old man steps through the blanketing dread and takes the old woman's arm, nodding apologetically as he tries to pry his wife from her dark perch. "Perdonarci, per-donarci," he begs. "Venuto, Maria, venuto."

Stiffly, whispering "la clemenza" like a skipping record, she gives in to his lead, yet her tortured gaze does not break until they are swallowed up by the throngs.

The ominous vapors diminish with her vanishing, returning Ravenword to the sights and sounds of the airport.

"Absolutely," Motisha trumpets as if the old woman had never appeared, snapping the company back to the contention at hand. "I come to Milan every spring. You go and do whatever it is you are planning to do for two weeks, and I will be 'vivere la vita Italiana.'"

"I can't believe you!" Agnot carps.

"Why didn't you tell us?" Vin presses T. J., who stands beside her sheepishly.

"He does not have to explain himself to you!" Motisha snaps.

"I didn't think it mattered," T. J. defends.

Charlie and Julia trade exasperated sighs as Parson tries to intercede. "I think Motisha is better suited to staying in Milan and shopping like the lucky bitch that she is while the rest of us have our own adventure."

"It's just that we RSVP'd for eight," Vin admonishes gently.

"One or two fewer persons will not make a difference," Motisha interjects, her flawless complexion flushing with anger.

"What do you mean one or *two*?" Vin checks, his own tropical cheeks reddening.

Motisha smiles at T. J. as if she were about to present him a surprise gift. "I've booked the accommodations for us both."

"What?" T. J. blurts, genuinely surprised.

"I knew you wouldn't agree to my making the arrangements if I told you in advance," she explains with bright, hopeful eyes, "but now that you're here, just think of what a wonderful time we could share."

"So all the arrangements we made don't matter," Charlie interjects.

"I don't see why you can't accommodate a little flexibility," Motisha replies in a saccharine tone.

"It's rude," Agnot carps.

"Oh no! You do not lecture me in that regard!"

The crack of a hardbound book slapping the marble floor silences the mêlée abruptly.

"What's your problem? All you guys did was bitch over being stuck with her for two weeks, so why don't you just shut the fuck up and let her do her thing!"

With that Billy grabs his shabby backpack and shuffles down the terminal, leaving Ravenword dumbstruck at his back.

VII

Motisha's face reaches through the window of the taxi to meet T. J.'s. Their kiss is brief, and while T. J. looks on her with tender regard, Motisha chances a fleeting glance at the company.

"You call me as soon as you change your mind," she says softly, squeezing his hand.

T. J. steps back as the cab pulls away to dodge and challenge the traffic beyond the line of coaches at the curb. The departure of the next coach eclipses her quickly, and he returns somewhat bashfully to the rest of Ravenword.

"Black?" Julia moans as the next bus pulls forward. "Why do we get the black one?"

"It'll only be a few minutes," Vin proffers. "The station isn't far."

Ravenword stand in the brisk morning air, watching reluctantly as the door of the polished ebony coach opens with a hydraulic whisper. The eager commuters behind them, however, provide no opportunity for hesitation. Sooner than they would like, their luggage is stowed, and the darkly tinted windows are subduing the bright environs of the city. Billy shuffles evasively to the back of the bus, where he crumples into a corner and hides himself behind the bindings of his book. The remaining six fill the first three rows behind the driver, unfazed by his petulance.

Giggles rise behind Vin and T. J. as Julia slaps Parson playfully. In the seats in front of them, Agnot and Charlie are relishing the Italian architecture beyond the windows in low and intimate tones. Beside him, Vin checks their itinerary, leaving T. J. to the full, uncomfortable brunt of the commuters filing past them. Like a parade of eyes, the boarding passengers stare invasively.

T. J. can feel his cheeks and ears warming and tries to distract himself with the finials Charlie is pointing out on a nearby building. Her voice, though, seems muffled and distant, as he cannot break his awareness of the Italians congesting the aisle. Not as quickly as he would like, the seats fill and the bus pulls away from the curb with a gentle tug.

Ravenword are suddenly ripped from their individual microcosms into the confusion of a disembodied cry, the lurching of the bus, and the screeching halt.

The howl of a banshee rises like a siren from the street, and the cabin explodes as the Italians leap to their feet, craning their necks to gawk at the tragedy.

The chaos expands exponentially as the commuters pour out of the coach behind the stricken driver. The seven, however, remain seated and stoking their collective denial. Charlie buries her face in Agnot's shoulder, and Agnot looks back at Vin and T. J. with haunted eyes. Julia and Parson simply stare past them at Agnot, sharing her stunned horror.

Whistles and sirens overwhelm the shouts and cries channeled into the bus from the open door. A moment later, a police officer is gesturing to the Americans. "Via dall'autobus, per favore."

Needing no translation, they stand and file out of the coach somberly. Their emergence into the sunlight is punctuated by their own involuntary gasps and a terrible squeal from Julia. The broken body of the crone who had shrouded them in her spell in the terminal is sprawled on the hot pavement. Her inconsolable husband is wailing over her.

Security and police keep the crowding bystanders at bay as Ravenword are ushered away from the awful scene by an officer. As paramedics rush past them, shoving gawkers out of their path, an unspoken accusation hangs over the company, and the old man falls strangely silent.

As a paramedic gently maneuvers the little gray man out of the way, the old Italian's eyes fall on the seven Americans. With his gaze, the collective attention of the crowd rests upon them, arresting the momentum of their retreat.

As if summonsed, they each turn to look slowly over their shoulders.

With eyes nightmarishly transfixed, the old man raises a crooked and incriminating finger at the seven. His mouth gapes with a grotesquely writhing tongue. A scream, as if the old man were meeting death incarnate, tolls from his hollow and tortured throat.

The men of the crowd rush in to catch the withered gaffer as he clutches his chest and swoons.

Women gasp and shriek.

Taking advantage of the terrible distraction, the officer sweeps the Americans behind the line of coaches and out of sight. Visibly shaken, he gestures to them to stay put and then rushes over to a group of coachmen waiting for clearance as if the death of a pedestrian were routine.

With hopeless resignation Vin looks at his companions. Julia is crying in Parson's arms with T. J. standing over trying to comfort them both. Charlie and Agnot are wrapped tightly around each other and shaking. It is then that Vin realizes Billy's absence. Panning their surroundings, he finds no sign of their disheveled companion but instead the recognition of an unexpected and familiar visage.

The agent who had threatened them with charges on the flight to Paris stands between the buses speaking with the young police officer, who is now pointing in their direction. His eyes meet Vin's and within seconds he is making his way to them with determined strides.

"A dead elderly woman and six screamers, and...?" the man observes, his tone grave and humorless. He turns to T. J. "You were with the hysterical woman."

"Yeah, sorry about that."

Vin and the other four tighten ranks around T. J., wearing similar expressions of curiosity and apprehension.

"What are you doing here?" Vin asks, issuing the question that could have been posed by any of them.

"You know him?" T. J. follows, surprised and puzzled.

"No," Agnot states abruptly. "Let's go."

The company is surprised by Agnot's interjection but doesn't challenge her. A wary bond unites them, but as they turn to find their new bus, Julia casts an apologetic glance back.

"Where are you headed?" he calls after them.

"Lucca," Julia pipes to the consternation of her companions, who check her with collective groans.

"What?" she exclaims in a hushed voice with her head low and cocked. "He's a cop. Don't we have to answer his questions?"

Agnot grasps Julia's arm and pulls her ahead of the group like an errant child. Julia doesn't resist, but her smirk communicates her annoyance and incredulity.

"We'll miss our train," Vin offers weakly, too tired to mediate. "I'll find Billy."

Charlie's gentle squeeze on Agnot's shoulder tempers her frustration with Julia, who jerks her arm out of the grasp and glares back at Agnot. Behind them T. J. and Parson try to keep an eye on the stranger as covertly as possible.

"Who told you he's a cop?"

Julia's face turns like a page in a book from resentful to confused.

Agnot waits, watching the gears in Julia's head turn.

Julia scrunches her nose contritely.

At the same time, Vin finds Billy standing at the edge of the perimeter created by the police. The doors of the ambulance are just shutting out Billy's view of the old woman's body when he turns and steps right into Vin.

"What the hell?" Vin rebukes, dismayed at Billy's repugnant brashness.

"What?" Billy rebuffs.

Vin blinks back at him, at a loss for words, the crowd around them dissipating quickly.

"Oh, we got a new bus," Billy notes with a chilling ease.

Vin can only gape as they hasten to board with the others.

T. J. steps back to let Billy climb into the bus as Vin follows close behind.

Vin steps onto the coach but pauses when he realizes T. J. is not coming up behind him. Turning, he finds the reluctant athlete fidgeting on the curb.

"What are you doing?"

"I'm not going," T. J. blurts, stifling the sense of betrayal.

"What!" Vin shouts, at the end of his rope. "You're going to stay here with her?"

"It's just getting too weird," T. J. asserts. "And now we're being tailed by that guy. I just can't."

"Fine!" Vin retorts. "Go *shopping*!"

Before he can rally a defense, Vin storms into the bus and the door shuts T. J. out of the company.

Ravenword stew silently on the brief drive to Milano Centrale. Five of them attempt to use the defection as a means to shake off the black accident. Unfortunately, that line of reasoning only brings them back to the dark odyssey that their journey has become, which, in turn, draws them full circle back to the accident. But it is the macabre disposition of the sixth that unsettles Vin the most and he wonders how well they really know Billy—or one another. A dark shadow sets on his brow as he ponders what might lie ahead.

VIII

Not even the warm and spectacular Italianate facades of Milano Centrale are able to lift the six remaining members of Ravenword from their despondency. Their silence contrasts the bustling voices and booming announcements as they navigate under the colossal vault of grand arches. The rays of the bright midmorning sun filters through the innumerable square panes of the skylights bridging the arches to fall on Vin's crinkled copy of their itinerary. He pauses to get his bearings, bringing the group to a halt like a brood of chicks beneath a mother hen.

Julia shifts her weight to one leg and cocks her pigtailed head upward to take in the golden blush of the neo-Renaissance walls while letting a deep sigh tumble from her lips.

"I'm tired of being creeped out and bored."

Her fellows remain quiet as Vin pans the cavernous station.

Julia repeats her propeller-esque sigh and shifts her weight.

"So," she begins slowly, testing the waters, "if he wasn't a cop...?"

Charlie, who is resting her head on Agnot's shoulder, looks up at her lover for signs of a response. Agnot does not oblige, choosing instead to imitate Billy and ignore the lure.

"Or," Julia continues, "a marshal...?"

Vin catches a passing attendant to get directions and Julia deflates over her failed attempt to pull them out of their gloom. Parson reaches over and pulls her into a hug, shaking his head and shrugging as Vin rushes back to the ensemble frantically tapping his watch.

"We've got to hurry!"

With that, he hurls himself into the station, pulling a startled and bewildered Billy by the sleeve.

"Come on!" he shouts behind him.

Like a diminutive stampede, they trail behind with their backpacks dancing over their shoulders and tightly packed duffel bags swinging to their frantic gait. Sweeping through the crowds like leaves through a picket fence, the six spill onto the platform cradling train 595 and dash to the closing doors with desperate shouts.

The platform is empty save an attendant, who stares at them with the rest of the passengers as the conductor steps out of character and holds the train for the young tourists.

His dour greeting does little to dampen their gushing gratitude as they file by. Checking their tickets, he points into the car without speaking and then scurries into the adjoining car as if the six were plague ridden.

Panting, they file down the narrow aisle one by one, searching for empty seats to no avail. Regardless of being late, the group quickly realizes the pitfalls of traveling on a general ticket. As they press past clusters of stalwart standing passengers, the concept of overbooking is added to their lesson. At the end of the car, a gap opens at the elbow, small but empty, where Vin turns to his companions after surveying the car ahead.

"Looks like this is it," he says over the racket of the wheels, dropping his duffel bag in the corner.

"Who cares, as long as we can sit down," Billy spouts, crumpling to the floor.

"That was fun!" Julia trumpets gleefully, falling onto her own duffel.

"We'll probably have to do the same thing in Viareggio," Vin announces, following Julia's example and sitting on his duffel bag. "We only have fourteen minutes to find our connection, and I'm sure the train will be just as packed."

"At least it's not too hot," Julia proffers.

"What is this, *The Amazing Race*?" Agnot grumbles, trying to catch her breath.

"One team down," Parson quips, jostling Billy for space.

"Parson!" Julia rebuffs, afraid the group will relapse into their somber malaise.

Billy, having no interest in anything outside his book, slides over, and Parson plops down beside Julia with a playful grin. "Maybe it's a speed bump, and they're corralling goldfish in bikinis down the catwalk!"

Charlie and Vin both let out a laugh amid Julia's and Parson's giggles. Agnot rolls her eyes but can't repress a smile, while Billy remains hidden behind the hardbound. It is only his irritation with Billy that brings the title of the book to Vin's attention: *The Castle of Otranto*. Vin marks the title but doesn't allow it to distract him from the refreshing joviality that has overtaken the group.

Their journey along Italy's west coast is engaged thusly and augmented with sneaking peeks at the spectacular vistas as they are carried between dramatic mountains to the east and the dreamy blue Tyrrhenian Sea to the west. Any recollections of the unpleasantness that has dogged them are willfully waylaid by jokes and jibes as the train rolls south to Viareggio.

Soon the line is sprinting past the bright little buildings of the seaside town and slows noticeably as it glides into the station. The six gather their bags eagerly as the cars on either side are engulfed in a cacophony of disembarking travelers.

"Jeezus christ," Agnot grumbles. "Is everyone getting off?"

The train empties more quickly than any of them expect and soon they are on the platform looking to Vin for direction.

The station is small and bright, allowing he and the group to find their way easily. The warmth of the sun paired with a cool Mediterranean breeze bolsters their spirits to genuine optimism, which even the posting regarding the connecting train does little to dampen.

"Six hours!" Agnot bemoans.

"What are we going to do for six hours?" Charlie sighs.

Eager smiles blossom on the faces of Parson and Julia simultaneously as they look at each other and then at their comrades.

"The beach!"

CHAPTER 3

The Beach

THE ARGUMENT THAT CREATED THE vacancy in the wooden chairs clustered under the vivid turquoise-and-white
umbrella, now occupied by Ravenword, still rises over
the skimpily clad throngs on the outstretched beach.
Unprepared for seaside recreation, the company lounges in
an array of makeshift beachwear. Parson is the only exception and is delighted to flaunt his fire-engine red, box-cut
Diesels and gym-wrought physique. Julia, in a pink bra and
the faded yellow short-shorts she sleeps in, giggles at the
bare breasts bouncing past them, while Vin and the lesbians recline under the umbrella in board shorts and T-shirts.
Billy's attire remains unchanged.

Looking from the delicious multitoned menu of bodies
surrounding them to the improvised casual-frump of the
straight and lesbian alliance, Parson stands and grabs Julia's
hand. "Let's go look at boys!"

Agnot rolls her eyes but joins Charlie and Vin in a
welcome chuckle as the two trot gleefully into the sea of
sunbathers.

"Thank god for broken-down trains!" Agnot yawns, relishing the respite of leisure with a stretch.

"Well," Vin hesitates, looking at his hands, "not really broken down."

Charlie's carefree expression quickly melts. "Do we really need to know?"

As if given permission to enjoy himself, he grins. "Should we go check out girls?"

Agnot and Charlie smile and look to each other for accord before shifting in their chairs to stand. As Vin rises, the three look to Billy, who, by all appearances, is too engrossed in his book to notice their uncertain invitation.

"Just go," he brays without looking up.

Much to Billy's satisfaction, the three disappear quickly, and he turns a page in solitary contentment. By the turn of the next page, however, a presence pulls him out of the gothic fantasy. His eyes rise slowly over the book.

Standing behind the vacated chairs is the mysterious man from the plane, bare-chested and in swim shorts. His muscular build belies the gray at his temples and taunts Billy's insecurity with his own pudgy physique.

Billy returns his icy-blue gaze, unflinching. "What are you doing here?"

"Same as you," he replies, crossing his powerful arms, his enigmatic smile doing little to lessen the hardness of his features. "Waiting for the next train."

"Wait somewhere else," Billy rebuffs.

"Give me your locker number and key," the man states in a tone that implies he is accustomed to giving orders.

"What for?"

He does not answer, choosing rather to prod the slovenly youth with his imposing mettle.

With a resentful smirk, Billy complies, lowering the book to dig through the grimy pockets of his maculated jeans. Crumples of tumbled paper and lint spill out with the key lodged between two of his fingers, and with a heave, he reaches across the shadow of the umbrella to slap the graven shard on a chair.

Rolling back into his recline like a slug on a leaf, Billy returns to his book with indifference. When he chances another glance over the pages, the man is gone. His shifty eyes pan the surrounding bodies, checking for his companions.

II

Ankle-deep in the foamy surf, Parson and Julia mark and ogle the finest of the male holidaymakers as they stroll between sand and sea. The saline shallows are a virtual pedestrian highway under the noonday sun, and they find themselves squeezing through several large groups, much to Parson's delight. Ahead, three sun-kissed brunettes in bright designer bikinis chatter like vivacious finches while assessing Julia with disparaging glances. Parson can make out a bit of French as they pass, but his focus on their language evaporates as they burst into derisive laughter behind him.

Shrinking, Julia blushes and crosses her arms to hide her bra.

"Fuck those bitches!" Parson snaps over his shoulder with the wave of his hand.

"Parson!" Julia snickers, her countenance brightening under his austere defiance. "I really should've worn something else, though."

"Says who?" he counters. "And drop your arms. You have a beautiful rack! Show it off!"

Julia recoils with gull-pitched squeals as Parson grabs her wrists playfully to pry her arms from her chest. At the same time, she spins on her heels just as a retreating wave sucks the sand out from underneath her and, in an explosion of splash and spray, she plummets into the surf, taking Parson down with her. They leap out of the sea foam, crowing joyfully and wiping the salty water from their faces. Parson's eyes widen a split second before howling with laughter so convulsive that his six-pack abs pull him into a bow. Julia's confusion is just as fleeting before gasping in horror and throwing her arms against her naked breasts.

Bellowing, Parson falls back into the shoals, reveling in the comedy of Julia's frantic pivots in search of her bra.

"Parson!" she yells, unable to suppress her own giggles. "Help me find it!"

Few of the beachgoers mark her dance of modesty and desperation, and those who do take little note. Parson's mirth and Julia's desperation, however, are quickly subdued as a golden Adonis with dripping black locks jogs to her side with her bra dangling from his sculptured hand.

"For you, bella ragazza," he offers in a dulcet tenor, extending the sopped garment with a caress of her arm.

A glorious thrill rifles through her, robbing her of her ability to either speak or tear her gaze from the rivulets running down his chiseled, sun-kissed chest.

"You speak English, no?" he asks, bowing his head to look into her eyes.

"Si," she sighs melodiously, staring into his speckled green eyes.

Behind them, Parson sits in the waves equally hypnotized by the Italian god's flawlessly contoured back, muscular legs, and tight, round butt that settles the question of why Speedos are still on the market. He shakes himself abruptly, realizing that if he allowed his gaze to linger on the contents of those white Speedos any longer, he would have to get waist-deep into the sea. Checking himself, he stands.

"Hi," he says, sounding like a good imitation of Julia despite himself.

"This is your boyfriend?" the noble Italian asks, giving Parson the once-over.

"No," they blurt in unison.

"Friends," Julia spouts, fingers waving between she and Parson.

"Just friends," Parson interjects.

"Traveling companions," she gushes.

"Nothing going on here," Parson insists.

"I am Aldobrandi. Aldo to my friends."

"Julia," she replies, realizing only then that he is still holding her bra, and she her breasts.

"Parson," he announces, leaning in to shake Aldo's hand only to realize it is occupied by the bra.

Aldobrandi smiles politely, "You are *omosessuale*, yes?"

The uncertain expression on Parson's face prods Aldo to scour his English vocabulary and try again. "You are gay?"

Parson's grin is tainted, and he and Julia exchange an uncertain glance before he answers, "Absolutely."

"Then you may help bella Julia with her bikini," he says, offering a gentle smile to Julia and handing the bra to Parson. "I will turn away."

"The beach, the beach!" Julia hisses, moving to use Aldo's magnificent form as a shield as Parson tries to help her untangle the straps.

"I can do it! Just help block me," she insists, slapping back his hands.

Parson's heart races to be shoulder to shoulder with Aldo, who is showing no sign of aversion. The question of which one of them he prefers is distracting, yet in no way impedes Parson's survey of Aldo's body, which stands as solid and magnificent as the great mountains that rise over Viareggio. Unfortunately, his inspection is short-lived as Julia bounces from behind them, extending a shy hand to Aldo.

"Thank you so much!"

"Of course, bella," he replies sweetly, taking her hand and kissing it.

Parson shifts on a twinge of jealousy before Aldo straightens and looks at them both.

"We may walk?"

"Absolutely," Parson cedes, giving Julia an excited, albeit envious, glance.

To both their surprise, Aldo steps between them and links his contoured arms with them both. With a round of friendly smiles, the three begin to stroll in the spindrift shallows.

"You are staying in Viareggio?"

Parson and Julia look around him to check each other with bewildered expressions.

"No, we're just waiting for our train," Parson replies, enjoying the feel of Aldo's arm against his and the cachet of being seen beside him on the beach.

"Ah, you go to Roma then?"

Julia takes Parson's hesitation to reply as her cue. "We're going to a castle!"

"Oh, si, si," Aldo nods, impressed. "We have many castles. Which do you visit?"

"Castello Nel Buio," Parson answers blithely.

Aldo halts abruptly and swings his powerful form around to take Julia's shoulders in his hands, yet fixing on Parson with a burning glare. "You must not go!"

Struck by his explosive reaction, Parson stands frozen, feeling suddenly conspicuous and naïve.

"You're hurting me," Julia squeaks meekly, prompting Parson to lay his hand on Aldo's arm.

But there is no thrill, as their fantasy has turned to fear.

"Perdonarci, perdonarci, bella Julia," Aldo stammers, releasing his grasp and caressing her arms apologetically. Yet he remains fervent and takes each of their hands. "This place is dangerous, some say it is evil. Many have been harmed there."

Julia places her hand over the one Aldo clasped to her own, and he eases his grip, his furrowed brows framing his green eyes with urgency.

"Hold the phone, drama-rama," Parson chimes, no longer concerned with winning him over. "Are you saying it's haunted?"

Aldo's eyes narrow on Parson, recognizing the condescending incredulity on his face, and steps back, throwing his hands on his marble hips. "No! I said it is dangerous place. You go because of the English writer, yes? But that is not why I say you cannot go. There is...crime there. Danger."

"Crime?" Julia echoes, the accusation staining her poetic preconceptions of the castle.

"Let us sit with drinks, and I will explain," Aldo offers, his tone softening.

"We didn't bring any money," Julia says sheepishly.

"We didn't expect to entertain a local...hottie," Parson quips with a probing grin.

Aldo smiles back at him, his brows now high. "Ah, yes. I see. Come with me. We will drink and talk to when your train comes or the sun goes down to the sea."

III

Billy's attention is once more drawn away from the woes of Lord Manfred, but this time by the clambering of Agnot and Charlie back into their chairs, each cradling a paper bowl of gelato. Irked by the interruption, he tries to return to the page.

"Hey," Charlie exclaims, pulling the plastic spoon out of her mouth. "Why is your locker key on the chair?"

Billy's head turns sharply to her indication. There, indeed, sits his locker key, having returned unseen.

"I was looking for something in my pockets."

"Are you going to leave it there all day?" Agnot chides.

Billy snatches up the key, quickly barring the lesbians behind the width of his hardbound, yet his indifference has been tainted by the implications of the key.

"Where are Parson and Julia?" Vin asks as he saunters through the sunlight to the shade of the umbrella before taking his seat in a brisk and cheerful manner. His matted black hair and the fine dusting of salt on his bronze Madhya skin betray his afternoon activities.

Billy stews, annoyed with the impertinence of the women and even more so with Vin's belaboring the interruption.

"Haven't seen 'em," Agnot states through a mouthful of gelato.

"We should find them before it gets too late," Vin says half-heartedly, reluctant to leave the shade of the umbrella. "We only have a couple of hours."

"They're big girls," Billy snaps, slapping his book shut and lurching out of his chair. "They know."

Vin and the lesbians sit in a stupor, surprised by his outburst and storming away.

"Do you think something's bothering him?" Charlie asks quietly.

"Hopefully his hygiene," Agnot retorts.

"Come on, Ag," she prods, "it's just not like him. And it's the second time."

Agnot's and Vin's eyes meet with significance.

"We're all pretty run down," Vin offers.

"Should someone talk to him?" Charlie presses.

"No," Agnot exclaims curtly before shifting to a gentler tone and demeanor. "I mean, what good will it do, babe? He's tired. We're all tired. Everything will be fine once we can finally get a fuckin' good night's sleep."

Charlie nods and takes another scoop at her gelato.

The reminder of their weariness threatens a surrender that descends on them like a spell, and Vin perks with willful defiance. "Should we go find them or trust them not to get lost?"

"Or kidnapped," Agnot chortles. She mocks seriousness, putting her spoon to her chin.

They exchange glances.

"Fine," Agnot relents. "I guess it's better than falling asleep in these fucking wooden chairs."

"What about Billy?" Charlie checks.

It takes a moment for Agnot and Vin to understand her point.

"He's a big girl," her lover punts.

Despite the afternoon heat, the sun on their skin and the energy of the surrounding beachgoers sweep away any lethargy threatening to thwart their first opportunity to enjoy themselves since leaving San Francisco. They amble down the bustling beach, chatting as Charlie expounds on points of interest with Agnot's arm hanging leisurely across her shoulders.

"Searching for a needle in a haystack," Agnot bemoans after twenty minutes.

"Well, if you were Parson, where would you go?" Charlie chimes with a wry grin.

"Besides a stranger's bedroom," Agnot retorts.

"Do you think he'd take Julia to a bar?" Vin wonders.

"Don't be fooled. That little Asian girl is not as innocent as she seems," Agnot poses cagily.

Scanning the beachfront cabins and hotels, Charlie spots an outdoor lounge under a bright-blue canopy. With a lighter stride, the three navigate through the golden forest of the beautiful and the bold to close quickly on the bar.

"Ya know, I could go for a nice cold gin 'n sin," Agnot sighs, before being halted abruptly by Vin's soccer-mom arm block.

He brings a swift index finger to his lips and then points past them.

Following his direction, the picture produces the same expressions of intrigue and suspicion in them as is burning in Vin's eyes.

In the portico of the adjoining hotel, the suspect air marshal is locked in a contentious row with an agitated young Italian man caught in nothing but white Speedos. A curt gesture by the statuesque Italian brings the conversation to a halt.

Fearing discovery, Vin nudges the lesbians to the bar swiftly.

Stepping under the canopied entrance, they find Parson and Julia easily, as they are sitting conspicuously at a little table in the center of a wide open-air window. Their gregarious giggles and the plastic Italian flags sticking out of their shorts exaggerate the frame of revelry, replete with fruity umbrella cocktails and American top forty overhead.

"Hey, ladies!" Parson cheers upon spotting their approach.

At the same time, Julia bemoans like a nine-year-old, "Aw, it's not time to go already?"

"Get up," Agnot spurs petulantly as the three reach the table. "We gotta get outta here."

Parson and Julia look at them with surprised, albeit tipsy, consternation.

Charlie throws a backward glance at the entrance while Vin tries to allay any overreactions Agnot's orders may have stirred.

"We just saw the guy from the plane," he explains.

Parson takes another sip of his nearly full cocktail before responding with a flip of his hand, "And?"

"*And?*" Agnot echoes incredulously. "The creep is following us, and we need to go!"

Parson sets his drink down gingerly and folds his wrists one over the other to lean on the edge of the table. "Girl, you need to learn how to dig in your high heels when a buzz cut shows up to spoil the fun!"

Julia's snicker is stifled by Agnot's glare, and Parson amends himself. "Or whatever the faux fellas are wearing this season. Do clodhoppers come in heels?"

"She's right," Vin interrupts, hoping to stave off Agnot's temper. "It would be a good idea to head back to the station."

"I'm not going anywhere," Parson retorts.

"Can we just finish our drinks?" Julia pleads sweetly.

"What if he comes in here?" Charlie presses, plying herself to Agnot's side despite the afternoon heat.

"Mary, Joseph, and *Hey Zeus*! What if he does?" Parson balks, shrugging his shoulders. "We haven't done anything. He can't arrest us."

"But he's following us!" Agnot insists.

"Okay," Parson states flatly, looking at them as if he were talking to kindergarteners. "Take it from someone who's been followed by a lot of strange men. First, there's nothing you can do about it. Two, they can follow all they want, they're not going to get what you're not gonna give. And last, our Italian stallion just walked in, so you bitches need to clear out."

Vin, Agnot, and Charlie look to the entry only to be surprised by the approach of the chiseled Italian who had been talking with their stalker.

Julia squeals, and Parson admires the play of the white linen shirt over his tan, muscular form.

"Buongiorno!" Aldo trumpets amicably, surveying Vin, Agnot, and Charlie with his arms wide as if ready to embrace them. "These are your friends, yes?"

Agnot's calculating eyes meet Vin's as her head tilts slightly. In concert, the two pull the nearest empty chairs up to the table.

"And who might you be?" Agnot smiles shrewdly, leaning back in her chair and folding her arms as Charlie settles in next to her.

"Aldobrandi," he answers happily, taking the seat between them.

"So tell me, Brandi—"

"Aldo. This is how my friends call me," he corrects politely, his smile somewhat faded under the bleaching brazenness of the young woman who looks harder than her age should allow.

"Whatever," Agnot dismisses, evoking gasps and reproaches from her friends. "What were you doing talking to that guy over by the hotel?"

Annoyed and embarrassed by her direct rudeness, Parson and the others erupt into apologies, only to be allayed by Aldo.

"No, no, it is fine. I understand she is being a friend to you."

"No excuse," Parson interjects, glaring at Agnot.

Having subdued them, Aldo leans into the group, wearing a grave expression that, to Parson and Vin, seems foreign to his handsome features.

"He saw me with bella Julia and bello Parsone and pulled me away when I go to change to my shirt," he begins, his voice no longer jovial but as grim as his countenance. "I know nothing to tell," he deflects preemptively, anticipating Agnot's interjection. "It was he who brought forward this cursed place you are to visit. I ask him to help you, to…dissuade you from going, but he did not answer. Then," Aldo finishes, lowering his voice so that the five must huddle to hear, "I tell him of l'Ordine degli Intercessori per i Maledetto Rosso."

His earnest eyes meet each of theirs one by one before translating, "The Order of Intercessors for the Red Damned."

Ravenword exchange puzzled and hesitant glances, unsure whether he is making fun of them.

"What is that?" Julia asks, unable to wait on his pause.

"They pray for the souls in the Englishman's story," he answers.

Agnot leans away, again folding her arms. "Now I know you're fucking with us."

Aldo's face widens, taken aback by her accusation. "No, no, some believe that the Englishman came away with this story as true when he visited the very same place."

"Do you mean Edgar Allan Poe?" Vin asks, correlating the "red damned" with the author.

"Si, yes, the writer from England," Aldo answers quickly, nodding.

The faux pas breaks the tension as well as Aldo's credibility.

"Poe was American," Vin corrects gently, hoping to avoid embarrassing the earnest Italian.

"And he never came to Italy," Agnot states flatly.

Puzzled by the contradiction, Aldo stands, surveying the group sincerely yet cautiously. "But I am told he came from England in eighteen hundred and twenty. Only then did he go to America."

Vin considers the possibility, knowing Poe had spent five years between Scotland and England before returning to the United States in 1820. "Well, for argument's sake, how can this Order help? We're going to have to get going soon."

"If you mean to go on to Castello Nel Buio, the Order must be told so they can help in protecting you. I will tell them of you, and they will help," he says, leaning into the table.

This simplistic answer does little to engender faith in either Aldo or his story, but Vin and the rest of Ravenword, with the exception of Agnot, respond with gracious smiles.

"How do you know all this?" Julia asks as if a light bulb has gone off over her head.

A hint of blush accentuates the richness of his bronze face, but he does not drop his gaze as he straightens. "I am from Badia di'Cantignano, a small town very near to the mountains where this place of yours is. We know much of the legends."

"So you do think the place is haunted!" Parson volleys lightly, giving Aldo a wink.

As the Italian stammers, Vin rises from the table and extends his hand to Aldo.

"Thank you," Vin offers sincerely, "for the information and…help. It was nice meeting you."

Aldo shakes Vin's hand and pulls him into a terse embrace with his great strength to whisper in his ear. "Find the dagger."

Before Vin is able to react or reply, Aldo kisses his cheek and then the other before exploding with joviality and kissing the others likewise. The scene is a happy chaos of voices, embraces, and laughter that is soon replaced by sun and drudging strides over the sand.

IV

T. J. sits in the nineteenth-century Lombard chair, luxuriously upholstered in red-and-gold silk, staring at the bags from

Gucci, Dior, and other fashion houses huddled on the bed like monoliths on a crimson sea. Behind him the architecture of Milan is muted by the gossamer sheers that drape the window and scatter the Italian light throughout the lush room.

"I adore the use of wood accents, but the red theme is a tad garish," Motisha observes as she enters from the bath suite, looking radiant in a lavish cream Lacroix dress suit. "Have you seen the vanity?"

The lack of a response from T. J. waylays her delving into the bags, and she turns to face him fully, studying his countance.

"Is everything all right?"

"Yeah," he replies pensively. "I just feel bad about leaving."

The smirk on her flawless face seems tantamount to drawing a mustache on the *Mona Lisa* and does nothing to ease the nagging regret in his mind.

"You can't be serious," she exclaims, turning to the first bag within reach. Her expression changes to a coy smugness. "I knew you'd choose me," she says with the sideways glance of a vixen.

T. J. offers her as reassuring a smile as he can muster and stands to helps her, rubbing his hands together enthusiastically.

"Oh!" she cries, withdrawing from the bag with surprise.

"What?" T. J. exclaims, rushing closer.

Motisha turns to him with a small black velvet box cradled in her hands.

"Was this supposed to be a surprise?" she asks through a gleaming smile and adoring eyes.

T. J. flushes and fidgets, unsure how to answer her.

"You are such a dear," she coos, reaching up to caress his cheek before giving him a tender kiss that exaggerates his clumsiness.

"Uh, I didn't get you that," he stammers, looking down at her with a wan and nervous smile.

Her brows furrow as she retrieves the small card within the envelope affixed to the underside of the velvet box. "You!" she sings happily. "It's your handwriting."

"Um, what?" he says taking the little card as she lifts the velvet top.

"Oh, Terrence!" she gushes as T. J. reads the card. "It's lovely!"

Dance with me…

It is written, indeed, in his own handwriting.

A chill runs down his back as she withdraws from the gift box, on bated breath, a delicate ruby teardrop pendant on an equally delicate gold necklace.

"Oh, Terrence," she gasps softly, staring at the stone as if hypnotized, "you really shouldn't have."

T. J. turns the little card over to find *l'Ordine degli Intercessori* written in tiny letters over an ornate watermark crest.

"Please, help me with it on," Motisha insists in a bright, soft voice as she turns her back to him, holding the pendant high on her chest. "I want to wear it to dinner."

"Maybe you shouldn't," T. J. replies, hesitating to take the ends of the gold chain.

"Why wouldn't I?" Motisha rebuffs, a hardness seeping into her tenor. She glances over her shoulder expectantly as she holds her hair aside.

"May you'd want to get it appraised—or cleaned—before wearing it out," he says, cringing the moment the words leave his lips. Hoping to deflect her reaction, he lays the pendant against her breast and clasps the ends of the petite gold necklace.

"Don't be foolish," she whispers, turning around to kiss him again. "I will always measure its value by this moment."

Motisha steps back to display the pendant against her lovely brown skin and extends her arms in invitation. "Dance with me."

Upon the invitation, the room is abruptly swallowed in cold darkness.

T. J. recoils.

A ghoulish, rotting corpse in tattered blue rags has replaced his beautiful lover.

Aghast in the void, his hand shields his silent scream.

A grasping, bony claw reaches out as it staggers toward him.

Horror-stricken, T. J. swoons, hands flailing for an anchor.

The ghoul's grimy fungus-spackled neck and jaw twist gruesomely, as if desperate to speak. The very desperation that permeates the black-stained hollows of decay once home to eyes pierces his soul.

A howl rises from T. J.'s throat, his eyes peeled madly to their margins.

"What is it?" Motisha shrieks.

Sweeping the bags off the bed, she throws him down and holds his contorted face in her hands frantically. "Terrence! Can you hear me? Terrence, answer me!"

His wild eyes suddenly languish and blink.

Motisha leans for the phone but is stayed by his hand on her wrists.

She looks into his eyes, grateful to find them fixed upon her.

Pulling her onto him, he grips her in an exquisite embrace.

V

The arriving train finds the six members of Ravenword waiting on the platform surrounded by those who did not make other travel arrangements to Lucca. Their unexpected excursion having bolstered their spirits, five of the six chatter and tease like so many siblings as the train whines to a stop and throws wide its doors. Overhead the fair blue of afternoon has deepened into the blushing azure of the sun's impending set. They are happy to find the train relatively empty as they board and quickly lay claim to a cluster of seats facing each other.

Having learned the need for expedience, Agnot and Charlie fall into the first two as Vin ducks into the row across.

Waiting in gloomy silence for Julia to decide which seat she prefers, Billy screens the boarding passengers ahead with steely eyes and then chances a glance over his shoulder.

"What are you doing?" Agnot checks suspiciously.

"Waiting," he replies, gesturing toward Julia.

"Ope! Sorry!" Julia giggles. She throws her backpack at Agnot's feet and alights in the seat opposite her.

Parson's descent, taking the seat next to her, clears the way for Billy to crumple into the window seat and use his book to wall off Vin and the rest of them. With no sign of the dogging agent on the train, Billy subtly positions the book so as to cast his survey on the platform.

There, in the queue of last stragglers trickling aboard, is the stern antagonist.

Billy's covertness is sidetracked by a sudden interest in the events unfolding on the man. Two police officers have waylaid the agent, one on either side, and a station security officer steps between he and the open doors. The detention prompts the commuters to rush the train with agitated backward glances. The agent shakes off their grasp motioning to the train, obviously arguing their reason for preventing him from boarding. Raising his hands as if to allay their fears, he reaches into the breast pocket of his blazer and retrieves what Billy can only assume is his identification.

The doors of the train fold with a hydraulic shush.

The amplification of the agent's insistence is evident on his face even from a distance.

The officers do not yield.

The initial tug of momentum announces the train's commencement. Before it whisks them out of the station, however, Billy follows the pointing arm of the security officer to an old woman huddled anxiously on a nearby bench. The scene quickly falls away in favor of vignettes of Viareggio and Billy returns to his book, pondering the ramifications of the agent missing the train.

"You think everyone's gay," Charlie scoffs lightheartedly.

Accustomed to Billy's reclusiveness, the five have continued their banter, unaware of the scene on the platform.

"Yes, Parson," Agnot parlays, rebuffing his exaggerated astonishment.

"In all fairness," Vin offers, "Parson has never accused me of being gay."

"He only thinks that about hot guys," Julia interjects innocently.

Her cohorts erupt in a storm of laughter.

"I didn't mean it that way!" she bellows.

"Oh, girl," Parson chuckles. "You're going to be the end of me!"

"Parson!" Julia giggles, slapping his knee as she leans across him toward Vin. "I'm sorry."

"I was on his rock-solid Roman god of an arm all day," Parson declares as Vin shakes his head with a smile and waves his forgiveness to Julia. "If that's not gay, I'll turn in my wig."

"Yeah, and Julia was on the other arm," Agnot counters amiably.

"I think that's just how Italians are," Charlie presumes.

"Who cares!" Parson sighs blissfully. "What a day, what a day."

"Wow!" Julia exclaims, her face mirrored in the window. "Look at that!"

Beyond the window, the fleeting landscape is a black silhouette beneath a torrid red band of sky that cradles the setting sun. The drama of Sol Invictus reclining through the blood of his conquests and into a dark Mediterranean bath mesmerizes the five. Nearly spellbound, they watch in silence. With every degree of his descent, the welling night seeps in to weigh upon their hearts and minds until the luminosity of their stolen day has been all but extinguished.

VI

Motisha and T. J. dine quietly on braised veal and risotto at an elegantly dressed table of silver and white. The champagne at Motisha's ruby fingertips is burnished gold by soft candlelight, contrasting her flawless sienna complexion, which is tarnished with composed irritation. The Milano-chic restaurant is a-hush with the beautiful, the stylish, and the wealthy and does little to ease T. J.'s sense of displacement. He casts his gaze from the bewitched teardrop pendant on Motisha's lovely breast to the arched panes of the neoclassical windows and shudders at the blazing scarlet ribbon ushering the sun beneath the horizon.

"I have had enough of this foolishness," Motisha says evenly, reaching to squeeze his hand in an attempt to belie the implied criticism. "There is no point in ruining our holiday simply because your friends have convinced themselves that they have been caught up in some sort of gothic horror story."

"What about the hospital?" T. J. insists, his eyes sharpened by dread. "The plane?"

Motisha lifts the crystal flute to her lips without breaking eye contact with T. J., indulging in more than a delicate sip. "We were caught up in the suggestive atmosphere of that *society*, nothing more."

With his mind's eye, T. J. witnesses the last shard of the blood-red sun drown in the black horizon and with it any hope or illusion he may harbor that things are not as they appear. He looks at Motisha's fresh and beautiful face, and his heart sinks even deeper into the convincing sea to face the leviathan of his cowardice. Like the last, desperate gulp of air, he acquiesces to her denial, squeezing her hand and offering as genuine a smile as he can muster.

"You're right."

Motisha's stern countenance breaks like the bright full moon through clouds, yet her chocolate irises continue to scrutinize his face for subterfuge. "Of course I am," she beams. "Oh! I can't wait to introduce you to the passeggiata! It's still a bit early," she chimes, checking the time.

"The what?" he stammers, distracted by the churning of his head and stomach.

"Bella figura!" she fawns blithely.

Her ensuing discourse is muted by the compulsion to join his friends now mounting a fierce offensive against his fears. Regardless of the freakish events, and those that may lie ahead, the strongest detractor in rejoining Ravenword sits across the table espousing of the romantic joys of Lombardy. Only in this moment does he realize that he truly loves her.

CHAPTER 4

The Castle

THE SIX MEMBERS OF RAVENWORD disembark travel-weary and anxiety worn. The night has taken deep hold on both their fatigue and the bus line that was to carry them to the village of Colle, as evident by the handwritten notice posted over the route.

"Now what?" Agnot grumbles under the withering of the group.

Irritated with their sheeplike demeanor, Vin lets the duffel bags slide from his shoulder to the floor to punctuate his exasperation. "Can anyone get a signal?"

"Not without the right SIM card," Billy rebuffs.

Vin's lips purse in suppression of his mounting irritation, and as he pulls off his backpack to rifle through one of the large pockets, the rest of Ravenword follow suit. Billy, however, pans the empty station as cell phones interrupt the night with the cheap jingles.

A grumpy and disjointed chorus of "Nothing," "Nope," "No," and "Told ya" tins off the adumbral walls as Vin pleads silently with his mobile. Defeated, he deactivates his phone and looks up to find the shambled eyes of his companions on him.

"So?" Agnot drawls.

Vin sighs curtly. "Find a pay phone!"

"Fuck you," Agnot barks.

A general agitation runs through Ravenword until broken by Charlie, who wraps her arm around Agnot's shoulder.

"Babe," she says before eyeing Vin and the rest of the group. "This isn't helping. We're not going to get to get some sleep anytime soon by being bitchy with each other."

Resignation permeates their nods and murmurs of contrition, passing from face to face until Billy's exodus dawns on them. Turning like lethargic cogs in their scan of the terminal, they find him stock-still and staring at the street-side exit. Despite the warm Tuscan breeze, a collective chill follows their gaze to the source of an unspoken heed.

On the other side of the glass doors, a figure stares back at them against the backdrop of pitch. Long, stringy hair exaggerates the unnatural gaunt and pale of the face framed in that thin black mane. Likewise, the ill-fitting, shabby brown suit creates a skeletal impression of the man's wiry build, which stoops as if the weight of an unholy curse were upon his shoulders. The most chilling feature of the aspect, however, is the inscrutable eyes, recessed so deeply under the shadow of his brows as to defy existence.

Seemingly autonomous, his left arm raises a bony hand to point into the darkness. Ravenword gape in silence as the arm sinks, and the specter recedes with a trancelike gait.

Before they can check one another, Billy lumbers toward the exit in pursuit of the creature. Parson, at the behest of his rest-starved body, tosses a resolute glance to his comrades, secures the duffel strap to his shoulder, and saunters after him. The rest of the company scurries to catch up, and soon they are on the sidewalk, blinded by the gloom of fatigue to the life and music of surrounding Lucca.

"Jesus hates us," Parson deflates upon reaching the end of the building.

The five gaze in defeat at the old, black-windowed, rusted green van blotched with gray primer, into the back of which Billy is now stowing his backpack and duffel bag.

"Do you want to get there or not?" Billy calls, leaving the rear panel doors open as he moves to the side of the van and, with a measure of effort, slides the door open.

"Not," Parson declares.

Vin steps out, with the rest of Ravenword in tow, and peers into the abysmal gut of the van. With the exception of a beaklike nose, the features of the driver are eclipsed by darkness. In the bench seat behind him, Billy is scratching in the shadows for a seatbelt.

"Where are you going?" Vin hisses, astounded at Billy's willingness to climb into a strange vehicle, in a strange city, with an even stranger stranger.

A raspy moan rises from the throat of the creature behind the wheel, imitating "d'castello nel buio" in a thick Italian dialect.

Billy's head tosses a swiveled nod to Vin with smug satisfaction.

"How do we know that's really where he's going?" Julia squeaks, curled up against Parson.

Billy lets his eyelids fall and looks at the group as if he'd like nothing more than to slam the door and leave them behind. "He's our ride. Who else would be going there?"

"How do you know that?" Vin presses.

"Jeezus christ!" Billy exclaims, ignoring the cadaver's protest. "Don't you think Fichtenberg would find some way of getting us there after the train delay and the bus not running?"

Billy returns to his search for a seatbelt, leaving Ravenword to their decision.

Vin, despite the massive cluster of reluctance snowballing in his chest, leads the others to the back of the van and begins loading their bags.

Within moments they are buckled in and lurching with the van as it pulls onto the road.

Sitting beside Billy, Vin whispers, "I hope you're right."

Without responding, Billy presents a piece of folded paper, holding it up between his fingers. In his surprise Vin fails to notice from where Billy had produced the page but takes it quickly and attempts to decipher the face of the parchment to no avail. Without speaking, Billy offers his book light. Bemused, Vin takes the tiny lamp, turns it on with a click, and holds it over the page.

"Why didn't you show this to me before?" Vin exclaims with exasperation.

"Because," Billy snaps, "this isn't a fucking field trip, and you're not our goddamned scout leader!"

"What is it?" Agnot asks, anger already bleeding into her voice as she leans forward to look over his shoulder.

Vin holds the book light over the message again. "Ravenword, please excuse the means of transport in delivering you to the abbey. It was the best I could arrange on short notice. Despite the disposition of the van and driver, both are sound and will provide you a safe journey through the mountains. I look forward to welcoming you upon your arrival. Sincerely, Fichtenberg."

"Goddamn you, Billy," Charlie rebukes as Agnot kicks the back of the bench behind him spitefully.

"Billy!" Julia cries disapprovingly from the back bench.

Parson, already positioning his travel pillow, tosses his hand in the air. "Who cares? At least now we know we won't get molested in our sleep." With that he props his pillow against the window and closes his eyes.

The communal grumbling continues only as long as they can spend the energy, but soon, one by one, they are lulled into slumber by the drone of the road.

II

Motisha falls against T. J., laughing amid the lights and music drifting through the streets of Milan as they walk arm in arm under the dazzling lampposts casting warm hues over the boulevard. Simply being seen strolling the passeggiata has lifted her sense of worth more than any excursion America could offer, and T. J. has rarely seen her so exuberant. The sight of her luminous face partnered with her uncensored laughter is an effective shield against the arrows of his foreboding, and he relishes the moment with a wide grin. Yet a fleeting flash of the ruby pendant catching the light slips through the moment of bliss to plant a splinter in his mind.

"Let's go to Café L'Atlantique!" she gasps happily.

"I'm not sure I'm dressed for it," he pauses, presenting himself with a self-conscious smile. "You said it's really chic."

Motisha steps back to assess him, her bright demeanor flickering with the examination. Although dressed in the black slacks and blazer she chose for him, the open-collared shirt gives her pause. "You may be right."

He teases her with a hurt expression, and she taps him playfully on the arm as they continue along.

"To be honest," she admits, "I could use a good night's sleep. We will have plenty of time to enjoy Milan's delights, and tomorrow we can tour the shops and find you something stunning for the most exclusive clubs in the city."

T. J.'s jovial response is abruptly cut short by the brazen lungs of a clock striking with a sound which is clear and loud and deep and exceedingly musical, but of so peculiar a note and emphasis that it riddles his heart with a dread that his denial cannot negate.

"Don't worry," Motisha says, her giddiness faltering at the sight of his tainted countenance. "Consider it my way of thanking you for this," she continues, kissing the pendant with her fingertips.

As T. J.'s eyes fall on the ruby teardrop, the disconcerting clang rings a second time, and the insinuation of the gem's true expression pushes against the shutters of his mind.

"What's the matter?" Motisha's eyes follow his burning gaze to the pendant on her breast as her joy evaporates.

The muting of her felicity brings T. J. back to his senses, only to be sacked by a third unnerving sounding of the toll. "Nothing," he soothes. "It's just that weird sounding clock striking the hour."

Motisha shifts stridently to face him. "Why must you insist on allowing your imagination to run away with you?"

A fourth clang scratches its fingers across the chalkboard of his brain, and he grimaces.

"We're in *Milan...together*," she pleads over the fifth resounding clang. "Why ruin it?"

"You hear it!" he exclaims, taking her shoulders.

"I hear nothing!" she retorts, pulling away, yet even she winces as the sixth toll sounds.

T. J. checks his watch urgently.

Midnight.

"Yes you do!" he growls back at her, his own anger at her obstinate repudiation surging.

Clang!

"You stupid man!" she rages. "You're too stupid to realize you don't have to hear it or see it or feel it if you don't want to!"

Clang!

"That's right," he shouts. "I should keep my brain locked up in your little ivory tower!"

Clang!

"How dare you speak to me like that!"

Clang!

"Yeah? Well, fuck you!"

Clang!

Motisha's eyes flare. *Smack!* claps the night air from her swift strike.

Clang!

T. J.'s cocked arm is caught and held by figures ambiguous in his rage, thwarting his balled fist.

His vision clears to find a crowd of gawkers encircling them as a gang of brawny men pull him from the sidewalk. Motisha's face is buried in her hands, cowed and comforted by a cloud of women chattering like a pen of agitated hens.

The venom spent, T. J. breaks and collapses. "Motisha!"

The men corral him into a chair at the street-side café, patting his face and searching his intentions while gabbling in Italian and French.

"Terrence!" Motisha cries miserably.

A clamor rises in the throng. Motisha pushes through the men caging T. J. and throws herself into his arms.

T.J showers her with kisses and impassioned apologies, shaken by the power of the spell.

The crowd disperses, but the men hold guard, wary of T. J.'s temper should they leave. The rescuing sorority, however, glare, prattle, pet, and fawn as they wheedle Motisha off T. J.'s lap. As the scene quiets, two glasses of water are set on the table for the stricken lovers by an intervening matriarch.

One of the men, her husband by the look of scorn she shoots him, sets two tumblers of bourbon next to them.

Grabbing the amber tonic, T. J. throws back the burning liquid in a gulp and is surprised to find Motisha doing the same. Sputtering, she waves back the bottle, which is poised for a refill, and focuses on T. J. with tearstained makeup.

"Take me home," Motisha pleads hoarsely, reaching across the table to clutch his hands.

T. J. nods emphatically, glancing at one of the burly sentinels as he replies, "I'll get us a taxi to the hotel."

"No!" Motisha exclaims, sending an uneasy rustle through her hovering guardians. "Home!"

Any allegiance to Ravenword in T. J. melts away at the grievous sight of Motisha so broken. His heart sinks as he yields to her grief with a somber nod.

III

Parson shivers against the draft antagonizing his slumber like icy fingers. His body's attempt to shift against the chill is thwarted, however, by a weight pinning him to the window.

Ca-lunk!

The abrupt and oddly familiar sound penetrates his unconsciousness to prod his lethargic mind from its nocturnal cocoon. His reluctant brain yawns to a dull stupor. Julia's petite form curled up against him is a Picasso-esque contortion of fabric, hair, and odd angles shrouded in the night. Bleary-eyed, he squints and blinks heavily as the setting begins to clear. An elusive peculiarity about the scene tugs at his atrophied facilities. Other than the breathing and murmurs of his slumbering cohorts, it is utterly peaceful.

His attention piques.

Where's the noise from the road and motor?

As his brain shakes off the grogginess, a strange sensation registers.

Gravel begins to crunch ominously under the tires.

"Are we here?" he mutters with a dry voice, trying to sort out the position of the driver.

There is no driver!

Parson's eyes flap to their margins like the window blinds in a noir film.

The van's center of gravity lunges, jostling the others out of their comfort.

A benighted world of blotchy, animated voids and nebulous shapes fills the windshield.

"We're moving!" Parson screams, struggling to free himself from Julia's rousing form.

Ravenword bolts to the alarm, dazed and confused by the violent pitching and jumbling of the groaning suspension contending with a pocked and pitted path.

"Brakes! Brakes!" Parson screeches at the bewildered faces of Billy and Vin.

As Agnot peers out the window, their plight becomes unanimously clear.

The cabin explodes with screaming mayhem as the building momentum dashes them against the innards of the van. Vin is fighting to get past Billy, who is grappling between the two front seats while Agnot scrambles over them both—each vying frantically to reach the controls. Julia sirens as Charlie recoils, pointing at the windshield in terror!

"Tree!"

Their collective perception slows to play out the remarkable scene in an exaggerated moment. Vin, Billy, and Agnot are tangled in a nightmarish constellation. Charlie is erect and reaching. Julia is shrinking behind the bench seat screaming.

The freeze-frame is shattered by a crash and a force that hurls them out of the suspension.

The ensuing silence is broken by Agnot's sharp exclamation. "Shit!" From the driver's seat, she rises in dismay and disgust in search of Charlie.

Beside her Billy has splattered the dash panel with vomit, the bile having been squeezed out of him by the seats between which he is wedged.

Charlie is already heaving the sliding door open as Vin moves quickly to pull Billy free.

His ashen face meets Agnot's as Vin strong-arms him out of the wedge, and each checks the other with a dazed nod. Ravenword pour into the open night as Parson confirms that Billy is uninjured.

"Hey," Agnot calls in a shaken and wounded tenor, "what about me?"

"Door, door," Vin rambles, indicating the driver's side door.

Agnot turns sharply, throws it open, and leaps out of the van and into a pummeled scream.

Ravenword race to the far side of the van only to be arrested by an inscrutable abyss.

"Agnot!" Charlie screams.

"Goddamnit," her voice trails over the blackness.

Relieved, her friends try to trace her to the exclamation blindly.

"Where are you?" Vin calls.

"How the fuck should I know?"

"Check the van for a flashlight," Vin directs Parson.

"Like that's going to happen."

"Fuck you, Parson!" Agnot's sardonic voice sails. "It's okay. I see a light."

"Don't go into it!" Parson quips loudly.

Billy taps Parson and Vin on the shoulders.

Charlie and Julia turn with them.

Standing on the meridian between the uneven ravine and nebulous pitch of sky, a cadaverous figure is illuminated by the yellow cast of the lantern it extends over the edge. The features of the gaunt face are disfigured by the stark radiation and exaggerated by the black frame of hair lost in the night. Its lower extremities are likewise relinquished as the creature peers into the abyss.

Vin steps from the wreckage, trying to reconcile the unsettling visage. "Romero?"

"Ravenword?" The voice carries as if drifting through the long years to seep into the shrill sphere of the fiasco.

"Professor Fichtenberg?" Vin calls in a wary tenor.

"I cannot come down," his frail voice, strained by force of volume, leaches down the slope. "Is anyone hurt?"

At that moment rustled footfalls and curses emerge from behind the tenebrous tree that had caught the van before it could plunge into the unseen depths. Hugging the trunk, Agnot circumnavigates the gnarled breast until finally stepping onto the narrow ridge upon which they had so unceremoniously been deposited. "Take a fucking picture," she growls at her gaping companions as Charlie launches into her arms.

"I think we're okay," Vin answers with a resolute shout.

Fichtenberg does not reply, nor does he move. Like Chiron on the bank of the river Styx, he stands extending the lantern as the six students pry open the back door of the van and collect their luggage. Within minutes they are scaling the tumultuous incline, tripping on stones, hollows, and branches.

Upon cresting the ledge, Vin finds the harsh and weathered face of their host, whose skeletal hand is held out in welcome. Taking the hand gently, Vin scrutinizes the haggard face.

"I assure you," the withered man muses, "I am Fichtenberg."

As the old man turns to greet the rest of Ravenword, Vin is struck by the semblance to Romero and the fact that Fichtenberg is not an old man.

"Where's that goddamned driver?" Agnot snarls, shaking the professor's hand as carefully as she can manage in her seething.

"I'm afraid I cannot say," Fichtenberg replies weakly. He lifts the lantern and pivots toward the road. "We mustn't linger outside the gates," he insists. "Come, quickly."

Only when they turn to follow are the black iron tendrils of the gate in the imposing stone wall impressed upon the company. As the margins of the great rampart recede into obscurity, the ruined towers and scowling facade of the stygian castle behind stare resentfully down on them against a mat of ashen clouds.

Crossing the road, which is no more than a stain of dirt and gravel, Fichtenberg leans against the iron bars.

A piercing screech splits the dank atmosphere.

A bead of frost trickles down the backs of each as Ravenword steps across the boundary and into the benighted expanse of the courtyard.

"I don't think I want to do this anymore," Julia squeaks.

Parson reaches around her shoulder and gives her a reassuring squeeze.

Billy looks back at the black gate. "Should I...?"

Before he can finish, however, the hinges creak, and the thick, scrolling bars drift shut with an unnerving clang.

The trespass on silence is answered by the rising call of a wolf not distant enough for solace. In seeming obedience, the light of Fichtenberg's lamp expires suddenly, swamping the Gothic landing in night.

"You gotta be fucking kidding," Agnot whispers, an uncharacteristic treble in her tone.

"Yes, yes," Fichtenberg warns gravely. "We are deep in the mountains, far from any villages. Wolf country. I would advise against wandering beyond the walls, even in the day."

A second howl seals the warning.

"Watch the steps," the professor directs.

A moment later Billy is heaving the heavy wooden door shut as quickly as he can manage as the company is swallowed by the cavernous foyer. A stone fireplace illuminates the chamber with the dancing light of a blaze substantial but, strangely, less comforting than disconcerting. Opposite the granite mantel, a massive staircase fashioned to complement the grandeur of the hearth rises to a landing of long shadows out of reach of the firelight. Appending the flight, a small passage sinks beneath a Gothic arch into enigmatic depths. Each of these features, however, is only briefly visited by the eyes of Ravenword. Looming from across the forbidding chamber, enormous and ancient ill-grained doors oppress their very senses as if ravenous with an evil and insatiable want.

The professor nods nervously, wringing his bony hands. "The original doors into the castle," he whispers, looking from the spiteful panels to the transfixed faces of his guests. "This entry house was built in the nineteenth century by a local baron who had hoped to restore the castle and open a spa."

"What happened to the baron?" Julia asks dreadfully, providing Ravenword with the reprieve of distraction.

The professor surveys the group as he makes to answer, but suddenly his eyes burn more keenly than his drawn features should present. "There are only six of you!"

The abrupt shift in his demeanor and the sharpness of his rebuke quells any ease massaging their harried minds. Amid the passing of anxious glances, Vin clears his throat, looking at the wizened professor, whose nebulous shadow shifts by firelight on the stone steps.

"Motisha chose to stay in Milan," he begins, watching for clues to the professor's reaction. "T. J. decided to stay with her at the last minute."

The haggard lines of Fichtenberg's face are suddenly transformed by craggy madness with eyes wild and raging. "Eight! Eight!" he screams as if accusing them of some heinous crime.

Ravenword stand dumbfounded, tightening their ranks.

"Not six! Eight!"

His shrieks reach a nerve-shattering crescendo that slaps every stony corner of the hall and tumbles into every black recess.

"Ruin!" he howls. "Ruin!"

With a knot churning in their collective gut, Ravenword watch in a harrowed stupor as Fichtenberg slumps into a stream of ravings. Pacing fitfully, he rants as if reviling some invisible presence until his mania is spent, and he subsides into a silence even more unsettling.

For a moment, the hall is animated by only the crackling fire.

"Professor?" Parson intercedes carefully, studying the withered man.

Fichtenberg lifts his tormented face, his eyes fading into a malaise. "Ravenword, yes, all is prepared." With a weary gesture, he ascends the yawning staircase to the disjointed cadence of a soundless dirge. Pausing midway, he turns stiffly to find the company framed by the glare of the hearth and staring up at him with faces awash in uncertainty. "Your rooms."

The six uproot their reluctance and follow him up the wide staircase as if marching to the gallows. They settle upon the landing with a marked unease to find the corridor hence stretching narrowly to a reclusive black window. To either side, the passage is lit by candles resting on pedestals that flank opposing doors lining the hall in succession. The passage is drab and comfortless with walls papered in a dingy pattern bereft of warmth even in the glow of candlelight.

"The power is untrustworthy here."

The six nod uneasily in the dim glow, remaining in their huddle.

"You will find your rooms assigned by name," Fichtenberg mutters with a hopeless sigh, shifting his form toward the descent.

"Where will you be?" Julia mewls.

"In case we need anything," Parson interjects quickly.

Fichtenberg pauses, his long black hair obscuring the features that remind the group forcibly of their missing driver. "You'll not be needing anything tonight."

The six exchange nervous glances as he descends like a decrepit phantom before turning to survey the rows of dark wooden doors. Vin is the first to step up to the threshold of the closest chamber to the left, where he finds Motisha's name penned rather elegantly on a weathered card that has been pinned to the grain. Grasping the knob as his apprehensive companions pool around him, he pushes against it as if braced for some ghoul waiting on the other side.

The door swings open on the creaking of atrophied hinges to reveal a room consistent in scale to most of those found in Europe. It is very small with an equally small bed and an ample window framing the nocturnal pitch. A small chest of drawers grimaces beneath the pane under a candle lantern that casts a strange hue to the coordinated midnight-blue dressings of the chamber. Beneath the tapestry draped across the wall opposite the bed, the glow of embers shines through the ornate grille of a small inset wood-burning stove.

"I smell a theme," Parson chirps from over Vin's shoulder, stepping across the narrow hall and opening the door opposite the blue room. The hinges whine likewise, and the chamber behind would pass for a mirror image of the first except that it is dressed in a purple lustered by candlelight.

"Built to suit," he chimes, offering Julia a reassuring smile while pointing at the card on the door. "Looks like someone knew you were coming."

"Don't say it like that," Julia bleats, stepping into the doorway to view the chamber as Parson delves into the hall. The rich purple hues wash over her in a wave of welcome despite her trepidation and the baleful odyssey of their journey.

Ravenword move to the next set of doors to find two tiny lavatories tiled from floor to ceiling with chipped and dulled mosaics depicting quaint scenes of refined country living. As

Parson checks the sink and tub for hot running water, Agnot leads Charlie, Vin, Julia, and Billy to the next set of doors.

"Green and orange," Parson calls over the gushing faucet.

"Green and orange," Charlie's confirmation sails back. "Me and T. J."

Parson shuts off the water and examines his weary image in the mirror. Tszujing his hair, he notices a series of letters tiled into the mosaic in the mirror's reflection. With a disconcerted frown, he turns and peers at the mosaic before returning to the glass.

Set within the depiction of the pastoral gentry is *agnus*. The unsettling aspect of the discovery, besides the inference to Agnot, is that it is written backward and can only be read from the mirror.

"Hey, guys," Parson calls, staring into the mirror as the creeps crawl up his neck.

"White for you, Parson, and violet for Vin," Julia's voice answers with the enthusiasm of one playing a game.

The lack of a retort from Parson brings Ravenword to the doorway of the tiny lavatory with curious but relaxed faces.

Parson looks to them, then turns and points at the mosaic. "Agnus."

Agnot growls at him, "I am way too tired to be fucked with, Parson."

"No," Parson insists, pointing at the tile. "It's written here—backward! Agnus."

The declaration sends a chill down Agnot's back and roots her to the floor.

Sensitive to the pale expression of dread on her face, Vin steps next to Parson and examines the tile. He looks back at Parson for any hint of humor. "You're pointing at a lamb."

"I'm what?" Parson blurts, confused. He pivots quickly to search the mirror, feeling Agnot's glare. Where he had read the word a moment before, a black lamb rests in the mosaic. Parson leans back, squinting. Agitated, he turns to inspect the tile directly to find the script has been replaced by the dark lamb in a cluster of white sheep.

"That's really not funny," Vin rebukes warily, assessing dreadful insinuations of Parson's confounded expression.

"I guess we're just too tired to carry that kind of joke," Parson placates, attempting a chuckle as Vin offers a supportive nod.

"Not cool, Parson," Agnot says, leading Charlie and the others back into the hall.

As their companions retire to their chosen rooms, Vin lingers. "You really saw something, didn't you?"

Shaken, Parson nods. "I thought I did. Who the hell knows? I'm so exhausted after all this shit that I'll be seeing Chippendales in the walls soon."

"Lamb," Billy announces from the doorway, startling them both.

"What?" they chorus.

"*Agnus* is Latin for *lamb*," Billy states, stepping in and pointing at the mosaic.

As the two men stand puzzling over the significance, Billy lumbers into the hallway and disappears, leaving them to ponder the disconcerting connotations before summoning the fortitude to take possession of their respective chambers.

"What the fuck?" Agnot exclaims from the end of the hall with an exasperated sigh.

Billy emerges from the black chamber bearing his name as Ravenword rallies around Agnot and Charlie, who stand at the grimy door opposite him.

"It's locked," Charlie explains.

"So everyone gets a room but me?" Agnot huffs irritably.

"Maybe there's a problem with the room, and he knew you and Charlie would most likely being sharing anyway," Vin offers, noting the absence of a name card on the door.

"Yeah, maybe," she relents, looking at Parson with an unsettled check.

"Don't get your tighty-whities in a twist," Parson quips. "With Miss Bitch and her beau off in Milan, I don't see why we can't have our pick of the rooms."

"I want to keep mine," Julia states quickly.

"Of course you do, sweetie."

"There were only seven rooms in the story," Billy alludes. "In the 'Red Death.'"

"So, what, I'm not supposed to be here?" Agnot spurns, unnerved by the dark, and increasingly personal, serendipities.

"Just sayin'," Billy retorts before retreating.

"Come on," Charlie heaves, leading Agnot by the hand.

The promise of bedded sleep and a fresh perspective vanquishes the imaginations, and the company disperses to their respective chambers to surrender to the night.

IV

Charlie wakes to the blue room, lost between the unyielding wall and the bastion of her slumbering lover. The anemic, gray morning waxes enough to brighten the cerulean wallpaper and prevent her from drifting back into the fretful and disjointed dreams now dissolving into the haze of consciousness. A sobering yawn betrays her stillness as well as the retirement of the fire sometime in the night. The hope of the clarity of a new day beckons, yet she is reluctant to abandon the warmth of her shared bed.

Within the false gloaming of the violet room deep in the gloomy hall, Vin is braving that snappy cold to stoke the fragile flames beneath a fresh bundle. Wrapped in a handcrafted comforter that matches the lurid pattern of the walls, he draws the blanket against the chill and relieves his soles of the aching frigidity of the floor with the reprieve of the bedside rug. With a stare symptomatic of the stupor between waking and alertness, he tries to will the fire to life. Regardless of his mental prowess, success follows in a span of time indeterminate to his grogginess, and the bowl of the stove is soon aglow and luring him back to shut the grille. Opening his wrap like a vampire his cape to glean the welling heat, Vin shivers under warm goose bumps and turns his head to gaze at the misty spine of mountains beyond the window.

Lulled by the increasing comfort and the smoky tendrils massaging the vista, he wonders if the van is visible from the vantage of his second-floor casement. Perhaps he'd be able to determine where it had left the road and piece together the circumstances of their harrowing deposit.

With a few icy steps, he is leaning over the chest of drawers and surveying the dilapidated environs of the medieval castle. The width of the fallow courtyard and height of the sagging wall encasing the abbey prevent a view of the road or the ravine, leaving the impression that he has come to the very edge of the world. Movement draws his gaze to a clear view of the huge black gates, where the waiflike form of Fichtenberg is crouched and reaching past the bars.

Vin's burnished brows furrow. He leans against the cold glazing.

Bang!

Vin's heart leaps to his throat.

An explosion of beating black and scratching and screeching throws him from the window. His startled brain grapples with breath and tangle as he topples backward.

The forbidding clamor translates, even as his backside hits the floor, into a sharp and spectral form.

A raven.

Vin's start eases, and the fists that threaten to rend the fabric of the comforter relax as the corvid finds its footing.

Expelling the fright with a nervous chortle, he moves to sit on the bed without breaking his gaze.

The unblinking raven cocks its head to track him with sinister intensity.

Vin bows over the foot of the diminutive bed to reach for his duffel but, as he turns away, the raven raps the glass willfully with its thick, stabbing beak.

He turns sharply and surveys the bird with an uneasy curiosity. The story of Bhusunda echoes as he retrieves his sweatshirt, but there is no sense of wonder in the ominous manifestation.

The watching raven remains in the scope of his vision, staring through the glass with a ruffling of feathers.

Allowing the blanket to fall around him, he pulls the green hoodie over his head and draws it down to his waist, revealing the university emblem.

A second tap at the window nags his attention, dogged by a caw muted by the watery pane.

Trying to ignore the increasingly unsettling scrutiny of the bird, Vin pulls his jeans to his waist before reaching back into the duffel and pulling out a pair of clean socks.

Again the raven taps, but twice and more resolutely.

Resolutely?

Vin scoffs at himself. Yet as he dons his socks and shoes, the corvid's agitation grows into harried, Morse code-like rapping, incessant cawing, and frantic ruffling of wings.

"Good gods!" he groans, rushing the window to shoo the annoying creature away.

His attempt only fuels the raven's mania until he can no longer tolerate its cacophony and throws open the window-panes and, in doing so, pushes the raven off the ledge and into the air where it swoops and circles before disappearing verbosely beyond the Gothic gables.

With a sigh of relief, he reaches out to close the panes when a glint on the stony sill catches his eye.

V

"Babe, grab my gun," Agnot grumbles, the frantic cawing of the raven stoking the annoyance that pries her out of her rest.

"I wish," Charlie whispers, sliding her arms around Agnot.

"Cold," Agnot yawns, nestling into the warmth of her lover's body.

"You want to call room service?" Charlie quips.

Agnot's body quivers with subtle laughter as she surveys the woodstove. "With our luck it'd be Parson in a French maid's uniform."

"Who cares?" Charlie chuckles. "As long as he can start the fire."

Agnot rolls over in the small bed mindfully and kisses Charlie before issuing a determined sigh. "I'll get it." She bounds out of bed and dances atop the icy floor, scouring the hearth for matches.

"There!" Charlie trumpets, pointing to an ornate box hiding on a reclusive shelf within the folds of a coordinated tapestry.

Agnot grabs the box with a shiver, finding wood matches within, and crouches to open the grille. "Ooh, we've still got some pretty good embers," she croons happily, reaching for the box of wood resting inconspicuously in the corner.

Soon the stove is welling with heat, and Charlie and Agnot are dressed with bare feet yearning for the comfort of socks. As Agnot sits on the disheveled bed, Charlie stands at the dresser to select a pair. Looking out the small window in an attempt to determine how the weather might turn out, she is struck by how starkly the castle and towers rise from the wild, patchy earth. From her vantage she can see the ruin of an elegant chapel and the spoiled cloister encased between the harsh walls of the castle. Interrupting those pale walls, like gaping black maws, arched windows follow the succession of the unseen pathways within.

Charlie's gaze lingers absently on one of the casings. The morning clouds have cast it in a somber hue, and she wonders if all castle windowpanes were painted in black. *Maybe it's tar to help seal the panes*, she considers. *It's strange that no light seems to reach beyond those black mouths. Perhaps it's a room and not a passageway.*

But it is a passageway, long and crooked, following the odd angles above the garish apartments garnished to host the masquerades of the prince's guests. *Come hither to the grand stair, and I will show you the varied colored parlors. The prince has such a mad eye...*

Blue, powder blue, cascading into a dress tied at the waist with a navy sash. Drawing closer, it seems worn. Not worn, but tattered. Her hair, not so chestnut nor kempt, frosts. Her face...! Her face!

Charlie gapes in horror at the spoiled beauty shriveled over a grime-spackled skull and gruesome jaw twisting in the ghastly narrative. Her quaking shriek, however, is arrested by an anchoring strength.

Agnot is shaking her by the shoulders. "Charlie! Charlie! Charliesse!"

The horrible face vanishes.

Charlie swoons, her eyes batting thickly through the passing of the spell. As Agnot whisks her to the bed, the full horror of the vision breaks over her, and she lunges into her lover's arms, trembling and choking back tears.

"It's okay, babe," Agnot coos, unnerved by the ominous possession. "It's okay."

VI

Vin's fervent fist knocks against the door to the blue room, but he is mindful to avoid sounding panicked. Parson and Julia, still in her Hello Kitty pajamas, stand on either side of him, their antemeridian stupor scrubbed away by the disconcerting quiet that has fallen behind that door. The three step back expectantly at the sound of the latch. The thickly grained door opens to the consternation and careworn features of Agnot. She slips into the hallway, shutting the door smoothly behind her as she meets their worried faces.

"She's okay."

"What happened?" Julia asks, wide-eyed.

Agnot shifts her weight, shaking her head. "I don't know. She was looking out the window, then got real quiet before freaking out."

Vin takes a deep breath, his determined expression offering Agnot an unspoken prod.

"Yeah," she says resolutely. "It's time to get some fuckin' answers."

"What about Charlie?" Parson checks in a paternal tenor.

Agnot sighs, her eyes glancing at the door. "She'll want to be in on it, but give us a couple of minutes."

The three nod, and Agnot slips back into the room, leaving Vin, Parson, and Julia thinly framed in the frail gray light intruding from the window at the end of the hall.

"I guess I should get dressed," Julia fidgets.

"I'll be right across the hall," Parson reassures. "Just come on over when you're done."

In less than half an hour, Ravenword are descending the grand staircase. With Agnot at her side, Charlie's composure belies any traumatic residue lingering from her esoteric encounter. Below, the expansive foyer is empty, and Vin is surprised to find the fire within the gaping hearth blazing just as fiercely as the night before. Julia leans into Parson under the oppression of the mammoth doors sealing off the original structure of the castle and shivers. As they reach the floor, the faint echo of voices leads them into the dim passage between the staircase and the Gothic threshold.

The passageway opens up to a large gallery paneled with embossed wood and adorned with molding paintings consistent in theme with the mosaic tile in the baths, namely pastorals. To the right tall, arched windows pour the sullen light of the overcast sky onto a long, bare dining table that could easily accommodate a score of guests. The backs of as many chairs rise like sentries along the perimeter where, at the end of the table, Billy sits across that width of the polished wood conversing with the professor.

"Good morning," Fichtenberg hails, his voice carrying even more thinly than in the night. "There is a kitchen of sorts," he continues, gesturing to the open gallery to the left. "It is well stocked."

His amiable countenance falters with the decided approach of his former students, who take up the chairs around him and Billy. Fichtenberg examines their collective demeanor wisely, facing off with their returned scrutiny in the dull light of morning. His long, thin hair, no longer black with the pitch of night, exaggerates the skeletal gauntness of his features and matches the gray stubble that peppers the face textured with lines and wrinkles too numerous and entrenched for a man of his age. Within the exceptionally deep and crinkled sockets, his once sparkling blue eyes, now prematurely faded, stare back at them with a cold hawkishness.

"What the fuck is going on here?" Agnot salvoes.

"I'm quite sure I don't know what you mean," he deflects, checking each of their faces.

"Ever since we left on this little excursion, horrible things have been happening to us," Parson states, making a concerted effort to sound less inflammatory.

"The world can be a horrible place," Fichtenberg replies pensively, as if his mind were suddenly wandering.

"Even before we left," Julia interjects. "As soon as we got the invitations."

The professor perks with the mention of the ivory notes.

"Nightmares, people dying in the streets, creepy drivers who abandon us to roll over cliffs," Charlie charges angrily.

Professor Fichtenberg nods slowly. "Pedestrian accidents are common in Italy. As for Romero, it was very foolish of him to leave the van parked along the ravine."

"Fuck Italian drivers and pedestrians," Agnot bellows. "We've been seeing things, fuckin' awful things."

"Perhaps your imaginations have simply taken hold of visiting this place."

Ravenword bristle at his inference, and Vin levels his suspicion at the professor. "Why did you bring us here? Was it to find something for you?"

The furrowing of Fichtenberg's brow is the first genuine indication of engagement. "What do you mean, Mr. Singh?"

"Are you familiar with the l'Ordine degli Intercessori?" Vin asks flatly.

Recognition blossoms on the professor's countenance, much to the satisfaction of Ravenword. But their gratification quickly turns to dread as the change in his features begins to exceed concession.

Darkness stains the frosty pallor of his irises like crude befouling a winter pond. Spreading from those defiled orbs, the shadows leach, blackening the recesses of their sockets.

With a collective gasp, Ravenword recoil as the maleficence seeps from the rings bagging his anguished eyes into the lines and features of the changing face. Even Billy is raked by the black manifestation bleeding into the gray of his hair.

Romero's tortured eyes widen upon the company. "La grazia di vita ci libera dal destino del nostro egoismo e dall'ignoranza!" he bellows like an induced confession. "La clemenza!"

Julia slaps her hands over her ears, tears streaming down her horrified face. Agnot and Charlie stand dumbfounded and shocked, looking a great deal like Vin, who stares with eyes blazing in terrible astonishment. Parson, cringing under Romero's agonized pleading, wrestles with his dismay as he backs to the wall, watching the emaciated figure lurch in the chair as if subject to unspeakable pain.

"La clemenza!" His wild screams resound through the gallery like a deafening chorus of phantoms. "La clemenza!"

"Help him!" Julia cries, throwing her pitiful stare to Agnot and Charlie.

Finding his wits, Parson rushes upon Romero, as the creature's frail form begins to convulse violently. He takes the man's face in his hands, peers into those tortured eyes.

"You're okay!"

"La clemenza!" Romero pleads, sweat and tears tracing lines in his contorted features.

"Si!" Parson echoes firmly, "La clemenza."

Romero calms, his haunted gaze fixed on Parson.

"See if there's any alcohol in the kitchen!"

Vin darts into the kitchen, pausing suddenly. "Antiseptic or drinking?"

"Drinking!" Parson shouts, waving Julia and the lesbians to assist him.

"We've got to keep him calm," Parson states urgently. "Rub his arms, try to make him feel safe and comforted."

Romero turns his pooling eyes and wet face to Agnot. "Perdonarci!" he begs, "Perdonarci!"

Not even Agnot can deflect the waves of despair and grief drowning the miserable soul. "Si," she chokes as she rubs his shoulder. "Si."

Vin arrives swiftly with a glass and bottle of absinthe. "It was the strongest thing I could find."

"That oughta do it," Parson quips softly.

Filling the tumbler quickly, he lifts it to Romero's tortured lips, still pleading in hoarse whispers. With his dark eyes begging the faces surrounding him, Romero draws from the liquor, wincing and gasping it down.

"Okay," Parson coos, petting Romero's hair as he administers the spirit in measured pours. "You're okay."

"Do you know where he sleeps?" Vin asks, turning to Billy.

"Yeah," Billy says, pale and shaken. "Well, I mean, I know where Fichtenberg's room is."

Romero soothes noticeably, and Parson gently pulls him forward in the chair. "That'll do.

"Help me get him up."

Agnot and Vin move quickly to support the creature's frame, realizing only then the true frailty of the man.

Billy leads them through the kitchen and into an adjoining hallway that is a nearly perfect replica of that which hosts their own rooms. He opens the first door on the left, where a small room dressed in blue receives them. As Vin and Agnot lower him onto the small bed, Parson cradles his head to the pillow.

"Glass," he urges, hand reaching.

Charlie, having taken up the bottle and glass, sets them on the chest of drawers next to the bed, where Parson pours out another measure.

Romero, semiconscious and muttering his supplication, lies listless on the blanket.

"Hasn't he had enough?" Vin checks carefully.

Parson throws him a scowl. "We need to get him unconscious," he replies like a mother speaking to her baby as he tips the glass at Romero's lips. "That's the most likely way of getting the professor to resurface."

Ravenword watch Parson's ministry with curiosity and awe. Romero's heavy lids droop and close before willing one last peer into Parson's eyes.

"Perdonarci."

Romero sinks into desperation, then into a frailty, and finally into an induced slumber.

Parson rises and turns to his friends. "I think it's safe to go."

Shaken and tearstained, his companions nod and begin to retreat into the hallway.

"Shouldn't somebody stay to watch him?" Julia whispers, still trying to catch her quivering breath.

Parson shakes his head as he closes the door, leaving the man to the bed. "Have you ever had absinthe?"

VII

"Where's the phone?" Vin asks as Ravenword shuffle back through the kitchen toward the extensive table.

"I don't think there is one," Billy answers, interrupting their survey of the rustic kitchen. "That's what I was trying to get out of him when you guys stormed in."

"Did he *say* there was no phone?" Agnot presses impatiently.

"Why were you trying to find out about a phone?" Vin follows too quickly for Billy to respond to Agnot.

"Are you gonna pull the fucking van out of that ravine?" Billy snaps under the crush of eyes. "Unless there's another car around here, we're shit out of luck without that van!"

The realization leaves his companions thunderstruck, the unimaginable expansiveness of the mountains dawning. Any sense of connection with the closest villages has now evaporated with the discovery that Romero is actually Fichtenberg, and neither seems to be in any condition to help.

Billy shoves his hands into the pockets of his grimy jeans, his steely eyes waiting on their answer.

"Maybe there is," Vin announces, pulling a bright brass skeleton key out of the pocket of his own jeans.

The declaration and production of the mysterious key fractures the group's growing dread as they gather round to gaze at it like the starved over the last morsel of bread.

"Where did you get that?" Julia gasps excitedly.

"Do you really want to know?"

Agnot and Charlie exchange expressions of incredulity.

"Hell fuckin' yeah," Agnot declares.

"You're not going to believe this," Vin sighs bracingly, "but a raven left it on the windowsill of my room this morning."

"Now why would we find that hard to believe?" Parson surrenders sardonically.

Ravenword manages half-hearted chuckles, the underlying truth in Parson's point exaggerating their apprehension.

"It seems pretty modern," Vin continues, eager to pull away from the implications of the key's delivery. "Maybe there's a garage or radio house somewhere on the grounds."

"He had to have some way of contacting the outside world," Agnot adjoins.

"Absolutely," Parson trumpets, taking a seat at the small butcher-block table in the center of the rude kitchen.

"Or," Billy interjects in a dry tone as he recedes to lean against the counter, "it stole it from one of the villages." The onslaught of silent reproofs prods him to explain, and he continues as if weary of being the voice of reason. "Ravens are attracted to shiny things."

"Why would it bring the key here?" Vin rebuffs, annoyed with Billy's latent sabotage of their enthusiasm.

"Castle ruins would be a pretty good place to nest," Billy retorts with a condescending glare.

"Have you seen any ravens nesting around here?" Vin spurns.

Billy crosses his arms and locks his gaze. "We haven't been outside yet."

"We will be when we search the grounds."

Vin's retort brings a wave of anxiety over the group, with the exception of Billy, who stares back at him defiantly. Julia shrinks into the chair beside Parson under the contention of the confrontation. Intrigued by the exchange, Agnot sinks back against the far counter, considering the weight of Billy's reasoning.

"Do you really believe this bird was delivering this key to you?" Billy scoffs incredulously.

"Um," Parson interjects, "have you been in la-la land since we left San Francisco?"

"Either way, we need to be sure just so it doesn't drive us crazy," Charlie mediates coolly.

"Fine." Billy sneers. "Then we should check the rooms first—unless you want to ignore the professor's warning about going outside."

Vin's contemplation is polluted by the struggle over relinquishing his argument. But as his reasoning can produce no justification for pressing the issue, he relents in a conciliatory tenor. "It would make sense for a phone or a radio to be close to his room."

"And it won't take long," Charlie offers.

"Providing that key works," Agnot amends, gesturing.

"Why don't we just wait for the professor to wake up and ask him?" Julia proffers, reluctant to be exposed to the openness of the courtyard.

"He was death warmed over even before he flipped over to Romero," Parson replies gravely, looking around at his friends, "and needs a doctor more than a sailor back from shore leave."

"He could still tell us when he wakes up," Charlie argues.

"That could be a while," Vin counters as Billy opens and closes the cupboards behind them.

"And it could be Romero who wakes ups," Parson adds. "Leaving us stuck in the same boat."

"He'll have a lot of explaining to do, whenever he does come back, but I don't think we should waste time hanging around and waiting," Vin states.

"What about breakfast?" Julia peeps from the chair between Vin and Parson.

"Well, there's plenty of food," Billy answers, gazing into the antiquated industrial refrigerator.

"Good, then let's have breakfast and get going," Vin prods enthusiastically. "Are there eggs?"

Ravenword spread out in the kitchen as Billy reaches into the refrigerator and retrieves a basket of chicken eggs.

"Hey, Parson," Agnot calls as she rifles through a cupboard for a frying pan. "How come you handled that freakiness shit so well? I almost shit a brick!"

Parson pauses over the drawer set with flatware in neatly contoured rows and looks at Agnot with a puzzled expression.

"Because he was a nurse!" Billy retorts, punctuating his disdain by thudding a block of cheese on the counter.

"I swear to fucking god, don't you people ever listen to each other?"

Agnot turns on Billy like a viper but is stayed by Charlie's hand on her arm.

"Student nurse," Parson corrects with a nod to Agnot. He scoops up a handful of spoons and counts them out, hoping against knowing that his friends will not pursue the subject.

"I thought you were in business school?" Julia chirps, her nose crinkled with puzzlement.

Parson sighs heavily, dislodging the burden of his scholastic history. "I am, sweetie. I started off in nursing but then transferred to business because I saw how fucked-up the system is. So, I thought I'd be helping a lot more sick people by running a place right than being under a bullshit bureaucracy."

"I knew it was something like that," Vin offered from a cupboard packed with spices, teas, and…"Coffee!"

"Oh yay!" Julia sings happily. "Where's the coffee pot?"

"I think this is it," Charlie says, holding up two glass carafes.

"This'll be interesting," Agnot adds, looking at the brewing system dubiously.

"You'll need to boil some water," Parson states quickly, eager to distract his companions.

Within moments Parson has left the kitchen to set the table, thankful to be free of the subject. Charlie and Agnot are at a butcher block, dicing vegetables as Vin stands at the stove trying to ignite the burner without causing an explosion. Julia, fanning her nose at the smell of propane, sits on the counter watching the vacuum brewing of the coffee with fascination. The setting brings a sense of normalcy to Ravenword, which in turn allows their fortitude to recover and their courage to mend.

VIII

"How are you going to find it?" Motisha asks somberly as T. J. packs his duffel bag on the elegantly dressed bed.

The warmth of the red and gold suite seems depleted under their long morning of deliberation after a night of especially restless sleep. T. J.'s insistence on regrouping with Ravenword was met by Motisha's plea for them both to alert the authorities before return to the United States. T. J. countered with the incredible nature of their story, which no one is likely to believe, insisting that Motisha return to California without him.

T. J. answers without pausing to look up into Motisha's sullen face. "I'm not sure. We were supposed to catch a bus to a little town at the foot of the mountains called Colle. There's got to be somebody in Lucca that knows how to get there."

Motisha sets herself gracefully on the edge of the bed next to him, bracing her composure and reaching out to lay her hand over his. The gesture stays his frenetic packing. "Why must you do this?"

Instead of meeting her earnest expression, he sighs and hangs his head. "Because," he states softly, "they're my friends. I know you've never thought much of them, but they've never made me feel like I have to be anything or anyone but who I am."

Motisha's rich brown cheeks flush, and she lowers her eyes. "I apologize if I've ever made you feel pressured to be someone that you aren't."

"Hey," T. J. coos, taking her hand and gazing into her face. "Don't do that. You make me feel like the man I want to be every day."

"Is that why you're going?" she asks carefully. "Out of a sense of nobility?"

"No," T. J. answers firmly, turning to seek out his backpack. "I can't shake the feeling that we were invited for a reason, that I've got to be there, like there's something I'm supposed to do."

"Are you implying that I should be there as well?" Motisha queries in a stronger tone.

Finding the backpack on the other side of the chair, T. J. rises and looks at her with an uncertain smile. "No. I think your invitation was more of a case of graciousness."

Motisha crosses her arms and glares at him as if he has just insulted her. "I see."

"I'm just saying." T. J. chortles, setting the pack next to his duffel bags and offering her a consoling grin.

"I understand what you are saying," Motisha counters indignantly.

"Look, you barely knew Fichtenberg," T. J. backpedals, entertained by her reaction. "And nothing will make me happier than knowing that you'll be on your way home by the time I get to Colle."

"Very well." Motisha relents, rising from the bed. "Since I have been relegated to the red-eye tonight, I will accompany you to the train station."

T. J. grins. "Fine, but go straight to the airport after," he insists tenderly, reaching out to pull her into an embrace and a kiss.

CHAPTER 5

The Baron

THE HINGES OF THE DOOR across the narrow passage from where Professor Fichtenberg now slumbers as Romero creak in protest as Vin intrudes upon the darkness. The room is a duplicate of the one he had first been introduced to the night before, yet bereft of the warmth and sundries of habitation. A queer sensation marks the bare mattress and candleless chest of drawers, as if he himself were a ghost gazing on the shuttered remains of a former life. Even the air feels void of natural resonance and threatens to syphon the vitality from his chest. The succubus in that uncanny stillness, however, recedes under the mirth of Parson's call.

"Phoneless."

"Nothing in the purple room," Vin calls back as a muted clamor draws his attention to the window. His senses prickle warily with the impulse to trespass. A giggle seeping through the casement dismisses the warning and he crosses in ease to throw wide the panes. Craning his head into the open air, he finds Julia poking her own pigtailed crown out from the neighboring chamber window.

"Sorry," she giggles with a wave. "I didn't think they'd open so easily."

Vin offers her a smile reminiscent of Motisha. "No radio?"

Shrinking back in bashful recognition, Julia offers an apologetic smile and shakes her head. "No. It's kind of weird being in an orange room, though. I mean, one just like upstairs."

Vin nods and withdraws, closing the panes and then the door of the somber purple room to continue searching those deeper in the hall. The pedestal-borne candles between stand coldly extinguished in favor of the dreary gray light offered by the windowed sentry as he grasps the knob of the next chamber entry. The prospect from the white chamber exhibits the weed-riddled courtyard and drab face of the encircling wall. "White, no phone."

Behind him Parson opens a door and scouts the violet room with disgust. "Oh my god. I'm so glad I didn't get this room. How do you stand it?"

Pulling the door shut, Vin is poised on a glib retort when a fleeting figure beyond the window seizes his momentum. Stock-still and staring, he peers at the vista through the white room.

"Now what?"

Vin spins on his heels with a start.

Parson assesses him wearily as Julia skips past them with the ebullience of a game.

"Nothing," he insists. "It's nothing. Just a shadow."

"Just," Parson echoes dubiously as Vin shuts the room.

Vin does not respond, and the two turn to find Julia standing between the last set of doors with shoulders shrugged and snickering, her fingers pointing at the thresholds on either side.

Parson's austere countenance gives way to enthusiasm as he crosses his arms thoughtfully. His eyes narrow as if calculating figures in the recesses of his mind and then he swings at the waist to review the hall behind them. "The door to your left should be the black room."

"So what's behind the other door?" Vin continues, following Parson's logic with a hopeful gleam.

Julia drops her hands and looks to the door with a thrill of anticipation. As Vin and Parson stride to her side, she takes the doorknob in hand.

"It's locked," she deflates, staring into the wood grain.

Her face blanches suddenly, and she leaps from the door.

Vin rushes to put his ear against the door, bringing a finger to his lips.

Parson stands beside them, his chest tightening.

Vin relaxes and looks at Julia. "It's gone."

"What's gone?" Parson asks, teetering between dread and annoyance.

"I heard a knocking," Julia whispers, hugging herself.

Parson deflects with a wave of his hand, "That could have been anything—the wind, the plumbing, Billy getting to know his right hand."

"It was all echoey and hollow and weird," she bleats.

"You didn't hear it?" Vin checks.

"No," Parson replies, annoyance winning out over dread. "Is that a key in your pocket, or is there something else you're fishing around for in there?"

Vin and Julia exchange bracing glances as he withdraws the shiny brass key and introduces it to the keyhole.

"It doesn't fit," he sighs, looking to Parson, who seems more relieved than surprised.

"Now what?" Julia moans, defeated by the game.

"We check the black room," Parson retorts, trying to meter his tone. "Then we see if the others had any luck."

Vin turns, tucking the key back into his pocket, and crosses the hall. "Might as well be sure." The door opens with a rusty whine, but easily, to reveal what they had expected, a chamber dressed in black. With Parson and Julia peeking in on either side, they share a moment of consternation in the discovery that this room, like the others, is devoid of any communications equipment.

"I guess it could have been the wind," Julia acquiesces timidly as the three withdraw, leaving the black chamber behind them and assessing the locked door.

"The professor must have the key," Vin insists pensively as they retreat toward the mouth of the corridor.

The three are quiet until they reach the door to the professor's chamber, where Parson pauses. "I should check on him. If he's awake, I'll ask."

Vin nods and leads Julia into the kitchen as Agnot, Charlie, and Billy enter with expectant expressions.

"Nothing yet," Vin says in answer, pulling out two chairs from the butcher-block table. "But the last door on the right is locked."

"Same thing upstairs," Agnot replies with a curious tone as she and Charlie join them at the table.

"But we heard this creepy knocking," Julia interjects, still spooked.

"That was us," Agnot rebuffs with a sardonic roll of her eyes.

Billy, meanwhile, ambles to the large door at the back of the kitchen.

"We already checked there," Agnot calls after him, annoyed. "It's the boiler room," she explains in answer to Vin and Julia's expressions.

"Where's Parson?" Charlie asks.

II

Upon closer inspection, the frailty of the body inhabited by the two men seems too severe to sustain either of them for much longer. Crouching beside the small bed, Parson monitors the anemic pulse palpitating through the tenuous channels in his emaciated wrist. The man's wan pallor and shallow breath concern the nurse in Parson, who lays his palm over the waif's forehead before checking his pupils. Lifting the eyelids, the listless irises stare blankly through constricted windows.

Parson sighs heavily, then stands. For a moment he casts a pitiful assessment upon what has become of one of his favorite teachers before the dire implications lead him to consider those stalking him and his companions. That consideration brings to bear the importance of finding the key to the mysteriously locked chamber, and he turns to the chest of drawers.

With the ginger movements of a considerate burglar, Parson slides open the two smaller drawers of the dresser. With the awkward task of sifting through the professor's underwear proving fruitless, he moves his search to the three larger lower drawers to find nothing but Fichtenberg's threadbare clothing.

Throwing a backward glance over the sleeping body, he pans the room. With the exception of a short and narrow bookshelf crammed with collegiate texts, the room is very much the same as the others. As he deliberates searching under the bed, a reclusive angle peeking out from the folds of the navy-blue tapestry at the end of the shelf catches his eye. With a thrill of anticipation, and illicit daring, he quietly draws the ornate box from the shadow's hollow. Parson takes a deep breath and lifts the lid of the delicately engraved case, only to have his hopes for both the key and the professor dashed. In addition to matches, he finds a syringe, a set of fresh needles, and several full glass vials rolling over a photograph carpeting the floor of the box. A set of familiar faces smile up at him in black and white.

On the bed behind him, the professor's eyes open.

Parson reaches into the box, carefully avoiding the drug paraphernalia.

Behind him, the cadaverous figure rises silently with a venomous scowl.

Captivated by the image of the Ravenword's younger selves, Parson examines the photo as he returns the box to its place on the shelf.

The addict joins his knobby hands in a conjoined fist and raises them over his head.

The hairs on the back of Parson's neck prickle as a shadow across the door catches his eye.

He turns.

The strike descends.

The blow strikes the crook of Parson's neck and shoulder, sending him sprawling to the cold granite.

Panting over him, his chest heaving in an excited agitation and horrible sobbish wheezing, the wretch grabs the box and falls back onto the bed, quivering with rage and rapacity. His taxed body curls around the case like an emaciated dragon, glaring at Parson with a vile and desperate spite.

Unable to determine whether it is Fichtenberg or Romero who cowers greedily in the nest of blankets, Parson backs away toward the door cautiously. Rubbing his bruised muscles, he shakes his head in pitiable homage to the miserable creature. He slips out of the chamber, breaking visual contact with the addict only when the heavy door separates them.

Still rubbing his neck, he steps into the cavernous kitchen, where Billy is gloating over the two keys dangling from a ring hooked by his finger. Upon seeing his friends in this setting, it occurs to Parson that the kitchen and dining hall are much larger than the twelve-room accommodations seem to need, and he wonders if there is another wing to the nineteenth-century addition.

"How is he?" Vin asks as Parson pulls out a chair to join them at the table.

"Stronger than he looks," Parson replies, wincing as he stretches his neck.

"What happened?" Julia plies, her eyes wide with concern.

Deciding against disheartening his companions further by divulging the professor's addiction, Parson tosses the black-and-white photo onto the middle of the table.

"Hey!" Julia cries happily. "That's us!"

Agnot and Charlie huddle over her shoulder, pointing at the photograph.

"Wow," Agnot exclaims. "Look how good Professor Fichtenberg looks."

A handsome, albeit gangly, man of fortysomething, wearing a spirited smile and wavy, clean-cut hair, peers out of the monochrome image with eyes bright enough to be striking even without the flourish of color. Around him, the founding members of Ravenword wave and pose with fresh, enthusiastic faces.

As his companions ogle the nostalgia of the image, Parson nods at the keys dangling from Billy's finger. "Where did you find them? Are they the ones?"

Billy answers with a satisfied smirk. "Don't know yet. I first noticed them in the boiler room looking for something to eat. I didn't know it was a boiler room."

"Where's Motisha?" Julia chirps, too captivated by the flood of memories to notice Billy's triumph as she squints at the photograph.

"Taking the picture?" Charlie suggests.

Billy grows sullen as resentment clouds his sense of accomplishment.

"That'd be the day," Agnot counters.

"Remember, she hadn't joined yet," Vin corrects, recalling the formation of Ravenword as a college club.

"Were they even together then?" Charlie asks, digging through her memories of T. J.

"We weren't," Agnot interjects, pointing at the picture. "Look how hot you were."

Circumventing Agnot's faux pas, Parson chimes in assertively as he stands. "Reminisce later, bitches. I want to make a call."

His exclamation rallies them to their feet, abandoning the photograph to the tabletop in favor of the key Billy is trying to liberate from the ring.

"What are you doing?" Agnot chides.

"We don't have to all go together," he retorts, annoyed with her incessant harping. "We're not lemmings."

Freeing the first key, he tosses it to Parson.

"Fine," Agnot snaps, extending her hand.

The two glare at each other like dogs sparring for dominance. Billy drops his gaze with a smirk, tossing the second key onto the table. Agnot grabs it and, taking Charlie's arm, heads out of the kitchen. At the threshold of the dining hall, they hesitate, whispering between each other, before turning around.

"You coming or not?" Agnot grumbles.

Billy crosses his arms defiantly but shifts his weight away from the countertop to plod behind them in a sulky gloom. A moment later the three are gone and Vin turns to Parson with a hum of anticipation.

With Julia between them, they return to the long and narrow hallway like intrepid explorers, eager to discover and yet cautious of the menace that haunts their denial. Despite the day reaching full strength, the light filtering into the hallway remains anemic and casts a somber hue on the doors and pedestals. The three continue in a communion with the silence that feels as inherent to the castle as the stones used in its walls. Approaching the locked door, they notice the ruins of the chapel standing beyond the glass panes for the first time. Like sleepwalkers they reach the door.

Vin leans his ear to the door as Julia steps back, her hands clasped at her breast.

Parson watches his face for a reaction.

Their eyes meet, and Vin shakes his head.

He then gives way to Parson, who takes a deep breath and guides the key into the keyhole.

It fits.

Vin creeps closer, his eyes fixed on Parson as he turns the brass head.

The latch clicks and frees the door from the frame.

In spite of herself, Julia rushes to Parson's side as he and Vin push against door.

The door swings open to reveal the framework of unfinished walls and a small window, familiar to all the rooms, staring back from across the rustic chamber. Yet it is the gaping black pit yawning between the margins of the exposed foundations that commands their attention and sends a dire shiver through each of them.

Absorbed by the impenetrable darkness of the void, Vin, Parson, and Julia stand transfixed by the creeping gulf widening in their minds as if the atramentous chasm were a consumptive contagion. A crackling frost expands in their chests as a voiceless, dispirited chill beckons from the imperceptible depths to lure their souls, warm with life, into the grip of its subterranean slumber.

A resonant "Holy shit!" startles them to their senses, pulling each back from the edge. Turning upward, they find Agnot, Charlie, and Billy looking down on the pit from the upstairs doorway. Vin notes the roof high above them. Though lacking a ceiling, it appears sound and provides no clue to the gutting of the chamber or the unnerving hole in the earth.

"Can you see anything?" Vin calls up to the three above, holding tightly to the frame.

"Yeah," Agnot says, her retort resounding with a hollow reverberation, "a big fuckin' waste of time."

Parson and Julia recede back into the hallway as Vin strains and grapples for the doorknob, his heart pounding like an adamant alarm against the snare of the pit. Catching the brass orb, he pulls the door shut and twists the key to secure the lock, leaving the gulf of their disappointment to the chasm.

"We're going to go unpack," Parson relents, taking Julia by the hand with a dismal sigh before sauntering down the drab hallway.

III

T. J. and Motisha evade the bustling shoppers while enjoying espressos under the reaching awnings of the Gucci salon. Behind them green hedges line the plate windows of the arched facades while tourists and natives navigate the pavilion en masse underneath the sheltering vaults encasing the famous Milano fashion district. Retail bags embellished with Dior, Armani, and Prada huddle at Motisha's feet as she watches T. J.'s gaze drift absently.

"Perhaps this wasn't a good idea," Motisha says, searching T. J.'s pensive expression.

"No, it's okay," he replies, offering her a reassuring smile. "Besides, it's a little late to change our minds, don't you think?"

A coy grin curves her lovely features, and she takes a sip from her cup with a flutter of lashes. "I wouldn't mind Monaco."

T. J. returns her smile and shrugs.

"That isn't fair of me, I know, but I can't abide going back without you. And if you get to have your holiday, then I deserve mine."

T. J. nods, and as his eyes fall on the teardrop ruby pendant adorning her breast, a shadow taints his countenance.

"It's a keepsake, and I will always wear it in Milan," Motisha insists, checking him with raised brows. "I am more sentimental than people give me credit for."

"I thought we weren't going to dwell?"

T. J. lifts the little espresso cup to his smile and glances into the crowd and his expression suddenly falters. His eyes grow sharp as his brain races to confirm the recognition.

The mysterious agent, whose dogging of Ravenword compelled him to abandon his friends, strides through the crowds.

T. J. tracks him, hoping to glimpse or project the agent's course.

Stricken by his distraction, Motisha shifts to turn around only to be stayed by T. J.'s swift hand reaching across the table. "It's nothing."

"Who did you see?" Motisha insists, her expression an amalgam of hope and dread.

"I'll be right back," he says as he rises. With a hurried kiss on her forehead, T. J. rushes into the throngs in pursuit of the agent, leaving Motisha to gaze after him contending with a will of her own.

IV

The long corridor hosting the various color-themed rooms is alive with the voices of Ravenword as Billy shuffles through with a cup of tea and a plate piled with cookies. Agnot and Charlie's muffled banter seeps from their door as he passes, as does the rush of shower spray from Vin's lavatory. The animated voices of Parson and Julia spill into the corridor with abandon, as they have propped open their doors in order to prattle like schoolgirls from their respective chambers as they unpack.

Having left his own door ajar in hopes of returning with hands occupied with morsels, Billy kicks it gently and it creaks open to reveal the black chamber. The room is already a disheveled collage of clothing and luggage with the wrinkled sheets and blankets of the bed churned in a haphazard bundle. Likewise kicking the door shut behind him, Billy sets the cup and plate next to the candle lamp on the chest of drawers and straightens.

His gaze falls onto the choppy sod cloister beyond the black-framed window. The imposing square tower that rises out of that weed-riddled lawn stares back at him under the oppression of the stewing clouds as if angry with his intrusive gaze. Billy's eyes follow the weather-beaten masonry to the inky window that interrupts the tower's weathered face. Stillness falls over him as he peers into that distant portal. Where such grounding would be a precursor to fear in others, in Billy it is akin to the posture of a pointer scenting prey.

Locked in place, he waits.

The presence in the black window of the tower stares back unseen.

Stolid and focused, Billy tries to will the watcher forth.

Nothing.

Billy turns his back on the window abruptly, having no patience for reticent ploys.

A raven caws brashly in the distance somewhere over the chapel wall, but Billy chooses to ignore the lure and moves to disembowel his duffel bag. Grabbing a fistful of underwear, he transfers them brutishly to one of the top drawers in the dresser absently. He continues until the contents of the duffel have been stowed before dragging his backpack across the floor and onto the rumpled bed with a lazy heave.

Pulling the zipper along the body of the pack, the main compartment splays to reveal toiletries and more clothes. Billy digs into it absently like a badger in the dirt until his fingers strike an object both hard and unfamiliar. Rifling quickly, he pulls a satellite phone from the shabby backpack. Astonished, he stares at the brick-size device, contemplating its usefulness and the intentions of the agent who had excised his key in Viareggio.

V

"I don't get it," Julia laments, standing before the tall windows in the dining hall and staring up at the overcast sky. The dull light of the somber day washes her skin in a pasty hue. "I thought Italy is supposed to be warm and sunny?"

"Eat your soup, Julia," Agnot deflects in a tone that sounds very much like an order.

"I'm waiting for it to cool down," she replies with a glance at her friends sitting around the end of the table.

Having unpacked and showered, Agnot and Charlie had returned to the kitchen to explore the pantry where they found several industrial size cans of various stews.

Considering the odd weather, they had busied themselves with preparing a main course of soup for the group. With stores of bread and several cheeses, they were able to surprise Ravenword with a nicely laid-out meal.

At the head of the table, Vin resists playing the part of mediator in favor of a torn chunk of bread soaked in rabbit stew. On his left Parson turns to Julia, patting the seat of the empty chair beside him. "Ignore the old woman," he teases. "Come sit next to young and pretty."

Julia giggles and takes the seat, offering a conciliatory smile to Agnot, who sits beside Charlie on the other side of the table.

"Sorry," Agnot replies, "I didn't mean to snap."

Julia's smile brightens, and she waves back to her. "Eff'n eff," she sings.

Agnot answers the inane reply with a dry expression, "Sorry, I graduated from high school."

"*Agnot*," Julia giggles.

"*Julia*."

A couple of empty chairs away, Billy pauses in his shoveling of soup and bread into his mouth to assess his companions. "Why do you think they brought us here?" he punts, after a thick gulp, shrewdly watching their reactions.

The lesbians exchange cryptic glances as Julia looks from Billy to Vin with a suddenly sullen wane. Parson, however, continues to sip from his spoon, unaffected, as Vin wipes his mouth with the cloth napkin supplied with the table dressings.

"That's a funny way of referring to the professor," Vin muses, "but I guess it's appropriate."

Billy pulls off a piece of bread and caps it with a square of cheese before stuffing it into his mouth with a shrug. "Um, okay."

"What the fuck does that mean?" Agnot snarls, leaning past Charlie to glare at Billy.

Charlie exhales wearily, dropping her spoon and looking furiously at Billy.

"What?" he exclaims. "Can't I ask a simple question?"

"You know why we're here," Vin interjects irritably.

"*Um, okay*," Agnot mocks with an overly exaggerated shrug. "You always gotta stir the goddamned shit!"

Parson's eyes dart from Billy to Agnot and then to Vin as he holds a slice of bread and cheese to his mouth, feigning a disinterest worthy of Motisha. Beside him, Julia sinks in her chair.

"So you're just going to live in denial?" Billy retorts.

"Denial?" Agnot echoes indignantly.

"Have you been fucking unconscious the past three days?" Billy sneers.

"Fuck you," Agnot roars, "and your fucked-up life!"

"Stop it!" Charlie shouts, bolting to her feet. "Both of you!"

Burnished by the rebuke, Agnot and Billy glare at each other with contempt.

"I'm not going to listen to you two argue for two weeks!"

A derisive chuckle trickles from Billy, who stares at his hands and shakes his head slowly. "I can guarantee you won't have to if you don't pull your heads out of your asses."

"Billy," Vin chides, checking him with an authoritative glare.

Billy meets Vin's domination with an austere defiance as he rises. "When you guys are ready to talk about this fucked-up shit, come get me." Grabbing his bowl and plate, he kicks the chair back and marches out of the dining hall.

"I think," Parson says delicately, "it's time we find that phone."

VI

Vin and Agnot push the heavy nineteenth-century doors open against the blustery gloom of the dismal afternoon. Tufts of overgrown grass and weeds in the courtyard, stretching out to either side of them, bow angrily to the abrupt harassment of the charging wind. Vin, Julia, and the lesbians step into the harried day and are quickly absorbed in the unseasonable morose. The incessant clanging of the huge iron wrought gate riddles the air angrily as if unseen hands were wracking them in a desperate bid to escape.

Turning, Vin shuts the door behind them with the aid of a sweeping gust. The door snaps tight with a thick and disconcerting thud, relegating them to vulnerability.

"At least it's warm," Julia offers weakly, hoping to stoke a gleam of optimism.

Overhead, mountains of murky billows tumble and churn as they scroll across the agitated sky. In the distance,

Jupiter gives voice to the tumultuous dome with a deep and booming rumble that resonates from peak to peak.

"We'll meet back here if it starts raining before we meet up behind the castle," Vin says, taking the lead and stepping off the granite landing. "Right or left?"

Agnot marks him with an expression devoid of enthusiasm as she passes, leading Charlie onto the bullied grounds to the right. "See you on the other side," she calls without turning around.

Charlie takes her arm and the two commence their search in an affectionate huddle.

Vin offers a bolstering smile to Julia, whose stout pigtails are no match for the will of the wind, and she skips down the worn and chipped steps to join him.

The facade that hosts the great Gothic entryway extends the entire length of the building to encase the formal dining hall and the themed guest rooms. Ahead, the desolation stretches far beyond the abbey until it is finally broken by the sagging western wall. The monotony of the vista is interrupted only by a tree, bent with age, struggling in the northwest crook.

As Vin and Julia meander under the reaching windows of the dining hall, a desultory rapping reaches their ears, piquing their reluctant curiosity and playing on their sense of exposure.

• • •

Agnot and Charlie, meanwhile, have turned the northeasterly corner of the building, where a cluster of ruined houses greets them. Under rows of watching windows high on the castle's eastern face, the shanties tell the story of their grim histories with dilapidation and ruin. The crumbling brick walls of many have pulled in the decayed remnants of their roofs. Even from a distance it is obvious that the emaciated doors, those that remain, have long since lost their purpose and leave no need for a key delivered on the talons of a raven. A drab greenbelt of reeds and mosquitoes winds from the far corner of the castle to an arched opening in the east wall, where the corresponding mire still drains into the alpine wilderness. Rusty fangs grin at them menacingly from the lip of the archway, the remains of the bars that had once fortified the compromise in the ancient bulwark. In the heart of the bleak setting, a small bridge of stone extends a faded pathway over the ribbon of muck to fallow fields and untamed orchards. Without speaking they proceed into the time-ravaged expanse of the service bailey like sleep-walkers stepping into an eerie canvas washed in sepia and monochrome.

• • •

With Julia pressed against the cold wall of the weather-beaten face of the dining hall behind him, Vin peeks around the corner as the unnerving tapping continues unimpeded. Images of guillotines and ax murders are subdued by the reality of a loosened set of windowpanes beating against the apartment by the will of the wind. He relaxes and looks back at Julia with mild reproach.

"You didn't close the windows, did you?"

Julia's nose crinkles with her knitting brows, unsure what he is referring to.

"When we were checking the rooms this morning," he expounds, stepping away from the building. "The orange room?"

"Oh yeah," she shrinks into shrugging shoulders. "It's not that big a deal, is it?"

Vin considers the supposition. "I guess not. But the last thing we need right now is something stupid to freak us out in the middle of the night."

Julia's eyes widen as they walk over to the open window. "Oh my god, I didn't think of that. And it's right under my room!"

"I don't know if I can reach it," Vin says, stretching his arms and body to grasp at the bottom edges of the window frames. "Nope, see if you can find a big rock or old stump."

Vin starts rummaging through the tall weeds and grass, brushing his hands through them. Julia, however, afraid of an unpleasant discovery, simply strolls to and fro and hugging herself as she inspects the wild lawn.

"I don't see anything," she sings against the gale that has risen suddenly to buffet her. Not getting a response from Vin, she turns and finds him examining a thicket of weeds.

• • •

In the service ward, Agnot and Charlie have been drawn to a tiny building by its relatively well-preserved condition.

Rounding the low stonemasonry wall, they find that, like the other buildings, it is lacking a door. As Charlie examines the entryway, she doubts there ever was a door.

"It's a well house," Agnot declares, stepping cautiously into its dark hollow.

Chills rise on Charlie's shoulders as she loses sight of Agnot in the darkness lording over the interior. "Let's keep looking, babe."

"You should see this," Agnot exclaims, her voice resounding in unearthly reverberations. "It's a lot bigger than it looks from out there."

"That's okay," Charlie deflects anxiously, pacing at the entryway. "Let's keep looking."

"It's so dark."

A rock clacks across Charlie's nerves as it prattles against the walls of the well. A dispirited plunk from the black depths follows, constricting Charlie's reason in the grip of an ambiguous fear.

"Get the hell out of there!" she spurns, stomping away from the well house.

Agnot hurries from the darkness and quickly wraps her in her arms. Charlie buries her face in Agnot's shoulder, trying to tame her trembling.

"Sorry, babe," Agnot whispers, "I just thought it was kind of cool."

"I know, but not being able to see you ten feet in front of me is not."

"I get it," Agnot consoles. "Let's keep looking."

• • •

"It sure looks like a tombstone," Julia demurs as Vin rests the hewn stone against the foundation of the nineteenth-century addition.

Panting, Vin looks up at her from his stoop as he tries to catch his breath. "Does it matter?"

"Why don't we just call to Parson?" she suggests. "He can shut it from the inside."

An image of Parson sitting in the kitchen as disembodied voices sail through the hall flashes through Vin's mind and he laughs despite himself.

"What?" Julia asks with an uncertain grin.

"What would you do if you were in there hearing someone calling your name when you knew everyone else was outside?"

Julia indulges in a mischievous chuckle. "Yeah, that would freak me out."

Vin nods with a grin before straightening and stepping up onto the stone. Leaning his body against the wall, he reaches up and brings the two panes together to a close. "We'll lock it once we're inside."

The momentary levity sets them more at ease. Vin springs off the block, and they continue along the face of the apartments. At the last window, the corner of the building recedes, and that levity is grounded by a sight that catches their breaths.

The imposing chapel cathedral rises out of the despoiled earth as if having rooted and grown from the bile of that desolation. Its yawning medieval archway and flanking towers are mottled with the stain of rain and lichen, sun and grime. Swaths of missing roof reveal decayed beams like the exposed ribs of a rotting corpse. Murders of black corvids swoop and soar in and out of the desecration on the invisible byways of the mad wind. Tumbled pavers plot a course through the weeds to the fractured steps of the entrance landing, where enormous doors, coated in the same spackled grime as the surrounding masonry, stand sealed by time and the elements.

Slowed by creeping apprehension, Vin and Julia trespass the sod breast of the once sacred bailey under the ancient scowl of the defiled church. A battalion of gales bully them like phantoms of angry parishioners as they approach the bare granite plateau of the landing. A menacing rumble thunders in the deep mountains to the north.

Reaching the corner of the steps with Julia on his heels, Vin ascends to the dust-swept platform. Behind him, Julia stares up at the decrepit cathedral with a cringe.

"Come on," Vin coaxes, having turned to find her transfixed.

Reluctantly, she takes his hand and climbs the steps.

Facing the ornate ironwork weeping rust and scum that frames the doors, Vin withdraws the raven's key.

• • •

"There's nothing here," Agnot huffs as she and Charlie plod over the soft dirt past the small bridge bowing over the murky channel.

The great hulk of the castle looms spitefully, and Charlie can't shake the spectral watching of the hollow, black windows lining the high walls of that oppressive wing. In spite of her willful intent, she pauses as if captivated and lifts her face and then her eyes to the series of stygian cavities. Relief seeps into her veins upon finding only emptiness in those repetitive frames.

Her solace, however, is short-lived. An ambient shift sets the atmosphere ajar, as if the moment has been immersed in an affectation of despair. Charlie turns, hoping to draw reassurance from her lover's brooding countenance, to find Agnot ahead by the stream. Her back is to her. The distance between them is a sudden gulf of grief. As if blunted and soulless, Agnot stands queerly slack against the bleak backdrop of tuft and bramble and tangle of forsaken fruit trees devouring the eastern wall in obscurity. The blotted strokes of cinereous storm clouds upon that dreary canvas deepen to malevolent gunmetal and descend like preternatural mountains of doom over the dispirited figure bewitched in a milieu of in-anima.

Once again the rapier of fear plunges into Charlie's chest. Nothing within her can *feel* Agnot's presence. Desperately open, her senses expand to reap only the oppression of the castle and its bereft bailey. Even the smatter of ruined out-buildings retain the impressionist echoes of the last days of life. Yet the shadowy landscape and dispirited cast of her lover defy vital resonance.

Charlie's pulse sinks with her heart as she struggles to face what horrors calling out may bring. She fills her lungs, her hands sweeping behind her for an anchor. Her will and her voice falter. She falls against the bone-like frame of a dilapidated bake house, silently pleading for a sense of life in her lover's form. Any hope lingering in the wider world bleeds away as if all of reality were suddenly blanched with desolation.

Unable to endure the ghastly ambiguity, Charlie regains her footing and steps forward with stifled whimpers. As she traverses the gulf between her and the changeling, she quivers under the sapping of her strength and weakening of uncertain knees.

The figure's demeanor is unchanged.

As she struggles toward the golem, memories of laughter and lovemaking mock Charlie's imagination, as if predicating an endless divide. She reaches for the shoulder of the dispirited doppelganger, but a thick dread smears the atmosphere with an impenetrable foreboding that stays her hand. Pursing her lips against crying out, Charlie steps abeam of the figure, resigned to the harrowing reveal. The hairs on the back of her neck rise.

A blast of white light suddenly blinds her upon a stunning thunder strike.

Crumbling to the ground, her scream is a thin tenor within the mighty crash.

"Holy shit!"

Charlie gapes, stunned and dazed, but buoyed by her paramour's exclamation. Agnot is in the dirt beside her. As her senses clear, Agnot is grabbing her and pointing into the field. "Look!"

Charlie pulls her bewildered eyes away from her resurrected lover to peer across the boggy stream. Fleeting shadows disappear through the drainage arch in the protective wall. Her blood curdles when one turns and stares back at them with brazen and ferocious eyes.

"Wolves!" Agnot exclaims. "They were in the orchard. I could feel them watching me," she finishes with a disconcerting drone, as if suddenly possessed once again by the golem.

Charlie scrambles to her feet, pulling Agnot up with a force beyond her gentle nature. "We gotta go!"

Agnot complies, throwing her arm over Charlie's shoulder. "You're shaking like a leaf," she exclaims, pulling her in to kiss her head as they quickly stride toward the south ward.

Charlie looks back over Agnot's arm, which provides her no comfort.

"Don't worry, babe," Agnot reassures, "I don't think they'll bother us, at least not during the day."

• • •

Julia clutches the bars of the iron fence caging an ancient cemetery that flanks the western length of the cathedral, pressing her trembling form against its unyielding anchor. "Can we go now?"

Vin, his face blanched by the crowning blast of lightning and thunder, answers with shaken reassurance before his eyes goggle. In a frantic charge, he grabs and pulls her from the conductive black stripes.

Overcome by his steel, she surrenders with a flutter of affinity and uncertainty as he sweeps her into the open bailey.

Alighting at the edge of the overgrown cobblestone road, his grasp eases, and he returns her gaze with soft and apologetic eyes. "Lightning and metal fences aren't a good combination."

"Oh," she sighs, before casting an absent glance on the iron palings. "Oh!"

Vin's arms release with her sudden astuteness and his cheeks warm as he withdraws to the relief of the open air.

Julia, begrudging the emancipation, turns to thank him only to have icy fingers rake the back of her neck. Vin is retreating slowly with a scowl fixed on the cemetery. Behind him the gnarled trees bracing the sagging wall howl and wave in the gales as if pleading with them to desist. She jogs to his side with a shudder, hugging his arm and searching the stark visage of the cathedral for the dreadful mark that has captivated him.

Granite headstones, from the tall and exquisite to the low and simple, populate the necropolis under the arches of the nave so layered in grime that the stained glass is nearly indistinguishable from the masonry. The imposing wing of the weather-bleached transept divides the ranks of those long departed, sequestering the humbler remains to a stretch of cankered sod tumbling back to the margin of the Lady Chapel. There, a stone wall juts from the cathedral to anchor the black spears of the iron fence.

Vin takes Julia gently by the shoulders of her fuzzy purple coat and leads her along his crab-angle course. From their shared vantage, the wall turns like a page to reveal a crude garden of lowly crosses, rust eaten or rot-wooded, hidden from the grace of the noble yard. Interrupting this lowly bid for absolution, a mausoleum crafted from marble finer than any found on the sacred ground rises conspicuously amid the modest ornaments. Like the formal cemetery, this small necromantic ward is barred by the continuing strength of the ironwork fence. An inconsistency in the pattern of these black bars denotes the presence of a hidden gate.

Vin returns to the perimeter of the black grille with Julia glued to his side. She lifts a fretful gaze against the wind to the menacing sky as Vin surveys the mausoleum, captivated by the cryptic inconsistency.

"Why is it back here?" Julia wonders aloud, looking from the marble house to Vin. "Do you think they ran out of room in the main cemetery?"

Vin shakes his head, the thrill of discovery coursing through his veins. "No," he explains eagerly, pointing out the various yards. "This isn't holy ground. See, look, the part of the cemetery at the front of the chapel was reserved for people of rank. The part behind the transept, that square part coming out from the church, was for common people—probably people who were important or prosperous but not part of the aristocracy."

Julia follows his hand as he pans over the small site before them.

"This little graveyard...shouldn't even be here."

She looks back at the churchyard cemetery and then at the mausoleum, cocking her head. "Um...okay. So why is it here?"

Like weaving an eager tapestry in his mind, Vin pulls the clues together as he drifts along the fence to meet the gate. His face reflects the brooding, yet energetic, mood of the turbulent atmosphere as his inquisitive fingers caress the frame of the secret entry.

"It was probably put here after the castle fell into ruin," he surmises, gesturing to the markers. "These graves surrounding it are set with crude markers, but they're not primitive, so maybe people from a nearby village buried their dead here, mistaking the placement of the mausoleum as holy ground."

"Okay," Julia exclaims with a tentative sigh. "So why is the mausoleum here?"

Vin reaches through the bars, his hand searching for and finding the latch on the other side. "Obviously someone significant came to the castle…"

The latch does not give way as he tries to pull it out of its cradle.

"Poe!" Julia proposes excitedly. "Aldo said Poe was here!"

"But he's not buried here," Vin counters, entranced and confounded by the unwilling gate. "And he certainly didn't die here."

Julia's fervor evaporates.

Vin pauses, turning to her with sudden fervor. "Don't you see? Aldo said that Poe came here and found out that the story of the red death was true. So someone had to have told him the story." The ghastly implications suddenly dawn on him, repelling him from the gate.

"What?" Julia asks reluctantly. "You think it's true?"

"What, Poe's story? That's ridiculous. But it might be based on a historical event known to the locals. Someone who knew the legend would have to've brought him here."

"And died?" Julia surmises dreadfully.

Vin steps back and surveys the uncooperative ironwork. "We've got to get in there."

Julia recoils at the thought of worming their way into a tomb.

"Let's just go," she pleads fretfully, hoping to avoid antagonizing whatever forces have been dogging them on their journey. "I think it's going to rain."

"We've been looking for the home of this key," Vin insists, presenting the brass key, "and mausoleums are usually locked."

"Aren't we supposed to be looking for a phone or radio or something?"

"Yes, but if this goes to the mausoleum, we need to know it."

Julia shifts her weight to question the significance of the tomb when black-feathered wings descend from the cheerless canopy and into the unhallowed yard. With a rustle and caw, the raven alights on the gable of the marble house, cocking its head to cast a beady eye on the two. Before either can comment, thin and ethereal rays of silvery beams reach through a crevice in the murky thunderheads to polish the ebony corvid and gray stone with an unearthly grace.

Faces wide with astonishment, Julia and Vin acquiesce to fate to join forces at the gate.

"It's rusted solid." The words press from Vin's lungs as he strains to force the arm of the latch out of its cradle.

"Oh my god!" Julia exclaims.

Vin's head swivels to find Agnot and Charlie rounding the far end of the corner of the castle at a full run. Their white and terror-stricken faces register on his brain even before he can process the scene.

"Run!" Agnot booms, her command penetrating the dreary air like a cannon through the mist.

A harrowing thrill rushes through both Vin and Julia as a pack of wolves rounds the corner behind them. Giving no heed to Julia's scream, Vin heaves her up onto the iron spindles, unceremoniously shoving her petite posterior over his head.

Grasping the daggered peaks of the black bars, she pedals desperately to pull herself up to the crossbar.

Vin clamors frantically behind her, using the atrophied hinges of the gate as footholds.

As Julia spiders down the inside of the iron, Charlie and Agnot burst onto the grille, throwing her to the ground.

With wolves at their back, the two grapple with the sinewy bars.

From an uncertain perch on the dragon spines, Vin grabs Charlie's coat at the back of the neck and, with all of his strength, hoists her to the crossbar and then grabs Agnot. As he heaves her from the sod, the wolves rush upon her, leaping with the wild ferocity of deprived fangs.

Agnot bellows as jagged teeth sink into her calf and tug loose her grasp.

Julia screams, palms at bloodless cheeks.

Vin and Charlie shout a communal rebuke at fate, grasping Agnot by the shoulders, lifting both she and a viciously tenacious wolf.

Agnot's instinctive kicking and pawing for a foothold beats the beast loose, and she explodes onto the iron spine, pushing Charlie and Vin to the unhallowed ground.

Both scurry away from the cage on hand and heel as Agnot teeters at the top of the fence with the wild dogs leaping and gnashing murderously after her.

Rocked by the onslaught, she leaps from the height and hits the ground with a cry of pain.

Vin and Charlie sweep her into their hands and out of the reach of the snapping jaws that lunge furiously between the bars for another taste of her flesh. Not waiting for her to find her footing, they drag her quickly along Julia's panicked path to the mausoleum. Behind them the wolves begin to throw themselves savagely against the bars.

Streams of rust fall from the corroded latch with every brutish impact. Soon it is loosed from the encasing grime and bouncing in its cradle.

With limbs racked by terror-charged nerves, Vin thrusts his hand into his pocket at the face of the mausoleum.

Julia is already wiping away a century of gunk with fingers frantically searching for a keyhole.

The latch of the gate bounces ever more freely under the collective barrage of beasts.

Sensing the giving of gate, the pack summon all the barbarity of their lineage to attacks the iron barricade.

The moment lingers.

Agnot is reassuring Charlie.

Julia's eyes are burrowing into the keyhole.

Vin is inserting the key.

His hand turns.

The latch of the gate jumps.

The door of the mausoleum gives way.

The gate is thrown open.

Agnot shoves her friends into the darkness.

The wolves are upon them.

Agnot screams, tearing her leg out of a saw-toothed mouth and shoving the door behind her.

The yelp of a crushed muzzle pierces the fray as the four wrestle the iron door of the marble house against the offending jaws and, finally, into its frame.

Vin wedges his foot firmly against the bottom seal of the door with a stomp and sets his weight upon it. Regardless of how heavy the barrage of lunging wolves, the door does not move.

"Agnot?" he checks through the pitch as his fingers find the keyhole and he locks them in the shelter of the tomb.

She hisses from the stinging gash before answering, "Okay. I'm okay."

The tumbled pounding of wolves throwing their bodies against the thick iron door is replaced by unnerving scratching and snorting and sniffing along the seams.

A light is struck, and Julia's breath is caught by the desiccated corpse lying between her and the lesbians. The flashlight tumbles from her quaking grasp. As it hits the cold marble floor, they are again engulfed by the blackness of the mausoleum and the onslaught of the wild wolves.

"Goddamnit!" Agnot hisses.

"It's not her fault!" Vin snaps before catching himself. "Sorry, sorry."

"No, you're right," Agnot follows quickly. "Sorry, Jules."

Light again emerges in the darkness at the hand of Charlie, who holds a small flashlight of her own. The closed space allows the light from its diminutive lens to adequately illuminate the tomb.

"That's my girl," Agnot chimes.

It is only with the steady light that the condition of each is apparent. Still rooted against the door, Vin is scuffed and scraped with a tear in his sleeve and an under-lying gash in his forearm where an iron bar caught him in his fall. Julia is equally plied with dirt with a purpling bruise swelling on her cheek. Charlie's hands, now bracing Agnot's stance, are sprinkled with stripes of blood. Agnot is worse by far. Both of her legs and feet are gnawed and bloody, torn deeply with the gashes inflicted by the primal tools of the carnivores.

Beside them all the grizzled remains of the enigma rest upon the stone bier covered in dust and decay as if hewn from the marble itself. The cast of the odd, angled light from Charlie's lamp stretches and exaggerates the features and cavities of the dusty remains into strange shadowed fancies consistent with every macabre imagination.

As their collective survey settles, Vin nods toward the wall opposite himself and the door.

The three women turn to find an inscription carved into the marble above the head of the eternal recline of the tomb's inhabitant.

Enrico Salvador Eliano Romero † Nobile dei Barone di Maledetto di Anno Domini 1779–1819

• • •

Parson sets what medical and first-aid supplies he could find on top of the chest of drawers in the blue chamber, looking out the window into the dismal day with somber resignation. In the bed beside him, the professor sits curled in his tangled nest of blankets and languishing in the semiconscious nodding of his narcotic euphoria. The rattling in his lungs began soon after Parson entered to check on him, culminating in bouts of choking hacks that leave Parson wondering if his declining health in this isolation was the real reason behind the invitations.

• • •

"I don't think the professor has split personalities," Charlie says slowly, contemplating the implications of Romero's name in the wall.

Julia recedes from the engraving with tears welling in her eyes.

"That's impossible!" Agnot retorts, the pain coursing through her making her impatient with even her lover.

With the wolves huffing and clawing in his ear, Vin stares at the inscription, trying to determine a reasonable explanation for the coincidence. "I wonder if Fichtenberg adopted the identity, or at least the name, for his other personality."

"Parson would know," Julia trumpets desperately. "Let's go ask him."

• • •

The tiny hairs on the back of Parson's neck prickle. Wary of another attack by the addict, his eyes dart quickly to the incapacitated wretch.

The professor has not moved, but his stillness does nothing to dissipate Parson's unease. Attributing the queer atmosphere to being alone in the apartment annex with the professor, he sits on the edge of the bed and takes Fichtenberg's hand.

The professor's heavy-lidded eyes roll to the heart of the room, where a gossamer wisp is developing like a ribbon of smoke.

• • •

"How long do we have to stay here?" Julia moans, tears tracing lines down her creamy complexion.

Vin follows the scratching and seething along the perimeter of the iron door.

"A long time," Agnot replies bleakly.

Vin's expression changes to curiosity as his eyes fall absently on the skeletal remains. "Agnot, you're Catholic, right?"

● ● ●

Parson pulls Fichtenberg's hand gently in order to extend his arm.

Gazing through the euphoric haze, the professor's brain fixates on the form developing over the shoulder of his former student.

Clasping his hand around Fichtenberg's frail wrist, Parson carefully slides back his sleeve.

● ● ●

"Not since my mom caught me with Kat Thrace," she quips, wincing under the triage of Charlie, who has ripped out the lining of her coat to bind Agnot's wounds. "Why?"

Vin nods toward the body. "Look at his hands."

Clutched in the withered bones of the folded hands, several cords lay under a layer of dust against the bare sternum, the ends of most having fallen between the hollowed ribcage.

● ● ●

Parson sighs heavily, disheartened by the pattern of blotchy lesions that dot the professor's sallow skin. Behind him, the phantasm takes the form of a terrifyingly unearthly Romero.

Fichtenberg lurches out of Parson's grasp with eyes wide in mad recognition.

• • •

"Scapulars?" Agnot frowns. "I've never heard of someone being buried with more than one."

"What are scapulars?" Julia asks, trying to avoid the corpse.

• • •

Startled and confused, Parson leaps to his feet as a feeble scream croaks from Fichtenberg.

Lifting his talon-like hand, he points chillingly past Parson.

Parson spins on his heel only to throw himself against the dresser, horror-stricken by the phantasmal presence of Romero's horrible ghost. Before he can react, the phantom is upon him.

• • •

Shovels slice into the damp earth.

A black void beneath encasing walls.

Romero is leading a man down a ladder into the pit.

The swinging lantern casts an orange hue on the worn features of the author Poe.

The two men are walking through a hall of grotesque monuments.

Desperate footfalls in a stretch of blackness are consumed by a snarl.

One man is scrambling out of a pit.

A roar and a scream and Romero is snatched.

A sick white mask stained with droplets of blood.

Huge arched and ill-grained doors slam shut.

Fourteen squares are coupled with golden cords and placed in cold and folded hands.

A marble mausoleum rises.

CHAPTER 6

The Pit

T. J. SHUTS THE TRUNK ON Motisha's Louis Vuitton luggage amid Milan's Late-Modern glass blocks of concrete, steel, and glass. His own modest bags hang from his fist and shoulder like anchors against the backdrop of Milano Centrale's roundabout plaza and grand facade. Pedestrians and traffic vie for dominance beneath a bright-blue Italian sky that washes all but Motisha's countenance in lavish sunlight. Pushing past the dark thunderheads clouding her features, T. J. wraps his strong and consoling arms around her.

She rests her face against his broad chest. "Are you certain?"

Her persistence feeds the doubt gnawing at his resolve. His heavy sigh bolsters his fortitude but does little to assuage the storm clouds building over his heart.

"Yeah," he whispers, kissing her hair.

It is only when she withdraws from the embrace to gaze into his eyes that T. J. recognizes the anguish behind her polished demeanor. Drifts of crystalline tears frame her lashes as she inhales briskly and reaches into her Rioni purse.

"Take my cell," she orders, handing him the phone. "Leave a message at my home number when you get to Lucca."

T. J. deflects the offering, shaking his head. "I can't leave you with no way of calling for help if something happens."

Motisha ices over, extending the cell with an insistent prod. "Nothing is going to happen. I'll buy a new phone when I get to Monaco and call you so you will have my new number."

T. J. relents with a diffident smile.

"I will see you in a few days," she states, setting her hands behind his neck and pulling him into a lingering kiss.

Upon the pain of release, she sweeps to the waiting door before his steel can delay her and, with a tearful glance, disappears into the back of the taxi.

The cab pulls away with an abruptness that leaves T. J. feeling destitute, conflicted, and relieved. Mustering another cleansing sigh, he bolsters his courage, secures his luggage, and strides across the plaza for the train that will hasten him to his fate.

II

Faces, drawn and pale, fill Parson's scope of hazy vision. Nausea and a throbbing head are the first sensations to coax his mind to presence. Vin, Julia, and the lesbians are worryworn luminaries hovering in the ether like so many moons while the frigid, unyielding floor orients the length of his backside. As his friends come into focus, a figure brooding over them sends his mind searching. By the time he has grasped the identity of the silhouette, Billy has already given himself away.

"How the hell should I know?" he retorts. "I was in my room!"

Images of pits and ghouls and graves flash through Parson's mind.

"Hi, honey," Julia chimes sweetly, smiling down at him. "Are you okay?"

Parson makes the mistake of trying to nod, rise, and answer at the same time. His head swoons and his body rolls instinctively to lurch the contents of his lunch all over the stonework.

His friends recoil with an involuntary chorus of disgust, except for Charlie, who kneels quickly to support him.

"I'm not cleaning that up," Billy declares as Parson rights himself and Charlie rubs his back.

A volley of unspoken rebukes befalls Billy as Vin stoops to help Parson to his feet.

"Uck! How unattractive," Parson quips weakly, obliging Vin's aid. "Sorry, ladies."

"Charlie," Vin directs, throwing his arm around Parson's ribs and shifting his weight toward the dining hall, "help Agnot. I saw a first-aid kit in the kitchen."

It is only when Parson's feet are shuffling across the cavernous foyer that he realizes he had been lying at the foot of the stairs directly in front of the ancient doors to the old castle.

"No, it's not there," Parson reports, looking to Charlie. The sight of a bloodied Agnot supported by her lover shocks Parson to sobriety. "Bloody Mary in a blender! What the hell happened to you?"

"It's a long story," Agnot grumbles, hissing as she limps against Charlie.

Vin pauses at the mouth of the corridor into the dining hall. "What do you mean? I saw it there before we left."

"I took the first-aid kit with me when I went to check on the professor," Parson answers, pulling away from Vin to test his knees.

"I can get it," Billy states, trudging into the hall without waiting for a response.

"I guess I can find a mop or something," Julia says with the enthusiasm of a beleaguered janitor.

By the time Vin and Charlie get Parson and Agnot into chairs at the butcher-block table, Billy is spilling the contents of the first-aid kit onto its surface.

"There's aspirin in there somewhere," Parson begins quickly. "Give her three or four tablets and grab the flashlight and check my pupils. I want to make sure I don't have a concussion."

Vin grabs the penlight from the jumble of supplies, clicking it to life quickly and checking Parson's eyes.

"They shouldn't look dilated and should constrict normally to the light," Parson instructs.

"They look normal to me," Vin replies.

Parson blinks heavily. "I'll take a few of those," he begs as Charlie deposits four tablets in Agnot's palm. Chasing the pills with a glass of water, he pulls himself out of the chair with labored exertion. "Excuse me, dear," he says, taking Charlie's place over Agnot's wounds. Charlie had propped Agnot's legs up on another chair and, as gently as she could manage, began to remove the makeshift bandages and her boots and socks. With bracing fortitude, Agnot endures the agony with stunted grunts and hisses as Parson takes over.

"Vin, boil some water. Charlie, I left the bottle of hydrogen peroxide in the cupboard where the kit was."

As the two swiftly comply, Billy stands beside Agnot, watching Parson examine the bloody gashes. "What do you want me to do?"

"Tell me what happened," Parson replies without looking up.

"I don't know what happened," Billy shrugs before being pushed aside by Charlie.

"Fine!" Parson snaps, the urgency of tending to Agnot before infection sets in putting him on edge. "What happened to *me*?

"Vin, water?"

"It's on," he calls back from beside the industrial gas stove.

"Find some hand towels and boil them in the water."

"All I know is I heard someone screaming like a banshee down here. At first I thought it was the professor, but something just didn't seem right. So I came out and saw you passed out at the bottom of the stairs. That's when these guys burst in the front door."

"I need a bowl." Parson looks to Charlie before posing his next question to Billy while Agnot sits wincing under his probing administrations. "Did you check on the professor?"

"Not till just now," Billy replies, his brow furrowing, unsure if the question was a veiled accusation. "Everyone was freaking out."

Charlie offers a clean white bowl to Parson, who uses it to catch the peroxide he pours over the gauze. At the same time, Vin is emerging from the long hallway with a pile of hand towels, setting them on the counter next to the pot on the stove.

"Where's that fucking absinthe?" Agnot barks petulantly, unable to bear the agitation on top of the pain.

Parson glances to Charlie with a nod. As she sprints into the dining hall to raid the liquor cabinet, Vin sets the pot of steaming water on the rustic floor next to Parson.

"I want you to be a big boy," Parson teases, hoping to allay her apprehension. "This is going to be uncomfortable."

"Fuck you, Parson," she ribs while trying to manage a grin through clenched teeth.

Parson coaxes one of the hand towels out of the hot water and tosses it frenetically between his hands until it is cooled enough to be handled. Embracing the near scorching, he wipes down his hands thoroughly, dunks it in the boiled water, and then spreads the towel out on the floor next to the pot. Quickly drawing another hand towel, he sets it on the other to cool as Charlie returns with an open bottle of absinthe in one hand and a half-filled tumbler in the other.

"Fuck the glass," Agnot bristles, taking the bottle and throwing it back like a pro. "Thanks, babe—fuck!"

Parson cleans her wounds with the hot cloth as Vin fishes out the next.

"So will someone please tell me how this happened?" Parson presses, hoping to provide a measure of distraction for everyone.

As one hand towel after another is bloodied, Vin recounts his and Julia's part of the story, with Charlie interjecting. Both are interrupted by exclamations when Agnot can no longer stifle the excruciating process of being cleaned and disinfected. By the time their stories have merged with wolves and the mausoleum, Parson is bandaging and then wrapping Agnot's legs.

"You're going to have to stay put," Parson orders brusquely as he secures the wrapping with sterile tape. "The kit didn't have sutures for stitches, and I don't want to have to break out my sewing kit—but I will if you don't do what I say."

"The mausoleum is Romero's," Vin declares, drawing reassurance from Julia and Charlie. "We found his body with an inscription."

The revelation stuns Parson and Billy.

Billy, pondering the implications of their ordeals, leans against the counter. "How did you get away?"

III

Like an eruption of ebony streamers, ravens poured from the weather-worn chasm in the roof of the cathedral chapel to churn into a swirling stygian typhoon. Screaming, they descended by the hundreds on that pack of wolves viciously vying for the mausoleum door where they had trapped their prey. In a storm of beating black wings and snapping black bills, the epic murder attacked the wild dogs. Between teeth and talon, the wild tempest was choired with snarling yelps and screeching caws. Where the wolves lunged and gnashed for a mouthful of feathers, the cold-blooded ravens clawed and dove for a beak-full of eyes. By sheer strength of number, the pitch-feathered avengers overwhelmed the savage might of fur and fang, routing the wolves back into the surrounding wilderness.

Unthanked, the ravens ascended victoriously into the unseen currents before returning to their colonies beneath the remains of the cathedral's sheltering pitch.

IV

Vin rubs his eyes with his fingers, squinting with the recognition of the dull and plodding thud in his head. With Agnot doctored and all of them safe within the walls of the annex, the tension has dissipated, leaving him feeling spent and overextended. A survey of the rest of Ravenword confirms their share in the condition. "I don't care why they left, I'm just glad they did," he yawns. "I'm done. I'm going to go lay down for a while."

"What about dinner?" Billy asks, being the only exception.

"Fuck dinner," Agnot replies, trying to stifle the contagious yawn.

Billy deflates at the prospect of going without a meal but knows better than to protest. He glances toward the dining hall where the somber light of late afternoon slants to caress the polished wood table.

"It's not that late right now," Julia chimes, reluctant to compound her fatigue by skipping supper. "Can't we be a little late with it so we can get some rest but still eat?"

"I tell you what," Parson says as he carries the pot of bloody hand towels to the sink. "Billy and I will have dinner on the table at eight. That will give you guys a few hours to rest up, wash up, and cheer up."

"I kind of have stuff to do," Billy says sheepishly, only to be met with a round of spurning exclamations.

"It won't take that long," Parson assures.

"What stuff?" Charlie chides in a suspicious tone.

"Here," Vin interrupts, pulling a tangle of golden cords from his coat pocket. At both ends of each cord, fabric tiles are sewn onto small woolen squares. They are the scapulars found clutched within the dead hands of Romero's corpse. "You can clean these up and see what you can make of them." He hands them to Billy as Parson moves to scrutinize them from over his shoulder.

V

Despite the potentially garish nature of dressing a room in green, the coordinated walls, tapestries, and sundries of the little chamber Parson and Billy have chosen as a work station is surprisingly soothing—the effects of which they enjoy as they sit on the bed with towels draped over their laps, gingerly cleaning and examining the scapulars as if the little squares were part of a research project.

"Well, I'm certainly not going to be able to figure these out," Parson mutters as he huddles over a scapular, carefully wiping away centuries of grime with a cotton swab. "I don't know anything about Catholic iconography."

Billy sweeps away the greasy strands of hair that had tumbled into his eyes as he scrutinizes one of the tiny images pressed into the square cradled in his palm. "Not a Dan Brown fan?"

Parson looks up at him with a sardonic grin. "Yeah, that's why I'm in a gothic book club."

The jibe is friendly and gives Billy a sense of comfort he rarely enjoys. He manages a tentative half smile but remains focused on his set of little woolen pictures. His heart begins to pound in his chest as he considers risking exposure. "My parents were Catholic," he offers with a low, constrained tone. "But I never learned anything about it," he amends quickly, hoping to deflect the line of questioning that typically follows.

Recognizing the unspoken volumes behind the offering and the courage in Billy's breach, Parson speaks without looking up from his task. "I'm not sure how you want me to respond to that."

"I never cried."

A dark shroud of pensive air falls over Billy, arresting the moment in a somber stillness that seeps into Parson like a cold damp.

"I watched them die."

Parson stares at Billy's haunted face and distant eyes.

"I was so glad…so relieved…"

Struck by the confession, Parson infers what he can.

"They suffered," Billy whispers.

Understanding breaks over Parson, washing him in a relief that brings with it compassion for the lowest member of their fellowship.

"It was horrible," he explains, suddenly lucid, with a face pleading for absolution. "That was the worst. I mean, when they finally died. I knew they weren't suffering anymore, that it was over."

"I'm sorry. I didn't know," Parson says softly.

Billy smirks defensively, restoring the internal buttresses that have isolated him from the world. Parson watches with resignation as Billy returns to cleaning the scapular in his hand as if the subject had never been broached. The affectation, however, suddenly abates, and he squints at the image being uncovered by his swab.

Parson looks up at him and knits his brow. "What's up, buttercup?"

Billy meets Parson's puzzled gaze as if the quip hasn't registered. The look on his face sends a chill down Parson's back. "It's a lamb," Billy states dreadfully.

VI

The weight on the bed shifts, and Charlie opens her eyes to find Agnot sitting up and looking at the door with determination.

"What's up, babe?" Charlie whispers through her drowse.

"Why do you have to go into the hall to get to the bathroom when it's right next door?" Agnot grumbles.

Charlie raises herself, yawning. "Okay, give me a minute."

"Nah, stay in bed," Agnot insists, patting Charlie's hip. "I can make it."

"Are you sure?" she queries with another yawn, already sinking back into the pillow. "What about Parson and his sewing kit?"

Agnot smiles at Charlie's sweet selfishness. "I'm not running laps."

"Okay," she whispers, snuggling the pillow.

Agnot tussles Charlie's hair before slowly setting her bandaged feet on the floor.

"Goddamnit!" she hisses as she hoists her weight onto those wounded limbs and stands uncertainly.

"Okay?" Charlie checks, rising quickly.

"Okay," Agnot winces. "Relax."

Slowly and tenaciously, Agnot hobbles to the door, setting her weight against the wall in hopes of a reprieve, however slight. With a deep breath, she leans back on her heels and pulls the door open to find the candle sentries in the hallway aglow, despite the will of the insistent dusk reaching in through the far window.

As Agnot lurches into the corridor on wince and grimace, a shadow darker than that of night retreats into the corner of the ceiling, having reluctantly resurrected the offspring of its nemesis to camouflage the span in comfort.

The origin of these quivering blades of flame, in Agnot's mind, leaves her wondering if the professor had cleared his stupor or if one of the other members of Ravenword had taken care of the candles. Her throbbing legs, however, convince her to accept the amber hues without further contemplation. She hobbles to the lavatory, smudging the floor with traces of scarlet. Above her, the shadow seeps into a dark crevice over the open end of the hall where the stairs descend into a dark foyer.

It is in the foyer, prematurely benighted by a lack of windows, where the low rasp of angry breath rolls across the floor. In the lower passage, a figure looms, crouched and silhouetted against the waning light in the first-floor hallway.

A muzzle rises to sample the still air.

In the tiny bathroom, Agnot sits on the toilet wondering what has gotten the ravens so stirred up, as their frenzied cries storm the walls to bombard her aching head.

A malefic and perverted nature delivers the scent of blood from smeared tile and stained bandages to the nostrils of the beast.

With wary malevolence, the wolf creeps onto the threshold of the foyer, panning the darkness for its prey.

At the great hearth, the Lady in Blue emerges from the ether like a beacon swelling in the night and commands a sudden and angry torrent of flames from the enchanted fuel.

Startled, the wolf recoils, but the ghost cannot sustain the intensity of the flames.

The blaze casts the beast in an orange hue but fails to deter. With another nodding sniff, it moves with piqued ears into the openness.

Muffled curses tumble down the stone stairs like an invitation.

The wolf pursues, stalking the grand flight.

A piercing wail sirens from the Lady in Blue to penetrate and set on the edge the deepest recesses of the annex as she shrivels and rots and fades back into the ether.

The bathroom door opens sharply, and Agnot pokes her head out, her face wan with an unnerved chill.

In the blue room, Charlie is sitting upright with senses bent on confirming the alarm. She is met with only silence.

Agnot shuffles her swollen feet past the frame, closing the lavatory door behind her.

With one fell swoop, the shadow clinging to the ceiling extinguishes the candlelight and dissipates into the darkness.

Seized by the inexplicable vanquishing, Agnot stands rooted the floor. Her senses expand with dread and return the heavy breathing of the beast. Her gaze is drawn by horrible instinct to the mouth of the hall.

There crouches the wolf, poised and hateful in its terrible intent, with head low and ears back and fangs bared. One horrible eye seethes with a barbaric desire rife with rage, the other a gory, weeping cavity echoing black-winged talons.

Strangled by terror, Agnot grapples with the unyielding bathroom door, her eyes and mouth gaping.

The wolf prowls closer.

Stirred by the dull clamor in the hallway, Vin rolls out of bed.

Abandoning the door, Agnot clamors for her own chamber, throwing candle and stand between her and the stalking beast.

The wolf takes little heed. With each step, it grows larger and more monstrous.

Finding her voice, Agnot pummels the door madly, her screams filling the hall.

On the other side of the three-inch separation, Charlie fights furiously against the wood, pulling and heaving and beating to no avail as her screams answer in horrible recognition.

Trapped in their garish chambers, each of the Ravenword hostages wages war against unrelenting doors. The black will of the shadow, however, cannot be broken, and only one door is loosed.

The portal to that gaping black pit creaks.

Pleading and pounding in horrible desperation, Agnot throws herself from door to door, her tortured eyes unable to pull away from the atrocious beast that has grown into a fiendish debasement of nature.

Behind her, the threshold to that horrible void yawns wide.

As the door gapes, the monster pounces.

Charlie, Vin, Billy, and Parson batter the doors of their chambers as the nightmarish cacophony of an unspeakable ravaging fills the annex. Their burning throats bellow a ghastly chorus to Agnot's mortal screams amid brutal roars.

An appalling quiet descends.

Ravenword are struck mute by the dire stillness.

The latch to each of their doors is loosened.

The company flies into the corridor, only to be repulsed. The entire breadth and length of the hall is soaked and splattered with blood and gore.

Only Billy is unaffected enough to perceive the door to the pit creeping eerily shut. His rush to catch it before it closes pulls the rest of Ravenword from their grievous stupor.

With collective momentum, they dash through crimson pools. Billy's hand is the first to grasp the handle, but even with the swift reinforcement of Vin and Parson, the door defies strength and pulls itself into its frame.

The three men strain on the handle with adrenaline-fueled might, Parson imprinting a bloody footprint on the wall in their effort.

The portal remains unmoved, as if fused to the stonework around it.

Vin slips on the carnage, inadvertently bringing Billy down, then Parson, into the sanguine muck.

Julia wilts against the frame of her chamber door and into a curled ball. Her wailing, however, is quickly usurped by a savage cry.

Charlie sprints wildly up the hall. Her footfalls spew ringlets of her lover's blood onto the walls as she hurls toward the offending door on the tail of an ax, whose head bites firmly into the malignant grain.

Vin, Parson, and Billy cringe and dodge as she rips the blade out of the evil wood, cocks the ax, and swings with desperate fury. As if possessed by a demon, Charlie bludgeons the door in a frenzy that is terrible and shocking. Her furious volley does not wane, despite the strength and age of the wood. Every heave is punctuated with her roar, and every roar takes a bite out of the ill-natured timber.

The face of the door splinters and the ax-head catches, having bitten clean through.

An unearthly howl that eviscerates Charlie's dire fervor reverberates from the pit behind the cleft to seize Ravenword with soul-riddling fear.

Charlie's roar is translated to sobs. Exhausted, she falls back to be caught by Vin, who sweeps her away from the threshold as Billy picks up the ax to exploit the breach.

Quickly spent, Billy is forced to surrender the ax to Parson, who pushes past his trepidation to exorcise his diffidence by demolishing the barrier.

"Come on!" Parson shouts, tightening his fist around the ax handle and launching himself over the splintered debris before Ravenword can mount an argument.

Billy scurries to follow but is pushed aside by Charlie, her eyes burnished with reckless resolve.

The remnant of the second floor is too narrow even for Parson's feet. "Shit!" Pivoting frantically against the pull of the yawning black gulf below, his footing slips, and he is swallowed by the terrible pit.

• • •

Parson rubs his ankle brusquely. Before him is the gaping stillness, its black and absolute emptiness coring his chest and laying his heartbeat bare and drumming against the shrill silence. The totality of the abyss radiates on his senses like the very angel of death, consuming the primal impulses of mob and gallantry. The palpable malevolence leeches the very heart from him. On legs bled of strength, he stands, stripped to his cowardice, baring both his senses and the blade. A cold sheen glazes him as his pores open with the prospect of trespassing that utter silence. A tumbling whisper from a parched throat is all he can manage. The ax-head pulls under the teetering of his quivering arms. Clenching his grasp tightly, he clears his throat. He takes a deep, bracing breath. "Come on down," he calls in a trembling voice.

Despite his anticipation, the abrupt deposit of Charlie behind him startles him so violently that he throws himself against the dirt wall with the ax raised to strike. Before his mind can clear, Charlie is hissing curses at Billy, who follows so closely that he knocks her under Parson's poised blade.

A deep rolling growl echoing beyond the void evaporates the discord.

Charlie can see the shimmer of the ax-head as Parson lowers it carefully.

"Get ready," Billy mutters.

Parson and Charlie atrophy under the terrible anticipation.

A sharp and penetrating silver beam pours abruptly into the void.

Parson's knees buckle under the threat of unshrouded horrors.

The light crowning Billy's forehead, however, reveals only earthen walls for as far as it can reach. As they indulge in their relief, Julia lands unceremoniously behind Charlie with a whimper and is followed quickly by Vin.

A second round of snarling with a hideous dragging quells their temptation to vent their apprehension.

To everyone's astonishment, Billy creeps into the cavern, his forehead book light fixed on a collection of artifacts piled in a shadowy hollow.

Parson recognizes the silhouette of the rusted pickax before Billy reaches for it. Shamed by the betrayal of his wits, he rises quickly but carefully to join him. Ravenword follow in a stew of terror, no more immune to the fear effects of the cavern than Parson.

Among the artifacts are several Davy lamps stowed between the rungs of a dilapidated ladder. Billy nudges each one with his fingers before taking one in hand, the subtle dins of their disturbance amplified to dinner bells in the unnerved imagination of Ravenword. He sweeps the void with the silver beam as he hands the lamp to Charlie.

They are both trembling.

Rifling through his pockets, he surprises everyone by retrieving a book of matches and revives the nearly two-hundred-year-old wick like a seasoned miner.

Parson wipes the base of the lamp with his fingers, presenting the sheen of leaking oil.

Billy replies with a fatalistic shrug.

The breadth of the new orange light, however weak, comforts their beleaguered minds but does little to bolster their courage.

Charlie snatches the lamp and forges ahead defiantly with a pickax lifted high. Her heart pounds in her chest. With every beat, it bleeds for her lover. Regardless of what her ears have heard and eyes have seen, she cannot acquiesce to the prescience of that bleak golem nor the watching blackness that haunted them in the bailey. The knots and crevices of the roughly hewn burrow unfolding with her advance draw long and strange shadows that are twisted and construed into a brood of evil spirits. A chill streams suddenly through her veins as a form, a framework, emerges out of the darkness ahead. Grasping the rung in hand lends substance to the ladder and the end of the tunnel. Charlie turns to her companions only to have her hope arrested by a seething in the darkness.

Ravenword spin on their heels, Charlie and Billy casting their lamps back into the cavern as terror grips them.

The rising growl does not resonate from the black void behind.

In frightful unison, they lift their heads.

Involuntary screams erupt from their gaping throats.

Leering over the ledge of the second mouth of the pit, the monstrous wolf with fangs and snout bloody and gore-matted glares down on them with ravenous ferocity.

Ravenword break into a bedlam of mad scrambling as the monster lunges.

Yet before the beast can fall upon them, an unearthly shriek from deep within the void repels its momentum.

The company swoons on confused terror as a blue form in the blackness blossoms into a horrid phantom.

Streaking out of the black channel with a face like hell's fury and form like a billowing demon, its waste-laying screech scatters the five. Shoving them against the walls of the pit, she soars high to confront the monster and command black-winged avengers.

The wolf rears with an angry bellow, rising onto its hind legs to reveal the full stature of its abominable nature. Not that of a wolf, but a monster of legend and stories and nightmares. Fangs and claws snap and sweep as the werewolf retreats under the onslaught of the raging phantom and a storm of diving ravens.

In the pit, Ravenword flee headlong into the void like bewildered mice.

"Parson!" Billy yells as he rushes back toward the ladder.

A figure is charging up the rungs.

The alarm catches Parson, who curses Charlie as Billy flies after her.

"Vin!" Parson calls, to no avail.

Julia has run blindly into the cavern, and Vin's impulse drives him to follow.

Parson sprints to the ladder, ax in hand, to clamor out of the pit. The sight that greets him curdles his blood and shatters his perceptions of reality.

The air is thick with a cacophony of ravens harassing the werewolf, who towers over Charlie with malicious bearing while she extends the reach of her rage with a swing of the pickax. The monster evades the strike before pouncing, claws first.

Taking advantage of the creature's intent, Billy runs at the raven-battered beast with his own pick raised overhead, only to be backhanded and thrown across the grimy floor.

On counterbalance, the werewolf swipes at Charlie just as she lets her pickax fly. A piercing yowl fills the expanse as Charlie rips the pick from the deep flesh of the monster's forearm as its reflexive swing swats the Davy lamp out of her hand.

Upon the werewolf's brief retreat, a sweeping current of rabid ravens encircles and barrages the villous monstrosity. As it bats them away with a roar, Parson charges with his ax ready.

The monster shifts quickly and bounds at Charlie. She dodges the beast, but its riposte snares her legs and sends her to the ground. Before the monster can recover her, Billy and Parson are upon the creature.

Picking herself up, the breath is robbed from Charlie's very lungs, and she crumples to her knees. Protruding from a dark recess, the bloodied hand of a motionless silhouette lies in the wan light. Around the wrist of the cold and pale flesh is the braided bracelet that Charlie had made for Agnot on their three-month anniversary.

The alarm of Billy's bellow draws her back to the fight and the werewolf looming over her, shrugging off corvids.

Billy is sprawled on the floor, reaching for the leaking lantern.

Parson and his ax are thrown from the monster's back.

The beast turns again on Charlie.

Julia screams from the rim of the pit.

Vin gapes in a stupor.

Billy grasps the lantern and flings it at the monstrous beast.

Charlie's eyes widen with those of the werewolf.

Flames erupt and spread across the creature's shoulder, scattering the mauling ravens. The terrible werewolf bays and screams, recoiling and beating the consuming fire as it throws itself against the floor.

As it rolls and writhes, Parson recovers the ax.

The air is a frenetic bedlam of churning black wings.

"No!" Billy shouts in wild command.

Yet momentum cannot be hindered and before Parson can even hope to pause, the blade of the ax rends deep into the neck of the burning werewolf.

The final, earsplitting yelp disperses the murder and heralds a comfortless hush.

Billy scrambles to his feet to meet Parson over the monster's body, where they are joined by Julia and Vin. Julia's sharp gasp punctuates their panting astonishment. Before them lies not a werewolf, nor a monster, but a simple wolf in a stench of blood and burning. Their confounded reason, however, is given no time to consider. A wail of pitiful mourning rallies them to Charlie, who sweeps and searches a shadowy recess frantically.

"No, no, no, no," she sobs.

Her friends encircle and coddle her, gently pulling her away from the empty shadows.

"She..." Charlie cries, "she was right here...Right here."

"She's in shock," Parson assesses, lifting her listless and sweat-glazed body.

Despite her own tenacious tears, Julia pets and holds Charlie as Parson and Vin move her to the shallow steps. As Parson and Julia console and tend to her, Vin is drawn to Billy, who stands in the openness, surveying their surroundings. It is only then that Vin's overwrought brain is able to acknowledge that they are inside the chapel cathedral.

Before them a file of derelict pews in every stage of decay litters the nave. But it is the bizarre representations of the saints lining the desecrated sanctuary that captures his imagination.

"Mary and the baby Jesus," Billy surmises, pointing at the dust and web-blanketed marble statue of a naked young woman in recline with legs spread wide upon the moment of issuing the divine infant. An arch of twelve stars encircles her head as she swoons against dour angels while a petulant cherub lays lilies between her ample breasts and enigmatic seraphim catch the newborn in their many wings.

The harshness of the enormous statue makes Vin uneasy and the prominent, erect nipples of the Virgin impress him with a lasciviousness that further mocks the sanctity of the iconography. But it is the flaking blue pigment that was splattered haphazardly against the statue in a distant past that intrigues him more acutely and leads him to examine the rows of statues flanking the defiled Virgin.

The three weathered relics on the left of the Madonna are equally disconcerting. The first depict two headless male nudes, their bodies slumped against each other with a staff rising between, around which two phallic serpents emerging from between their legs are coiled. It, too, is hewn starkly and is blotched with a purple dulled by time. The second is a male nude accosted by dismal orange. It is easily recognizable as a Roman soldier, one caught in the instant of death. His powerful physique is listing, his scorpion-crested shield slipping from his grasp. A quiver's worth of arrows impales the figure from head to groin with an almost modern horror sensibility, while a sinister angel is set above the martyr to crown him with a ring of fire. The next, and that closest to Vin on his right, is smeared with gaudy violet. The work is also a male nude, depicting an old man crucified upside down. The heads of golden keys protrude from his hands and feet as if the wounds were keyholes to latches waiting to be unlocked. The perineum of the victim is conspicuously contoured so that, with the testicles and hanging penis, the genitals create a lewd cross.

An anxious caw from the host of ravens overhead pulls Vin from his ruminations to find Billy standing before the statue directly right of the idiosyncratic Madonna and Child. While Vin stood fixed in uneasy examination, Billy toured the enormous icons to ponder and glean what he could.

The corvid calls again as Billy scrutinizes the pear-shaped nude of a headless female standing on a bundle of kindling with a young lamb across its shoulders and brandishing a flaming sword. Like the Virgin, the nipples on her delicate breasts are protrusive and licentious and splattered with drab green. His survey, however, is waylaid by the insistent raven's shriek being joined by another and then another until the bare rafters are a discordant squall of excited birds.

The loud thud of a heavy door slamming reverberates through the chapel.

Vin spins abruptly to throw his gaze into the dark depths beyond the choir.

Parson and Julia jump to their feet as the mass of black wings flee through the foul haze and out the gaping maw in the roof.

Stock-still and honing their frayed senses on the depths of the cathedral, Ravenword stand suspended in terrible anticipation. Their dread is twisted with wonder by an eighth colossal figure, but it does little to ease their bated apprehension.

The mighty angel rises on a large bier before the rood screen, locked in combat with a writhing serpent. His great wings are spread wide as he holds the jagged mouth of the evil viper at bay with a daggered hand while plunging his robust sword into the enormous coils strangling him at the waist. Unlike the other bizarre representations of the saints, the depiction is unstained and wrought in the purest translucent marble striated with clouds of quartz and onyx. Yet for all its perfection, a series of chipped and violent scores in the wrist of the hand grappling against the fangs mars the relief, as if attacked by some desperate vandal.

An insistence nags at Vin's blunted brain, but the oracle is muted by the ply of fear.

"I'm done," Parson quips in sharp abandon, cradling Charlie's shoulders and pulling her up. Taking Julia's hand, he ushers them toward the tunneling pit.

Vin shifts his weight to join them.

Billy lingers, enthralled with the pattern adorning the border of the base that supports a statue of a male nude whose marble has been splashed with a contrasting, aged, crackled white. Kneeling on a pile of rugged stones, the figure's horridly gaping mouth and eyes are swollen and wrought in agony. Standing over it is an unsettlingly unfinished figure, save for the massive club poised to bludgeon the wretch.

"Billy!" Vin carps.

Before Billy can respond, a disembodied wail harrows Ravenword's momentum.

A cold and unnatural heaviness descends as the cry evaporates in the shadows.

Parson and Vin exchange apprehensive glances in the arrested moment.

On wings of heart-pounding defiance, the company breaks the spell and rushes to the waiting hole in the transept floor only to be seized again by dark and grimy spectral rings blooming from the stone.

Emerging like rust and weathered sprouts, chains rise from the two fixed anchors to shackles and, from those braces, beseeching phantasmal hands. Expanding between, like some ravenous mildew, an apparition blossoms.

Ravenword gawk with minds reeling as the humble robes and forlorn visage of a mad and sallow friar appears between them and their escape.

"Aw, fuck," Parson whimpers as the mouth of the consecrated deceased gapes grotesquely wider and wider.

The company cringes under the black and maniacal glare, braced for a scream that does not come. Their suspense is shattered violently as the candelabras in the chancel behind them crash to the floor. To their dismay, utensils and ornaments explode from their dusty graves, clamoring and clashing in a dispirited tumult of cyclonic rage as the phantom thrashes against the spectral chains.

The friar's head writhes on a twisting neck, craning and lunging in wild desperation.

Ravenword recoil instinctively, seized by a helpless stupor.

The phantom's face is a mask of yawning terror.

The torrent of supernatural debris rains down suddenly in a cacophony of extinguished animation.

A queer silence ensues, setting their hearts to pounding until trespassed by a whisper, pitch and tenuous and resonant, like a parasitic worm slithering through the brain.

Charlie wrings herself from Parson's embrace, turning on him with blazing eyes and a face as white as the friar's ghost.

Julia begins to cry, sinking into Vin's arms.

With a face like mortal fear, the phantom dissolves into the silence, leaving the void staring up at them like Satan's spite.

The unseemly hiss rises from the pit once again to press the silence with Charlie's name.

Ravenword fall back aghast, the horrible address arresting even Billy's macabre indifference.

Compounding their terror, a disembodied scream, like the echo of the friar's mute visage, explodes over them to shatter the grimy stained glass of the rood screen and push Ravenword back into the dilapidated nave.

The hideous voice from the pit counters with the mounting venom, repeating its invocation.

The rough arms of the ladder reaching out of the pit quiver abruptly, as if someone or something has taken hold to ascend.

In the heart of the chapel, the unseen phantom continues to shriek and pillage the chancel.

The cohesion of Ravenword unravels, their tortured minds spent. Each paces on the verge of panic, scanning frantically for an escape.

The stiles clatter against the rim of the pit as the wicked voice, now clear and harsh and derisive, taunts Charlie.

Invisible chains clatter violently as the unseen poltergeist topples benches and launches the podium at Ravenword.

It splinters at their feet.

In a flash of insight, Vin takes hold of it and heaves.

Parson rushes to lift the other side.

Together they fly to the south transept, over the smoky corpse of the wolf, and hurl the dais through a turbid pane of stained glass.

Charlie, Julia, and Billy are hard on their heels, each catapulting themselves through the rupture without care or thought for the biting shards or the fall beyond.

The heinous torment from the pit rockets across the nave after them.

Parson picks himself up off the mangy tufts of the rampart, glad for the light of day, however gray, and scrambles to check Julia and Charlie as Vin catapults from the window behind them.

Charlie scrambles to her feet with palms pressing her ears against the horrible anticipation of the ghoulish siren that rises over the tumult of the angry ghost to the chapel.

Vin clamors to his feet as Ravenword bolt over the wrought-iron fence and into the bailey with the last of their strength.

Behind them, the windows of the ruined transept explode in a nebula of grime and debris as the entity reaches the boundary of its prison.

CHAPTER 7

The Phone

Julia stains the shoulder of Vin's sweatshirt with her tears, sobbing within his embrace as they sit at the dining hall. The night has blackened the high windows yet is chased from intruding by the pair of candelabras on the polished expanse of the dining table and the fire in the simple hearth behind the head of the table, where Billy sits with a sullen and downcast stare.

"It's my fault!" Julia bellows, her voice hoarse with grief.

Vin tightens his arms around her. "Don't be ridiculous."

"I left the window open!" she cries.

"It's not your fault!" Billy shouts, pushing himself away from the table and standing so forcefully that his chair is thrown back onto the marble floor. "It's my fault!"

His outburst causes a reprieve in Julia's sorrow and throws a mask of astonishment on Vin's face. A selfless confession from Billy to allay another's grief seems inconsistent with his character, and Vin's surprise melts into a draft of suspicion.

"Did you know we left the window open?" he asks slowly as Billy paces in front of the fire.

Billy shakes his head miserably, looking as if he, too, were on the verge of tears.

A disconcerting sensation that Billy has done something terrible grips Vin, and he sets Julia upright in her chair to rise from his own. "Then how is this your fault?"

Billy retreats from Vin's creeping approach. "I have a phone!" he blurts, avoiding Vin's eyes.

"You found the phone?" Vin roars incredulously.

"No, I have a phone in my duffel bag."

Like a pointer scenting prey, Vin stalls. "You can get a signal?"

Billy stares at the floor as he backs away along the table, wringing his hands. "No," he says in a low tone that sets Vin's nerves on edge. "I...I have a satellite phone."

Thunderstruck by the revelation, Vin glares at Billy with eyes blazing with rage. "What?"

"The guy you guys thought was an air marshal put it in my bag when we were at the beach," Billy confesses in a ramble saturated with remorse.

In one swift charge, Vin is upon Billy, knocking him to the floor with a balled fist.

Billy spits crimson as Vin grabs him by the collar with both hands and wrenches him to his feet. "What have you done?"

"I'm sorry!" Billy bawls, his face wet with tears and blood.

"What-the-fucking-god-up-the-ass is going on?" Parson shouts from the threshold of the hall, shattering the atmosphere of contempt.

Vin shoves Billy to the ground brutally while Julia cowers in her chair. Awash in anger and disgust, he storms past Parson.

Bewildered, Parson turns to follow, and Billy picks himself up from the floor to rush after them.

Shaken by the explosive scene and terrified by the prospect of being left alone, Julia scrambles to catch up. As she flies into the hearth hall, Parson and Billy are bounding up the stairs after Vin, who is shouting obscenities with all the volume his lungs can muster.

"Vin, quiet!" she bawls. "You'll upset Charlie!"

Vin snaps his jaws into a clench but yields none of the forcefulness in his charge to Billy's room. Shoving the door open, he is appalled to find the room so disheveled it looks as if it has been ransacked. He rummages through the knots and bundles of clothing in a rage. "Where is it!" he barks as Billy and Parson reach the chamber.

Billy hurls himself into the black room and pulls open one of the top two drawers of the dresser. "Fuck!" he shrieks with Vin on his heels.

"What the fuck did you do?" Vin roars, grabbing him again.

Having had more than his fill of trauma, Parson throws himself between them. "Stop it!"

Vin relents, turning away as Billy falls onto the mess of his bed, crying, "I didn't do it!"

Parson looks into the drawer and is shocked to see a satellite phone resting on a bed of Billy's underwear. His elation, however, is swiftly dashed by the tendrils of wires sprawling from the casing. Pursing his lips, he looks to the ceiling and takes a deep, bracing breath.

"Can someone please tell me what the hell-on-earth is going on here?" Parson shouts.

"You tell him," Vin spits. "I've had enough of this shit."

As Vin sweeps past her at the doorway, Julia spurns Billy with a sad reproach before receding into the hallway.

Parson looks at Billy with cocktail of concern and irritation. "I don't even want to know," he sighs wearily. "Save it for the morning." He tries to muster a reassuring smile, but fatigue, adrenaline, and uncertainty quell the offering. "You gonna to be okay?" he asks, indicating Billy's bloodied lip.

"Yeah," he shrugs, wiping the blood on his sleeve.

Parson nods and heads for the door but is stayed by Billy's somber insistence.

"I didn't wreck the phone."

Parson sighs and grabs the door knob as he looks to Billy with a disappointed countenance. "You can explain in the morning," he says before closing the door on the battered wretch.

II

Charlie stirs. Her swollen eyelids part apathetically. It is still dark, and the wall she faces is nearly lost in shadow. Entwined around her are the tangled blankets meant to comfort her. Tossing amid nightmares has twisted them into knots. The pillow is still damp with her devastation.

A sound worms into her ear.

The softest scrape, as if someone were sliding a hand across the dry wood grain of an old desk.

She strains to listen. The compulsion to roll over and survey the room is stifled by the quite rational fear welling inside of her, born of their harrowing odyssey.

The constriction of her suspended muscles begins to melt as the chamber is drained of sound completely. With ears piqued, all she can hear is her own breathing and the drumming of her heart.

Her breath is caught suddenly, however, by the scrape repeating.

Against her door!

Her eyes widen. She can hear breathing, yet she has not exhaled.

It is coming from the other side of the door!

With goose bumps rising, Charlie swallows her fear and slowly rolls onto her back, bracing herself for whatever horror her eyes may meet.

The sight of an empty room fills her lungs.

She stares past her feet at the door.

A hushed collage of unintelligible syllables seeps through the seams.

Charlie's heart is pierced again, struck with the possibility that Agnot has somehow survived and used the last of her strength to return for help!

Slowly, Charlie sits up and slips her bare feet to the icy floor.

She rises from the bed, craning to glean any noise from the door.

Her first trepid step reaps only silence beyond her pounding pulse and bated breath.

Charlie leans forward with the second. She restricts her lungs.

She can hear only the pounding of her pulse.

Her exhale is chased by a deep draw as she steps closer to the door.

She pauses before it.

Palms flat against the ancient grain, she slowly presses her ear to the wood.

Nothing.

Creeping to the frame, she can feel the cold body of the knob in her hand.

Her heart thunders in her chest.

A cold sweat washes her face.

Drawing her eye to the crevice between door and frame, she turns the doorknob.

The door dislodges to the rasp of breathing, heavy and terrible.

Confusion swamps her.

Peering through the crack, she cannot see the hallway.

Foul, wet breath blows against her lips. An inch from her own face, a disfigured, bloody eye peers monstrously back into her cornea!

The momentum of her shoving the door as her throat disgorges a siren scream sends her falling backward.

The rebounding force prevents the latch from catching and the door flies open.

As if drawn from Charlie's nightmares, Agnot's corpse fills the doorway. Her head is gruesomely splayed open, and her blood-soaked clothes swim in an invisible wind. Ghastly, ruptured eyes fix on her from a face of sickening pallor and violent lacerations. The gore of bloody gashes quivers in the hollows of her neck and chest.

Charlie flails in abject terror against the back wall.

Ribbons of black tendrils radiate around the corpse of Agnot as it levitates into the room. Its gruesomely shattered jaw twists as if to speak, but whatever words it intended are issued in garbling globs of coagulation that drift into the horrible ethereum enveloping the phantom.

Charlie wails in horror so forcefully that blood sprays from her throat. In a frenzy of terror, she claws at her own eyes.

The apparition shatters with the rush of Vin, Parson, Julia, and Billy into the tiny chamber.

Stricken at the sight of Charlie's fit, the four fall to her aid.

In her terror, she fights them off.

It is only when Julia throws her body against Charlie to wrap her in an embrace that she is subdued.

"Light! Light!" Parson screams.

Vin, shaken by the blood and claw marks, hesitates only a moment before flying to the doorway and throwing the switch.

The little chamber is washed in warm and welcome yellow light.

"Did you bite your tongue?" Parson asks Charlie loudly, looking sternly into her reeling eyes. "Charlie! Look at me! Did you bite your tongue?"

From Julia's shoulder, Charlie's haunted gaze fixes on Parson, and her head shakes frantically.

"Okay, okay, honey," Parson continues in a paternal tone. "We're going to take care of you. You've scratched yourself up a bit, and there's a little bit of blood, but you're going to be okay. Can you open your mouth for me?"

With Charlie's nod Julia relaxes and shifts to cradle her as Vin, Johnny-on-the-spot, hands Parson his penlight.

Parson pinches Charlie's chin tenderly, and she opens her bloodied mouth. With a tender, trained hand, he examines her tongue and inner cheeks, thankful to find no indications that she has bitten herself.

"Can you stick out your tongue and say 'Ah' for me?" Parson asks tremulously.

With her compliance, he understands the source of the blood. Her voice is frail and rough and her swelling throat raw and coated crimson.

"She's going to need some aspirin and something to keep her asleep," Parson says, looking to Vin. "I'm going need the first-aid kit."

Vin turns quickly to Billy and is stayed by what he finds, his startled expression causing Parson to turn also.

Billy is standing by the foot of the bed staring transfixed at the doorway as if gazing into a preternatural television screen.

"Billy!" Vin barks.

Billy snaps out of his trancelike fixation and turns slowly to answer Vin's call.

"Go downstairs and get the first-aid kit. And bring a bottle of water! And that bottle of absinthe!"

"I have aspirin," Billy replies in a mesmeric tenor.

Vin and Parson exchange furtive glances.

"No, the first-aid kit!" Parson snaps.

III

"Why did you have to hit him?" Julia sniffles, picking somberly at a simple plate of sliced cheese, ham, and toast while a sickly fist of churning grief garrisons her stomach.

Vin forces down his remorse with a hard swallow as he sets a mug of coffee next to her plate and navigates the end of the table with the decanter, shaking his head sheepishly. "I just couldn't help it," he bleats, taking the mug from Parson, who sits across from Julia with a dispirited gaze over his own plate.

The three drift in and out of their fractured individual microcosms, consumed by the dire blackness of Agnot's harrowing death under the superficial gloom seeping in from the high windows of the dining hall.

"I just couldn't take it after...everything," Vin concedes, taking Parson's coffee mug.

"He deserves an apology," Parson interjects with an austere edge in the quiet tone of his despondent sigh.

Vin fills his mug. "He deserves to be thrown to the—thrown out!" Vin growls, the tide of his emotions having turned suddenly to disgust as he sets the mug on the table with an abruptness born of this translation. "The guy had a phone the whole time! Even worse, he's been working with that…that…whatever-the-hell-he-is behind our backs!"

Julia's face lifts and falls in timid nods behind the coffee on which she suckles, carefully avoiding their responses by filling her vision with the mocha swirls within the mug.

"Uh! God's teeth," Parson exclaims, his weary survey passing from Julia to Vin, who is taking the seat at the end of the table. "Stop beating your chest, Tarzan. You're getting Cheetah here all wound up."

"Parson," Julia huffs.

Vin throws an impatient glare at Parson before brusquely slicing his ham steak.

Parson brushes it off coolly, looking at Julia with one brow lifted high-mindedly. "May I remind you, darling, and this isn't an accusation, so don't get your panties in a bunch, that you were more than willing to blab all of our plans to him."

"I thought he was a cop!" Julia cries, the words striking her harried mind like a slap.

"I know, I know. I'm not trying to hurt you," Parson insists in a conciliatory tone. "But why would that matter?"

Julia's hand falls to the edge of the table as she cocks her head and gazes back at Parson with brows raised. "Because if a cop tells you to do something, you do it. Right?"

Vin bristles at his chair, surprised and impressed by Parson's tact.

Parson returns his attention with an air of satisfaction. He sits back in his chair and crosses his arms. "Precisely.

And since we don't know anything about him, we don't know anything about him."

A puzzled smirk contorts Julia's flawless complexion. "Um…I don't get it."

Vin's head bobs in a slow nod to Parson's logic. "Yeah, yeah, you're right. He could be anything, military, Secret Service…"

"Interpol."

Billy's seemingly disembodied announcement startles them, snapping their attention in concert.

The weight of their eyes stings nearly as much as his bruised and swollen lip. He avoids those stares and lumbers toward the kitchen, having no interest in a futile attempt to explain.

"Come join us," Parson hails gently, pulling out the chair next to him.

"We have coffee," Julia coaxes sweetly, blushing under the guilt of her unfounded prejudice.

Billy risks a furtive glance at Vin and continues traversing the dining hall without speaking.

Parson prods Vin with a stern glare.

Vin stands and takes a tentative step toward Billy, who pauses but does not look up.

"I'm sorry for—"

"Punching me?" Billy chides in a low pitch of disdain. "Or going through my stuff?"

"I shouldn't have touched you," Vin begins, shame burning his neck and ears. "I shouldn't have jumped to conclusions either. I'm sorry."

"Whatever," Billy mumbles, staring at the floor through greasy strands under the crush of the horrible consequences of his omission and the ostracism it engendered.

"Come have some breakfast," Parson urges.

"Yeah, have some coffee," Vin adds quickly. "I'll get your breakfast."

Before Billy can protest, Vin is sailing past him for the kitchen. Reluctantly, he shuffles to the chair Parson has pulled out for him. His guts churn as he struggles to reconcile his need for their acceptance, his revulsion for being so weak as to want it, and the overwhelming glut of guilt. With a reclusive slouch, he sits in the chair and turns over the coffee mug sitting upside down at the place setting.

Parson reaches for the carafe and gingerly lifts it over Billy's cup, offering a reassuring smile as the rich aroma of the coffee dilutes the sullen atmosphere. By the time he is returning the decanter to the trivet, Vin is entering the hall with an abundantly provisioned plate of toast, cheese, ham, and condiments.

Billy fidgets uncomfortably, unaccustomed to such generous attention, and with the consequences of his capitulation eating away at him, the graciousness only accentuates his anguish. He leans back, still without looking up, as Vin sets the plate before him and then hands him a knife and fork. "Thanks," he mutters.

"So," Parson pipes up carefully as Vin returns to his seat, "now that the pussy's out of the pouch, we'd sure like to play with it."

Billy takes a gulp of coffee. He tries to convince himself that disclosure would be a way of gaining allegiance rather than pandering to his want of inclusion, but the affectation won't take. Disgusted with himself, he chooses not to care about their reaction either way. "I wasn't allowed to tell you guys because he didn't know if you'd tell the professor."

"Um, before we go there," Vin interjects as tactfully as he can manage, "who is he?"

Billy's eyes flit from one curious face to another before settling on Vin with a twinge of indignant reproach. "Agent Grayson? He's a tool," Billy smirks. "He's with Interpol, drug-trafficking stuff."

Perplexed, Vin leans over his plate. "What does he want with us? And why would it matter if we told the professor?"

"The professor is a heroin addict," Parson states frankly, seeing no reason to withhold the information any longer.

"What?" Vin exclaims, taken aback by the declaration.

"How do you know?" Julia follows, wide-eyed with astonishment.

"Have you seen him?" Billy interjects sardonically, nodding as Parson continues.

"Oh, I found his stash, and he's been using. That's why he's locked himself up in his room."

"Grayson thinks he's been using the deal with the castle as a cover to run drugs," Billy explains.

"Does he think we're involved?" Vin presses, aghast at the prospect.

"No," Billy chuckles as he shoves an inordinately large piece of ham into his mouth, quickly wincing at the painful reminder of his lip. The humor is short-lived as his face grows serious.

"What?" Julia presses dreadfully.

Billy leaves them in suspense as he tumbles the meat between his teeth. With a heavy swallow, he clears his mouth before continuing. "Nothing."

"You might as well spill it," Parson sighs.

Billy's cold, gray eyes alight from one to the other as he risks proffering his supposition to what remains of Ravenword. "Just thinkin' drugs are the least of our worries."

"And?" Parson prods.

"And the real question is why are we really here? What does the professor need us for?"

IV

Charlie wakes. A nebulous dull gray light filters from the window as if to complement the dull gray ache in her head. Her forehead and cheeks pinch as she knits her brow, searching the room for an unknown presence. Parched and prickly pain burns her throat as she swallows with the recollection of a nightmare, the fact of it rather than the images. Her head is pierced through the temples and her limbs bound by the thick lethargy of sedatives as she attempts to rise.

She acquiesces to the pillow and mattress before drawing a deep breath and repeating the effort. Throwing off blankets that feel as if they were woven from lead, she coerces her feet off the edge of the bed and rises with a raspy groan. She massages her throat unconsciously as the iciness of the stone floor prods a sobering reminiscence. Her stiff muscles protest as she thrusts her weight to rise from the tiny bed and stands, bolstering herself against the headboard.

She stares at the door, trying to penetrate the amnesic tugging in the recesses of her foggy brain. Her pursuit of the elusive images, however, is distracted by the grate of cotton antagonizing her swollen fingertips. She looks down to find herself in a Hello Kitty nightgown and wonders how she could have ended up in Julia's pajamas.

The hope of making sense of it all is abruptly stripped away as her gaze falls upon the braided bracelet lying at the threshold of the door.

With stifled and stunted steps, she forces her weary body to kneel over the circlet of entwined cords. As if drawn from the cold stone beneath her, ice rushes through her veins as her throbbing fingers sweep the memento into her grasp. As she examines it, that ice spills from her pores in one synchronous contraction.

Agnot!

Charlie's blood curdles as the nightmarish vision of Agnot's corpse rises, shrieking through the corridors of her mind. Clenching the bracelet, Charlie bows under the crushing weight of the revisited horror as her diaphragm squeezes an involuntary sob from the depths of her. The buckling grief swells until it is translated into barking screams that claw at her throat.

The horror pours into her consciousness like a hellish brew of evils, throwing the chamber into a grotesque spin around her. Lunging for the door, Charlie falls against it, struggling for an anchor. Finding the cold knob transports her instantly. Fighting tides of panic, she clasps her eyes tight and throws the door open. Not waiting for sight, she hurls herself into the hall and runs frantically past the chamber doors and candle stands to the gaping staircase.

With her bare feet slapping the stony steps, she descends into the grand foyer and flies past Vin, Parson, Julia, and Billy, who are just emerging from the passage. Before they can react, she throws open the main doors and bolts into the courtyard.

"Charlie!" the four shout in a chorus of dismay.

They rush to the threshold to find her between the weather-beaten blocks of the ancient wall, rattling and pulling at the reluctant bars of the gate like a desperate lunatic. As the four spill into the cold, wet courtyard, the bars relent and Charlie slips through and onto the gravel road.

Parson and Vin are the first to cross the overgrown span to battle with the iron. Running up to them, Billy yanks the gate violently, opening it wide as Charlie reaches the far side of the road and steps off.

Charlie drifts down the slope like an ethereal sleepwalker, staring pale and dumbfounded as her tortured brain tries to reconcile the inscrutable testimony before her. The rest of Ravenword, having rushed upon the ravine's rim behind her, stand arrested by the absurd suspension of reality-splitting bewilderment.

Before them lies the van, just where it came to rest on the fateful night of their arrival, the bumper and grille still crumpled against the gnarled tree. Yet the van has been impossibly transformed.

The hull is a rusted shell standing out of a thick of weeds like an ancient, weather-beaten mausoleum. The dark green pigment has long since peeled under the bleaching hand of the elements, leaving only tenacious flakes sprinkled in crevices that have not yet succumbed to the cancer of rust. A few shards of grimy yellow glass remain in the dried-out seals that once held the windshield and the other windows.

Charlie descends to the decaying bulk and reaches for the blemished chrome handle of the side passenger door, her heart pounding in horrible anticipation of what lies behind. The handle sticks. Using her weight to force it, she digs her bare feet into the foul soil now rolling up between her toes.

The latch gives, but the door refuses to slide.

Now at her side, Parson and Julia draw her away in favor of Vin's attempt to open the slider. With his heart in his throat, Vin's quivering arms flex and strain.

The door gives, but only an inch.

Handing Charlie off to Julia, Parson steps in on Vin's second attempt, prying his fingers into the separation and pulling at the door.

With a grating moan, the door slides open.

Vin and Parson straighten and gaze, stunned, into the gaping hole.

Charlie and Julia creep up behind them.

"How?" Vin grapples.

Billy leans into the hollow of the van, scouring the surfaces with his eyes, desperate to find discrepancies that would reveal a hoax.

Traces of both the lining and the upholstery cling to a skeleton of rusty springs. Tangled webs droop in the dark corners, and tattered weeds push up through holes eaten into the floor.

Vin watches expectantly as Parson runs his fingers across the seam of the door as if waiting for confirmation.

Parson meets his gaze and shakes his head.

Julia shivers against the damp gray morning, looking at them both with eyes framed in dreadful resignation. "Can we go back?"

Her plea pulls Vin out of his stupor, and it is only then that he realizes that Charlie is no longer with them. His start at the discovery startles the others, and they spin on their heels to find her breaching the lip of the ravine.

Her strength, taxed by the climb, surges upon crawling onto the shoulder of the cold and empty road. Bounding to her feet, she hikes the nightgown and sprints in long and wild strides into the gloomy forest byway. Voices rise as the sagging wall and ruined castle shrink behind her.

Her pulse and footfalls thunder in her ears as the frigid air sears her dry throat and burns her heaving lungs. The unfeeling trees fencing the dank woods scroll past her against the battleship clouds staining the alpine vista. With base determination, Charlie peers through the dizzy collage of her ransacked awareness to chart the road as it scrolls beneath her, biting her feet with stony teeth.

Running with all of his might, Vin hands the mental baton to Parson, whose gym-trained physique allows him to swiftly outpace him. Yet Vin pushes himself to keep Parson in sight for fear of whatever monsters lie in wait. Images of mad wolves flash through his mind, and he forces the brisk air deeper into his lungs to stoke the furnace of his exertion. Rounding the bend, the road stretches out before him to a sight that steals the breath from his very lungs.

Charlie is beating the ground with her fist, convulsing in what he hopes are sobs. Parson slumps over her, falling to his knees.

The necessity of haste now vanquished, Vin slows and allows his body to recoup its resources before bending to the release of his emotional floodgates. Behind him, he can hear the footfalls of Billy and Julia and tries to rally himself to manage their reaction.

They catch up with Vin just as he crouches to comfort Charlie. Their momentary relief shattered by the registry of the two forks, one descending into shadows to the right and the other continuing before being lost in a bend and the other halfway down the straightaway.

Their defeat is complete in the knowledge that each of them had slept the entire journey up the mountain.

CHAPTER 8

The Relic

BILLY SHUTS OUT THE VACUOUS and dispossessed world with a heave, the heavy door swinging reluctantly into its frame. Behind him Ravenword huddle like a knot of withered wraiths within the yawning Gothic foyer whose hearth fire crackles and dances yet provides no comfort.

Unable to bear her weight any longer, Parson gently delivers Charlie's feet to the floor, but her cold and trembling arms refuse to retreat from his shoulders. Stayed by her need, his arms remain around her shivering form, and he whispers to Vin as if fearing to wake a sleepwalker, "I should get her to bed."

Shuddering fiercely from her stupor, Charlie recoils with sharp and pleading eyes imbued with the haunting distance of the netherworld. "N-no. No," she stammers, her arms coiling around Parson's neck. She is the very countenance of fear, pale and dreadful, leaving her friends little choice but to keep her in the cradle of their company.

Julia, still wrapped around Vin, is very nearly a doppelganger to the tragic lover, the veneer of safety having been stripped from her psyche like the leaves of a wind-whipped tree.

Without speaking, Billy ushers them to the fire.

Parson sinks to the floor with Charlie, welcoming the hot breath from the flames and the stone tiles they have warmed.

Billy, having less concern for Julia's state than that of Charlie's, gestures to Vin and then steps away.

Vin offers Julia a reassuring smile before releasing her to the company of Parson and Charlie. But before she withdraws, Julia rises up on her toes and presses her lips firmly against his. A surge having nothing to do with the hearth warms his surprise. An awkward grin frames his flushed features as he retreats into the corridor with Billy, who notes the event with a misanthropic roll of his eyes.

Julia snuggles up to Charlie and Parson as the two men disappear into the hallway bridging the dining hall. Cast in orange, the three huddle in silence to glean comfort from the warmth of the fire and the bonds of survival.

"You gotta keep them downstairs for a while," Billy states plainly. "Make them dinner or something."

Vin follows Billy through the dining hall, unsure of his direction, both literally and figuratively. "Why? What are you going to do?"

Billy doesn't reply as he crosses the kitchen for the boiler room. A moment later he emerges with a mop and a bucket loaded with cleaning supplies.

Vin draws a deep breath and nods. To Billy's surprise, however, he does not acquiesce but passes him swiftly and returns from the boiler room with a push broom and a resolute countenance. "Parson will take care of them."

II

The bright afternoon lavishes the small gift card in sunlight, beautifully inscribed with *l'Ordine degli Intercessori*, and draws to prominence the watermark on the other side upon turning. *"Dance with me..."* scrolls beneath the artful castle with a teardrop in the center, encircled with twelve stars. T. J. lifts his gaze to San Michele, a striking white Pisan Romanesque church set in the heart of picturesque Lucca. It was the only lead Agent Grayson would give him. Armed with hope and the memento, he navigates through ambling pedestrians and meandering cyclists for the church steps.

Two rows of pews and the hush of sacred space greet him, and his entrance is given little attention by the few faithful sitting in silent prayer or meditation. The tumbling whispers of tourists provide him with unwanted camouflage, even as a priest stands with an old woman adding a votive to the altar overshadowed by a saint unfamiliar to T. J. Each step feels like a trespass as he makes his way to the shrine in hopes of catching the priest. As a fallen-away Protestant brought up in the Church of Christ, the Catholic ritual is mysterious and fascinating, but even in his disbelief, the tradition feels beautiful and substantial. His ruminations, however, are interrupted by the stare of the priest and the woman, which are fixed on him expectantly.

"Oh, mi scusami," he whispers, proffering an uncertain smile. "Sto cercando per la direzioni."

"We do not have visitor information here," the priest announces loudly with an articulation betraying a history of English.

"Oh no," T. J. chuckles, unnerved by the curt response. "I was wondering if you had any information on this," he amends, handing the priest the gift card. "Or maybe direct me to someone who can—"

"This is nonsense," the priest interjects, returning the card brusquely before excusing himself from the old woman in genteel Italian.

Taken aback, T. J. stands in a momentary stupor as the priest retreats stridently.

"You must excuse him," the old woman says in a tone much more robust than he would have expected from one so petite. Her keen sense of fashion and impeccably dressed white hair attest to a woman of the world rather than a provincial crone. "Some days there is not enough wine in all of Tuscany to ease his temper. So what is it that you are looking for, young man? You are certainly no tourist," she assesses with a shrewd cast.

T. J. hands her the card with a tepid smile, uncertain of her humor.

Her eyes herald a terrible dread that blanches her complexion suddenly and she shuts them tightly as an earnest prayer is traced in the air by her thin lips. The dark cloud is chased by resignation until peace raises the painted lids. Her gaze fixes on T. J. with a veracity that sends a shiver through him.

"If you mean to do this, I know two people. One is a fool! The other is a superstitious old witch who lost her mind years ago! Che Dio abbia pietà." Without waiting for his response, she aims for the Foro outside, her high heels clacking on the ancient stone floor like a New York fashion mogul. "Come!"

Feeling suddenly carried away, T. J. follows the grand dame into the broad and sunny square at the heart of the romantic medieval city, where she commandeers their path with choice bellows.

Seated inconspicuously under the arch of Pasticceria Taddeucci, Grayson watches. Indulging in a final swig of espresso, he tracks their course before rising in stealthy pursuit.

"Sto camminando qui!" the old woman roars, deflecting two star-crossed cyclists unfortunate enough to have their enchantment intersect with her intent as she busies herself with her cell phone. Prattling into the cell in what sounds to T. J. like a verbal boxing match, the feisty virago leads him into a tiny lane lined with flowers, shops, and cafés. Long before she has finished the call, he has determined her to be the winner and listens attentively as she turns to him. "One of the idiots will be at my house in an hour. You can wait with me there."

"I can wait at a café if you'd rather—"

"Why would I invite you to my home if I'd rather you wait at a café?" she retorts, her eyes welling. "I will have my housekeeper make you a cappuccino, and we will wait."

"Are you all right, signora?"

"Have you had buccellato?" she replies brusquely, waving away his concern.

III

"Is this seat taken?" a sultry voice interrupts with a thick French accent.

Accustomed to the European convention of sharing tables with strangers, Motisha raises a polite smile over her magazine to find a chic kindred in a blue spring-print Dolce & Gabbana dress smiling back at her.

"The café is so crowded today."

"Please," Motisha invites before returning to the article.

"So many travelers," she says as she alights into the chair and sets her matching sapphire clutch on the small table with her latte. Her rich lashes levitate as she surveys Motisha. "Are you catching the train as well?"

Motisha quells the rising annoyance with a terse smile. "Yes, actually—"

Staring up from the young woman's open neckline, a delicate ruby teardrop pendant catches Motisha by surprise.

The vixen kisses the pendant with her ruby fingertips, her green eyes glancing at its twin on Motisha's breast, then meets her gaze. "Of course this is why I wanted to sit with you. It is a rare and precious thing. We will be fast friends and loathe each other like jealous debutantes," she announces spritely. "I am Coquette."

"Motisha," she grins, taking her hand briefly and assessing the bright young woman. "Is that your real name?"

"Of course not!" Coquette gushes. "Given names are so boring! Don't you think?"

Motisha laughs.

"We will have to find you something to call yourself," Coquette chimes, then quickly deflates. "But you are going... where are you going?"

Motisha's pragmatic nature bristles at the question, stoking the inherent distrust that prompts her to retreat behind her infamous smile. She sweeps the tailoring of Coquette's dress, the clutch, and her accessories and can find no fault in their audacity. Yet the integrity of the presentation does little to assuage her reserve.

The ruby pendant stares back at her.

"I'm going west."

"I don't know how you can do it!" Coquette exclaims. "Leave Milan on the cusp of Fashion Week? It is a crime!"

"But I understand this," she continues, opening her sapphire clutch and retrieving a calling card. "I have many friends in the industry who would adore you and you they. I would tell you to change your mind, but who am I? Some lunatic you met at a train station."

Motisha proffers an apologetic aspect, considering that she may have misjudged the free spirit.

"Next time you are in Paris or Milan," Coquette bids, setting her calling card on the table as she rises, "or...if you change your mind about 'west,' you call me, and we will give you a new name and see all the runways together, eh?"

"Merci," Motisha replies. "C'est très gentil."

"Oh! Et elle parle français!" Coquette trumpets blithely. "But of course you do!"

Motisha beams, nodding graciously.

"Au revoir, mon amie!" Coquette sings. Having planted the seed, she sashays to the exit.

"À tout à l'heure," Motisha calls after her, unable to resist.

Coquette turns, sends a coy wave, and then disappears into the world.

Motisha, still processing the encounter, lifts the calling card. Her breath catches suddenly, and her eyes dart quickly to the exit.

IV

Parson monitors Charlie and Julia from the landing at the top of the stairs as they huddle under a blanket in front of the fire, lost in a comforting stupor. "I don't know, boys," he demurs, turning to Vin and Billy. "I don't even know if I want to sleep up here."

Both men sag, their features drawn in shadows that accentuate the dark circles and weary lines that exaggerates the haggard cast of their faces. Billy fidgets impatiently, his rapport with Parson straining under frustration.

"What? We just spent hours cleaning this...everything for nothing?" Billy insists in a terse whisper.

"The rooms downstairs are identical," Vin follows quickly. "What's the difference?"

Parson looks past the two, down the damp and naked corridor washed in the orange hues of the impending sunset to the black sheet pinned over the demolished remains of the last door on the right.

Vin follows his gaze and then leans against the wall, a dire resignation forcing him to face the terrifying truth. He stammers, his battered consciousness reluctant to acquiesce, and turns away to face the wall.

Shy of initiating an embrace, however necessary, Parson steps up behind Vin to squeeze his shoulders.

"We aren't safe anywhere," Billy acknowledges, saying what Vin cannot.

"Maybe not," Parson retorts resolutely, patting Vin on the back. "But at this point, every little bit will help get us through the night.

"Come on, gents," he coaxes. "We've got one more chore before dark."

• • •

With a final clanging chink, the door that had kept the purple chamber for more than a century slips from its atrophied hinges. Parson and Vin heave the weight of it as they lower it into a carry. Behind them, Billy is pressed against the grain of its counterpart at the blue room and the desolated host within as the two men maneuver the thick panel into the kitchen where Charlie and Julia watch from the butcher-block table. As the beleaguered women look on, the two thread the door into the narrow-arched passage with Billy as the clumsy satellite.

Charlie's glassy stare falls absently to the table.

Julia rubs her forearm, lost on how best to console the woman who has always been such an exemplar of strength. "Would you like some soup?"

A braided band of dyed hemp is revealed with the blossoming of Charlie's hand. Caressing it between her fingers, she languishes in silence.

Julia takes her hands and, with a tender squeeze, draws the bracelet to Charlie's wrist.

The shattered lover's eyes well above quivering lips as her friend ties the stringy ends of the memento around her pale and listless wrist.

"*Khi tes*," Julia proffers sweetly.

Charlie checks her with somber yet grateful eyes.

"It's a Hmong thing…" she replies with a shy smile and crinkled nose, shrugging through her diffidence.

"For protection?" Charlie surmises vaguely on a heavy breath.

"Sorta," Julia nods uncertainly.

Charlie straightens, her features drawn with a decisive and haunting sobriety. Her forlorn stare passes from Julia to the rustic cabinetry. "You need one, too," she whispers terribly, as she shifts to rise. But her momentum is stayed by a creaking yawn.

Dread meets dread as their eyes meet under an icy draft.

Charlie clutches Julia's fists. Her head turns to follow Julia's stricken gaze.

A vacuous emptiness consumes the corridor, as if the void of the pit has extended its spectral reach into the annex.

Mesmerized by a terrible and compulsory fascination, they shudder to their feet with hands clasped and eyes locked.

A moan rises from the professor's room as if beset to give voice to the contagion.

As the women back away, the length of the corridor opens to them.

Charlie crumples on their gasps to the cold floor in hoarse sobs.

Sapped by the sight of the door to that black pit standing open like a demonic usher, Julia sinks beside her.

A stir in the depth of the bewitched dusk furrows her brow as an unearthly chill scrolls across the stone.

Mopping her eyes, Charlie levels her gaze in defiant witness.

The singular effect blooms into a roil of morbid tendrils.

Helpless against the paralyzing spell, Charlie and Julia cower tightly in horrible anticipation as the specter takes shape.

A countenance, at once graceful and unnatural, like the remnant of beauty within the desolation of despair, defiles the threshold. The apparition congeals into the visage of a young noblewoman in humble loveliness, her chestnut hair set and braided like a medieval portrait, her ornate blue dress draping from a delicate navy sash, and her supple face weary in its beauty as if burdened with a terrible truth.

Charlie gapes, nerves stretched, immersed in the frosty ethereum of otherworldly recognition. It is the Blue Lady, the same manifestation that reached out to her from her chamber window on the chill of that first morning.

The dark and delicate gaze of the supple ghost rests on them as with hope and longing.

Charlie and Julia answer her unspoken hail with eyes wide and mesmerized.

A singular tenderness overcomes the Lady's regal demeanor. Her hands, clasped at the waist, loosen, and she rests her palms against her abdomen. She bows her head. Tears, from eyes translated to insufferable grief, stream from the beauty. Once they were tears of joy, when Prince Prospero's face was lit by elation. Despite his regard for her condition, he lifted her high with celebratory arms. Life had come to a world benighted by Death and his plague. Blithely, she fell into his embrace as her laughter resounded through the abbey. Taking his strong hands, she beseeched him, "Dance with me."

Charlie and Julia swoon as Beauty's radiance changes abruptly to abject terror.

Her arms rise against some unforeseen onslaught, and her beautiful form rots.

A shared scream sirens from their convulsing embrace.

The devastated phantom issues a waste-laying screech and vanishes.

Amid frantic footfalls, the dark hold of the corridor is vanquished by the candlesticks bursting to life in consecutive pairs culminating with the slamming of the evil door.

V

Renata Diometi's scrutiny from her settee, upholstered in a rich cream satin, forces a hard swallow from T. J. Her freckled hand retires the cappuccino to the diminutive table between them, a ring of sooty foam staining the cup as it rattles on the saucer.

"So you believe l'Ordine degli Intercessori per i Maledetto Rosso can help you when the polizia cannot? You are a fool as well, I see. Finish the buccellato!"

"I'm not sure. It's all I've got to go on," T. J. replies, transferring another slice of the sweet bread to his dessert plate obediently.

Blanketed with a sudden frailty, the old woman casts her gaze out of the window between them, drinking in the sunlit vignettes of the lane.

T. J. waits in polite silence.

"Not true," she replies darkly, meeting his gaze with a renewed vigor. "A man does not pursue such a thing without faith, nor would he seek the Order if he did not believe in their mission."

"I don't even know what their mission is, Signora Diometi," he says carefully. "I just want to find my friends."

"You don't know," the old woman muses. "You don't know because you are afraid to see. The time for wavering is past, Terrence. You cannot do these things with your eyes closed."

The admonition passes into him like a spirit loosing the cords of denial. T. J. allows the spell to fulfill its purpose, searching the lines in the old woman's resolute face for faith to borrow.

The patterns of those lines shift as she returns the pensive survey beyond the window. A whispering recollection brightens her face, and she returns to him with a sagacious smile.

"You're part of the Order?" he presumes cautiously.

"No," she answers flatly. "I do not waste my prayers."

"But you know something," T. J. leads.

"I know what you know," she retorts, rising from the settee, suddenly careworn. "No, no," she waves as he begins to rise from the elegant Rococo chair. "But," she continues in a tenor that strikes him as both reluctant and resigned, "I do have what you do not." Renata crosses the opulent little sitting room, passing the entrance to the rustic butler's pantry, to an antique credenza where she pauses, lost in a faraway reminiscence. "Santa Maria, un segno, è lui quello giusto?" she murmurs, suspended in the trepid deliberation.

An odd thrill of curiosity and fascination ripples through T. J. as she draws open a drawer hidden in the side of the credenza and retrieves an ornate box. Roughly the size of a large jewelry box, the carved wood case is longer than conventional dimensions and ancient in the extreme.

"Signora!" a stern voice rebukes.

• • •

Aldobrandi meters his pace, careful not to draw attention to himself, his earnestness perforated with amiable salutations to neighbors and shopkeepers along the narrow lane. But the sight of Agent Grayson sitting outside the café across from Casa di Diometi evaporates both caution and charm, and he rushes upon him. "Why are you here?"

Grayson looks up at the flushed and panting Italiano with indifference. "Italian soda," he deflects, gesturing to the bubbly concoction. "Although I think it could use some-thing a little stronger. Don't you?"

Aldo's ferocity falters, "You have found something!"

"I found your great-aunt," the agent replies.

Confusion tightens the young Italian's face. "She knows nothing."

"Then why are you here?"

Grayson takes a sip of the soda while Aldobrandi tries to divine the agent's intentions.

"She said a *compagno* of my American friends has come."

● ● ●

T. J. spins out of the chair and onto his feet. He is surprised to find the priest from San Michele standing at the entrance to the sitting room.

"This is not yours to give," the priest says, piercing the old woman clutching the case with a condescending glare. "The bishop suspected it was you who held this holy relic."

Renata pales, but her resolve is undiminished. "Marcello, you were always a sneaky boy. How did you get into my home?"

Behind the petulant priest, Renata's contrite house-keeper risks a furtive and apologetic glance, a handkerchief balled to her fretful mouth.

The old woman's eyes drift thoughtfully out the win-dow, where they alight on an impassioned Aldobrandi amid the flowers framing the patio across the narrow lane. "But today," she sighs wearily, "you are expected."

The priest advances boldly only to be blocked by T. J., whose powerful frame provides a potent warning.

"Gallant American," the priest simpers with the guile of a serpent, stepping back cautiously, "forgive my impetuous entrance. Signora Diometi and I are very old friends. I would do nothing to injure her."

T. J. confirms with a glance to the old woman, before relaxing.

"You always had the tongue of a snake, Marcello," Renata chides with a dismissive wave.

"You must understand," the priest insists, "the relic belongs to the church."

"It belongs to my family!" Renata rebuffs angrily, her Italian accent deepening with emotion. "You cannot hide it in obscurity for another generation."

"You would rather give it to this boy so he can take it to America and sell on eBay?"

"Now hold on!"

"He cannot go to the Order without it," she states ominously.

"Misericordioso Dio, give me strength," the priest groans. "Signora, why do you believe such things?"

"What I believe," the signora begins gravely, "is that the night the relic was passed to me, Santa Maria came in a dream saying that on the day of my death, a *corvino* would come from across the sea with a priest on his back..." She falters as her housekeeper sweeps to her side from the butler's pantry. "Niente, niente," Renata coos before continuing. "And then it would be my time to pass on the relic."

"Signora!" the priest exclaims, dumbfounded

"I am old, but the day is long," she rebuffs. "You have time to prepare for last rites."

Equally stunned, T. J. stands dumbstruck as Signora Diometi directs her housekeeper with a nod.

The woman retreats, her face blotched with grief and cheeks stained with tears.

"You are being ridiculous!" the priest carps, his own complexion waning. "You are fine! You are healthy! You have beaten pickpockets in the streets!"

A pleased grin interrupts her sober countenance. "We will know by day's end." Her sharp eyes look past the priest to Aldobrandi, who rushes past him and T. J.

"Are you not well?" he cries, kneeling to search her face before scanning the room frantically. "What is this?" he demands, unnerved by the presence of the priest. "What is going on here?" His burnished eyes fall on the case in his aunt's freckled hands and then on T. J. "You are the American!"

Behind T. J. and the unsettled priest, Agent Grayson steps into the tiny foyer.

"Come, Terrence," she says, bringing Aldobrandi to his feet by lead of her hand on his elbow.

T. J. obeys under a cloud of terrible wonder.

"Aldobrandi, this is Terrence," Renata begins, looking him squarely in the eye. "Together you will find your friends."

"Si," Aldobrandi replies softly, shaking T. J.'s hand.

"You are good boys," she says, her strong voice quavering. "Take this to the Order," she nods, extending the ancient case. "They will help you."

Emotion forces T. J. to clear his throat before quipping gently, "I thought we were fools?"

Renata laughs, nodding wisely before imparting her final gift. "Every hero is a fool until he proves himself."

VI

Deciding against cluttering her Louis Vuitton handbag with the magazine, Motisha sets it on the café table in favor of the calling card left by the enigmatic Coquette. Retrieving her clutch, she lingers on the card, contemplating the Parisian's effervescent invitation. Terrence's pursuit of Ravenword has afforded her the liberty to do what she wants, and attending Fashion Week was an indulgence not conducive to his tastes. The touching of her thoughts on the mysterious plight of their friends, however, sobers her. Motisha checks the time on the dainty diamond-encrusted bracelet watch adorning her delicate wrist and then rises to collect her luggage from the Club Eurostar Lounge.

Every step through the bright and teeming station fuels her internal deliberation. Even after procuring a porter and trolley for her luggage, the closer Motisha's approach to the platform, the more compelled she feels to pursue Coquette's invitation.

She finds herself settling into a seat on the train by the window, casting her contemplation under the great canopy of the station. Her heart pounds with equivocation. The seating of a fellow traveler next to her strikes the impending departure like the toll of that dreadful clock, and Motisha springs out of her seat with brash apologies and dashes to the end of the car. The attendant's finger is closing in on the button that will seal them in.

"Attendez, s'il vous plaît!" Confounding the steward, she pushes past him with the grace of a cornered gazelle.

"Signorina, per favore!" he stammers as commuters gawk.

Motisha leaps like a child into a puddle with stilettos nailing the platform precariously. The train pulls away, leaving her feeling as if she'd just escaped some horrible fate. Beaming in her newfound spontaneity, she turns gleefully for the splendors of Milan when suddenly seized.

"My luggage!"

VII

"Are you sure you're all right?" Vin presses at the butcher-block table as Parson sets bowls of soup in front of Julia and Charlie respectively.

"Yeah. It was just kind of the last straw," Julia mewls, her haunted gaze alighting on Charlie, who stares absently into the bowl from which she raises a spoon to her mouth. "You know?"

"I'll say," Parson retorts wearily, ladling a bowl of soup.

"What are you thinking?" Vin asks him, taking the cue.

"I'm thinking we pack our shit and get the hell out!" Parson exclaims, setting the bowl in front of Vin like a disgruntled waitress.

The kitchen is abruptly blanched by a strobe of lightning born from the umbral clouds framed by the windows of the dining hall.

"How?" Billy challenges from the counter on the far side of the kitchen, a corresponding rumble of thunder following hard upon.

His misanthropic remonstration forces them to acknowledge the dereliction of the van and their enigmatic course through the mountains. Julia allows her spoon to sink into her soup as Vin sets his elbows on the tabletop to rub his eyes deliberately. Charlie, however, continues the monotonous pace of her meal as if deaf to the discussion.

"I have no fucking idea," Parson wilts, looking to Billy defeated.

"We're trapped," Julia whimpers.

"No," Vin refutes with charged determination, "we've got to figure out which road goes to the next village."

"And how are we going to do that?" Parson rebuffs, already knowing the awful answer.

"Tonight?" Billy blurts over Parson.

"Of course not! We'll wait until morning," Vin replies with finality.

"And then?" Parson prods, crossing his arms and looking at Vin dubiously.

"We split up into teams of two, each team taking one of the three roads," Vin replies as if solving an equation.

"Teams of two?" Billy frowns. "There are only five of us."

Anticipating Vin, Parson piques. "You're not suggesting we take the professor? You've met him, right?"

Julia's beleaguered eyes scroll to Charlie, who continues completely disengaged.

Vin runs his fingers through his thick black hair, trying to assuage the suffocation of the walls as another flash of lightning bursts over them. "We have got to find a way to get help," he insists, leading Julia with a metered nod.

Submitting to the inevitability of necessity, Julia nods back with a bolstering sigh.

Recognizing the exchange, Parson takes the fourth chair at the table, and Billy slides off the counter to hover behind him, each knowing and determined. The sky roars an angry affirmation and Ravenword set to hone a plan with renewed fervor.

VIII

A quiet falls upon Casa di Diometi. Renata's forlorn house-keeper is serving Nocino in the sitting room to the somber Americans and Padre Valeriani. The cat, Venere, lashes a lazy tail upon the secretary in the hallway, her heavy hazel eyes drawn silently to the stairs.

"Are you certain?" Aldobrandi checks softly as he escorts his great-aunt through the sheets of golden light pressed onto the steps by the sun setting in the tall transom window. "The time to sleep is hours away."

"Not for me," Renata surrenders, patting his hand.

"Zia!" he cries miserably as they reach the landing.

Renata turns to face him squarely, peering into his eyes with a resolution maternal and sober.

"I will gather the family, si?" Aldobrandi proffers, his own eyes welling with tears.

She pats his beautiful face before continuing down the hall on his arm. "No, I have lived in a quiet house and want to die in one," she insists. She pauses at the doorway to her bedroom, a revelatory sense of apprehensive liberation expanding through her upon gazing at her richly dressed bed.

"Zia?" he whispers.

"Niente," she murmurs.

The room is welcoming and warm as she enters, seemingly imbued with peace. She surveys the chest of drawers and clothed tables bountiful in ornately framed photographs old and new. Her fingers caress the opulent vanity passed down from her grandmother, glistening perfume bottles and personal sundries set just so before the mirror that has held her image for half a century. The bed cradles her in soft, familiar comfort beneath the portraits and landscapes that have greeted and encouraged her upon waking and soothed and consoled her upon retiring.

Aldobrandi takes the plush chair bedside to hold her hand.

The lines around Renata's wisdom-laden eyes deepen as she offers her nephew a gentle smile. She turns to the window where the cumulus clouds billowing on the horizon beyond the terracotta roofs are painted in hues of fuchsia, orange, and gold. A warm stillness seeps into her limbs, spreads through her body, and lulls her contented mind.

The Lady in Blue stands smiling solemnly from the center of the room, corporeal and lovely. Her chestnut hair set and braided, her ornate dress drapes from the delicate navy sash, and her supple face glows gracious in its beauty as if burnished with unfathomable gratitude. She gestures with the slightest nod.

Renata returns the token, squeezing Aldobrandi's hand. "It is time for Padre Valeriani."

A sob gushes from Aldobrandi. "No, no," he cries, burying his face in her hair.

Sympathy and tears wash the visage of the Blue Lady, who watches and waits.

"Be a good boy," Renata whispers, kissing his ear.

Aldobrandi caresses her hair, returning the kiss to her forehead, his tears anointing her passage.

"Go," she coos, her own tears trailing.

Aldobrandi straightens out of the sob and turns reluctantly for the door.

The matriarch's countenance is transformed to emblazoned rapture as the Lady in Blue is joined by Renata's husband and parents, family and friends long departed from this world.

Beauty extends her hand, and Renata accepts the invitation.

The phantom recedes into the unknowable depths, and Renata Rosetta Romero Diometi melts into the welcoming embrace of her loved ones.

IX

The oppressive gray dusk ushers a spiteful and ravenous night as spectral gales set the eaves, byways, and hollows of the castle howling. Thunder usurps the churning cauldron of crepuscular clouds, riddled and gutted by the venom of stark lightning.

Having secured the apartment shutters and windows against the bane, Ravenword distract themselves from the unnerving onslaught by preparing the blue room as their collective lodging for the night.

The stone floor growls as Julia drags a chest of drawers into the hallway where Vin, Parson, and Billy pass her with duffel bags under their arms. Gently, they set them on the small bed upon which Charlie is curled. Without coaxing her from her nest, Parson and Vin pull the bed from the wall and set its length against the wall under the window. Julia enters with her own duffel and, grabbing Charlie and Agnot's from the floor, sets them on the bed as Parson and Vin sweep past her. Charlie jumps, startled by the door swinging open abruptly as Parson and Vin burst in carrying a second bed. Careful to avoid the candles on the hearth, they lower it to the floor and scoot it against that on which Julia reassures a trembling Charlie. Billy follows, setting a large, thick, and waterlogged cutting board in the narrow gap between the foot of the second bed and the woodburning stove that has been fed and stoked to keep them through the night without tending. Lightning freeze-frames him as he exits swiftly, and the suffix of thunder punctuates the entrance of Parson and Vin with a third bed. The confines of the chamber force Vin onto the center bed, and Julia lays Charlie low and out of the way as Parson kicks the door shut. They maneuver the frame into what little remaining space their preparations have left. As they slide it snugly against the center bed, Billy's entrance strikes the footboard, forcing him to squeeze between the door and its frame. The restricted swing of the door, however, is a comfort for the harried and traumatized companions.

"Well," Parson chimes wearily from the center bed, "time to consider the little practicalities."

"I think the girls should take the bed in the middle," Vin anticipates.

Parson attempts a patient smile, "Actually, I was thinking of midnight potty breaks. I think it would be a good idea if we tried to get that taken care of sooner rather than later. I, for one, don't relish the thought of escorting anyone into that hallway tonight."

The prospect sends a collective shiver upon them.

"I'm fine," Billy says flatly, only to be scrutinized by Parson. "What? I just went." Sequestering himself behind a book, he activates his reading light with a terse click and settles against the headboard.

"Are you sure you want that bed?" Vin asks, intruding on Billy's microcosmic bastion.

"Somebody's going to have to sleep by the door," he answers without lowering the hardbound.

"Yes," Vin replies uneasily. "I just meant that until we're all settled, it might be hard with us having climb over your bed as we go in and out."

Billy lowers the book and cocks his head and sweeps the air in a sardonic invitation to proceed. Without waiting for a response, he pulls his knees up and buries himself behind his book.

"Ladies?" Parson addresses, swiveling on the center bed to assess them.

Julia is already steadying her feet on the mattress as she pulls Charlie up by the hand. The two navigate over the beds like uncertain toddlers as Vin breaks their path into the corridor. Parson follows as they slip through the narrow exit, pausing to check with Billy.

"You going to be okay here?"

"I'll scream if I need you," Billy quips darkly, attempting to muster some facsimile of a grin.

Parson receives the satire bracingly but manages a smile before crabbing through the door.

The corridor is cast in the illumination of a single candle. The anemic light stokes the anxiety burning in Vin's chest like the fuel in the wood stove as he stands guard outside the bathroom.

Julia's gratitude for electricity has not prevented her from having taken the companion candle from the corridor in with her and Charlie. "A hot bath would be so nice right now," she chirps.

Charlie, upon the toilet, does not respond.

Julia moves to the mirror and runs the hot water, both to mask the sound of Charlie's relieving herself and to draw a measure of physical consolation. Burying her face in the hot water cupped in her hands, Julia relishes the luxury with a gratified moan.

"You okay in there?" Vin checks from the other side of the door.

"Yeah, just washing my face."

She turns to reach for the towel and jumps with a gasp.

Charlie is standing beside her, staring at her blankly.

"You sure?"

"Yeah," Julia says, spooked by Charlie's silent rise. "Just a little freaked out."

Charlie looks down at the running water.

"It feels good," Julia prods meekly, making way.

Charlie slips her hands under the flow.

Julia flushes before taking Charlie's place on the toilet, watching her apprehensively.

Charlie draws the reviving water to her face and hangs her head to rub the warmth into the back of her neck.

Her shoulders slump as the rigidity bleeds from her body.

She straightens.

Her body cramps in horror!

Agnot's corpse, with head splayed open, looms in the mirror!

Charlie roars on a gasp, smashing the mirror with her fist!

The door bursts open.

Julia screams.

Vin and Parson rush upon the fitful Charlie.

Parson pushes Vin into the corridor, where Billy tumbles from the constricted doorway stricken and pale.

"Girl time!" Parson trumpets, swiftly assessing Charlie's hand.

Her revival shattered, she sinks.

Parson catches her, hoisting her with a grunt. "Sorry, sweetie," he offers Julia, who dodges Charlie's feet from the toilet.

"Vin! Close your eyes and open the door," he calls.

Carrying Charlie like a tortured bride across the threshold, Parson pushes past the rattled Indian.

The door is shut on Julia abruptly.

Shaken and whimpering, the separation from the others expands around her. Droplets hang on her lashes as she surveys the lavatory and the shards littering the floor. Her quivering breath grows loud in her ears until it, too, becomes a source of fear.

The knob turns.

Julia begins to tremble violently.

The door opens.

Darkness falls around her.

"Whoa, girl!" Parson exclaims, rushing to steady her.

"Shut the door!" he barks. "I got her!"

The door snaps shut behind him.

"Okay, sweetie, come on," he pants, tapping her face firmly.

To Parson's relief, she rouses quickly, and he helps her clean up before carrying her across the jagged remains of the mirror.

"I think we're done with that bathroom," he charges under a flash of lightning, bearing her across the corridor, where he is grateful to set her on her feet.

Julia crawls onto the center bed to curl up with Charlie, both desperate for the solace despite the stove-induced swelter.

Billy, however, stifles under the heat. He shifts his weight but then pauses thoughtfully. "You guys don't mind if I open the window for a minute, do you?"

His only answer is the voice of thunder rolling over the castle.

The windows shift and rattle under the badgering storm as Billy lumbers across the beds.

He frees the latch.

A malevolent gale snatches the pane, pulling him waist-deep out of the window.

Wolves fill his pupils and harrow his nerves.

The cloister below is thick with the beasts. They lunge and snap in ravenous anticipation, their horrible eyes glowing with the devil's light.

Wrestling the two panes, Billy reels himself back to a secure base.

A burst of lightning strips the castle of its benighted veil, piercing Billy to his core with revelatory dismay.

Within margins of that celestial flare, a ghoulish corpse stands in every black and gaping lancet in the castle, staring back at him as if summonsed from his nightmares.

Billy recoils with a gasp, the casings slipping from his fingers.

The clamor hammers Julia and Charlie from their bed and rallies Parson and Vin from the corridor.

Billy meets them with an ashen face apparent even through the darkness.

"Sorry," he stammers as Parson flies over the beds.

Behind them, Vin is fighting the invading gusts to relight the candles. "Shut the window!"

Parson and Billy grapple for the rapping panes as the dome of heaven belches a spiteful roar.

Another blast of lightning replays the ambulatory corpses.

Parson and Billy mirror each other's harrowed faces, grasping the panes and slamming them shut.

"I think we'll need the shutters tonight," Parson declares as he and Billy bar the window with the panels.

Vin does not argue, his face a mask of his presumptive imagination in the glow of the first candle as he moves to reignite the others.

"One candle will do," Parson breathes as he and Billy slump onto the bed. "I'm ready to end this day."

Vin sets the candle on the mantle, looking to Parson with a bashful demeanor. "I've been rethinking our sleeping situation," he begins.

"I thought you might," Parson replies through an amused sigh.

"I'm not worried about anything, or anything. It's just…"

Billy passes an indignant expression from Vin to Parson.

"No one wants any awkward misunderstandings," Parson elaborates.

"Jeezus christ," Billy grumbles. "With all the fucked-up shit we've been through, you're afraid of Parson's boner?"

Before Vin can defend himself, Parson interjects quickly to safeguard their cohesion. "It's not unreasonable, and I can bunk with Charlie, if Julia doesn't mind."

"I don't," she whispers, sitting up and offering Vin a coy smile.

"That worked out," Billy chides, shaking his head as he crawls across the beds to the one allotted him.

Parson takes Julia's place beside Charlie as Julia and Vin settle into the next bed.

The candle and flame stand unflinching on the thick shelf above the stove, providing a warm and glowing touchstone for their badgered emotions. The room is still and quiet, save the rustle of bedfellows and the irregular prattle of the harried window. A flash of lightning streaks through the slats of the shutters to herald the trespass on quiet by booming thunder.

"I wonder why it isn't raining," Julia murmurs with the subsided thunder.

"What do you mean?" Vin whispers.

"Well, it's a pretty bad storm."

"Because rain brings life," Billy rebuffs grumpily.

"Billy!" Parson hisses in rebuke.

The declaration, however, succeeds in silencing Ravenword and soon the gentle tide of slumber begins to well in them.

Vin is stirred from this borderland by the sudden trembling of Julia's body.

A wail, pitiful and resonant, descends on his ear.

He rolls over to find Parson propped on his elbow and Billy sitting up and staring at the door.

The anguish, bellowing from some indeterminate part of the annex, is consumed by thunder.

The rumble dissipates, leaving Ravenword to task their ears.

Billy turns to his companions, unsettled by the lull.

Julia gasps as the horrible rue resumes, but from the corridor!

The confused intonations of the unnerving dirge coalesce into a drawn and pleading call: "La clemenza!"

Billy leaps from his bed to Charlie's and shoves it against the door with his legs.

As dragging footsteps close in, Parson coaxes Charlie to the last bed as Billy leapfrogs to join Vin in reinforcing the barricade with the center bed.

An impotent thud seeps through the grain.

In a storm of whispers, Ravenword manages the last bed across the thin gap.

The latch shimmies as the doorknob twists slowly back and forth.

"La clemenza! La grazia di vita ci libera dal destino del nostro egoismo e dall'ignoranza!"

Ravenword huddle on the far bed watching the door, as their fear gives way to pity. That sympathy, however, quickly transforms to anxiety.

"Ruin!" Fichtenberg screams, beating madly against their door. "Eight! Eight!"

Ravenword constrict, exchanging fretful and weary expressions as the professor's shrieking begins to resound in the corridor. As if making rounds, he can be heard beating against the doors of the other chambers amid his ranting. Ravenword remain tight and quiet, waiting to see how long it will take the frail addict to spend his manic rage

"Lost! Lost! Lost!" he roars like a deranged soloist in the mad symphony of wind and thunder.

A crash, more violent than his diminutive frame can deliver, hammers their door, jolting both the bodies and hearts of the company. The men exchange knowing glances, thankful they had decided to remove all but one of the pedestals in the corridor. As if disembodied, Fichtenberg's delirious ranting reverberates through the annex, waxing and waning like an oppressing tide until Ravenword can no longer track his location. The five friends amble back to their pillows, resigned to the resonant haunting of Fichtenberg and Romero.

That resignation is short-lived.

The jarring crash of shattering glass once again rips them from their beds. Stock-still and peering through the candlelight, they strain to hear through the tempest. The howl of wind marauding through the annex convinces them that at least one of the great windows in the dining hall has met its doom. Yet another sound rises amid the tumult to set the ice loose in their veins.

Claws on stone!

The horrible clattering sails into the corridor with snapping jaws and snarls.

Ravenword scramble for the far wall, wedging themselves in the narrow gap and setting their feet against the bed frame.

Claws scratch and dig at the margins of their door.

Hot and heavy snorts blast under in frenzied bloodlust.

Stark and fleeting sheets from lightning beat through the slats of the shutters, Fichtenberg's maniacal shrieks churn in the wild winds, and the ferocious tenacity of the wolves ravage their harried faculties.

Thunder booms spitefully, as if hell-bent on breaking them.

Vin clutches Julia, his weary head pounding.

Julia is beyond tears, and her trembling is wasted with abject fatigue.

Even Billy, his legs trembling, is pierced by the verity of their ordeal. His gaze is emblazoned on the wolf-infested door.

Parson's chest burns with an irrational irritation as his beleaguered mind fixates on contingencies should the beasts somehow breach their barricade.

Charlie begins to shudder violently.

A fresh horror is added to the desperate nightmare, passing from the bereft lover to the rest of the company.

That heinous, damnable voice rises over the din of claws and shrieks and wind and thunder to hiss her name like a merciless bane.

The wolves begin to pummel the door as if suddenly rabid with the cantor of that hideous intonation.

The bed frames lurch and knock, shocking their knees as they use their collective weight to bar the assault.

The terrible invocation of Charlie's name continues to slice through their minds like a diseased razor.

Charlie suddenly falls still.

Ravenword watch in horror as she rises to the summons.

The door thunders ferociously in its frame, trapping Ravenword in their bracing defense.

With a grace terrible and perverse, Charlie crosses over the three contentious beds as if they were mediums of tranquility.

Overwrought by the sight, Julia slumps unconscious, leaving the men to contend with the onslaught.

That grotesque voice beckons like an insatiable yearning.

Charlie reaches for the knob.

Parson, Vin, and Billy's legs burn.

Charlie's head falls back on her shoulder, her mouth gaping.

An inhuman moan blasts from Charlie's throat, merging the terrible cacophony into one harrowing harmony.

The wolves abandon their assault to possess her howl.

Somewhere in the annex, Fichtenberg's scream rises.

Parson, Vin, and Billy cringe under the harrowing chorus.

The hellish accord crescendos under a cannonade of thunder and explodes into an earsplitting cacophony that shakes the very stone around them until their overwrought senses succumb helplessly to darkness.

The Order

V<small>IN WAKES TO GRAY DAYLIGHT</small> that twinges his pupils as they focus upon Billy opening the shutters. Parson is stretched across two beds beside him, while Julia remains unconscious in the gap where she sank the night before. Twisting stiffly, Vin stretches as he leans over to wake her.

His intent, however, is arrested by a shrill dread.

A vacuous stillness encases her, as if imbued by a void bereft of vital essence.

The unnatural sallowness of her features freezes the very heart of him.

Reaching through grim trepidation, his fingers find her as cold as the stone upon which she lies.

His crashing grief is usurped by sudden horror as some unseen thing tugs at her—from under the bed!

Under the rasp of a hideous roar, she is gone!

"Julia!"

Vin bolts upright with a gasp.

Julia gapes in startled surprise from atop the mounds of duffel bags piled in the corner.

His head swims in the lingering tendrils of the incubus as he winces against the morning light spilling into the room as Billy opens the shutters.

"Are you okay?" she gasps.

Billy shakes his head as Parson pats Vin's shoulder with a bemused sigh as he toddles to the center bed to check Charlie.

The tenacity of her slumber is unsettling to both Parson and Billy, who had moved her to a comfortable repose. "What do you think?"

"I think we let her sleep as long as she needs to."

Vin shakes off as much of the chill as his groggy mind can manage, focusing on the condition of his friends and the aftermath of their night. He can hear nothing beyond the door, still barricaded by beds.

"You all right, there, woody?" Parson jibes with a wry grin.

The tenting of his trousers is already waning and, while blushing, the bond of their peril-forged camaraderie abates his embarrassment.

"Yeah." He checks their faces one by one before continuing carefully. "Has there been any—"

"No," Billy answers quickly. "It's been really quiet. We've been waiting for you to wake up before checking things out."

"Why didn't you wake me?" Vin presses. "How long have you guys been up?"

"After last night we all needed as much rest as we could get," Parson interjects. "So we weren't waking anybody up. Besides, I don't think anyone is too eager to open that door."

"Do you think anything's still out there?"

Parson and Billy share resolute demeanors.

Julia busies herself with the duffel bags.

"We've been up awhile," Parson sighs. "If anything were out there, it would have heard us by now and been on that door like—"

"A pack of wolves?" Julia chides, her curt interjection surprising and silencing them.

The revelation of their isolation amplifies the enormity of their plight and the dire risks in their intentions to set out. A patina of despair creeps over them, threatening to immobilize the company before they start.

Parson, determined to find a way of escaping the dark clutches of the castle, shakes off the lethal frost and adopts as carefree a demeanor as he can manage. "How about we go survey the damage?"

"All of us?" Julia checks.

"The more the merrier."

"What about Charlie?" Vin considers. "I don't think she should be left alone."

"She's sleeping," Billy carps, eager to get out of the room.

"So we leave her to wake up alone in an empty room?" Vin rebuffs.

"God's teeth!" Parson exclaims. "Can we please not bicker?"

"You guys!"

Julia's admonishment draws them from contention to Charlie, whose languid eyes survey them one by one.

"Sorry, sweetie," Parson whispers gently, squeezing her hand.

"We were just about to go down and make coffee and breakfast," Julia proffers sweetly.

Charlie rolls toward the wall without speaking, pulling the blanket over her.

Billy nods at Parson and then to the door.

"Sweetie, we're going to need to move the beds to get out. Is that okay?"

Charlie does not respond.

Assuming her silence is acquiescence, Vin and Billy move the farthest bed against the wall. They are careful to do so quietly. Parson climbs over the footboard to stand alongside Julia as the two men gently lift Charlie's bed. With Parson and Julia in the cramped corner, they finish by removing the final bed-frame blockade.

The liberation of the door taints the insulating atmosphere with apprehension.

The company hesitates.

The suspension is broken by Vin, who meets the door as the company braces themselves.

He opens the door to an uncertain silence.

A draft of morning damp drifts from the corridor.

Vin slips slowly out of the egress. He is followed closely by Parson, who notes an angry gash in the grain with gratitude for the hardiness of the wood. Like silent phantoms, the four members of Ravenword seep into the exaggerated openness, studying the shambles with prickled senses.

The podium, splintered and scarred by momentum and wolf claw, lies in the center of the hallway as if it, too, had been murdered by the castle's dark forces. The doors to the surrounding rooms and lavatories hang ajar in violent angles, save the cursed portal barricaded with nails and desperation. All is still, yet they cannot shake the impression that something monstrous waits in one of the surrounding chambers.

Vin puts a finger to his lips as he gestures to his friends to stay. He crosses the corridor on guard, peering past the door to the purple studio where a toolbox waits on the floor. Laying his palm against the door, with a checking glance at Parson, he pushes it back on its hinges. Their squeaky protest riddles his nerves.

The chamber is a fortress of shadows lording over the anemic light filtering through the shuttered window.

Despite Vin's direction, Parson crosses to guard him as he crouches over the toolbox. With the stealth of a thief, he lifts a crowbar from the bin and hands it to Parson before appropriating two screwdrivers and the hammer.

Behind them, Billy and Julia watch anxiously.

Vin nods to Parson as he sweeps across to hand Billy and Julia the screwdrivers. Again, however, he motions for them to stay put.

Tracking Vin's intent, Parson waits at the door of the purple room on taut muscles. On a nod, the two men mirror each other along the walls to the next set of opposing doors with their makeshift weapons bared.

With his heart pounding in his chest, Parson pushes the lavatory door.

Vin follows suit.

The shattered remains of the mirror, creating a disjointed collage, lie undisturbed. The shards crunch under his feet like a bitter grievance as Parson crosses to release the shutters.

Silver light brightens both lavatories with the unbound windows but yields no comfort.

With Julia and Billy as wary sentinels, the two men proceed hence to each of the doors. Upon the illumination of each, their tension ebbs. The last vestiges of apprehension, however, mount a counter surge as Vin closes in on the black chamber.

Parson fixes his stance in front of the hated door as Vin pushes that of the black chamber open.

The room is an abyss. The tepid light seeping through the slats of the shutters is of little consequence to the chamber's ebony dressings.

Tightening his grip on the hammer, Vin disappears into the stygian cavity.

Parson extends a staying hand to Billy and Julia.

A gasp barks from the chamber!

An abrupt thud and clamor pull Parson from his post.

Vin yelps in the darkness!

Scurrying back on hands and knees, Vin meets Parson in the doorway, shouting frantically, "Stay back!"

Billy, catches Julia swiftly by the arm.

"Billy!" she pleads, turning on him desperately.

"Stay there!" Vin barks as he clambers to his feet.

Horrible understanding dawns on Parson as the stench slaps his nostrils.

Billy is already digging his book light out of his pocket as Parson jogs toward him with a forbidding expression. Billy nods as he hands Parson the light, keeping Julia firmly by his side.

"What is it?"

Vin shushes her sharply.

Billy's book light is just strong enough to reveal the corpse sprawled on the cold flagstone.

Vin holds his breath and, taking the tiny lamp from Parson, steps into the room and over the body to open the shutters and window.

The new light reveals the fate of their slaughtered friend in such ghastly detail that it fells Vin to his knees.

Her torso has been ripped open to expose a raw ribcage that frames the hideous cavity from which desiccating intestines spill into a mirror of stale crimson. A grotesque and gaping gash in her cold and bloodstained neck exposes gore and bone. Her head is splayed gruesomely. Yet it is her brutally battered face, frozen in an expression of horror so abject it defies nature, that shatters the defenses of the spirit. One sunken eye stares in cloudy death, the other a slashed and gory hollow.

Crushed, Vin vomits and chokes.

Parson, blinded by stinging tears, struggles to tame his dizzied brain even as his diaphragm begins to convulse.

The sight of his desolation conveys the terrible discovery, robbing Julia's lungs.

Billy catches her even as strength bleeds from his legs.
Cradled in grief, the two slide to the floor.

Within the blue room, tears pour through Charlie's enchanted slumber as if witness to the atrocious nightmare.

Vin jerks the black damask from the bed that had been Billy's as Parson presses through his anguish to position the ravaged corpse's grisly limbs to a restful repose. Gasping through grief and revulsion, the men cover the remains of their friend and then roll the body to wrap it in the raven shroud. Bundling the ends, they lift her onto the bed of the black chamber to rest in as much peace and dignity as they can provide.

II

White lace ruffles and curls as a delicate handkerchief is tucked under folded hands entwined in rosary beads. Aldobrandi's hand lingers upon those that had provided a familial refuge to him so often. His face is wetted by the memories. The reminiscence, however, is short-lived as he is nudged by one of the many matrons who weep and prattle as they set the final dressings on Renata's body.

Much of his family had come during the night on the wings of mourning and pragmatism that only an Italian family can muster in moments of loss and grief. While the women tended to their departed matriarch, the men necessitated the removal of her bed in favor of the ivory casket that cradles her. Now, the golden morning sun reaches through the window to set her aglow as the women fuss and bicker over final touches.

They have clothed her in the embroidered champagne dress she bought for a cousin's wedding, which, Aldobrandi knows from her own admission, she never cared for. Her white hair remains as impeccably set as it had been the night before and wreaths an expression of wise contentment that stings him. Leaning over her, his tear anoints her head. "Grazie, zia," he whispers, kissing her brow. "Grazie."

Aldobrandi turns away, his intentions set on the living. He finds the hallway empty but swamped by a tempest of voices. The stairs are littered with bored and fidgety children. Below, relatives and neighbors press between one another in and out of the entry as they circulate through the house. A din of cell phones ring incessantly above the commotion as he navigates past the bewildered moppets, his aching heart set on rooting out the Americans and vindicating Renata's sacrifice.

Plunging into the fray, he is petted and kissed and consoled in a tsunami of hands and faces and tears as he wades through the sitting room. "Padre!"

Father Valeriani answers with a scornful eye from a fortress of widows.

"Scusi, mi scusi," Aldobrandi interjects politely as he squeezes past mourners to dour priest. "Padre, have you seen the Americanos?"

"Thieves!" the priest spits. "They have no regard for your family! Insolent Americans!"

"Yes, yes," Aldobrandi deflects impatiently. "Do you know where they have gone?"

"They have taken the relic!" Valeriani reviles. "I do not know where!"

Aldobrandi turns back into the tide and allows the current to shower him with comforts as their procession carries him through the house and, after not finding the Americans, out the front door. A poster announcing Renata's passing has already been pasted at the café across the lane, closing it and prompting its patrons to gather outside her house. Stepping out of the crowd, movement farther down the lane catches his attention, and Aldobrandi turns to see the two men rising from a rustic bench.

"Sorry," T. J. offers as the noble Italian jogs up to him and Grayson, "we didn't want to intrude."

"Grazie," Aldobrandi replies, reinforcing his tender emotions against sentiment with a deep breath. "Do you have it?"

T. J. lifts his satchel, patting it as he sets the strap across his shoulder.

"Then we must go, now," Aldobrandi insists.

T. J. is surprised by his declaration and hesitates as the momentum of Aldobrandi and Grayson shift. "What about your aunt…the funeral?"

"You heard the man," Grayson interjects, sparing the noble Italian the pain of doubt. "Let's go."

III

Julia wipes an apprehensive tear from her milky cheek. "We'll be okay," she insists bracingly. The annex and its recessive apartments seem more expansive and cavernous with the prospect of being alone, and she wraps her arms tightly around her chest. "We'll stay in the room."

Vin nods, shrugging under his rucksack and avoiding the fact that her legs are trembling. Billy stands beside them at the entryway likewise packed and cringing over the inevitable display of desperate affection. A grimace marks Billy's face as Julia launches into Vin's arms. He pivots on disgust toward those ancient and ill-grained doors as their lips collide.

"Oh my god!" Parson exclaims, hurrying out of the passage from the dining hall.

His declaration pulls them out of the vignette, much to Billy's satisfaction.

"You guys have got to see this!" Parson trumpets, grabbing his backpack swiftly and pushing into the openness of the courtyard. "Come on!"

Despite the monotonous gloom of the umbral sky, the brisk gust that buffets them is refreshing and adds to the thrill as Parson leads them past the shattered window of the dining hall. Ahead, the harried tufts are strewn with rubble. As they round the end of the apartment annex, their excited charge is abruptly halted.

"Holy shit!" Billy exclaims.

The four members of Ravenword gape at the fresh ruins of the collapsed chapel cathedral. Jagged peaks jutting through mountains of debris and splintered beams are all that remains of the walls.

"All of God's horses and all of God's men aren't going to be able to put that church back together again!" Parson quips over the wind.

"This is what we heard last night," Julia reasons with terrible wonder. "Louder than thunder."

"All those statues," Billy laments, to the surprise of the others. "What? Do you think you'll see anything like them anywhere else?"

"Fuck!" Vin snaps, startling his friends.

Recovering, the three press his outburst.

"Sorry," he covers quickly, but the imagination of the great sculpted angel lingers. Deciding against poisoning the already tenuous momentum of their plan with an explanation, he buries the image deep in the recesses of his denial. Yet as they stand marveling at the devastation, the implication of the failure congeals in his gut like a cold stone.

A rumble in the dark and wind-whipped clouds descends upon them with the weight of the dire mission and their enthusiasm for ogling the spectacle dissipates like a tear in the desert. One by one, they turn and plod reluctantly back toward the great hall.

A figure in the shattered window catches Julia's eyes.

She looks up and gasps!

Billy and Parson can't help but do the same.

Fichtenberg stands in the black cavity, forcibly reminding the two men of the spectral corpses filling the castle windows within the bursts of lightning the night before.

"Ravenword," the professor calls down with a voice too frail to compete with the angry gate. "You should not be out. Wolves," he moans, gesturing to the shards riddling the panes of the lancet. "You see what they have done."

Vin offers a half-hearted wave as they regain their stride.

"I was hoping I hadn't woken him up," Parson offers, shaking his head. "Sorry, sweetie."

Julia shrugs helplessly. "You couldn't leave without checking on him."

"He probably broke the window himself," Billy grumbles before branching off for the clanging iron grimace.

With nothing left to delay them, Vin takes Julia into his arms, sending Parson across the fallow courtyard to join Billy. The warmth of her accentuates the chill of the wind, a chill that transcends temperatures and anchors the foreboding his chest.

Savoring the sense of safety in his arms, Julia lingers until drawn out by those arms and Vin's resolute voice.

"Go inside. Take care of Charlie."

The rolling of Billy's eyes punctuates his disdain as Julia kisses Vin again before slipping back into the comfortless hall. Pausing at the door, she watches the valiant Indian join Parson and Billy. A dour and piercing pitch rings clamorously into the wind as they shut the gate behind them. With a final wave, the three men tread the gravel road, feeling suddenly small in an exponentially expansive odyssey.

The weather-beaten ruin of the van scowls up at them like a brooding inmate as they pass between the sagging rampart and the murky ravine. The men deign little appreciation for the openness until it is eaten away.

"I feel like I should be wearing a little red riding hood," Parson quips darkly as the forest swells around them.

"Not helping," Billy retorts.

They continue with only the crunching of their footfalls to interrupt the eerie hush of the surrounding woods. The profundity of the stillness creeps along their necks, yet they are loath to intrude upon that quiet for fear of provoking some unseen evil.

The men round the bend. The sight of the straightaway and the forks ahead quickens the pulse of each. The three exchange uneasy glances, asking the unspoken question of who will take the first divergence.

Vin peers down the descending branch, which is little more than a broad path, bracing himself for the plunge. His deep breath heralds his decision and he turns to Parson and Billy with his hand extended. "Good luck."

Hesitant, Billy takes his hand and shakes it firmly, unsure of a consensus.

When Vin turns to Parson, his hand is pushed aside in favor of a solemn hug.

"Last one home is a rotten egg," Parson quotes as they withdraw.

Vin nods at his two friends, swatting Parson against the shoulder before marching into the decline. Ahead, a tenebrous hollow of crooked limbs and resentful thickets yawns as if to swallow him. Despite his resolve, he looks back and is bolstered to find Parson and Billy standing on the rise, monitoring him. Vin lifts his left forearm and taps on his watch.

Parson nods, grudgingly stepping away.

Billy follows.

Vin is quickly lost to brush and topography.

The legion of trees surrounding them groan and creak under the rise of the wind that fills the forest with malevolent whispers, setting both Parson's and Billy's nerves on edge as they stride willfully toward the second fork. The men slow as they approach the split. The road before Parson stretches into the trees until lost to the acrimonious woods, while that bearing before Billy curves along a shallow incline and is quickly obscured.

They pause.

Resigned to his fate, Billy extends his hand.

Parson pushes it away. "C'mere, you lump," he goads sweetly, pulling Billy into a fraternal embrace.

Billy flounders in ambivalence, surprised and uncomfortable with the display but needing and welcoming the gesture nonetheless. His hands rise slowly to reach around Parson, patting him on the back awkwardly. A bulwark in his soul buckles. "I'm afraid."

Parson withdraws but retains him by the shoulders. "Um, duh," he retorts with a weak chuckle. "One surprise squirrel, and I'll be shitting blue Twinkies."

Billy laughs in spite of himself.

Parson's face takes on a reflective cast as he releases Billy. "I think the farther away from the castle we can get, the safer we'll be."

Billy nods. "Good luck, Parson."

"You too, Billy."

They follow each other's progress as long as they can and fare each other well with a final wave as the divergent roads segregate them to their respective paths.

IV

A volley of caws draws Vin's gaze past the gnarled and caging branches to the squadron of ravens soaring over as if to break his path. The gloom of the dreary sky deepens under the shadows born of those comfortless boughs to cast the rustic road in hues of melancholy and despair. His senses raw from vigilance, Vin's rhythmic panting and steady footfalls begin to impede his concentration. The trees lining the road seem to tighten their ranks like paltry Dryads closing in on hapless prey, their limbs so entwined that a black roof is soon woven over him. The temptation to retrieve his flashlight is tempered by the compulsion to do nothing that would draw the attention of the wilderness. Thus, he advances into the dark arbor tunnel, relying only on his harried faculties. The aphotic drudgery, however, begins to add itself to the roster of oppressions and the wormhole through the woods presents no indication of relief.

Deciding a respite of water and a sandwich would do both his body and his senses good, Vin surveys his path for a sod shelf or small boulder on which to pause. He notices a large elbow at the root of one of the larger trees that has collected enough soil to create an appealing little plateau. The prospect of a cheery seat, however, is dashed.

A mass of black seizes his imagination with sinking dread.

Spread across the road, the blight is a physical thing that undulates within rambling margins as it clings to the ground like some inky brume.

He runs his fingers through his hair in weary consternation and looks back to confirm no means of quick escape. A surge of despondence rifles through him, but it is broken suddenly by a terse caw. Vin blinks under a furrowed brow, stepping cautiously toward the mass.

A second caw validates the nature of the shape—or rather, shapes, for the teeming black mass is actually a murder of ravens congesting the trail like unfortunate commuters.

Vin indulges in a puzzled grin. A few of the birds cock their heads to study him with a beady eye, but none ruffle a feather. Charmed by their curious comfort, he continues slowly into their company. Ravens hop out of the path of his feet as he advances as if ushering him into their murder. Strolling through the pool of sable feathers, his beleaguered mind revels in the reprieve of the enchanted moment.

A muted thud, however, agitates the ravens and pulls Vin out of the spell to peer back at the road behind.

A fair turtledove flounders at the far end of the hollow, constricting in the final grips of death.

The shrill fear that has become so familiar regains its seat in his core as his instincts descry the ominous demise.

The dove's mate tumbles to the ground beside it.

The corvids squawk querulously, nipping at his feet with bristled feathers and beating wings.

Vin stands gaping in horrible astonishment as sparrows rain down from the branches in a flurried wave that rushes toward him as if death itself were sailing through the branches.

The murder explodes in a flurry of beating wings, screaming in alarm.

Through those beating wings, Vin can see the tide of evil blackness rushing at him through the canopy.

The ravens dive and pivot, clawing and pecking at him wildly.

Needing no prodding from their metered assault, he bolts into the verdant wormhole.

Infused with terror-stoked adrenaline, his furious legs lead the frenzied tempest of ravens as the nebulous blot of pitch lunges from the canopy to pursue them like a fist of demons.

Vin's feet drum the ground as his eyes, peeled to their margins, plead for a sign of escape. His lungs burn as they suck the icy air. His ears whip him with the screams of ravens being ripped from the vanguard as the hellish phantasm gains.

A shimmering orb of silver gray impresses his harried brain.

Ravens begin to beat past him as the black ghoul presses.

A surge of desperate energy lashes through him as he realizes the bouncing orb is a clearing yawning with his approach.

Striding madly in a squall of black driving wings, the hairs rise on his neck on the frigid breath of the closing bane.

In a burst of screaming ravens, Vin erupts from the fearsome hollow and onto a hillside washed in the filtered silver of midday.

The threat at his back is thwarted.

Vin turns with heaving chest to find a trail of dead ravens and the abysmal stain seething deep in the canopy. What remains of the murder circles above him, cawing incessantly as if to prod him onward.

As he turns to consider the road through the scrub and hills ahead, the nebulous black phantom slips from the tangled branches and disappears between abetting trunks.

Vin tries to quell the shudder induced by the lurid specter's egress, but the awareness of some conscious vindictiveness in the thing beckons to his primal fears. Like wary prey, he returns to his course, shakily cognizant of being stalked.

V

With the exception of the thunder rolling across the low and tenuous clouds looming like islands of ash in the sky, Parson's trek through the mountains is not unlike his hikes through the Sierra foothills. Granted, he is not likely to run across any tantalizing excursions like the Yuba River or the Auburn Ravine, but he does marvel at how reminiscent the rugged alpine terrain and flora are to the gold country. The comparison, however, quickly leads his imagination to bears and mountains lions.

"Okay," he says to himself, "That's enough of that."

A branch of lightning imprints itself in the gunmetal expanse above a distant peak and Parson counts—one-one thousand, two-one thousand—for the rumbling suffix. Now well accustomed to the sky's profanity, when it does clap through the range, he suffers not a twinge of apprehension. He suddenly realizes a sense of lightness, as if he were finally out from underneath the castle's sinister spell. The satisfied smile tempting his features, however, is dampened by the sobering knowledge that Julia and Charlie are still hostages to that nightmare. An abrupt downpour emphasizes the point, and Parson issues an exacerbated sigh. Continuing through the barrage of liquid bullets, the seasoned old road proceeds into another incline and Parson lifts his face to the rain. Refreshed, he begins the ascent. His quadriceps and calves warm with exertion, triggering his appetite for a good workout, and soon he is marching up the increasingly steep slope with the fervor of an endorphin addict. Cresting the hill with deliciously burning legs, he is forced to a halt.

"Oh Jeezus, really?" he groans, throwing his hands on his hips. "You really need to get over this bitchy deity thing."

A growling boom resounds behind the clouds as the rain begins to penetrate his shirt.

"Whatever," he retorts. "It's so unattractive."

The hill falls away before him into a deep ravine, the edge of which the road skirts as if tasked in preventing the forest from sliding into the drastic valley. At the shallow base of the hill, where the path more or less levels out, an old wash has rent the road with a wide and craggy gully that now funnels the rainwater into the chasm.

Parson traipses through the increasingly heavy shower to see what he is up against. He folds his arms with an austere leer over the plumbing gulch, scrutinizing the soggy clay and boulders breaching the swollen stream for suitability in supporting his crossing.

The prospect is dubious at best.

His second option, he supposes, is to merely jump the seven or so feet that the cavity has stolen from the road. He is convinced that with a running start, he could easily make the leap, but stopping without sliding into injury upon landing gives him pause.

In the debate between potential bruises and a definite dousing, the lesser of two evils is the one he can control the most. His confidence in his ability to mitigate the consequences of a spill sends him backtracking while assessing the appropriate lead with a calculated eye.

Parson sets his mark with several deep and deliberate breaths.

The encompassing landscape is abruptly bleached in white light.

Upon the corresponding boom, Parson bolts from his starting line.

His determined footfalls build his momentum over the soggy asphalt.

The breach races toward him.

Parson shifts his weight to lunge; his right foot strikes his launch point.

Pushing from the wet pavement, his tread slips.

Parson's arms sail wildly as he tries to correct his pitch.

His eyes gape as the opposing concrete edge of the gully rushes up at him.

A blow to his abdomen jars his ribs, crushing the breath from his lungs.

He gasps amid a sea of stars, flailing onto his backpack into the rushing waters.

Pain racks his pelvis and neck as the unforgiving boulders surrender him to gravity.

The icy spray slaps his senses, which riddle him with terror.

His mad plummet is broken by a snare catching his foot, flipping him headlong into a bludgeoning tumble.

Grappling madly in the dashing, his bloodied fist clenches a root.

His desperate grasp is taxed by his own weight fishtailing to dangle over the precipice.

Parson's agonizing pants are stuttered as his free hand scrambles for a hold.

His fist numbs in the frigid water.

The shrill stab of mortal fear breaks over him.

His grasp weakens.

He claws at the slick stone.

His fingers loosen.

VI

The worn road grumbles under the roiling of gravel as Billy falls sprawling and sliding across its weather-beaten face. He wastes no time, however, in hauling his stout frame to its feet. Securing the straps of the backpack, he spins on his heels with wild eyes.

At the far periphery of the lane, wolves glare and pace as if eager to continue the chase. The alpha emerges from the stewing pack to level a low, malevolent scowl on him with a spiteful snarl that resonates with every primordial fear in Billy's genetics.

His chin is smeared with blood that stains his heaving chest as he savors every precious second of the fleeting respite. With acuity resurrected from the base memory of the species, he gauges the movement and disposition of the predators.

The powerfully built alpha stares savagely, the malice of his ravenous fangs reaching across the breadth.

Billy does not break the calculated gaze he casts back at the creature.

Able to spare a labored breath, and hoping against hope to secure more, Billy shouts with all the bravado he can muster. "Get out of here!" he bellows, waving his arms wildly. "Go on! Get out!"

The threatening pose of the alpha does not abate, nor does the frenzy of the pack.

Primal anticipation floods Billy's veins.

The terrible alpha rounds on the pack, his viselike jaws snapping ferociously.

With obedient yelps, the canid agents slip into the surrounding foliage.

The alpha leers at Billy, posture and muscles tightening.

Billy turns and bolts.

Images of wolves sweeping through the surrounding woods with their master closing in behind him harry Billy's pummeled imagination.

That waking nightmare is somehow penetrated by a cue.

Billy grapples against primal instincts to keep hold of lucidity, putting his ears to task as his brain races to confirm the call.

"Help!" he bawls.

An unmistakable call, distant and tenuous, returns his wail.

A thrill of exhilaration shoots through him, fueling him with mad vigor.

His lungs burn as the voice, ringing clearer, calls through the woods again.

The comfortless forest flies by as his legs find their stride, and Billy charges down the road with a will of iron that masters both his fear and his form.

His heart leaps as, rounding a bend like a derby stallion, his eyes catch sight of a wall.

His stride falters.

His perceptions shatter.

The gravel road again races up at him.

Pain sears his palms and racks his wrists.

He rolls, disgorging a wail that would freeze the soul.

Before his harried body can recover from the bruising tumble, his eyes are ogling through the dust.

"God damn you!" he screams. "God fucking damn you!"

Billy's tortured roar crashes against the wall, over which Castello Nel Buio looms like a scowling fiend, its clanging black gates yawning horridly to welcome him.

VII

A robustly outfitted Range Rover pulls off the country lane, its pearlescent shell flashing in the bright afternoon sun as it comes to a stop in front of ornate gates hung between opposing pillars that frame an old and rustic terracotta wall. Beyond the ironwork, an equally rustic villa heralds an estate that has graced sun-washed Tuscany for hundreds of years. Yet as Aldobrandi exits from the passenger seat, the aged manor exudes a queer and incongruent energy that impresses T. J. with a foreboding that defies the idyllic setting.

Before Aldobrandi can reach the gate, a raven sweeps from the leafy branches of a flanking tree to catch a cord in its beak and, perching atop the pillar, tugs the line to set the bell at the other end ringing.

"Clever bird," Grayson observes as Aldobrandi reacts to the stunt and corresponding attention from beyond the gates.

"Is this some kind of cult?" T. J. wonders aloud at the emergence of an old nun, whose striking scarlet and white habit mocks the reverence of conventional piety.

Grayson studies the persona with calculating scrutiny as the crone greets Aldobrandi from behind the bars. The extraordinary nun shifts her gaze to the Rover as Aldobrandi gestures, listening intently to his emphatic oration. Her eyes narrow shrewdly as he finishes, her thin lips barely moving in her reply. Aldobrandi turns and hurries to the back passenger-seat door.

"The relic!" he insists as he pulls the door open and extends an eager hand.

T. J. passes the case to Aldo without thinking, carried on fervor of the strange drama. "What's going on?"

His query, however, is stifled by Aldobrandi slamming the door.

The noble Italian presents the ancient wooden box to the old vestal.

Astonishment washes over her craggy features upon his opening the case and she crosses herself quickly then retreats toward the manor and out of sight.

A moment later the Range Rover is pulling through the open gates, circumnavigating the modest garden roundabout and delivering the three men to the antiquated facade where the scarlet-red nun waits in the recess of weathered doors. Her urgent prodding as they exit the Rover betrays her grim enthusiasm.

A crucifix, inlaid with a teardrop ruby at the heart of the tortured figurine, resting conspicuously against the starched white guimpe of her habit begs their attention as the three men are ushered into the villa.

Aldobrandi, T. J., and Grayson cross the threshold into a spacious hall that, either by purpose or contrivance, emulates the sanctity of a sequestered chapel. An ancient table, spanning the length of the peculiar nave, stretches out before them between arched colonnades that host recessive passages.

The singular nun closes the door behind them to lead them silently into the curious sanctuary. T. J. notes with a sense of reminiscent unease that the seven sets of opposing columns are draped in tapestries colored in the lurid hues of Poe's seven chambers. As they pass, his attention falls to the statuettes stationed on pedestals before those seven vivid tapestries. Each is a cast of saints, beginning with the Madonna and Child set against the blue. Slanted beams of golden sunlight pour through square stained-glass windows high above the arches to bestow uncanny halos upon the icons. At the opposing colonnade, as if placed within the line of sight of the saints, shrines alit with prayer candles set the tapestries aglow. The coordinated effect of the design frames the chancel ahead dramatically and taints the air of sanctity with a mad flare.

As the old crimson nun ushers the men toward the chairs lining the final end of the table, it is the striking effect of that chancel that usurps their fascination. The curved alcove rises through amber hues to a round vaulted arch that hosts a single source of light whose silvery ray descends upon a bizarre figure seated in a golden chair and dressed in a crimson robe that spills out onto the floor like a pool of blood.

The right arm of the life-size icon is absolute white with a hand laid over the heart position boasting fingers ringed with gold and silver set with bright and precious jewels. The left arm, painted to imitate a mottled black serpent, lies under the right to wrap the torso like the primeval tempter. The neck and face of the icon are patinated in a queer shade of pale green under sculpted hair wrought and twisted into blunted limbs in imitation of an ancient and dying tree. The lids of the serenely clasped eyes are inlaid with painted coins, gold over the right eye and silver over the left. Around the curious figure, incense smolders in rustic bowls, sending trails of aromatic smoke ascending in ribbons before dispersing in the distilled atmosphere.

As they take the seats indicated by the aged abbess, T. J., Aldobrandi, and Grayson cannot help but survey the surreal representation with a strange reluctance, as if committing some egregious trespass. Grayson notes that, although the icon is occupying the chancel dais, it is situated at the head of the spanning table. Their scrutiny, however, is interrupted by movement in the recesses beyond the reach of the sunlight cast against the colonnade.

Aldobrandi sets the ancient case on the table but keeps it well in hand as two silhouettes within the nebulous depths of the archway stare back at them from eyes hidden in hooded blackness.

• • •

Ebony-winged battalions scream over a thicket from which Vin explodes, his feet beating out a frantic rhythm. His black hair fans as he checks over his shoulder with eyes burnished with fear and determination. In the openness of the road, his pace surges, and he scours the course ahead for shadow sign and pitch. Ravens swoop and circle through the low-reaching branches, harassing and betraying the aphotic phantasm that continues to dog him. Despite the burning in his overburdened lungs, Vin does not relent. The waning afternoon, filtered to gloom by the deepening clouds, stretches the woodland shadows to provide increasing liberty to the ghoul, yet Vin has no intention of being snared when the meridian turns to its favor. Gratitude washes over him as the descent of the road steepens and curves around a bend in which the dark side of the woods gives way to deep and open slope that unveils a panorama of the Tuscan mountains.

• • •

The rays of sunlight from the high windows evaporate as if night has descended suddenly, leaving Aldobrandi and the Americans to the glow of enshrined candlelight and the singular beam that frames the strange chancel figurine with a blazing aura. The unheralded reappearance of the crimson nun compounds the disquiet welling in both T. J. and Aldobrandi. The resounding crack of her slapping hands after setting a tray of eight candles on the table does little to ease their discomfort.

On the echoes of that abrupt clap, the two hooded figures emerge from the deep passage, revealing monastic cloaks of deep crimson. The aged abbess distributes the candles as the enigmatic monks carry away the adjoining segment of the long table to leave the three men to their own island. Grayson, his exacting eyes trained on the two laboring monks, is thwarted by the shielding darkness of their hoods as he monitors their exit into the tenebrous passage. It is into this abyss that the old nun disappears, leaving the three men alone in the vast sanctuary.

● ● ●

Vin hangs his head.

In the dismal heights, the murder swirls like a blot of stirred ink, their ebony ranks swollen on urgent caws that serve to prod him through the mire of despair.

On a curt sigh, he heeds their prodding and lifts his head to assess the impossible obstacle.

Gnarled and thickly woven branches overshadow brush-riddled walls, quarried in some aged past, as they reach across a cleft rent into the hillside to accommodate the road. Black shadows curse the lane, marrying its stygian gullied margins to found a murky atmosphere that stains his weariness with the despondence of defeat.

It is the perfect snare.

That aphotic phantom lurks unseen, yet its presence presses into his raw instincts like a barb.

Vin's head bows once again, his shoulders crumbling beneath as his beleaguered body bends forward in a miserable avalanche. The waiting of Julia impels him to stifle the surrender, perching his palms on his knees.

The atramentous passage seethes with the menace of that black phantom, as if ordained for victory by the very forces that have held captive all the damned souls at Castello Nel Buio.

• • •

The crimson crone emerges from the arched recesses with the two robed enigmas, passing between the glowing shrines to set a bounty of food and drink at the end of the long table. As T. J. contemplates the bread, cheese, fruit, and pitcher deposited across the gap, the two strange monks place chairs on either side of the setting. His assessment, however, is circumvented by the startling crack of the staunch nun's insistent clap.

Grayson, growing impatient with the theatrics, crosses his burly arms as a monk places a chair beside him at the foot of the blunted table before joining the second peculiar abbot.

The two stand behind the vacant chairs but do not sit as the crimson nun takes the seat delivered by the subjugated monk.

A dark stillness settles once again over the company.

The bizarre monks bow their hooded heads as the old woman in the profane habit closes her eyes, raises a rosary in clasped hands to her mouth and begins to pray in low, ardent murmurs.

T. J. and Grayson both look to Aldobrandi for interpretation, but at a loss, he can only shrug.

As the fervor of her prayer intensifies, the two monks mirror her gesture with rosaries of their own.

The intonations of the cantor nudge a familiarity from the recesses of T. J.'s mind, but its nature remains elusive.

A press of lightning's stark light flashes through the sanctuary's high windows, charging the arcane atmosphere with a welling urgency that amplifies the prayers of the intercessors. T. J., Aldobrandi, and Grayson sit in rigid anticipation, unnerved by the bizarre scene as the burgeoning prayers take on the cadence of a chant. A roll of thunder impedes the resonance of the chant, but as the roar abates, the collective drum and pitch of the intercession becomes clear. "Om tryanmbhakam yahamahe, sugandhim pushtivardhanam, urvarukamiva bandhanan, mrityor mukshiva maamritat."

• • •

Vin straightens.

The shrill squawks of the encircling ravens crash through his trepidation to set his determination free.

His hands ball into fists.

A mantra burnished with ancestral fortitude rises from his latent memories, "Om tryanmbhakam yahamahe, sugandhim pushtivardhanam, urvarukamiva bandhanan, mrityor mukshiva maamritat."

Imbued with new resolve, he glares into the mouth of the vindictive pass.

As if called to battle, the churning armada of ravens screams down from the sky.

Vin lunges toward the gaping shadows.

He can feel the phantom tighten its abysmal snare.

The chant rises brazenly in his throat.

The black-winged allies become an enveloping tempest.

The black snare yawns, blitzed by a raven-winged offensive.

Beak and talon turn on him.

His hands flail to protect his eyes as sharp jabs and scratches penetrate the ebony wings beating him in the face.

Shrieking caws disorient his ears and balance as they are bitten and wrenched.

Enraged with the betrayal, Vin lashes out at the corvids in his determined push forward.

His legs and torso are clawed and pulled, then bruised by limbs stronger than those of birds.

Vin's charge, however blinded by the treacherous ravens, is undaunted.

The black-feathered blizzard dissipates abruptly, and Vin finds himself chest-deep in quaking shrub brush.

The light is gloomy but unimpeded by the waving limbs of surrounding trees.

Elation and gratitude sail through him like the whirling wind as the panorama beyond those trees heralds the realization that the ravens have corralled him past the snare to the crest of the cloven hill. That euphoria is compounded as his eyes fall upon a generous estate gracing the wind-whipped Tuscan countryside below.

"Yes!" he trumpets, lifting his head and hands toward the swirling murder above. "Blessed are you among all birds!"

A barking squawk arrests his blithe pause, reminding him that he is not out of the grip of the phantom and whipping his legs to task.

• • •

Lightning orchestrates the rising wind, now howling outside the walls of the sanctuary.

T. J. and Aldobrandi can't help but cringe under the ensuing boom that interrupts the dispirited wail.

His prowess stoked with the increasing tide, Grayson's sharp senses catalogue and correlate the unfolding drama toward the conclusion that they are being masterfully manipulated.

The wind slams against the entry, vanquishing all their suppositions.

An ensuing barrage against those double doors bursts them from their frames. They fly open, wrenching the men from their chairs as the intruding gale bores into the nave, harassing the tapestries and extinguishing the candle-laden shrines.

Emboldened, the intercessors lift their emphatic chant above the squall.

T. J.'s eyes are stricken wide with astonishment. Without remiss, he flies toward the lopping doors, his burnished gaze locked on the figure racing to him through the courtyard.

Aldobrandi dashes after him.

Grayson stands braced and watching.

"Shut the doors!" Vin shrieks, spent and panting, as T. J. catches him. "Shut the doors!"

Harrowed by his raving, T. J. pulls him into the sanctuary, kicking the door in a vain attempt to shut it.

As it bounces back from its frame, Aldobrandi rushes upon the entry. His face blanches as he bears the brunt of the wild winds, struggling to close the doors against a trailing tempest of pitch and raven.

The terrible and churning phantasm breaks free of the murder and lunges.

A concussion of hellish malevolence, like tendrils from his darkest nightmares, explodes within inches of Aldobrandi as the phantom crashes against a sacred barrier. Despite his noble bravery, he recoils with a roar of fright.

Bolstered against the hideous strength of the aphotic phantom, the doors are slammed shut and braced against it. Panting, Aldobrandi nods his thanks to Grayson, who mirrors him in laying his weight against the door.

Grayson returns the token, and the two strain adrenaline-piqued senses for reprisal. It is upon the relief of silence and safety that they relent and relax.

Hanging onto T. J.'s strong shoulder, Vin's harried mind spins in dreadful fascination with the strange sanctuary's motif as he is ushered to the tray of food. Although overcome with exhaustion, he is powerless to tear his gaze from the exalted saints, as each bears a conventional resemblance to the grotesque effigies in the cathedral chapel that have so marred his psyche and those of the friends he hopes to rescue.

T. J.'s strong arms relieve Vin of his backpack and steady him into the chair. "Easy, easy."

"How…" Vin huffs, his doe-like eyes searching T. J.'s face through a grimace glazed in sweat. "How are you here?"

"That doesn't matter right now," Grayson deflects, crossing his arms.

"Where's everyone else?" T. J. presses anxiously. "Are they still at the castle?"

"He needs rest and food," Aldobrandi insists, pouring a glass of water as Vin shakes his head emphatically.

"We left to get help—me, Billy, and Parson. I don't know where they are!"

"Help?" T. J. exclaims. "What happened?"

"We each took a road…" he gasps before succumbing to a disconcerting stillness.

Aldobrandi sets the glass before Vin, whose eyes fill with a sudden haunting, and calls to the nun, "Vino! Avete del vino?"

Vin's eyes well quickly upon recollection, the freedom from the castle's spell driving home the horror of the fantastic events. He falters, his overloaded mind exploiting the safety of friends and shelter to process the avalanche of traumas. He swoons.

"He's going into shock," Grayson exclaims, rushing T. J. to interject himself. "Get a blanket!"

"Vino! Vino!" Aldobrandi roars as Grayson pats Vin's face firmly.

The robed hoods shuffle into the recesses as the perplexing nun continues to intercede feverishly, fixed in her seat with mysterious countenance locked on the bizarre figure.

"Come on, come on!" T. J. prods fretfully, bounding to one of the occult monks to snatch the blanket.

"What's your name?" Grayson barks as T. J. wraps the wool blanket around Vin. "What's your name?"

"Kulvinder...Kulvinder Singh," Vin murmurs, lolling against T.J.

"What's your address?"

Aldobrandi extracts the cork and pours the ruby vintage with a swift and trained hand as Grayson coaxes Vin's brain from its insulating cocoon.

"Do you know where you are?"

Comprehension transforms Vin's face as clarity returns to his eyes. "Yes...and no."

Grayson gestures to Aldobrandi for the goblet.

"We are in the house of the Order of Intercessors," Aldobrandi begins carefully.

Vin brings the wine to his lips, nodding slowly as he drinks.

"Remember I told you about this when we met at Viareggio, yes?"

Vin's gaze, bewitched by trauma, meets Aldobrandi's. "You were right," he levels in a low, chilling voice. "About Poe...the castle..."

The noble Italian pales, exchanging a grim glance with T. J. as the verity of the legends takes root.

"What happened?" Grayson presses.

"But there's…more…more than anyone knows—"

"Give him a break," T. J. interjects gently, afraid his friend might slip into another stupor. "He needs to eat something."

"Yes," Aldobrandi insists, "he must eat."

The agent acquiesces in silence, a silence that permeates the dark, uncanny sanctuary.

The muttered prayers of the old crimson nun have ceased, drawing the attention of the three men, who turn to find her sitting with her back to them. The two monks sit in the chairs opposite each other at the end of the table, their hooded heads bowed.

An incidental serenity wraps Vin in a solace that ushers his overwrought mind from its retreat, and he breaks the bread on the tray before him.

Grayson and Aldobrandi move to flank the crone, leaving T. J. to take the chair across from Vin.

"Be still," she bids in a meditative tenor, her eyes closed. "Still!" she commands, with prescient anticipation of Grayson's interjection. The decree is issued in an accent thick on broken English, yet it rings clear and arresting, checking the robust will of the agent.

A curious awareness dawns in the corner of Vin's consciousness as he rebuffs his exhaustion with water, fruit, and bread. A subtle sensation of otherliness, like the unnerving feeling of being watched, draws on the fulcrum of his coherence. This curious cognition is not of an external entity but an awareness that his thoughts are being observed from a strange other within his own mind. On a compulsory drive, his intellect gravitates to the conundrum.

"Are you prepared?"

"Yes," Vin answers aloud, breaking the long silence and startling his companions.

Before they can question, the crimson nun beckons. "It is time! Take your seats."

A distant thunder rumbles as Vin rises to follow T. J., Grayson, and Aldobrandi to the sequestered table at which the intercessors now wait before the surreal figure on the chancel dais. The four men take the four vacancies, two sitting across from two beside the affected monks with the equally idiosyncratic nun at the foot of the table facing the abstract effigy.

The crone, her crinkled and age-weathered face imbued with an arcane aura, surveys the men one by one before resting her sharp gaze on the worn wooden case patinated with centuries of waiting. "The relic," she bids.

Aldobrandi looks down at the carved box. With eager hands tempered by foreboding, he passes the case to Grayson.

The box is lighter than the agent had expected, and he follows the nun's unspoken lead and sets the small chest before her.

"Father in heaven, you have made us your children and called us to walk in the light of Christ," the crone begins, her prayer rising and falling on fervent intonations that resonate through the shadowy nave like souls long rent from their corporeal form. "Deliver us from darkness and keep us in the light of your truth."

The abrupt invocation prompts the four men into uncertain humility intended to mirror that of the two mysterious recluses bookending the table. "Called in that light, we ask for your guidance." Yet the nun's bearing does not stray from the inclination toward the white and black armed figure before her, as if she were not praying to god but to the icon. "Shape our path in your truth, your love in our hearts."

Beyond the sacred incantation, a candlelit dusk from the starlike tongues of flame clustered on the seven shrines sets the nave in an eerie glow and closes a Delphian sphere around them. "Through the holy Eucharist, give us the strength of your grace that we might walk in the light of Christ and serve him faithfully."

The four men are pulled from the postulant cast by a match being struck. It is only as the crimson nun extends the flame to the candle situated as a centerpiece that T. J. notices it is the only white candle among the surrounding black.

"Infiammare," she entreats, gesturing to the black candles.

Despite the two monks merging black-candled wicks in the flame of the white, nothing is revealed beneath those inky hoods by the amber light.

Anticipation swells under the glow of the seven black candles as the freckled hands of the crone move over the casing of the ancient wooden box.

So drawn to the climax is Aldobrandi, his imagination suddenly aflutter with a lifetime of family stories and suppositions, that he inadvertently crowds Grayson.

"Easy there."

None of the company, however, is immune to the fascination.

Without ceremony, the venerable hands lift the framing lid.

Aldobrandi is unable to contain his gasp.

T. J. and Grayson stare, stunned by the implications.

Vin, ashen faced, casts a stricken expression on the elderly abbess.

Secured within the bed of the case rests a visage made so nearly to resemble the countenance of a stiffened corpse that the closest scrutiny must have difficulty detecting the cheat. The broad brow, with all the features of the face, is bespeckled with the scarlet horror of Poe's avatar: blood.

Even the staunchest devotee to the mission of the intercessors is moved by the appalling mask staring eyelessly up from the cradling box, touching the mind of the crimson nun reactively.

With the emancipation of the harbinger of mortality, a sublime resonance, like the ether of the netherworld, seeps into the sphere uniting them.

A collective chill exploits the gap wherein the company is rendered dumbfounded.

The countenance textured with the lines of time and framed in the crimson wimple resigns to an aspect so devoid of emotion that the nun quite closely resembles that mask of the red death.

Riddled with terrible awe by the uncanny transformation, Vin and his allies follow the course of her hazel eyes, peeled to their margins, past the obeisant monks to the amber-hued chancel.

So startled are the men by what they meet upon the dais that both Vin and T. J. leap from their seats.

Aldobrandi is stayed only by the agent's firm hand on his forearm as Grayson issues an astonished expletive.

Brazen irises, like cold sapphires, stare in like manner into those of the crimson-habited nun. The eyes are wild and unblinking, fixed yet imbued with a distance that defies the company and in their white pools contrast the green patina.

Unable to pull away from the mind-bending revelation, Vin and T. J. sink into their seats.

That verdigris face lengthens as the mouth languishes with the lolling back of the extraordinary persona's head. The bejeweled alabaster hand rises from the heart position, as does the mottled ebony serpent from the trunk of vivid red robe to alight gingerly on the golden armrests of the chair.

"We listen, spirit."

The nun's exclamation is so abrupt that it, too, startles the men so completely that T. J. nearly knocks over the black candle burning at his hands.

"Give your guidance to those treading in the shadow of death!"

The bizarre medium's head twists on its neck.

The lips constrict in articulation.

The white hand rises.

With ascension of that immaculate palm, the clanging of dispirited chains echoes throughout the encompassing shadows, sending Vin's mind swimming in the nightmarish recollection of the ghastly chapel cathedral.

His friends pique at Vin's swooning, and T. J. grabs his hand to squeeze it in solidarity.

The altruistic warmth and reassurance of his comrade's gesture speed through Vin's veins to ground his senses and call his harrowed psyche back to the esoteric sphere that would challenge even the most rational of intellects.

"La bestia è stato sciolto in casa della paura!" the medium wails in a voice as unearthly as the rattling chains.

"The beast has been loosed in the house of fear!" the crone interprets, her unnerving countenance unchanged.

Grayson looks for understanding in Vin's tormented features as the surreal medium bellows again.

"I sette morti sono preparate e l'agnello immolato ora condannato a eseguire gli ordini della paura!"

"The seven deaths are prepared, and the slain lamb now damned to do fear's bidding."

Vin shakes his head in dreadful answer to the agent's questioning gaze.

"The dagger!" Aldobrandi erupts, his fiery eyes set insistently on the fantastical mystic. "Where is the dagger?"

The ornamented persona is unresponsive and by all appearances deaf to his earnest entreat.

Having his expectation of the relic disappointed, Aldobrandi bristles at losing the opportunity to discover the weapon of lore and turns with hot frustration on the crimson intercessor.

The consternation in his face is washed away as the nun relays the question to the exalted channeler.

"La casa di Dio è caduto!" the spirit laments sonorously with an equally booming howl.

"The house of God has fallen," the catatonic nun whimpers as the echoes recede.

A deep, resonant, and soul-shaking moan creeps from the throat of the medium. As the company gawks dreadfully, the muscles in the channeler's painted neck constrict and choke the morose cry.

Fear for the medium descends on the watchers, but their impulse to rush to the mystic's aide is swiftly replaced by revulsion.

That pained neck twists and travails as putrid bile rises from the yawning mouth. In a chilling display of spectral wonder, the viscous and undulating corporeity spreads into the air above on the disgorging column.

The men recoil as the looming gelatinous mass convex and churns, taking shape and commanding their reluctant fascination.

An impression, embellished by prolific and writhing tendrils and dark and deepening folds, coalesces to form an image in vile sepia.

Vin gasps as if bluntly winded.

The abhorrent rendering of a chapel nave registers on his stricken mind as the cast of the great archangel strangled in the coils of the serpent flashes through his memory. As if pierced by Gabriel's very sword, Vin's heart constricts on the terrible confession that he had seen the dagger in the grip of the statue and had failed to recognize it despite the admonition of the Aldobrandi in Viareggio.

A teeth-jarring scream shatters the ectoplasmic rendering!

The crimson crone is a caricature of horror, gripping the company in dismay as her gaping throat exorcizes the intrusive possession.

The white hand falls, toppling off the golden armrest to limply hang as the serpentine limb strikes out into the air.

The medium lurches then slumps.

"Rovina! Rovina! Otto! Otto! Otto! Rovina!"

"Ruin! Ruin! Eight! Eight! Eight! Ruin!" the stricken nun shrieks.

"Romero!" Vin blurts.

A base chill, like the frigid waters of the drowning sea, descends on the company, subduing their fervor and suffocating the candles. The ensuing darkness, fended only by the chancel beam, is consumed by the inescapable presence. The surrounding shadows quiver under its lurking.

"I see beyond your mask, Beautiful One, and I fear you not."

The dulcet voice, steeped with age and wisdom, drifts from the lips of the diminutive medium. But as the company looks to her, the elaborately decorated persona wilts, and she is taken by the cold hand of that unfathomable presence.

CHAPTER 10

The Eight

THE EMBATTLED GUNMETAL SKY, MARRED by ethereal wind-driven clashes and arches of blinding artillery, galls idyllic Tuscany and abets the dark oppression whispering doom to Vin's pummeled psyche. He cringes under the carp of acrimonious thunder and pleading gusts as T. J. and Aldobrandi escort him from the doors of the Order.

Grayson breaks their path through the contentious atmosphere to the perceived liberation of the Range Rover, ghostly white beneath the tempestuous dome. His steel-blue eyes mark the jet raven perched on the gate, untroubled by the storm and scrutinizing the company as if charged with their policing. His fist tightens around the keys.

Vin is ushered gently into the back seat by his friends. Vin's bleary eyes press the bullied environs as the coldness of its tenacity seeps into his veins. The certain threat of that aphotic demon looms in the ambiguity beyond the window as T. J. takes his seat beside him. As the gates open, the raven takes wing, and the window transforms into a reel of landscape and trees blurred by velocity and exhaustion.

The men ride in silence. The impending dusk deepens the somber gray of the expiring afternoon like a snare falling around Vin's tortured imagination.

Aldobrandi turns, observing Vin's grasping of T. J.'s hand with a face blighted by desperation. His eyes attest to the abyss upon which his mind teeters. The noble Italian reaches out and his hand is met quickly by Vin's. The men exchange reassuring nods as Vin drinks in their fraternal strength like a rescued castaway.

"The radio?" Aldobrandi proffers, trusting to the aid of music.

Reluctantly, Vin releases his grasp. A cascade of euphonic piano pours moodily through the surround sound chased by Rihanna's haunting refrain. Pressed within the background of the pensive melody, the brazen lungs of a clock strike with a sound which is deep and peculiar but so intertwined with the rhythm of the ballad that it chimes ineffectual. The recognition of the song resurrects the arrival of Fichtenberg's invitation, and Vin succumbs to the torment of hindsight.

Grayson's stern eyes peer at him through the rearview mirror.

"You okay?" T. J. asks carefully, concerned with the shadow passing over Vin's features.

He nods.

"How are you holding up?" the agent checks from behind the wheel as the headlights begin to cast sharper shadows on the road ahead.

"I'm okay," Vin eschews, the momentum of a pronounced curve pushing him against the door.

"Any of that business back there make sense to you?"

"I don't think we need to go into that right now," T. J. interjects sharply.

"I didn't ask you."

"You didn't need to," T. J. retorts. "You aren't in charge."

"We should not be arguing," Aldobrandi interjects.

"It's okay," Vin insists, hoping to pacify the company.

"You can keep telling yourself that, but you'd be up shit creek without me!" Grayson rails, taking the ensuing curve as if testing the agility of the Range Rover.

The needle of the European speedometer flirts with the fifty marker.

Aldobrandi, however, needs no gauge. "Rallentare! Slow down!"

"You haven't done a damn thing!" T. J. digs. "And we could've rented a car!"

"Agent Grayson!" Aldobrandi barks, alarmed by the dangerous glare in his eyes. "Slow down!"

The use of his title triggers Grayson's discipline, and his foot eases off the accelerator.

The SUV responds immediately, but the deceleration cannot compete with the advancing hairpin turn. The tires squeal and the men are pressed by centrifugal force as the agent applies all of his training. Harrowing dismay riddles the company, their eyes screaming as the SUV fishtails into a straightaway, where a hapless figure tumbles from the shoulder bank.

Grayson slams on the brakes!

The silhouette is consumed by the rushing headlights.

The radials screech with abandon as the agent throws the SUV into second gear and yanks on the steering wheel in a heart-stopping attempt to avoid the drifter.

The Range Rover roars in protest before coming to an abrupt halt, appropriately directed in the opposite lane.

"Fuck!" Grayson bellows, hoping the bootlegger's maneuver spared the wretched pedestrian from a deadly strike.

"Holy shit!" T. J. exclaims, exploding out of the SUV and rushing the staggering wraith.

As Vin and the others pour out of the Range Rover behind him, T. J. grabs the man by the shoulders. "Parson!"

Bloody and beaten, Parson gazes at his friend with a blank and glassy stare. "I could use a cocktail." He crumples into T. J.'s arms.

"On the ground!" Grayson shouts, scrambling back to the SUV.

With Vin and Aldobrandi huddled to help, T. J. lowers their injured friend onto the pavement.

The agent sweeps Aldobrandi out of the way, kneeling over Parson with a flashlight and first-aid kit. "Flares!" he orders Aldobrandi brusquely.

"Cosa?"

"Flares, goddamnit! For the road, traffic!"

Cursing himself, Aldobrandi flies to the SUV.

"How is he? Can you tell?" T. J. presses as the agent sweeps the glare of the flashlight over Parson's languishing eyes.

"Shock, concussion," Grayson answers urgently as he begins to slowly survey and probe Parson's body for internal injuries. "I can't tell how bad yet.

"Vin, blanket!"

Shame burns T. J.'s neck and face as he watches the agent tend to the friend who, despite their differences, has grown dear to him over their years in Ravenword. "I'm sorry about what I said."

"What?" Grayson retorts.

"In the car."

Grayson reproaches T. J. with a glance without pausing in his ministrations. "I think he'll be okay. No signs of internal bleeding or broken bones," Grayson announces. "Help me get him into the car. Don't let him fall asleep.

"Come on, buddy," he coaxes, lifting Parson to his feet.

As they walk him to the SUV, Vin wraps Parson in the wool blanket stowed in the well-equipped cargo bay. As he does, a sudden prickling revisits his trauma.

"Diometi!" Grayson calls. "We're going!"

Vin's pulse answers the voiceless herald with thunder, turning to find Aldobrandi in the dark distance.

His heart leaps into his throat!

Behind the noble Italian, that stygian malevolence swells from the tree line.

A fierce defiance explodes in Vin.

As the aphotic phantom rises to strike, Vin hurls himself into the SUV.

"Hey! Cosa stai facendo?" Aldobrandi exclaims, shielding his eyes from the blinding high beams.

The phantom recedes under the glare but does not relent.

Vin charges the seething ghoul, snatching the noble Italian. "Get in the car! Get in the car!"

The primal siren in Vin's command sends the men piling quickly into the SUV.

Beyond the headlights, the aphotic phantasm billows spitefully despite the glare. While the company gawks in terrible astonishment, Grayson punches the car into action. The Rover spins on screaming tires and darts into the long shadows of twilight.

"What the fuck was that?" T. J. roars.

"You don't want to find out!" Vin pants.

Parson swoons between them as Grayson pilots the SUV like an ace over the twisting mountain road. A glance in the rearview mirror stokes his verve.

The roiling abyss trails them like a malicious avalanche, betraying glimpses of hellfire in its anima.

The relentless drilling of Grayson's Interpol indoctrination relieves his intellect from the impossible task of identifying the menace, enabling him to use all his faculties in outpacing the threat.

The Range Rover shrieks on the asphalt slalom.

Aldobrandi prays wildly in the passenger's seat as they are pushed and shoved by gravity.

T. J. pats Parson's arm manically, stuck on a loop of "Hey, hey," as his hammered mind battles the unearthly fear force-fed into his brain.

"I got it!" Parson spurns wearily, brushing T. J.'s pelting hand off his arm. "Stay awake. Monster. Certain death."

Vin can't help but surrender a hysterical chuckle. Turnning in his seat, the seething nemesis of his flight fills the rear window like a pyroclastic surge.

Acceleration presses them into their seats as Grayson anticipates the road opening ahead.

To their dismay, the phantom does not lag.

Grayson pushes the agility of the SUV as it careens around the bend.

Masonry rushes the headlights!

A shrill stab of fear swamps the men!

Gravel roars under the braking tires!

Grayson rolls the wheel to no avail!

The Rover is a chorus of howls as it crabs into the colossal stone wall, crushing the front quarter panel with a terrible crash! Momentum throws the SUV up and over, shattering the windows as it rolls onto its top and slides to a roaring stop!

Stunned and dangling, and desperately aware of the predator, the men scramble to free themselves from the seatbelts.

Blanched faces meet them in the ruined darkness.

Billy and Julia are already upon them as the men clamber out of the wreckage.

Vin's brain spins at the sight of them, and Julia launches into his arms.

T. J. stares with grim wonder at the castle scowling down at them from against a crepuscular sky.

"Oh hell-shit-fuck-damn," Parson groans.

Grayson nods his recognition to Billy as the hairs on the back of Billy's neck prickle.

"Inside!" he shouts as nebulous shapes in the benighted woods register quickly on his brain. "Get inside!"

Abandoning the SUV, the company stampedes through the protesting gate and into the comfortless great hall of the castle annex.

Billy heaves the heavy nineteenth-century doors shut as quickly as he can manage. The glower of the oppressive doors to the ancient castle amplifies their despair as Ravenword and allies succumb to the emotional and physical repercussions of the horrible day in the blazing cast of the grand stone fireplace.

"Triage, anyone?" Parson quips. The offer, as if proffering cocktails, pulls the group from the absorption of the frenzied moment. "Billy, would you be a good boy and get us the first-aid kit?"

"For all the good it'll do," Billy replies, shaken by Parson's bruised and bloody visage as he heads toward the dining hall. "There's not a lot left."

"I've got a fresh kit in the car," Grayson declares, shifting his weight to stand.

"You can't go out there!" Vin blurts.

"Can you get us out of here?" Julia squeaks at his side.

Pausing on the question, Billy turns with the resurrection of Vin's knuckles splitting his mouth stinging his memory. "I guess that was the plan," he sighs dubiously, nodding to the Italian. "Maybe that guy can help."

"I am Aldobrandi," he chimes in with an uncertain smile.

"We know him from the beach!" Julia says, her countenance brightening on the recollection.

"Triage," Parson sings, sending Billy into the little hallway and the dining room beyond.

"I can get us *all* out of here," the agent affirms brusquely with odd emphasis. "But not without getting to the car. There's more in there than the first-aid kit."

"Where's Agnot and Charlie?" T. J. asks, unsettled by their absence.

The circle of friends exchange crestfallen glances, the gravity of which Grayson reads with ease.

"Charlie's sleeping," Julia mewls.

"No," a voice calls softly from the dark landing at the height of the stairs. "I'm here."

The unexpected interjection startles the company, and they shift in concert to find Charlie descending the flight like a fair apparition. The Hello Kitty nightgown helps to offset her wan and pale aspect but cannot dispel the aura of tragedy enshrouding her.

"Where's Agnot?" T. J. presses dreadfully, rounding on his friends.

"Come on," Grayson intervenes brusquely, swatting T. J. on the shoulder while casting an astute gaze over his dejected companions. "We can sort everything out once we've gotten what we need from the car."

In an uncharacteristic demur, T. J. hesitates with a sharp protest. "Why me?"

"Because," Grayson retorts gruffly, "I know you, and you're the least...injured."

T. J. stands with a defiant bearing, glancing from Aldobrandi to Charlie.

"I need someone I know and trust to watch my back," Grayson explains, tempering his tenor in an effort to engender cooperation.

Charlie hurries past the threshold of those awful castle doors to kneel in the firelight beside Parson.

"They can sort things out while we get what we need."

Vin stands as T. J. relents with a somber nod.

"We must also find the dagger!" Aldobrandi insists, his fervent green eyes alighting on Vin.

"No," Grayson barks.

"We don't have time to waste," Vin argues. "You don't know what a night in this place is like! If we have to stay until morning, we're going to need everything necessary to get us through."

Impressed with the young man's fortitude, Grayson nods but does not yield as he meets Vin's gaze with unspoken authority. "That can wait. The fewer of us out there, the better. You have business to deal with here."

Vin looks to Julia, who nods sadly.

II

The plot of orange firelight stamped onto the cold stone landing shrinks against the intruding shadows of T. J. and Grayson and then further into a sliver that surrenders to the black as the heavy door shuts behind them. The air is brisk and murmuring. The men survey the fallow environs of the benighted courtyard, ignorant of golems and ghosts and monsters and the undefined yet palpable enmity of that aphotic phantom filling the night with a hateful want.

Grayson nods to T. J. and steps down to the coarse sod, his senses honed.

Every shadow is a threat and the slightest movement a banshee.

T. J. follows, panning the black expanse as fear picks at his heartstrings. "Flashlight?" he nudges, only to be dismissed by a curt wave.

The enormous wrought-iron gate clangs lazily, as if intent on lulling the two into a sense of ease, and opens without protest.

The dauntless agent pauses in the gap, peering into the open abyss as T. J. closes beside him.

The SUV lies exposed, its roof so crushed that even Grayson wonders how they managed to escape unscathed.

He closes the gate and steps back into the courtyard to assess the derelict wall. "Can you climb?" Grayson inquires in a low voice, setting the industrial-weight flashlight in the sparse tufts.

"Climb?" T. J. echoes, the prospect of such complete vulnerability hollowing his core. "The wall?"

"I want a high lookout."

"And I want to get out of this without being the token brother who gets it in the second act!" T. J. scoffs, shifting his weight.

Grayson catches his arm firmly, leading T. J. into the deep shadows of the sagging rampart.

"Really?" T. J. balks as Grayson crouches.

"Your foot, my knee."

Succumbing to the agent's mettle, T. J. hesitates, exposure compelling him to peer into the shrouded lengths of the slumping fortification. The ambiguous expanse does nothing to reassure him and, with a sigh, he mounts the agent's back.

"Left knee, left shoulder," Grayson grunts beneath T. J.'s weight.

The young athlete climbs, albeit awkwardly, impressed with Grayson's brawn.

"Right foot, right shoulder, then push—"

"I got it," T. J. chides, the agent's whispers tolling like clarions to his ratcheted brain. Using the wall to steady himself, he plants his left foot on Grayson's broad shoulder.

"Ready?"

"Yeah."

Grayson struggles to stifle his roar as he straightens to a precarious stand.

T. J. grapples for the lip of the wall. Gaining both height and a hold, he pulls himself off the rugged man's stalwart frame and onto the narrow shelf.

Grayson stretches with a grimace before picking up the flashlight and makes his way silently to the iron bars.

Heady with the nebulous elevation, T. J. shimmies cautiously to the towering plinth.

The agent watches the young athlete secure his footing and then tosses him the light.

With the beam searching the darkness, Grayson slips past the iron bars to the SUV. A crystalline pattern textures the safety glass of the cargo hatch and, risking the attention of whatever forces are set against them, he shatters the window with his boot. The crash penetrates the enveloping night, and he clears the tenacious shards quickly under the prospect of a swift and menacing reply. Groping urgently, he recovers the blanket and first-aid and emergency kits quickly.

A visceral perception, as if every nerve were suddenly extrasensory, pulls his attention to the abyss at his back. He stifles the hounding apprehension but is unable to keep himself from panning the darkness as he sprints to the black bars.

Depositing the supplies behind the gate, Grayson returns his intentions to the ruined Range Rover and the one indispensable tool left therein. The collapsed roof is most severe at the windshield, and the agent is reluctant to attempt retrieval by that avenue with a threat upon him, even though it seems the most expedient. With his faculties scouring the ambiguous surroundings and the blanket in hand, he latches the gate behind him and creeps swiftly to the SUV.

T. J. is casting the reach of the flashlight into the ravine, where he pauses on the carcass of the old van. A surge of ice opens his pores.

Sharp and glowing eyes flash in the margins of the beam. "Wolves!"

Stung by the alarm, Grayson pulls his legs into the cargo bay. His fingers grapple blindly for the center seat release.

The backrest gives as a storm of padded footfalls rake the gravel. Cursing the snare, he pushes his robust frame through the narrow gap.

Snarling fangs descend on his feet. Jaws trained on blood snap with ravenous ferocity as the frenzied beasts inundate the crushed Rover.

With adrenaline-honed agility, Grayson bludgeons those perilous snouts with the thick of his heels.

The pack, however, does not relent and quickly encircles the SUV.

Grayson slides over the biting shards, kicking wildly to keep the savage maws at bay.

Mad, gnashing jaws burst through the fractured windows. Teeth and breath and throats rage on all sides.

The collapsed roof thwarts the broad build of the rapacious beasts, the shoulders of one flank crushing those of the other as their attack rocks the wreckage.

Grayson reaches through a blitz of lunging muzzles for the glove compartment as the backrest falls back into place, locking out the dogging fangs.

A monstrous head bursts through the windshield! The insatiable wolf thrashes barbarically for the agent's unyielding reach.

Grayson roars as jagged teeth tear into his forearm. The searing pain stokes his determination, and he musters his great strength against the mauling to pull open the center compartment.

• • •

Boom! Boom! Boom! Boom!

The cannon fire jars Ravenword and Aldobrandi to their feet with the violence of twisting hearts and bludgeoned senses. On limbs slick with sudden and chilling sweat, they bound in a tumult of shrieks for the door.

Billy throws them open like Hercules bursting through the gates of Hades.

Aldobrandi and Vin rush onto the landing with brazen eyes and bodies primed to charge.

Julia, however, can go no farther and cowers against the frame. Her sopping eyes find little relief in the retreat of the last of the wolves beyond the baleful bars of wrought iron.

Parson, meanwhile, finds the excitement of gunplay little motivation to upset his well-earned reprieve and maintains his convalescent recline in front of the crackling fire with Charlie tending to his wounds.

"It's okay!" T. J. insists invisibly from atop the column. "Take the supplies inside," he urges his stricken friends.

Seizing the opportunity, Vin and Aldobrandi nod a covert confirmation to Billy.

Billy endorses their venture by shooing them into the shadows.

Braced against the curse, the men slip into the nocturnal veil.

"Julia, come on!" Billy prods with his hand outstretched.

With a bolstering inhalation, she dashes toward the repulsive gate.

Stunned by the hammering discharges, Grayson crawls over a bloody wolf and out of the wreckage. He swaggers to the back of the ruined Rover and drops to his knees.

T. J. shimmies down the wall and rushes to him.

"No, no," he shouts over ringing ears. "No time!"

With the athlete as sentinel, the agent crawls back into the cargo compartment and breaks open the floor panel.

III

Within the encompassing bailey, Vin and Aldobrandi peer into the expanse of shadowy desolation from the corner of the apartment annex. Night remains a monotonous hostage to the pernicious will of the moonless dome, and rubble from the devastated cathedral rises in the gloaming as pitch and nebulous mounds. Beyond, the bent and waving tree in the black crook of the rampart is pressed against the crepuscular sky as if warding them back.

Vin lifts his flashlight enticingly.

Aldobrandi shakes his head, the voices of Grayson and T. J. perforating the darkness behind them.

Vin nods and, with a thrill of trepidation, creeps into the openness of the bailey with the noble Italian at his side. Both catch and guide the other as they strain to decipher and dodge the aphotic brail of the tuft and pitted field.

Running ahead, past the debris-littered steps that adorn the once grand facade and bell towers of the chapel cathedral, Vin turns and finds the noble Italian eerily captivated.

Gripped in a preternatural fear, Aldobrandi stares back into the void between the annex and the cloister wall. The primal impression of some malignant presence lurking within that abysmal cavity consumes his imagination.

A branch of lightning rips away the darkness, as if in sudden answer to an unspoken prayer, breaking the spell and vanquishing the fearsome imagination siphoning his courage.

Revived, Aldobrandi darts across the bailey beneath the ensuing thunder.

With the noble Italian at his side, Vin navigates the littered steps. Climbing onto the portico, he peers into the black sea of swamped ruins. Lightning once again comes to their aid as Vin uses his outstretched hand to plot the resting place of the archangel against the few wall remnants rising into the night. A glint in the strobe vanishes just as his gaze falls upon it.

He nods to Aldobrandi and, upon resolute breath, they forge into the devastation with flashlights bursting to life. As Vin sweeps the mounds, the beam illuminates the warped spine of the wrought-iron fence pushing through the crushing debris. The unyielding wind whips dust into tall swirls that play on his mind like the corpse of that disembodied voice.

"This is very dangerous to climb," Aldobrandi whispers fretfully.

Undaunted, Vin treads carefully onto the heap of devastated masonry and begins to navigate toward the obliterated transept. The cast of his flashlight sets such a glaring contrast on his precarious path that it robs him of depth and soundness—an unnerving affliction shared by Aldobrandi, who tests his footing carefully as they progress.

With each step the grating protests of disturbed offal serve as spiteful warnings. Against the towering backdrop of the stark and bitter castellated abbey, more repugnant and hateful than the fancies read within the pages of gothic romances, the two men scale the piles and troughs to penetrate the decimated nave.

A wave of accomplishment washes over Vin as his flashlight falls on a swath of transept floor. Scrambling down the pile of rubble, he stands very nearly on the spot where he had once scrutinized the bizarre representations of the seven saints. From that vantage, as Aldobrandi descends on uncertain strides behind him, Vin can discern where those effigies were consumed in the atrocious demolition.

"Here!" Aldobrandi calls in a strained whisper.

Vin turns to find the Italian deep in the heart of the ruin. His beam is illuminating a large, contoured bulb protruding from the chancel remains. The alabaster marble, however, proclaims its true nature. "Angelo!"

As Vin steps across the darkness, Aldobrandi's beautiful face blanches, and the hairs on the back of his neck bristle ominously.

A whisper, low and tenuous, leaches from beneath the rubble.

Fear, palpable and penetrating, blossoms in the aphotic atmosphere.

Seized, Vin turns with his heart in his throat.

The ghastly hiss subsides.

Stock-still and silent, Vin and Aldobrandi strain to listen past the pounding in their chests.

Again, that hideous voice filters through the debris.

Vin and Aldobrandi face each other, pale and glazed, with one mind.

An unnerving grating and knocking, as if someone or something were struggling to worm through the weight of tumbled masonry, sets them to task.

With desperation of mortal consequences, Vin plants his flashlight and joins Aldobrandi in heaving away the fractured blocks from around the head.

Shaken to his very core, Aldobrandi taxes his powerful physique to pull, roll, and hurl debris clusters from the statue.

With bare and frantic hands, Vin sweeps and probes the granite rendering.

"The face is down!"

"Shoulder!" Aldobrandi announces, his frenzied digging drowning out the ghastly creeping.

"Kulvinder..."

Vin's name slinks in a hiss so venomous and arresting that it defies the crushing debris to paralyze him with terror.

Aldobrandi throws a clump of masonry aside and grabs his friend's arm.

Vin nods, only to have the consolation robbed.

"It is broken!" Aldobrandi gasps. "The arm is not here!"

Vin paces in manic frustration, the devastation swimming around him under the wash of his panicked light.

Rubble grates and knocks.

"You saw it!" Aldobrandi insists, grabbing him by the shoulders. "You must think! Think!"

Vin nods through his stupor, his lolling eyes falling below the protrusion.

Bricks and rubble tumble as black tendrils rise from the crevices of the mound, heralding the abominable ascension of the ghoul.

Vin falls to his hands and knees, shoveling with bare and frantic hands as the unrelenting displacement creeps ever closer.

"I found it!"

As the men claw desperately to free the alabaster fist, the curling black tethers rise over them.

Again, that hideous voice wheezes Vin's name.

The address falls on the valiant Indian's ear and tunnels to the very heart of him on a course poisoned with terrible recognition.

Aldobrandi shudders as Vin turns.

The coalescence of those stygian ribbons fills Vin's eyes as if floodgates to horror.

A visage of Agnot, grotesque with trappings of cursed death, floats above the sea of devastation with ethereal black ribbons and globs of coagulation drifting in the horrible atmosphere of the ghoul. Her once lovely eyes are now black, and her mouth, stained with gore, twists to choke out his name.

"No!" Vin wails, snared in the terrible enchantment.

The men writhe in mad panic, blind to everything but the looming monstrosity.

Malevolence spreads over them like the rays of a nightmarish sunrise.

Their own screams fill the men's ears as the necromonster closes on them.

A sudden rattling of chains, somehow melodious in the face of such horror, rises above their hysteria.

From a part in the resentful black clouds falls the purest moonbeam to defend them from the ghoul.

Set shimmering within the silvery grace, the priest who rose from chains at the mouth of the pit impedes the phantom and dilutes its spell.

The foul wraith recoils, spewing its protestation in a vile and abhorrent scream.

"Fretta! Fretta!" the guardian calls, impelling Aldobrandi in rustic Italian.

The noble Italian shakes Vin vigorously.

The golden dagger glows in the ethereal light from the disembodied fist of the angel.

Together they pull the treasure free.

The ghoulish specter wails angrily and charges.

"Singh! Diometi!"

Vin and Aldobrandi force their gaze to the hail and find Grayson standing on a high mound, his cool blue eyes captivated by the impossible apparition.

"Andate, figli miei! Sii veloce!" the spectral priest exhorts, prodding them to flee.

With the dagger in hand, Vin and Aldo scramble furiously up and across the rolling rubble.

Behind them the rebuke of the ghost upon the ghoul fills the malignant night air. "L'eterno riposo dona loro, o Cristo, nostro Signore, e la luce perpetua risplendere…"

Without a backward glance, the men fly past the agent like stallions whipped by lightning on strides graced by that benevolent ghost. Grayson, hesitating in cagey wonder, turns and flees with an intellect bursting with new reconciliations.

IV

Vin and Aldobrandi explode into the hall only to be arrested by those enormous and oppressive ill-grained doors and the vacancy in the golden cast of firelight. Voices tumbling through the narrow passage lead them into the dining hall, where the tall broken window has been mended with makeshift boarding, to find their friends sitting about the adjoining kitchen like so many cats.

"Did you get it?" Billy exclaims, rushing upon their entry.

Aldo presents the dagger, clenched in the marble fist, and sets it on the table, beaming with accomplishment as Vin rushes to catch Julia up in his arms.

Amid gasps of surprise, wonder, and excitement, Vin kisses her with an insatiable passion.

Billy, feigning nausea, retrieves a hammer from the boiler room. With a swift strike, he shatters the impeding marble.

Julia leaps out of Vin's embrace, blushing.

"Jesus on a stick, moment killer!" Parson exclaims, having just entered from the narrow passage.

Billy shrugs as Aldo picks the remaining fragments from the dagger.

Ravenword gather as the noble Italian takes the chair next to Charlie and rests the prize between the two first-aid kits.

"Where's that man?" Julia asks, staring down at the dagger. "He went to stop you."

"He was just trying to keep you from getting killed," T. J. interjects from the corner of the counter.

"He was just behind us," Aldobrandi answers over Vin.

"He did a good job of it. How's the professor?"

As if on cue, Agent Grayson enters from the passage and assesses each of them swiftly.

"Apparently, he's used to cars crashing and gunplay in the middle of the night," Parson quips.

"Fichtenberg?" Grayson asks rhetorically, having little doubt that the object of his investigation is holed up and plotting a means of escape.

"Fichtenberg, Romero, who knows?" Parson sighs, his bruised and swollen features unable to mask his weary expression.

The agent spurns Vin and Aldobrandi with a silent rebuke as he moves to the kettle on the stove. The two men are only reprieved when Grayson turns to pull a mug from the shelf above the stovetop.

"Are you sure that's it?" Parson asks darkly as he assesses the blade.

T. J. and Aldobrandi exchange a forlorn glance as Vin replies, "Pretty sure."

"Well, hopefully," Parson declares, leveling his gaze on Grayson as the agent turns to meet the scrutiny, "our stalker can get us on the road before we have to figure out who we're supposed to be plunging that into."

Grayson appraises Parson with a clear and pragmatic countenance. "Speaking of roads, how did you end up in front of my headlights—in that condition?"

Parson demurs, his expression faltering. "I'd rather not go into that right now."

"Come on," T. J. presses. "You said you guys didn't even go in the same directions. You can't leave us hanging."

Parson bristles at T. J.'s metaphor, his eyes alighting on Charlie before turning to Billy.

Billy, sitting on the back counter, nods and scoots over to give his friend center stage.

Parson takes as deep a breath as his tender ribs will allow and gingerly lifts himself onto the counter next to his slovenly friend. "It won't be easy to hear, or believe, but I guess we're past that."

V

Having caught the root in a bloody fist, Parson found his grasp taxed by his own weight fishtailing over the precipice. Dangling in open air, the rugged wall of the ravine yawned beneath him. Pain stabbed at his ribs, catching his stuttered breath as his free hand grappled desperately for a lifesaving notch or nook with which to anchor himself. Yet the runoff, chilled by rock and wind, quickly numbed the fist he clenched around that miraculous and hardy root.

The shrill terror of his mortal end broke over him, undermining his desperation.

His grasp weakened.

Upon the ensuing panic, he clawed at the slick stone draped in the icy runoff.

His fingers loosened, defying his will to live.

"Parson! Take my hand!"

His gasp was nearly his undoing.

Agnot, flush with life and determination, bending over an unseen shelf with her reaching arm lowered to his aid was too much for his fortitude. He must be dead already, his spinning brain insisted.

"Goddamnit, Parson! Take my fucking hand!"

Acquiescing to his fate, Parson obeyed. His hand sailed through the cool air to clasp her wrist.

Agnot's cold fist wrapped around his, and she hoisted.

His expectation of some glorious afterlife, however, was quickly disappointed.

Beside him, the swollen creek snaking along the floor of the ravine rumbled prosaically. His bloody body shook, overcome by very physical cold and pain. Thunder growled in the distance. Yet in all the ordinariness of his impossible survival, Agnot stood before him as if never having stepped foot in that cursed castle.

He must have been dead.

"You're not," Agnot countered.

"I'm not what?" Parson droned as his bewildered brain slowly crashed.

"Dead, dumbass."

Irreconcilable, his brain insisted, so confused that his words stammered before he could even utter them. "But...how?"

"I'm bound to the castle but also to all of you."

"What?" Parson dithered, struggling to grasp the proposition.

"Quit being a fucking retard!" she rebuked angrily. "I need you to remember this! I am bound to the castle by the curse but bound to you guys by...love," she explained, characteristically reluctant to expose her vulnerability even in death. "Now listen up! When bound by the castle, I am a slave to its will. It will use me any way it can to get at you. Just like..."

An insufferable grief overcame her, evoking a lamentation she could never know in life.

Moved to pity, Parson released her. "I'll tell her, Agnot. I'll tell her it wasn't really you!"

As the portion of hell lifted, she leveled an insistence against him. "No. Tell her *why* it was me. But tell her that when any of you are outside the castle's influence, I am right by your side...right by her side. Oh shit," she exclaimed, punching Parson with fear.

"What?"

"Sorry," she amended in a tone that eased his agitation. "I gotta go."

"Wait! Please!"

"I can't," she countered. "Just don't give in to fear!"

Parson groped for words to no avail.

"That way," she pointed as she began to fade. "The road is that way...go left..."

VI

Charlie's sobs fill the kitchen. She clings to Julia, who, like the rest of Ravenword, has been reduced to irrepressible weeping. Even Billy cannot escape the impact of the remarkable history. Parson unbinds his grief, yet finds it tempered by the wonder and hope in Agnot's visitation.

Their allies, however, sit in uncomfortable silence. Aldobrandi's heart is moved, his faith allowing for the miraculous, but even he struggles to process the incredible story. Grayson sits with his hands clasped at his waist in somber observance, reserving his skepticism in the face of Parson's head injury, knowing the catharsis will pave the way to cooperation.

Exorcising his own demons, Vin shudders under heaving tears as Charlie flies to Parson, wrapping him in an embrace, and delivers the consolation of Julia's comforting arms around the overwhelmed Indian.

T. J.'s grief leads him to Motisha. He balls his fist against his lips as if suppressing a prayer of thanks for her refusal to join them. His eyes close under a furrowed brow as the agony of Ravenword insinuates her anguish should his foreboding come to fruition. Yet the implications of that digging insistence prove too terrible for his mind to foster and provoke a defensive resoluteness that charges his limbs and barricades his fortitude.

Grayson's bristly brows rise as T. J. strides purposefully out of the murky hall. His interest, however, translates to consternation as the brash athlete returns with his backpack in one fist and the agent's emergency kit in the other. Grayson stands warily, allowing the scene to unfold with guarded acquiescence.

T. J. sets the two vessels on the table.

Billy slips off the counter to follow Parson and Charlie to the butcher block, wiping away their tears as T. J. unzips his backpack.

T. J. reaches into the pack and withdraws a long and ornately engraved wooden box.

Julia can feel Vin's body tighten and looks to the case with dire apprehension.

A viscous repugnance turns in Charlie's gut, as if the small chest were somehow in league with the dark forces that have rent her so deeply.

T. J. lays the chest beside the golden dagger.

The monstrous anticipation is broken when he turns over the carved lid.

A collage of gasps tumble from Ravenword, stricken at the sight of the mask made so nearly to resemble the countenance of a corpse bespeckled with blood that their veins run cold.

"The mask of the red death!" Billy gasps in absolute astonishment.

"*The* mask?" Parson yelps, the antiquity of the relic permeating his captive gaze.

"That's not possible!" Charlie cries.

Julia moves quickly to coddle her as the company languishes in a stupor.

Billy pulls his stare from the will of the mask to the agent with new and eager zeal. "Is that it?" he presses, pointing at the red emergency kit.

"Yes."

Eager to prove Billy's hope, T. J. opens the red case and pulls out the satellite phone and places it next to the graven wood box.

A wave of full and invigorating relief washes over the company.

"Let's go get our stuff," Billy cheers, slapping Vin on the back amid the giddy jubilance.

"Make the call!" T. J. insists in a tenor sounding very much like an order.

"I've got business to take care of first," Grayson rebuffs, to the consternation of the company.

"There is no way in hell we're spending another night in this place!" Parson contends with a round of ardent affirmations from his friends. "You have no fucking idea what we've been through!"

"Calm down, all of you! I'm here to make an arrest. I didn't anticipate this turning into a rescue. I'm going to have to provide a report with that call, which I can't do until I question the suspect."

"How long will that take?" Julia bleats.

"Not long. But it'll take the response team at least an hour to get up here, so get your things together and let me do what I need to do."

The company flies out of the kitchen on exuberant wings, with the exception of Parson, who is stayed by Grayson's brusque address.

"Praed."

Parson pivots, laying his hands on his hips after reassuring Charlie with a flitting wave. "How is it that you know everyone's name?"

Grayson crosses his arms with a raised brow. "What can I expect?"

Unflappable, Parson crosses his arms and considers the agent with a raised brow of his own. "Obviously you know he's a heroin addict," he reports. "And I'm assuming you know he's a victim of AIDS—"

"I don't know if I'd call him a victim," Grayson interjects coldly.

Chafed, Parson indulges a drawn pause in order to quell the anger stoked by the callous retort. "At any rate, he is literally skin and bones. I don't know how he's managed to live this long. He's weak, listless, incoherent most of the time, and, oh yes...possessed by the ghost of the baron who used to own this place. Does that help?"

"Is he a danger?" Grayson returns, unaffected.

"I don't think he has it in him," Parson finishes sadly.

The agent throws out his hand, inviting Parson to lead him.

"God's teeth," Parson sighs. Without masking his disdain for the agent, he ushers Grayson to the rough grain of Fichtenberg's apartment door.

Grayson's prodding does nothing to ingratiate the man to Parson, who relents and knocks on the wrinkled wood.

"Professor?" he calls. "I have someone here who would like to talk to you."

There is no response.

Parson checks the agent with a glance and then sets the door ajar to peek in. "Professor?"

"Come, come, Mister Praed," Fichtenberg beckons in a voice so thin that it is barely audible.

"There's a...someone from Interpol here to talk with you," Parson warns gently as he opens the door wide to reveal Grayson.

"Yes, yes. Come in, officer. I know why you are here and am in no condition to refuse you."

Despite Parson's description, Grayson is not prepared for the decimation that greets him upon his entering the small blue room. He flinches at the sight of the creature, which seems to hold the visage of a ghost more convincingly than the fancies he faced earlier. He turns to Parson, who lingers at the door. "Would you mind bringing me a chair?"

The withered creature wadded up in the tangle of blankets returns Parson's chary expression with a nod before focusing its weak, sunken eyes on the agent. "I'm afraid I'll not be much use to your courts, mister...?" he proffers as Parson disappears from the open doorway.

"Grayson. Agent Grayson," he replies, the exchange with Parson not escaping his notice. The agent waits.

Fichtenberg, wisely astute, follows suit.

Parson arrives at the door with one of the kitchen chairs, which the agent relieves him of quickly. "Thank you. Please close the door."

With pitiful resignation, Parson retreats reluctantly.

"He seems loyal," the agent begins.

"Mister Praed is an exceptional fellow," the professor replies with a voice not much louder than a whisper. "But I hope you'll not make the mistake of trying to implicate him in my affairs. He is completely innocent in that regard."

"And the rest of them?"

"And the rest," the wizened addict assures.

"Unlike yourself."

"Unlike myself."

"You used the reputation of this place being haunted to keep people at bay so you could warehouse and traffic drugs," Grayson accuses directly.

"Oh, I can assure you, this place is quite haunted," Fichtenberg attests, a hint of a grin teasing his thin white lips. "The narcotics enterprise served my purposes for a time but has since ceased by my directive."

Grayson assesses the professor with a cynical glare. "Your directive? Why would a cartel take orders from you?"

A soulless smile crackles across the pale and weathered face of the addict. "Fear, Mister Grayson. The fear of death."

Grayson considers the diminutive man, impatience blossoming across his own features.

"The fear of this place is absolute and worked just as you say—and will continue to do so long after I am gone," Fichtenberg asserts with a frankness that chips the agent's skepticism. "Obedience to my 'orders,' as you call them, is simple acquiescence. I will soon be dead…trying to coerce more trafficking out of me would be futile indeed. The contraband has been delivered by horseback on intervals of my design from a drop site higher in the mountains."

"I appreciate your candor," Grayson states coldly. "Care to provide names and locations?"

A hard glare issues from the professor's feeble eyes. "You will have all you need when you deliver Ravenword to safety."

"Ravenword?" Grayson echoes. "I'm not here to make any deals. What was your purpose for bringing them here? Did you think they would abet you somehow?"

The ever-dimming light in the professor's eyes grows distant. "Life, Mister Grayson. They need to make contact with the living. If they can do so, the curse might be broken. But…" Fichtenberg retreats reclusively into the shadows, grumbling acridly, "…eight. There were supposed to be eight! I was assured. Everything was in place. Ruined, everything is ruined. Eight, not six! Six could never survive! Ruined! Ruined!"

The rising madness of the broken man dawns on the agent with the shrill realization that his arrival with T. J. and the noble Italian brings the number of souls in the castle to the very number upon which the addict is fixated.

The cold, sinking realization of a sudden snare riddles him.

Abandoning the ravaged criminal to his ravings, Grayson flies from the room, dashing into the kitchen to find it empty and the table cleared.

His explosive entrance into the great entry hall jars the company, where Billy is stowing the relic and dagger in his backpack as the other men of the company stow their luggage against the wrinkled grain of the front door.

Grayson sweeps past them to grab the emergency kit.

"What's wrong?" T. J. exclaims, unnerved by the agent's agitation.

Julia shrinks into Vin's embrace.

Parson, Billy, and Aldobrandi stare in terrible anticipation.

Grayson pulls open the kit and yanks the cumbersome phone from its bed. He lets the case falls without care as he activates the phone and dials.

On Julia's gasp and the abrupt diversion of the group, Grayson spins on his heels to find Professor Fichtenberg standing like a reanimated cadaver within the passage.

"Eight!"

An uncanny stillness, perturbed only by the dancing light of the fireplace, falls upon the cavernous hall.

Grayson stares with the phone to his ear.

The receiver crackles and sounds with a chime that is clear and loud and deep and exceedingly musical but of so peculiar a note and emphasis that it riddles Grayson with a dread that his denial cannot negate.

Fichtenberg emerges, ghostlike, from the passage.

Grayson throws the phone onto the luggage.

Drawing his gun from his jacket with the swiftness of a trained killer, he takes aim.

Ravenword are crushed with a collective gasp as the brazen lungs of a clock striking with that clear and loud and deep and peculiar chime resound from some mysterious depth behind the enormous and ancient ill-grained doors that have oppressed their senses from the very beginning.

Unaffected, Fichtenberg continues into the great hall.

Grayson stalks him with the gun poised as his brain spins on the chime. "How are you doing this?"

Fichtenberg alights beside the great fireplace with the hateful doors to the castellated abbey looming menacingly behind him. The golden glow of the fire bestows a peace to his countenance. "Eight."

Clang!

"Don't do it!" T. J. shouts at Grayson.

His attempt, however, is cut short by the agent throwing out a hand to silence him.

"I know what it does to you," T. J. presses, inching forward. "Don't let it."

"Can it, Elders!" Grayson barks, his eyes locked on the professor. "Tell me how you're doing this!"

Clang!

Fichtenberg grins, a grin so blithe and disconcerting that it silences both T. J. and Grayson. "Eight!" he cheers, his voice soaring as if free to spend the last of his strength. "Eight! Ha ha!"

Clang!

The horrible sound consumes the hall but cannot quell the professor's manic glee.

"Eight!"

Ravenword watch in dismay as his jubilant expression turns.

Perceiving the moment, Billy stoops quickly and grabs up his backpack.

Fichtenberg seizes as if stricken.

Clang!

Those ancient and malevolent doors begin to shake as if a horde of angry fists were beating their way out of the abbey!

Dust and grime spill from the encrusted frame and rusted hinges!

A legion of desiccated fingers, like skeletal talons, claw at the black gap beneath the doors.

Fichtenberg screams, his eyes twisting blindly!

Ravenword cowers into a huddle.

Dumbstruck, Grayson lowers his gun and backs away.

Ravenword cry out, lurching forward vainly as the professor's frail body is thrown to the floor.

Grayson dives for the suspect, his hands outstretched!

On a soul-shattering shriek, Fichtenberg is dragged by invisible hands to the doors that tremble with ravenous hatred! Pulled beyond their reach, Grayson and Ravenword gape in horror as the professor, clawing and scratching, meets the spiteful grain.

The hall is a concert of screams!

Ravenword watch with mind-shattering devastation as Fichtenberg is pulled, impossibly, under those evil doors! Convulsing and spewing blood, the doomed waif thrashes beneath the castle's revenge!

In a final cacophony of crushed bones, he is gone, leaving a gruesome pool of blood.

Grayson lies on the flagstone, shocked by the reality of the curse.

Ravenword cowers in a knot, their brittle courage bludgeoned.

The venomous rancor is replete as the flames are abruptly snuffed from the great hearth to leave the company in chilling darkness.

CHAPTER 11

The Blue Chamber

BLINDNESS, TERRIFYING AND ABSOLUTE AND wholly possessed by shrieking hinges, is silenced by a profound thud
that penetrates the abyss with vile mockery and delivers the
tragic company from their senses to seal them in the doom
of the diseased castle.

Trembling, they huddle in the aimless blackness.

The darkness shifts with a flicker of anemic amber, and
they are themselves again. The uncomely glow of unseen
torches attest to forbidding passages in the abysmal reaches
to either side, yet the company feels no invitation or solace
in the illumination.

Julia's whimper is caught suddenly by a black form rising
before them.

"Calm down. It's just me. Grayson."

Before Ravenword can respond to his uncanny station,
an invidious melody of ill-tuned orchestral strings rises.
Upon that cankerous symphony, spectral doors, livid blue
and hinged in scrolling black, congeal before them as if
conjured from a desecrated mausoleum. As the apparition

actualizes into the wall, the company recoils from a slick of black crimson stretching like a grotesque carpet to the seam of the ghostly threshold.

Their disgust is arrested, however, by gossamer tendrils of phantasmic luster blooming on either side of the spectral panels as if woven from the dank atmosphere. Writhing, the two ghosts wail as they are wrought in corporeal form.

"So far...no good..." Parson moans at the sight of the ghoulish court jesters.

Rot-faced and rankled, costumed in eviscerated flamboyance, the two ghastly buffoons fulfill the vocation of their damnation and open wide the empyrean doors of Prospero's grand suite with gruesome and skeletal grins.

A riot of raucous voices, as if the very revelers of hell have been unleashed, clashes against the sickening tide of the discordant symphony. The din of disembodied debauchery and the loathsome melody swamp Ravenword. Hands clasp ears against the invisible bedlam as the company cringes under the auditory barrage. The crushing cacophony screams to a horrendous crescendo, then dissolves into eerie silence.

One by one, Ravenword and their allies open reluctant eyes to the bizarre indigo ballroom of the castellated abbey.

A surreal cosmos of sickly stars expands infinitely beyond the nebulous walls as if those smears of navy and shadow were but an illusion. Opposing panes of two comfortless windows encased in the center of those murky sheets do nothing to impede the breadth of the hideous constellation.

The soulless dance of torchlight filtered through their cobalt glass stuns the company with the illumination of a mob of rank corpses at the center of the hideous hall.

The impossible scene of ghouls lathering themselves in putrid gore with the fervor of desperate centuries breaks Ravenword and they fall back against the doors, unable to tear away their harrowed gaze. Beyond the sanguine orgy, the aphotic phantom is unveiled in the murky distance, costumed in the very mask, deathly white and bespeckled crimson, of the red death as told in Poe's account.

The frigid and penetrating glare of the looming Masked Death squeezes the breath with which they would gasp and retch. Choking on terror, they turn on the ill-grained phantasmic panel, beating and clambering for escape.

Grayson, his arms wide in an instinctive effort to shield the youths, swallows the nausea of denial that his gut roils to expel as several of the blood-bathing cadavers rear withered heads toward the commotion. With untamed strength, he yanks the wild company from the doors. "Stand back! Stand back!"

Ravenword disperses with the gleam of Grayson's pistol poised on the atrophied latches. Covering their ears preemptively, they cannot help but check the ravenous undead at the end of the bloody trail. He squeezes the trigger.

Boom! Boom! Boom! sends a quiver through the dismal constellation.

The company rushes upon the doors behind Grayson, to find them unscarred.

Behind them, the sanguine wallowing of the terrible wraiths ceases. In one chilling turn, the entire horde of corpses set their rotting faces upon the clamor of the living.

In disbelief, the agent pulls at the handles with all his great strength.

Above, the pinpoints of bilious lights begin to reel in their foul firmament.

The doors do not yield.

Like despoiled shrews rising from a mass grave, the revenants find their footing. Lurching through imbrued vestiges of chemises, kirtles, and gowns, the damned matrons advance.

Julia's scream alerts the company to the stuttering onslaught, and Grayson steps out on the wake of his gun.

Boom! Boom! Boom!

The agent's brain is slapped by irreconcilable realities. The power of his gun hammers through his muscles with each squeeze of the trigger and his steely eyes attest to the striking of his targets, yet the hideous creatures do not fall.

The chamber spins suddenly as the eidolic stars churn and swarm like ghoulish fireflies caught in a tempest.

The horde of entrail-soaked hags close on Grayson in a riot of shriveled and exsiccated features, gnashing hisses, and clawing talons.

On concerted strides, he advances and fires again.

Behind him, Ravenword swoons.

The corpses advance.

Fixed on the descending current of repugnant stars, Billy rifles through his backpack desperately.

The Masked Death looms, filling Grayson's imagination. He recoils under the terrible scrutiny and turns only to be caught in the arms of the beautiful phantom in blue.

Grayson sprawls upon the grimy stone and into the blackest day of his life. Lifting his head, he is stricken by the sight of his mother standing in the flush of youth. Somewhere beyond the desert heat-shimmer mirages, a radio crackles "Hotel California." A gang of thugs from the South American cartel crowd her. A gun is held to her neck. Her horrible and tearstained gaze is fixed on him. The slithery gunman tugs her close and sneers at an unseen adversary. Grayson cries out! His voice, however, is that of a terrified boy, and the weight crushing his chest is not merely his mother's tortured gaze. His bleary eyes follow the boot up to the brawny gangster pinning him to the ground. Another fiend crushes his hand into the dirt with a red-hot branding iron poised over his forearm. A world-shattering boom bludgeons his senses as the scope of his vision is filled with the crimson spray of his mother's exploding throat. The glowing brand plunges into his flesh with a blinding pain that cannot rival the witness of his eyes. His howl resounds and fractures as it fills his ears. Translating within the scream, he finds that it is no longer his own but the collective terror of Ravenword as the tide of hideous stars avalanche upon them.

Grayson rips open his sleeve, the memory of his branding still searing. A shudder rifles through him at the sight of the symbol from the first scapular blistering into his forearm.

With the mark laid bare on his arm, the stampede of corpses renders Grayson no heed as they mass on Ravenword.

The cosmos of wan and ghastly pinpoints pour into the youths as if their bodies were merely vessels for the supernatural deluge. Convulsing under the horrid engorgement, the seven are helpless to repel the onslaught of decayed madams pressing in around them. As Grayson bounds to Ravenword's defense, the mouths of each stretch into wide and abhorrent cavities on faces contorted into atrocious and unnatural masks.

Grayson attacks the mob with brazen fury, hurling the animated dead to the floor like a mad barbarian. His zeal, however, is bled cold by generations of infants baying from the mouths of Ravenword as if channeled through the haunted centuries. The grotesque roar of innumerable wailing infants, acrid and petulant and vile, pours from those piteous youths to stir the maternally bereft carcasses into a desperate frenzy.

Through the reaching and clawing of ragged and desiccated limbs, a violently shaking and entangled fist lifts the baron's seven scapulars over the fray.

Grayson plunges anew into the melee with ferocious zeal, carving a path to the exalted sacraments like a lion routing prey. Casting the last blockading corpse into the eviscerated throngs, he meets the will and fortitude that cannot be repressed by a thousand marauding phantoms.

Even as the spectral stars pour into him and the cacophony of infantine shrieks scream from his gaping throat, Billy has managed to emancipate the scapulars. Through eyes wild and transcendent, he pleads.

As if tugging the cords from the atrophied fist of a cadaver, Grayson yanks the scapulars from Billy's grasp with a gentleness born of fresh respect. Upon a resolute nod, he dashes out of the broil and into the soulless firelight seeping through the cobalt windows. Sifting through the tiny squares, his harried brain scrambles to identify the significance of their images under the appalling oppression of the company's torment.

His hands seize in their shuffling upon the excitement of a symbol, identical to that burned into his forearm: lilies crowned by twelve stars.

A glance at the ravaged youths whips the labor of his reasoning as Julia wilts and falls under the barrage.

Stuffing the supernumeraries into his waistband, Grayson hurries to examine the square's counterpart on the other end of the cord. He squints through the pale-blue light to make out the fanciful image on the second patch.

Stricken with understanding, his intellect pans the room under the lashes of urgency to scrutinize the tall, dark niches set into the murky walls at regular intervals.

Grayson flies into the gallery while the invading ghostly spheres congest the bodies of Ravenword, vying and jostling contentiously for the beating heart of each. As one spirit slips through the heartstrings to displace another, a new persona of enduring bitterness and spiteful longing resonates through the living aura to contend for the supremacy. Yet the effort is futile as no one bantam poltergeist can hold back the legion of others. Thus their contention continually disrupts and shocks the living essence of the tortured and unwilling host. With each supplanting an impression of the character and nature of each thwarted spirit, had they been given the opportunity of conception, is ceded to the souls of Ravenword.

The desecrated shells of their ineluctable mothers vie in like manner to paw and pet and fawn on the tormented youths with fingers of bone and desiccated kisses. In their desperation to finally coddle the children they were robbed of by the precipitous curse of the Masked Death, the deprived fiends scratch and crush the supple flesh of the captive avatars in dead ignorance.

The tide of spirits in the endless celestial eos descending on the living dulls suddenly. An aromatic mist expands through the dismal indigo atmosphere and vanquishes the marauding sprites caught within the gossamer drift of the charm. The extinguishing of the spirits registers with the decimated progenitors, who turn from their convulsing victims to hiss and claw at their approaching doom.

A pair of billowing thuribles swing wildly on Grayson's charging gait, belching plumes of smoke from smoldering frankincense and myrrh as they hang from his powerful fists. Like a rider of the apocalypse, the agent storms the sprawling mob of bewitched corpses to dispatch them with the very caress of the sacred incense. The ghouls dissolve by the dozens in the diffusing bouquet and the heinous assembly clamors to evade the enchanted banishment.

One by one the members of Ravenword drop to the floor, released from the possessive influence of the pernicious never-born now being vanquished by the thousands. Grayson quickly sets a thurible on either side of the company to tend to the youths as phantoms scream into oblivion. The floor around him is a mass of quivering bodies, as each struggles to regain psychic equilibrium.

T. J. and Parson are the first to recover and find Grayson kneeling over Charlie's shuddering form. Shaken and trembling, the two men sit up and survey each other with renewed appreciation. Aldobrandi is the next to rouse, his awakening warmed by the sight of T. J. and Parson helping each other to their feet and embracing like lost brothers. Both men then extend their hands and pull the noble Italian from the filthy flagstone. The ensuing round of hugs is punctuated by Charlie's recovery and, with grateful and hopeful eyes, they turn to Grayson, who hovers over Julia.

Their elation is crushed by her motionless body and the agent's grim expression. They rush to her side as Vin stirs behind them.

"I can't find a pulse," Grayson whispers somberly.

"No, no, no!" Charlie bleats on tumbled breath.

Parson rushes to join them as Aldobrandi and T. J. move quickly to intervene upon Vin's recovery, bracing for the sting of his grief.

Looming black and motionless in the deep recesses of the ballroom, the merciless stare of the aphotic phantom divests the very atmosphere of any grace exuded in their affection.

Vin's bleary brain is ushered into the soulless blue by the faces of T. J. and Aldobrandi looking down upon him.

The bleak cast portends tragedy and, still prostrate, he rolls swiftly onto his belly to seek out the bane. Vin can feel essence of sweet Julia ebbing before his eyes can process the scene of Parson fighting to revive her. "Julia!"

Billy wakes to the pungent billows of incense and Vin's anguished wail. Sitting up, his heart dampens at the sight of the valiant Indian frantically gathering Julia's petite and listless form into his arms. As Billy stands to join his devastated companions, a lurid and sickly purple stains the impossible stratosphere of above the heart-wrenching scene.

The foul cast spreads like plague to consume and define the vaulted ceiling on the terrible clarion of the brazen clock, whose enchanted herald resonates throughout the infected indigo with a clear and deep and peculiar *clang!*

"Shit!" Charlie bleats. "What do we do?"

"Can you lift her?" the agent presses.

"Of course!" Vin bellows, shifting Julia in his arms and heaving to his feet as his friends stand ready in fearful anticipation.

"What the fuck is that?" Parson exclaims, catching sight of the grotesque purple blight creeping down the margins of the ceiling like a diseased hem.

Clang!

The dreadful fascination with the bruising walls is thwarted by Vin's sudden cry.

Julia's small form is rent from his cradling arm to rise suspended as the vile contagion stretches the creeping periphery.

"Oh my god!" Charlie gasps as Julia's body rises into the expanse.

A clamor of futility overtakes the company, scrambling and grappling and leaping in desperate hopes of reaching her.

"What the hell is this?" Grayson stammers in disbelief. "What the hell is going on?"

The noble Italian drops to his hands and knees beneath her levitation, shouting to the company. T. J., the tallest and most athletic of them, climbs atop the Italian's strong back swiftly but to no avail. Julia is now far from reach.

Clang!

Billy watches as the mottled contagion recedes into the hollows of eight tall divots and frames the two lofty panes of the cobalt glass, turning them a base shade of bruised purple. A cold pit sinks into his stomach upon realizing the translation and the vanishing of the great masked phantom.

"We've got to do something!" Vin roars, watching miserably as Julia continues into the heights like a drowned child adrift in the sea.

"Don't move!" Billy crows wildly. "Don't move from this spot!"

Clang!

"Why?" Grayson demands, ramped on suspicion and rage. "What's going on?"

The mass of blemishes stretch the divots into long and deep niches as it closes around the bottoms of the changed glass. Billy points as it continues toward the floor, genuinely afraid of what reaching those flagstone pavers might bring.

Clang!

The company gawks apprehensively as the maculated purple rash meets the floor to close the walls in around them.

"We've got to get out of here!" Grayson shouts as the snare sets.

"To where?" Billy counters.

A fresh cocktail of desperation washes over the ice in their veins as the aberrant flush is unimpeded by the borders between wall and floor.

Clang!

CHAPTER 12

The Purple Chamber

RAVENWORD'S INDUCTION INTO THE SECOND grand gallery is arrested by the putrid fetor of the creeping infection wafting over them with a fetid pungence that sickens the soul. The company chokes in the miasma, cupping hands and sleeves over their faces to fend off the noxious tolling. Billy, pressing a well-worn handkerchief against his face, tries to corral the others against the encroaching blight.

"Don't touch the walls!" Parson shouts, his fervor muffled by his sleeve.

The company recoils from the quivering stratum of ripe and oozing disease to pace the shrinking flagstone island like caged animals. Their welling panic, however, is quelled by the uncanny cessation of the contagious drift. Confounded by uncertain relief, they fall well back from the invisible boundary under the torment of Vin's irrepressible grief.

"What the hell is this?" Grayson scours the shadows with eyes hardened by experience, sensing a particular horror within one of the far and arcane alcoves.

Infused with the garish purple cast, the reclusive niches of the lurid chamber coddle hues so deeply perse as to mimic the blackness of death. That darkness steeps in the hollow of the enormous Gothic ballroom with a malicious obscurity that infects every tender memory of Julia.

None can answer, for the loss of Ravenword's sweetest and the ravaging of the blue room is still too fresh.

As if the violation has cleared the fields of their souls, the vast chamber seeds an utter emptiness that roots to their very core to poison their hearts with despondency and their minds with the terror of exposure. Inciting these wounds, the rank air tortures their senses like a manifestation of their grief that even the Interpol agent is unable to escape.

"The legend is true," Aldobrandi breaches in a low and dreadful tone. "The curse of Prospero and the Red Damned."

His exposition, however trepid, is muted by the prickly chill of a creeping prescience. Heads turn with uncanny awareness and harrowed eyes to the cruelest desolation of the castle's malevolence. A small and solitary figure floats in the center of the ballroom within the diffused shimmer of the vile purple windows.

Disgorging his grief, Vin bolts in dauntless rapture only to be sacked by the agent's brawn and the rush of his friends.

Vin stares in numb anguish as the petite and pale aspect of Julia, singular and forlorn, gazes back across the breadth of the overwhelming chamber with the pitiable countenance of a soul lost. A tender confusion hangs on her wan features. Her pallid lips quiver, as if fearful to speak.

"But," Vin whimpers, "she's alive!"

Charlie looks from his earnest face to the sad spectacle. "Remember Agnot."

"But she's right there!"

As if to contravene his hope, the Masked Death emerges from the recessive gloom to overshadow the wretched waif like a profound and merciless master.

The declaration stokes Vin's defiance. Trembling in the arms of his friends, he glares at the aphotic phantom spitefully, determined to spare his paramour Agnot's fate. To his dismay, Julia's expression contorts as her head jerks and bobs as if straining to regurgitate life.

"Help...me..." she chokes.

Enflamed, Vin bridles against the embrace of his friends. "Let me go!"

His fervor, however, is extinguished by a sudden cold and consummate oblivion as if the very nature of death has been unleashed to extinguish the naked anima of existence so completely that the shadows draping the cornered recesses seem enlivened by contrast.

The company bristles under the hopelessness of absolute cessation personified in the morgana of their friend. For, despite the visage of Julia and the phantom before them, the abysmal ballroom remains an absolute void bereft of any essential resonance. Even Vin, whose tormented heart longs to believe his fervid eyes, can feel nothing of Julia's gentle nature.

Grayson, relying on his own stubborn compass, repulses the effects of so liberal an intimidation with cagey and tactical denial. He takes a bold step forward.

His bravado surprises the company, and a bolster shuffles through Ravenword to pierce the residue of the neverborn with a ray of tenuous courage.

Shrewd even in the dismal contagion, Billy once again stays T. J.'s shift to join the agent with a firm grasp of his arm.

Aldobrandi, shrinking under all he has been told of the curse, can find no such fortitude. With a complexion burnished with shame, he recedes under the burrowing abyss behind the eyes of that terrible, watching mask.

T. J. yanks his powerful arm from Billy's grip, rebuking him with an indignant glare.

"You can't!" Billy chides in a terse and apprehensive whisper.

"Oh Jeezus," Parson groans as Charlie gasps beside him.

"He's right," Grayson asserts, rubbing the mark burned into his forearm without inclination toward Parson's interjection.

"Guys," Charlie presses with a faltering voice and blazing eyes.

As Grayson pulls the scapulars from his waistband, he follows Parson's and Charlie's appalled faces to Julia, where the diseased gore beneath her roils with erupting boils that issue raw and squirming tendrils. Like base and fouled tentacles, they rise in reach of her unstained flesh. An epidemic of startling and fearful cries sets the agent's intention on the solitary apparition, and he hands the sacraments to Billy.

Julia's horrible visage schisms, obscuring her devitalized features with a second ghastly face as the slimy cords lash around her feet.

Billy, forcing himself to ignore the frenzy of the company, blocks the agent and holds up the knot of scapulars. "One for every chamber," he explains, handing the scapular matching the mark on Grayson's arm back to him. "With a symbol for every one."

Grayson's incredulous gaze passes from the sacrament to his branding to the distorting visage of Julia and then to that of the looming Masked Death. "Bullshit," he reviles, provoked by the macabre and fed up with the superstitious affectations.

"You need to fucking listen because your life depends on it!" Billy chides. "Each mark on these things matches the patterns of the wallpaper in our rooms!"

Grayson scoffs at the ludicrous connection.

"We were each assigned a specific room!" Billy insists. "I also found the marks on the borders of statues in the chapel! The same saints represented by these and the marks all match!"

"I wasn't assigned anything, and I still got your asses out of that clusterfuck!" With steely resolve, Grayson forsakes the stunned company and steps stridently into the openness, his gun flashing in the incandescent purple as he draws it from the holster.

"Billy's right!" Parson shouts, stepping out of the company while trying to ignore the specter of Julia, whose skin now writhes with the seething contagion. "We went through them together as we cleaned them."

"So who is assigned to this hell?" Grayson retorts incredulously.

Parson and Billy's distraught gazes pass to the tortured apparition.

"Jeezus christ!" the agent growls, pushing Billy out of his way.

The contagion bloats and purples Julia's neck as it consumes her. Convulsing under the onslaught, she raises her hands to Grayson's approach as if desperate for release. A contortion of her sickly features, however, stutters his stride as Ravenword cry out upon Julia's head cleaving into a second carriage of her diseased aspect. Primed with sudden resolve, the company implores the agent as he reaches the margin of the quivering purple pestilence.

In a burst of blind heroism, T. J. charges the agent.

Parson and Billy pounce like wild cougars.

Leveling his aim on the aphotic phantom, Grayson steps across the boundary as T. J. is tackled behind him.

Webs of tangled veins whip around the agent's boots from the grotesque muck as venous tendons fly from Julia to lash him.

Her unearthly scream rocks Ravenword to their core.

Grayson twists and strains under the hematic cords wrapped around his thick arms and powerful body. Against those viscous strands, he heaves his aim past the tortured girl to level his gun on the towering black caricature of Death.

Boom! Boom! Boom!

The company dives to the floor.

The snared but valiant agent struggles against the grotesque cords as he is pulled deeper into slimy plasm.

Boom! Boom! Boom! Boom! Boom! Boom!

The thunder permeates the gallery and eclipses the defiant roar of Grayson as he is consumed alive until the vile and voracious pestilence renders all silent.

The trembling company lifts trepid faces from the icy flagstone, harrowed to find the agent a quivering cocoon and the deadly contagion advancing on them unhindered. Boils blister and weep on the clammy walls as they clamber to their feet.

Julia is trussed in the putrid sinews and calving ghastly, roiling, disease-riddled doppelgangers from her tortured form like plumes of twisted reflections. Ravenword's screams join those of an anguished and violated chorus of Julias to consume the hideous purple gallery with resonant horror.

Compounding their dismay, abrupt and fleeting apparitions of Julia in various and ghoulish stages of disease burst within inches of each of them as she struggles to break free from the vicious oppression of the deathly specter. With each abrupt and fleeting visitation, a word belches from each defiled version of her.

Parson's own shout supercharges his reasoning as a leering, pustular ghoul blanches his defenses, blurting, "Arms."

He turns swiftly to Vin. "What did it say to you?"

"'Your!'" he shouts hoarsely, throwing his terrified gaze to Billy.

Riddled by the ravenous contagion closing in around them, Billy's mind has no room for riddles other than the scapulars. He rifles through the sacraments with flustered fingers as the blistering pustules explode with grappling tendrils on the walls around him.

"If that belongs to Julia, then what do we do?" T. J. shouts.

"Here!" Billy calls, holding up the second sacrament.

Aldobrandi is drawn from the company huddling around Billy by the vacant glare of Death's ghastly mask beyond the ever-expanding sphere of contentious phantasmal Julias.

"Are those jars?" Charlie presses shakily, squeezed between Parson and Vin.

"And a box?" Vin adds, forcing his beleaguered mind to block out the torment of his paramour in favor of the clue that could save her.

"Snakes around a pole?" T. J. indicates, pointing to the opposing sacrament.

"Around the mark!" Billy corrects.

"That's a medical symbol," Parson interjects. "It's a medicine chest!"

Ravenword are so focused on the tiny patches of wool, the noble Italian's absence is only discovered when a pox-riddled visage of Julia blinks between Parson and the wall. The abrupt vanishing of the ghoul alerts Parson to the atrocious writing tentacles grabbing for them from a vomiting boil. Blanching, he shoves his confounded friends toward the advancing boundary and scrambles to account for the noble Italian.

Aldobrandi, enveloped in a queer and comforting peace, feels the attention of the company and turns through the turmoil of the pestilence to meet Parson's gaze. "The sacrament passes to me."

"You can't!" Parson bellows.

"He has to!" Billy counters somberly. "The rest of us already have our assignments."

Stepping out of the dumbfounded company, Billy retrieves a Sharpie from his backpack as he hurries to pass the scapular to the noble Italian.

"It must be blood, my friend," Aldobrandi exhorts, pulling a Swiss Army knife from his pocket. "Would you please? I cannot cut myself."

"Parson!" Billy hails.

Parson is at their side in an instant.

"You must hurry!" Aldobrandi insists, the contagion having already consumed half of their safe ground.

With a deep breath, Parson swallows his emotional affinity for the beautiful Italian and appropriates a clinical demeanor.

Aldobrandi's face tightens against the pain as Parson carves the symbol of the second scapular into his palm.

"Now be clear of the pestilence!" he shouts, taking the scapular from Billy.

The very air pulses with malevolence as the noble Italian turns to face Julia in the center of the vast gallery.

The aphotic phantom looms over her, yet the masked specter is unmoved.

As Ravenword watch on bated breath, Aldobrandi steps to the encroaching contagion. Drawing the gold necklace from his collar, he kisses the small medalion thereon, crosses himself, and steps into the domain of the Masked Death.

Tendrils spring from the caliginous plasm but shrivel instantly upon wrapping around the noble Italian's leg, sending a thrill rippling through Ravenword. With each cautious step, the pestilence withers, dries, and turns to dust beneath his feet. The constriction of their lungs eases with the slowing of the contagious tide under the noble antigen. Even the sphere of ghastly doppelgangers mocking their Julia begins to fade.

Nebulous billows, like wings unfolding in the power of the aphotic phantom, ruffle as it overshadows Julia and Aldobrandi, throwing fear into the gallery like a wicked deluge. As the impulse washes over penned and pacing Ravenword, a hue of malignant satisfaction can be felt in the foul and riveting aura.

On the crest of that terrible wave, the brazen lungs of that malicious and arcane clock strikes from Ravenword any remnant of comfort with the first ill-noted *clang!*

A chill runs down Aldo's back. Lifting his palm, the crimson inscription weeps down his arm. The fear breathed into the expanse by the Masked Death finds a doorway into the noble Italian's soul. Purpling welts, like blossoming bruises, rise between the streamlets of blood from underneath his skin.

A similar portal is born in Ravenword as Aldo turns to them with a forlorn expression. With the contagion creeping at their feet and the wall behind ejecting plague and tendrils, the waning of the noble Italian's lustrous olive complexion acts on their nerves like the herald of their doom.

Aldo sets his sight on the riddled Julia, held carnage-bound like the prey of a spider in a web of diseased sinews. Her desperate eyes meet his and lower them to the flagstone pavers liberated by the withering of the contagion.

Clang!

Beneath the dregs and dust of the banished bane, patterns appear.

Comprehension strikes Aldo like a bolt of lightning even as fever dulls and bakes his brain.

Ravenword gasps in their frantic retreat as the patina of disease manifests bluntly on his sallow features. His once tan and virile neck swells and purples. Helpless against the barring tide, they cry out as his shoulders slump and he staggers.

Desperate in the face of his own mortality, the noble Italian draws from a well of love bestowed to his deepest heart by family and friends. With a heavy sigh, he allows his weakened limbs to deliver him to the flagstones stamped respectively with the images of the seven sets of scapulars.

Ravenword mewl and gasp, aching against futility to rush to his aid even as they dive under the exploding pustules and contusing flagstone.

Clang!

Sifting through the grime and dross as fervently as he can manage under the fever, Aldo anoints each of the engravings with his own blood as his hands sweep in search of the serpents coiled around the cryptic symbol on a bed of kindling.

Within the tangled starburst of the grotesque tendons, Julia, so consumed that she is nearly lost to the wicked artifice, writhes violently to both capture his attention and again reach beyond her bounds.

Like a tongue of fleeting fire, a ghastly expression of Julia flashes between Aldo and her tormented self. "Here!"

Scurrying like a rodent across the floor, Aldo rushes to her vanishing.

Clang!

The aphotic wings of the Masked Death erupt like malicious tempests to throw the fury of its malevolent will against Aldo and the company.

The noble Italian does not yield to the hateful barrage, even as pox blossoms on the splotches marring his beautiful face. Beneath the gale of black rage, he claws the seams of the paver bearing the mark.

In their aphotic pen, Ravenword cower as the torrent of pitch pushes their harbor into the wall.

As the noble Italian pulls away the flagstone, Agnot's admonition to Parson supernovas in Billy's consciousness.

With a faith desperate and alien to his nature, he digs his heels into the stone.

"No!"

Pummeled and whipped, Aldo throws his arms forward and drags the carved chest to the base of Julia's slithering and sinewy cage.

Ravenword gawk, utterly astounded as Billy's thundering defiance holds back the cyclonic rancor of the Masked Death's black wing.

Aldo opens the lid, bolstered by her countenance to find the two clay vials cradled among archaic and tarnished instruments.

He can feel life bleeding away.

The noble Italian summons the last strength left to him to stand and extend the vial scarred crudely with the sacred symbol to Julia's blistered lips.

His thoughts turn to Renata and his family.

"What are you doing, Aldobrandi?" Renata rebukes, the glory of her fierce spirit raining upon him in the eternity resonating within the final strike of that terrible clock. "Take the medicine, you fool!"

Lying across the stone, Aldo draws the second ampule to his lips on a remnant of will. He is smiling at the pigtailed American girl standing in the bubbling surf under the bright warmth of the Tyrrhenian sun. With a holy kiss, she turns into the glittering waves and is lost in the radiance of that speckled glory.

CHAPTER 13

The Green Chamber

THE TEMPEST OF PITCH AND fear from the aphotic phantom's nebulous wings dissipate to reveal a dismal gallery. Lichen, moss, and mold from centuries of decay brindle the surrounding walls in a patina of the drabbest green broken only by the striated haze hanging from the oppressive heights. Sallow echoes of illumination from the viridian windows fluctuate in the dismal brume yet intrude too feebly to penetrate the compounded veils condensing across the floor. Standing in a morass so thick upon the floor that it obscures the flagstone pavers, Ravenword can discern nothing in the morass of the Julian ghost or Aldobrandi—only their pounding hearts and Vin's weeping.

"No!" Charlie bemoans, intruding on the melancholy as five pan the gallery for a sign of the noble Italian.

"But he drank the medicine!" T. J. charges, an arsenal of frustration building in his muscles. "He drank the medicine. Isn't that what he was supposed to do?"

Scanning the murky profundity with scrupulous eyes, Billy recedes from the confounded company. Piquing his senses, he pings the dismal expanse with his will.

Malevolence seethes from depths to descry the hidden specter of the Masked Death. To either side dark niches mirror the intervals of the former galleries as they sink past the rank walls. Lying within these spiteful recesses, a low and abhorrent wanting leaches lasciviously into the chamber like the damp of the dank mist.

The gauntlet of vile intention sends a shiver through Billy. With a fist of tangled scapulars, he pivots to face his friends.

Charlie's fragile restoration wilts as her beleaguered eyes fall on the tangle of sacramentals, and she leans, quivering, into Parson. Tapping the cold emptiness of a life without Agnot, she reaches through the dire anticipation and raises her sleeve to offer her trembling forearm.

"No!" T. J. barks, pushing back her arm. "There's nothing here! Nothing between us and the doors!"

Ravenword turn reluctant gazes through the murky ribbons to the doors that stand abeam of the inky void at the far end of gallery. The unspoken dread of what lies beyond spreads between them like the contagion of the previous chamber.

"Like it'd be that easy," Parson rebuffs as Billy's calculating eyes shift to the sallow, viridian windows.

"So, we don't even try and *still* end up like Aldo?"

The sting of T. J.'s rebuke perforates their morbid resignation and sobers Vin, who looks at him with a burnished gleam.

"Guys," Billy starts.

"No!" T. J. spurns, unable to quell the impulse to escape any longer.

The protests of his stricken companions fall away swiftly as he taps the vexation in his veins and sprints headlong into the gloom with Vin hard on his heels. Knots of fog harass his equilibrium and plot with the enveloping nimbus to thwart his stride. Hideous faces, veiled in the obscurity of the inumbrated alcoves, sneer as the two men cut through the mist beneath them. The clamoring of Ravenword haunts the unwholesome vapors like disembodied spirits, but their desperate determination does not yield. A surge of excitement courses through T. J. as his eyes catch sight of enormous and opulent doors. The sweet relief curdles, however, under the emergence of the masked and spectral presence of Death from his station in the blackness.

Sterile and callous, the looming figure stares down upon T. J. and Vin through the stale drifts with an aspect so devoid of natural essence that it stuns the men midstride.

His sturdy form betrays him, and the bold athlete sprawls into the putrid fog as Vin's timbering form disappears beside him.

"The doors!" he pleads, groping for those delivering panels as footfalls rush upon him.

"Get back!" Billy shouts, yanking Parson from the perimeter of Masked Death's liberty.

"Fuck!" Parson yelps on a wild backpedal, grappling for Charlie's hand.

"Shit! Get up! Get up!" she exclaims as she tugs on the men, her very vitality ebbing under the cold draw of the aphotic phantom.

T. J. kicks wildly as they scramble in retreat.

"Get off me!" he barks, throwing back Charlie's hand.

Knowing the desperate competitor will not capitulate easily, Billy surveys what he can of the murky ballroom as the company meerkat in an anxious huddle beneath the morbid hues of the enormous and garish windows.

"It's impossible!" Vin moans, rubbing his forehead in a futile attempt to erase his despair.

"Maybe not," Billy retorts, handing the sacrament imprinted with a lamb and a sword over a burning bushel to Charlie, and then doling the rest to their assigned victims.

"No way! You can keep it!" T. J. demurs in a tenor that well mimics Motisha's.

"We're each assigned a hell," Billy retorts in a somber tenor that shrills the company with terrible foreboding, "We might as well be as prepared as possible."

"'I!'" Charlie trumpets, turning to Parson. "Arms!"

The company returns her sudden outburst with puzzled expressions.

"That's what..." she begins, setting a gentle hand on Vin's arm. "Sorry, but that's what Julia's ghost said to me."

Justin Michael Greenway

"She was giving us a way out?" T. J. begs.

"'I,'" Vin clarifies with a bleak and crumbling demeanor, "as in, 'I died in your arms.'"

"That's what she was telling us," Charlie explains sadly, pointing to each respectively and quoting the words as they were given to them. "I. Died. In. Your. Arms. She wanted Vin to know that…who…*what* we saw wasn't really her."

Vin's shoulders tremble.

"How does that help us?" T. J. presses.

Charlie shakes her head thoughtfully. "I don't know…it's like she was telling us we're been fucked with."

"No shit!" T. J. chides.

"It's like what Agnot told Parson," Billy interjects.

"We can't believe what we see. We can't give in to it!" Charlie proffers. "*That* helps us."

"How the hell does that help us? Watching our friends die is not a ploy, it's real!"

T. J.'s censure is answered by stirring in the shadows that freezes the company's blood.

"Shit!" T. J. exclaims as they tighten their circle. "What do we do?"

Charlie starts as Billy rifles through his backpack and pulls out his cell phone.

"Did you get a signal?" Vin blurts as Parson and T.J. stare hungrily.

"Yeah, right," Billy scoffs, nodding to the yawning pane glistening grotesquely with the dancing light of a veiled torch. "How old do you think that glass is?"

350

Vin clutches the shoulder of T. J.'s jacket, wringing it in his fist with harrowed eyes locked on the pair of ghouls spidering out of the shadows on either side of the black abyss shrouding the Masked Death.

As Billy cocks his arm and hurls his cell phone at the towering pane, Charlie turns to Parson. "Cut me!"

With a loud bang, the technological projectile shatters against the vile viridian glass.

The window remains unbroken but is scarred with a small chip.

Vin gasps as he recognizes the ghouls creeping across the walls like monstrous roaches.

Sacrificial blood streams down Charlie's arm as she hisses under the bite of the blade, and T. J., shaking himself free of the Indian's grasp, catapults his phone through the dreary haze.

The phone explodes on impact, but the chip becomes a pock.

In an instant, cell phones are poised on ready hands.

Charlie slaps Agnot's phone, which she could not part with, into T. J.'s palm. "The last pitch."

Cardinal cracks web from the pock with Charlie's effort and, as Vin is pulled into service, she moves closer to the pane at Parson's prodding. The sight of Julia, Grayson, Romero, and Fichtenberg twisted into fiendish forms worming down the walls, however, seizes her in a terrible stupor.

Vin whimpers as his attempt misses the mark, and the four desecrations find the floor.

Resurrecting summers of innocence and Little and Lavender League softball, Parson shifts his stance and pitches his phone.

Like the others, it shatters on impact but sends a fatal fault racing through the very length of the green glass with a sharp *pop!*

"Charlie!" Parson snaps. "Get ready!"

As the four depraved monstrosities close in on them, T. J. forces his mind to clear and focuses on the heart of the fracture. He can hear the gruesome approach and smell the stench of fouled mortality yet pushes past his harried senses and drives Agnot's cell phone into the angry breach.

The glass, which had been stained so ghastly a shade of green in antiquity and spanned centuries in its vile casements, shatters in a cacophony of shards.

Ravenword's elation, however, is short-lived, as they find themselves surrounded.

The carpet of fog pulses and roils.

"Go!" Parson bellows.

Ribbons of grime fall from the casement as Charlie clambers onto the thick pane with no heed of the biting shards or the doom that has marked her fate. Behind her, the gallery writhes with depraved anticipation, while before her is a pyre that yields no warmth and consumes no fuel blazing upon a massive dish supported by four thickly wrought legs. In the center of the pyre stands a sword. The sight is a literal translation of the image on one square of her scapular. In contemplating her strategy, her eyes pass from the lamb on the second square to the bloody symbol carved into her arm.

As the four men square off with the four fiends, Vin's blood runs cold in the violent want radiating from the diseased and bloated specter of his paramour. Likewise, shrill and eviscerating recognition twists Parson's gut at the hard and hungry glare from the ghoulish imitation of the powerfully built agent. He can't help but surrender to the prospect that what they are in for will be very bad and that the other men are not prepared. Yet Billy, whose experience in life may be limited, has no illusions as to what is likely to soon befall them.

Standing at the base of one of the quadpod's thick legs, Charlie's test of its sturdiness is waylaid by a voice calling her name. Straining to listen, it falls on her ear again from within the darkness. Although it sends chills down her spine, it is not the hideous voice that ravaged her grief in the chapel but the impossible, comforting voice of Agnot.

"There you are! Come on, let's get outta here!"

Charlie stands transfixed by the figure that has swept in from the black depths of the corridor. Everything she can perceive tells her it is Agnot, alive and vital, but the reality of her anguish remains a sobering sliver in her mind.

"What's the matter with you? I've found a way out!"

Charlie slides behind the pyre's thick beam. "Are you a ghost?"

"Come with me."

As the visage lifts a beckoning hand, waves of young love and sunshine and the comfort of cuddling on Sunday afternoons wash over Charlie like an enchantment waking her from the tendrils of a nightmare.

"Come on."

Charlie steps out from behind the post, the stain of the castle fading in the newness of Agnot's love.

Screams shatter the spell suddenly, and Charlie finds herself alone in the great emptiness. Mustering her strength and agility, she shimmies up the pillar amid the horrible cries of the four men she left in the haunted gallery. With her pounding heart prodding her, she reaches up and trusts her full weight to her grasp of the lip of the great dish that hosts the fire. Resisting the urge to look over her shoulder to her friends, she heaves herself up with a roar until she is squirming precariously between the edge of the dish and the flames. Finding her footing, she turns to discover the horror of the men.

Each is stripped and laid bare and held by spectral bonds in positions most accessible to the hordes of figures that ravish them in a ghostly orgy. Pressed on all sides, warmth is bled from their bodies in the assault to invigorate and vitalize the grabbing, thrusting, pushing, penetrating fiends. The violence of phantoms vying for contact swamp the men like ocean waves, for the longer their carnal congress continues, the more corporeal and insatiable for sensation the phantoms become. Thus, as their four bond masters laugh and jeer, the four men scream beneath a crush of the ravenous nobles cursed to the numb damnation between the pleasures of life and the bliss of mortal release.

The heinous scene stokes Charlie's rage, and she turns and grabs the hilt of the sword. But even as her grip tightens, the steel and the flames become instantly blistering. In the shock and pain of her recoil, she slips over the edge but catches herself at the expense of several ribs. Amid the screams of her friends, she dangles, with a mind racing for a solution.

"Come on, Charlie, I've found a way out!"

"No!"

Slithering back onto the dish, now scorching hot, she carefully rounds the edge until the wall is at her back. Despite the inevitable fall, she bridges the gap between the margin of the pyre plate and the masonry behind her with her body and pushes.

The great torch crashes over the window casement to spew fire and cinder across the stone floor in a spray of sparks. The heat of the living flame vanquishes the dank mist and sends the horde of lustful damned clamoring in retreat. Those that can, recede into the ethereum of their spectral state, while those who have indulged too much in flesh of her friends are set ablaze by the wild and unrelenting rage of Charlie. With torch in hand, she pulls the sword from the embers and charges the four ghouls that guard as bond masters. Set afire and howling, the flight of the four fiends is cut short by Charlie's swift blade.

Amid the unearthly shrieks of the burning damned, Charlie gathers up the men's clothes and rushes to free them.

"Come on, babe."

Charlie turns to find Agnot, flush and beautiful, beckoning once again. Behind her, the doors to the previous chamber are wide, but instead of a cesspool of contagion, golden sunlight pours from the aperture. Relishing the warmth of light and love, Charlie stands and moves blissfully toward the promise even as her friends plead. Agnot opens her arms in welcome, and a tear of peace rolls down Charlie's rosy cheek. Without regret, Charlie raises her arm and pushes the blade through the mockery of her lover coldly.

With a piercing scream the imposter vanishes with the shackles holding her friends.

Despite having vanquished the vision and the bonds, Charlie's name once again reverberates through the amber-fire expanse as the four men rush to cover their shame.

The dreadful trepidation rippling through her is compounded by the lungs of that brazen clock striking clear and peculiar in tenor and emphasis with the first heralding *clang*!

As the flames continue to spread impossibly through the ballroom, the aphotic robes of looming Death open like curtains of malevolent shadows. From that pitch and shrouded gate, a figure, black and shapeless, emerges on wingless flight through the building plumes of smoke and haze.

Riddled with terrible anticipation, Charlie tries to rouse the men as her stricken eyes watch the specter's ethereal advance.

Shrouded in a flowing ebony sheet, the specter forces air through ruptured cords to spew Charlie's name into the expanse as it approaches unhindered.

Charlie stands, tightening her fist around the hilt of the sword in her right hand while brandishing the flaming torch in the left.

Clang!

Curtains of fire billow on the walls, framing the phantom as it stops and lifts an accusing hand. The black shroud drapes beneath that extended indictment to incite Charlie's valor once more. Leading with the torch, she lunges to ignite the rank shroud.

Flames swiftly consume the cerement of death, yet the ghoul neither shrieks or recoils. As the burning remnants fall away, the specter presents itself to Charlie in all its ghastly horror as if punishing her for rejecting the more merciful offering.

A brutally battered face frozen in a state that defies nature. One sunken eye stares in cloudy death, the other a gory hollow. A gash splays the head. Another exposes the gore of her ravaged neck. Her stripped ribcage frames the hideous cavity from which desiccating organs hang.

Clang!

The blatant visitation shatters the bulwark bravery bolstering Charlie against her grief, and she sinks to the floor sobbing.

The terrible monstrosity looms over her victoriously.

Charlie abandons herself to the eternal torment and, with the mournful howl of the unforgiven, bounds into the air.

The head of the macabre corpse falls to the stone floor, followed quickly by the mortal remains of her lover.

Clang!

CHAPTER 14

The Orange Chamber

T. J.'s RAVAGED BRAIN GRAPPLES THROUGH the tumbled quagmire of a psyche stripped of the insulating estate of self to grasp the fervid shouting of the woman standing over him even as his frantic hands seize on his clothes to cover his disgrace. Fire registers beyond the voice and casts a cognitive anchor on the chamber engulfed in an insufferable inferno. Lying beside him, Parson and Vin groan in the swoon of shock and shame that prioritizes the shelter of clothing.

"Shoes, shoes!" Charlie barks, as she throws the rescued jackets to the three men. "Fuck the shirts! Come on, guys! Push through it, push through it!"

Prey to the torment of his assignment to this preternatural Hades, T. J. scours his pillaged soul for the courage he once knew as his dexterity returns but finds only the hollow wake of the ravaging.

Billy rises against the backdrop of fiery oppression fully clothed, holding his head as he staggers through the remains of ego to retrieve his battered rucksack from the hot flagstone. With the consolation of the backpack, he gravitates through the oppressive heat to Charlie.

A visage of a soul bereft of all but grief, her fervent glare marks a face stricken by devastation and determination.

Billy surrenders to the necessity of an embrace, hoping to glean what comfort he can from her strength. Her trembling body, however, remains rigid and unyielding, with steely arms that prime his detached nature. As Parson and Vin continue dressing, Billy turns his head reluctantly to follow Charlie's gaze.

Rising out of the billowing flames like a black tower, the Masked Death surveys the unleashed manifestation of its hellish malevolence with an abysmal and penetrating glare.

The fearsome display is impotent against Billy's blossoming resignation, for what potency is there in the threat of hell after being gang-raped by demons? A witch's brew of anger, repugnance, and resentment spills into his chest, resurrecting his resolve and stoking his want for vengeance.

The clanging of the tarnished sword against the hot flagstone antagonizes T. J.'s stupor as Charlie falls to his side, taxing his tattered brain. "I can't," he stammers, his voice hoarse and quivering as Billy kneels beside them. "I can't."

"You have to!" Vin hisses desperately, furiously resentful of the cowardice that exposes his own.

T. J.'s eyes open with wide and consuming dread. "There's only one thing waiting for us!"

"The professor didn't bring us here to die!" Billy insists, stinging sweat adding to the trail of tears on his burnished face.

A deep and resonant and horrible growl erupts from the palisades of flame in which the Masked Death looms to rattle the snowy soot and let fly the chariots of adrenaline in the veins of Ravenword.

Vin and Parson launch to their feet and scour the rolling flames with dire urgency for the embodiment of the thunder.

"I can't," T. J. cries, unable to perforate the boundaries of his surrender.

Charlie's fist tightens around the hilt of the sword as she pulls T. J. to his feet with a ferocity that defies her stature. "You *can't* do this to Motisha!"

The admonition breaches his mental barricades, his vitality revived by the rage pouring from Charlie's vehement glower.

A second malicious roar explodes from the inferno.

With an uncertain nod, the athlete turns to Billy. "Time to bleed."

Parson's intervening scalpel is punctuated by a hulking form stepping out of the margins of the blaze. A single eye, as red as Satan's hatred, bores into T. J. as his blood anoints the stone. Smog, black and roiling, spews spitefully from nostrils glowing like a stoked ember on a muzzle of fire. A vicious grin of bloodthirsty fangs gnashes teeth as hot and bright as molten iron.

Ravenword gasp and recoil in concert.

"Now what?" T. J. checks boldly.

"You'll know," Charlie growls, lifting the sword with eyes locked on the fiery beast.

Imbued with the inferno, its very mane wind-whipped flames, the werewolf that met its end in the ruined chapel seethes like a challenger glorified in hell. The atrocious monstrosity lifts its fiery head and disgorges a courage-shattering howl that scatters the company. Bounding like a demon loosed from hell, the charge of the attacking beast shakes the very stones, sending burning timbers and rubble raining down from the ceiling. With every thundering footfall of the combusting fiend, sparks and embers are dashed into the expanse and transform into smoldering scorpions with charred exoskeletons and glowing red joints as they fall against the flagstone.

T. J. stands boldly in the path of the pyroclastic beast with a heart grappling for faith and a brain praying for deliverance. As if in answer, an avalanche of debris crashes down on the monster, startling the bold athlete so violently that pain arches through his chest. A shower of embers fortifies the ranks of demonic arachnids and the fiery pattern burning through the flagstone in their wake.

The blazing beast erupts ferociously from the wreckage, roaring madly and batting away beams and rubble as Charlie broadsides the athlete. The sack throws him to the floor and out of reach. Charlie shifts her stance and, as Parson rushes in to pull T. J. from the fray, challenges the charging beast with the sword poised to strike.

The werewolf roars as it lunges for the diminutive champion.

Charlie does not falter, roaring back in contempt of all that has been set against her.

Claws forged in flames flex and widen as they sweep into the thrust of her unyielding sword.

Both claw and blade, however, are thwarted by an intervening plank spiraling from the ceiling.

The great arm of the fiery werewolf bats the beam in an explosion of arachnid embers, propelling it against Charlie's ribs and pinning her to the floor.

Harrowed by the dire consequences of Charlie taking up his mantle, T. J. rushes in with Parson and Vin on his heels.

With its prey in reach, the great infernal monster rears triumphantly with a vicious howl that crescendos over the roaring devastation. Its victory, however, is stilted by Billy's brazen call.

"Come and get it, motherfucker!"

The demon swings its great flaming bulk toward the herald, screaming with rage at the sight of the golden dagger brandished brazenly and gripped for a fight.

Crevices born of the pyro-active scorpions wind between Billy and the beast like defending motes. But even as the monster levels its horrible eye on the hero, those teeming minions turn to rush upon him and his friends.

T. J. and Vin steamroll the scurrying tide of scorpions with the rustic beam as Parson pulls Charlie clear.

Billy can feel the demonic werewolf's lust for the dagger as it charges. Dashing on mortal terror, his lungs are seared by the torrid air as they expel a wail so harrowing that it drowns out Parson's frantic calls. It is only when the rest of the company joins the concert that Billy can hear his plea.

"The backpack! Billy! Throw me the fucking backpack!"

Without thinking, Billy rolls the pack off his shoulders and slings it over the expanding crevices and across the gallery.

Parson rips into the bag to brandish the ancient case containing the dreadful relic. Dodging a falling timber, he knows the ceiling will not last much longer, and bellows at the monster.

Beyond the infernal werewolf's quivering rage, a pocket of serenity opens in the scorched atmosphere and calls to T. J.'s heart as it hollows a temperate pass to one of the recessed niches in the wall. Beneath the shelf an angelic figure beckons to him with hand outstretched.

"I see it! I see the way out!"

Terrible anticipation swells within the suspended moment. The five mark one another's positions.

The moment is shattered by Charlie's shout, driving T. J. from his hesitation. "Go!"

The great athlete bolts for the hidden passage, tasking all of his training to hurdle over blazing debris and ever-yawning chasms.

As the fiery monster pivots after him, Billy and Parson sweep toward Charlie.

Billy lands at her feet, but as Parson sails over a smoldering crevice, the demon deviates abruptly, its flaming claw belting him squarely out of the air.

Parson crashes amid the cries of his friends, burned and crushed, at the creeping edge of a chasm.

The ornate box tumbles across the flagstone.

The werewolf lunges for the relic.

Vin grapples up the box midstride like a fumbled football and flies to the ushering athlete with the seething beast at his back. As he is caught in T. J.'s strong arms, the men vanish into the orange flames.

Charlie and Billy gape as the thwarted monster screams, turning quickly to unleash its wrath on defenseless Parson.

Too stoked to heed the searing pain, Billy hurls a burning block at the beast as Charlie taunts it wildly with the sword.

● ● ●

"Go," T. J. insists, wrestling Vin through the fiery passage.

"Parson!"

"I'll get him! Just go!"

Vin's flight is thwarted by unrelenting flames. "I can't get in! I can't pass the fire without you!"

● ● ●

Baited by dagger and sword, the great monster thunders across the maze of hellish crevices.

With its savage intent focused on Billy and Charlie, T. J. sprints from the wall of flames to his charred and broken friend.

"Get ready to run," Charlie growls, her fierce eyes burning with rage and fixed on the charging monstrosity.

Billy's fists tighten, strangling the dagger, as blood primes his body.

The terrible and blazing beast lands before them in a spray of embers and a soul-shattering roar.

Undaunted, Charlie thrusts her long blade into the very chest of the beast.

"Now!"

As the monster shrieks, Billy flees.

Charlie dodges the defensive wipe of the enraged were-wolf and bites deep into its arms with the blade.

Billy's mind is filled with the sight of T. J. fleeing toward Vin with Parson in his arms and a desperate hope as the ceiling begins to fall, crashing down around them. T. J. disappears into the fire with Vin on his heels and, as Billy clears the last of the chasms, he follows his valiant friend to the margins of the protective enchantment.

"Charlie!" Billy cries.

T. J. rushes to the mouth of the pass, ushering Billy through before dashing back into the fray.

Charlie staggers, locked in battle with the beast. Her chest and face blistering gruesomely, her anguished eyes studying the flagstone floor crumbling into the chasm of fire like shingles from a roof.

"Charlie!" T. J. roars, rocketing to the edge of the burning crevice. "Come on!"

"Go!" she thunders.

"It's supposed to be me!" he cries.

"I'm changing the goddamn rules! Go!"

Charlie leans into her assault, memories of new love and summer and innocence fueling her rage and sacrifice.

Wooden waster swords crack loudly under the hot California sun.

"How do I know you're not cheating?" Agnot teases.

"Join the club and you'll find out."

Agnot retreats with a chortle. "Is this a date or recruitment?"

Charlie lowers her waster with a wry smile, Agnot's robust allure filling her eyes. "Don't you think we should have common interests?"

"Oh, we've got that covered."

"Outside of that!" Charlie laughs.

Agnot tosses her waster to the grass to wrap her arms around Charlie's waist.

The intimacy sends a thrill through her.

"I tell you what," Agnot whispers, teasing Charlie's lips. "You join Ravenword, and I'll join your Renaissance sword-play thing…"

Charlie surrenders to Agnot's magnetism, and the world around them falls.

Money and want and loneliness crash like a burning barn. Sparks fly like embers, and the lovers are swept into bliss on a kiss that lasts forever as an avalanche of cinder and flame swamps the howling monster and the raptured hero-ine in a fiery torrent.

T. J. dives for the enchanted passage, dragged into its shelter by his friends. Compounded grief pierces his heart like a quiver of failures and stuns his senses as they clamber for the alcove.

Above the roaring din of the inferno, the clear lungs of the brazen clock strike on a tenor deep and malignant that forces the men's harried minds into hellish acquiescence with its vile *clang*!

Scrambling into the mystical void of the niche behind his friends, T. J. finds Parson laid across Aldo's lap like a vision of the *Pieta*. Overwrought by his agonized writhing and their tragic loss, the three men fall at his side.

Leaning over Parson, Aldo's tear anoints his head. "Do not fear," he whispers, kissing his brow.

"Oh fuck," Parson moans, panting to stay conscious. "Now I know I'm a goner."

Aldo smiles down on him. "Do not fear, bello Parsone," he consoles, kissing Parson sweetly on the lips.

"How are you here?" Vin stammers through his grief, taking Parson's hand as he sets confounded eyes upon the noble Italian.

Aldo does not reply. Placing his hand between the flaps of Parson's open collar, he presses his palm against the chest of his wounded friend.

Clang!

Parson bucks, as if stung, as the void around them is consumed by fire.

"Do not fear," Aldo insists as the three men wrestle uneasily with Parson's anguish.

As the infernal compass fades, the noble Italian removes his hand, and the three men of Ravenword are astonished to find the symbol of the fifth scapular burned into Parson's chest.

Like a gentle angel, Aldo passes Parson to his friends and stands.

"You can't come with us?" Billy presses as the sensation of falling washes over them.

"Only the woman in blue can deliver me from limbo," he answers serenely.

Clang!

CHAPTER 15

The White Chamber

THE FOUR MEN OF RAVENWORD are delivered to an alabaster
floor on the gentle wings of that enchanted void. Tumbled
on grief, desolation, and translation, their harried senses
clear to reveal a white ballroom stretching out in a vast
expanse crystalized by a pristine and untainted atmosphere.
That imbued clarity relieves the bitter residue of loss and
purges the frailties of blame. Billy and Vin surrender to the
administration and languish on the cool stone to allow the
sublime balm to soothe the wounds of fire and spirit.

T. J., however, can find no such absolution. The death
of Charlie and the shame of his cowardice are unyielding
and parasitic accusers. His only hope of consolation, however impotent, lies in tending to Parson, who lies beside
him badly burned and panting in shallow breaths. Delirium
has taken him, and T. J. leans over to rest his palm against
Parson's blotched and beaded forehead.

The touch is cool and bolsters Parson's resistance to
the fever spreading in his veins. Even in his senselessness,

he sets his will against the infernal surrender usurping his consciousness.

Unnoticed, a great eternal presence vested with infinite understanding observes the Ravenword men in their reparation from beyond the cursed walls as if they were no more than silver veils. Colossal and austere, the archetype radiates omniscience from a golden celestial throne, robed in ruby glory that expands into an indigo cosmos. The right arm of the thrilling manifestation is absolute white with a hand laid over her heart and boasting fingers ringed with vitality and essence and grace set with dazzling stars. The left arm, mottled with disease and pestilence and the perversion of will, lies under the nurturing breast of the majestic elemental as if held restrained. The neck and fiercely beautiful face of the inspiration are pigmented in a deathly pallor but adorned with the green and variegated palette of life in the blush of the cheeks, the blossom of the lips, and the dressing of eyes that flash like molten gold and penetrate like a perfect symphony. Upon the exemplar's pallid forehead, an all-seeing star shines like a beacon of hope under the tree that grows from her fiery hair in branches both withered and blossoming to crown the paradigm with the paradox of mortality. Yet for all of her majesty, crude and heavy chains hang from her shackled wrists.

Contrasting the glorious visage, the Masked Death looms like a stark obsidian monolith at the opposing end of the pearlescent gallery reeking with the want to unleash its vile instruments.

As Vin's scars melt under the healing properties of the chamber, his heart heeds the glorious consideration resting upon them. He rises slowly with a trepid gaze and is rewarded by those radiant eyes. In a fumbling stupor, he taps T. J.'s arm. "Can you see it?"

Looking up from Parson, the athlete turns to meet the glorious annihilator of his preconceptions, which suddenly seem as counterfeit and cartoonish as the Order's bizarre medium. "What...what is that?"

The exclamation rouses Billy, whose curiosity is usurped by sudden and wild dismay. His scrambling fingers find the dagger secure in his belt, but nothing in their frantic search can find the wooden case in the smoldering backpack or their tangled huddle. The relic is gone! A profound and harrowing loss riddles his innards. The dreadful agitation, however, fades under those sublime aurelian irises as the imperious features turn to address the men with a voice like the singing wind, lovely and uncanny. "Be well and beware, sons of Life."

As the colossal criterion rises from her celestial throne to gaze down upon them through the airy ceiling, the rattling of the grimy chains mocks her splendor, yet they cannot suppress the wondrous and elusive familiarity imbued in the mighty cast.

Still, the three men shrink in terrible awe.

On the other side of the gallery, four huge ghouls bound from the nebulous shroud of the aphotic phantom on identic chains as if the Masked Death were dispatching a scourge for each man. On bent limbs and twisted bodies textured in frayed and weeping gashes, the gray and bloodless fiends scratch across the floor, leaching bile from fanged and tarry gouges that suck and gnash.

With their terrible advance, the chains of the great empyrean grow taut, and the three men of Ravenword grovel beneath her in desperation even as Parson begins to rouse.

His strength consumed by the fire of the scorpions, Parson squirms to face the starry beacon radiating from the colossal criterion with little fear of the monsters clawing their way to his feet.

Vin, cultivated in the rich mythologies of the subcontinent, knows no equal to the providence emanating from the demigod, and in his reverent cower, trusting that strength against the ghouls, risks understanding. "Who...who are you, Highness?"

"I am liberty, neither judge nor justice. By the mercy of my right hand, suffering is ended, and by the tyranny of my left, hope is cut short. Your entire world has been created and endures by my hand, yet I am loathed by all creatures. I am the eternal womb and the final breath," she answers as if taking pity on his ignorance, standing suddenly beside them with the bearing of a wizened queen. "I am beauty beyond comprehension and ugliness beyond madness."

Upon her fearful manifestation, the four horrible creatures are yanked on their chains, riddling the men with dread and relief and humility.

"In my bosom all must lie," she continues, striding toward the four enormous fiends before turning to set an austere gaze on the men. "I am thief, reaper, and recompense, but I am not your enemy."

As she walks, her chains tighten, and the four grotesques are dragged thrashing and choking back to the black wings of the Masked Death.

"Your enemy is the spawn of your imagination, the purgatory that stands between us, the Great Tormentor. He is my terrible consort, to whom mankind has wedded me," the noble exemplar declares, seemingly indifferent to their plight as she points spitefully to the aphotic phantom.

As if in obedience to an unspoken command, that black specter recedes to the deeper confines of each lurid ballroom.

"It is he who would destroy you and he who revels in the power you grant him. Yet that transference is inherent to your nature and even the bravest cannot escape the yielding. Not even I can circumvent that transaction, nor can I deliver you from his might, though I have dominion over even him."

Billy falls to his knees, exploiting the reprieve to check Parson as the ghouls test both chains and her command ferociously.

"I just need some sun…" Parson allays weakly, following his craving toward that nurturing light.

The goddess stares in stern and expectant majesty. "Does this not comfort you? Do you find no light in my exhortation?"

"Comfort?" T. J. scoffs brazenly, the profound insignificance of their plight seeping into his humiliated heart with more venom than the purple contagion.

"We fear oblivion," Vin interjects quickly, stricken by her fierce and sudden survey of T. J.

"Oblivion for many, translation for some, and rebirth for those with consciousness," she sings expansively as she swells to address the bold athlete. "You will need that courage, child, to know such heights."

"Do we not all have consciousness?" Vin interjects reverently, recognizing the root of all faiths and eager to glean as much as he can.

The great paradigm laughs, translating to human scale beside them. "Oh, man, how can you believe such a thing? Where is consciousness in the murderer, the warmonger, the soul that sees nothing in all that breathes but gain and exploitation? No, small one, such may be strong enough for translation, but none capacitate consciousness. It is the way of things, by their own choice, for all creation would perish if such were to propagate beyond the veil."

"I know who you are," Parson declares on labored breath, "and you are beautiful to me."

His address pleases the elemental vision, and she sweeps past Vin to answer his trembling and beseeching arm.

"Can you save me from his curse?" he pleads as she stands over him.

"None who find me on this defiled ground can escape his hold. Yet those blameless of his judgment may find the key to the prison door, and once opened, all may pass," she coos, suddenly face-to-face with the poisoned Parson. Her alabaster hands rise to caress his face, but the gesture is arrested as if remembering herself before translating to a stand with a stern tenor.

A pulse of enmity and fury from the aphotic citadel of Masked Death surges through the white gallery like a noxious concussion, and the lips of the great paradigm adopt a gratified curve. The illumination of her eyes sets upon stricken Parson like rain in the desert.

His mind is swallowed by those glorious irises and discovers within their warm solace the seven symbols scrolling around the sagacious pupils like sapphires cast in light. "That's why we're here!" Parson rants in terrible wonder. "That's why the professor brought us here! To open the door!"

Fear rages abruptly through the expanse in a seething spray of bile from outstretched wings of the Masked Death to slay both the revelation and the hope kindled in the hearts of the Ravenword men. The fierce and noble exemplar retreats in the fray, driving the villain's device into their souls to resurrect their anguish.

"No!" Parson bellows, reaching desperately past Vin and T. J. as they shield him against the onslaught with hearts drowning as the magnificent empyrean fades.

"Now what?" T. J. rages as Parson writhes to free himself.

Chains rattle in the obscuring tempest. A talon, gnarled and pale, sweeps out of the billows, grappling for prey.

The men tighten their ranks, yet Parson continues to crawl as though the terrible squall weren't swamping them with fear and blindness.

Billy recoils from a second attack as Parson's desperate fervor breaks over him. "Do you see it? Do you see the symbol?" he implores, grabbing Parson by the shoulders.

The vision of that marvelous empyrean upon her resplendent throne fills Parson's eyes. His soul sings as her luxurious lids bow, entreating him with the promise of passage as those lashes rise to display the symbol of the fifth scapular.

"I can go!" Parson exclaims above the tempest. "I can go with her!"

"Let him go!" Billy shouts, pulling away the hindering arms of their friends.

The storm parts to Parson's procession, even as the ghouls claw through its currents behind them. Billy and Vin and T. J. follow closely, the bold athlete guarding against the fiends.

The balm of honeyed mortality draws the fiery poison from Parson's veins with every blunted step toward the beam of amber light descending from a high and lavishing star. As if breathing in the very essence of life, he can feel vitality returning to him. "It's so beautiful. It's…"

"T. J.!" Vin and Billy cry in unison as Parson faints, the weight of his robust form dragging them to the floor.

The nightmarish hurricane closes in around them, silhouetting the ghouls on all sides.

Parson cries out suddenly, cut off from that draft of luminous vitality.

The great athlete scoops Parson's body into his arms and glares into the torrent.

The marred and defiled face of a ghoul lunges with a sneer.

T. J.'s heart thunders against his ribs.

The fiend presses the margin of the fray with dead, black eyes and claws grasping.

Fear saps the strength from T. J.'s legs, but anger refuels. He steps forward boldly, and the storm obeys, sweeping the ghouls out of his path. With Billy and Vin flanking him, T. J. rushes forward. He can feel Parson fading in his arms.

The three men are harrowed upon the white stone wall rushing out of the fog before them.

"No, no, no!" T. J. growls, enraged by the abandonment.

With the last of his strength, Parson pushes himself from the arms of the athlete.

As Billy and Vin try to break his fall, T. J. rotates in hopeless dismay as their doom closes in to take them.

Parson staggers to his feet with the blessed beam pouring through the veil. As it cascades into his heart, his very being explodes with illumination that washes over Billy, Vin, and T. J.

The friends stand dumbfounded by his revitalization and the glorious revelation of the elemental's wonderful grace.

Vin bows his head.

That marvelous mercy answers with a smile that sets Parson's spirit afire.

"I feel like a happily-ever-after!" He sighs blithely, untroubled by the confounded faces of his friends or the claws digging their way through the roiling barrier.

"So..." T. J. stammers, "you're okay?"

"Are you kidding me, dishalicious? I could give that delicate flower of yours a run for her money!" he laughs, his gaze drawn into the light.

"You always did," T. J. poses softly.

Parson's smiling eyes return to find Billy's welling. "What's the deal, will of steel?"

"Nothin'," Billy sniffles, wiping his nose with his sleeve. "Do you see it?"

"Yeah! It's up there!" Parson chimes. "I better get to it," he adds, nodding to the monsters pushing through.

"Yeah," Billy retorts, his voice breaking as irrepressible tears trace the frame of his face. "We don't have all day."

Parson's grin falters only slightly, and he reaches out to pull Billy into an embrace.

The thrilling warmth of bliss, however, cannot allay Billy's grief as he sinks into the farewell.

"We're going to get through this," Parson assures him gently, allowing his hold on Billy to linger. "And we'll be flying home before you know it."

Billy withdraws from the hug, nodding, but cannot bring himself to look Parson in the eyes.

"I've really got to go!" he insists, his wide smile untarnished as he pulls Vin and T. J. into brief and beautiful hugs.

Billy blubbers with miserable abandon as his friend is released to ascend into the column of golden light. Vin wraps his arm around Billy, and the three men watch the miraculous ascension.

The ascent ends upon the striking of a clock with a clear and loud and deep and exceedingly musical chime but of so peculiar a note and emphasis that it sends a disconcerting *clang!* rippling through even Parson's bliss. Before him a book lies on an emerald pedestal standing on the edge of a limitless and shimmering expanse.

Stepping up to the book, adorned with gold embossing and corner guards just like the one on his scapular, he turns the cover. Pages flutter through gemstone hues as if enchanted to settle on a violet aurora. That bejeweled eos starbursts into a vivid and consuming glory.

Clang!

CHAPTER 16

The Violet Chamber

THE AURORA RECEDES, REVEALING A ballroom cast in lurid violet and fermenting with a garish and dismal and raucous bacchanal of bloated ghouls costumed in tattered and mocking visages of the bizarre. Ravenword's final three recoil against the abrupt ugliness of the rage as the macabre jesters that ushered the company into the castellated nightmare entreat them with low and scurrilous bows. The men are stricken with shock and pity as the fiendish buffoons are no longer obscured in anonymity. The cadaverous faces of Fichtenberg and Romero grin wickedly beneath those grimy and tattered tapers of drab and opposing hues to steal the breath from their lungs and the heart from Vin's tenuous fortitude.

Billy shrugs off Vin's arm, his soul retreating into the numbing refuge of detachment, to read his stricken expression with shrewd eyes. Steeling his emotions from the pitiful relegation of his mentor and the baron, he grabs Vin's wrist and slides back his sleeve to lay bare the bronze forearm of the stricken Indian.

Vin's blanched face meets Billy's. "Parson had the knife!"

Billy squelches the cold sinking in his stomach by reaching for the golden dagger but is swiftly stayed by T. J.'s wary and astute hand.

Any thought of protest is waylaid by the abrupt and terrible appearance of Agnot's black-shrouded corpse like a rigored banshee. The apparition hammers the tenuous reconciliation of her terrible death from the bastions of their psyches like a blitzkrieg. The men quake and cower in a pitiful huddle under the harrowing as a grave and unnatural ethereum envelopes them in the spell of the curse. Ribbons of black tendrils radiate around the imposing corpse to cage them as the vile phantom extends a tarnished tray with cold white hands. Upon that dreary platter lie three ruthless stilettos stained with the allure of the darkest temptation.

Billy contemplates the chilling visitation with a mind harried by compounded loss and wearied by the consolation of reason. But a shred of reason remains a staving glimmer that rebuffs lure of the spell.

Vin's soul, stricken down as if the black phantom were a manifestation of his own desolation, pleads with Vishnu as the tainted blades whisper the promise of release from his consignment to this hell. Even as he turns away, the bewitching worms its way into his beleaguered consciousness.

T. J., however, still imbued with the fortification of the glorious empyrean, defies the ploy and strikes through his fear, sending the platter careening from the hands of the foul goad. The utensils of temptation clamor beneath the raucous din and, in a burst of spite, the shrouded specter vanishes as abruptly as it appeared.

"Fuck!" Billy bellows, shivering in the wake of an insidious foreboding.

"Keep it together, guys," the bold athlete rallies, shaking off the haunting and turning to Vin. "You okay?"

Even as the question falls from his lips, the answer is apparent. Vin is shrouded in a stupor and trembling with his dark and glassy gaze cast absently into the teeming throngs of grotesque revelers.

T. J. shakes him by the shoulders. "Don't do this, man."

Vin's face is awash with sudden soberness, and he looks to his friends with a reluctant cast. "Are we sure we need to draw blood?"

A terrifying hush falls over the revelers upon the crimson reference, seizing the men in their conspicuity as the entire crowd lifts flaring nostrils hungrily to scent the dank air. Left wanting, the dull and misshapen bacchants descend back into the mad Saturnalia with heavy, exaggerated features contorted into vicious and cankered grins.

Like momentum in a nightmare, the gruesome assembly of damned souls swallows the men, pressing them on all sides and drowning their senses in the roar and rank and gaud of their festive torment. Aspects painted and powdered and rouged according to the convention of their bizarre and dingy costume shriek and bellow in mad gaiety. Their wildly dressed eyes, which strike as disturbingly small and dull for their enormous aspects, dismiss the jostled little men with disdain. Black wine sloshes from tarnished goblets in the rambling current of bodies to dribble over spidery fingers tipped with long and needlely nails. Towering above them all, the great and dreadful Masked Death surveys the churning horde like a beacon of manic fear.

With a terrible yelp, Vin is grappling for his friends. But before they can react, he is pulled between two jeering revelers and consumed by the fray.

As if swamped by a suffocating riptide, Vin paws for an anchor as the crush of revelers sweeping through the heart of the ghastly gallery threatens to trample him. His head spins under the kaleidoscopic torrent of debauches seething with needle-toothed grins, molestations, and twisting heads. The disorientation of his dizzy brain unhinges the margins of mind. Mania, dank and bizarre, seeps like brine through the planks of a sea-battered boat. His throat opens to unleash a delirious bray but is choked suddenly by Parson's face in the carnal tempest.

Vin's heels dig into the flagstone, and the entire party seizes with his arrest.

Staring under the queer stillness, his bulging and unblinking eyes scour the vile crowds until they are drawn to movement overhead.

From the inky heights of the foul chamber, Agnot's shrouded corpse descends like icy madness. With tray in hand, it alights before him to proffer the three stilettos with a cold and splayed and ravaged glare.

Within the suspended moment, those blades gleam with longing and rest.

The trickle of mad liberation poisoning his mind coaxes his reluctant hand.

"Vin! No!"

The cry pulls him from the spell. Yet just as his eyes find T. J. waving over the crowd, the crushing reanimation of the frenetic and depraved waltz recaptures him with terrifying might.

T. J. shouts with dismay from atop a drab banquet table as Vin is lost in the crowds circling the center of the gallery like roiling masses of an unholy Mecca. His frantic gaze fixes on Billy, who stands likewise across the chamber. "Can you see him?"

Nodding fervently, Billy points into the vile orgy.

"Don't lose him!"

The pace of the wild dance quickens and, with it, the comfortable surrender spreading through Vin's soul. Soon he is flying hand in hand with his fellow celebrants on fleet feet and carefree. Absurd abandon opens his throat, but his untamed crow is translated quickly to a scream as his gay glance finds Charlie, charred and blistered and beaten, leading him by the hand.

His howl brings the revelry, again, to a standstill.

His crazed abandon is shattered as he yanks his hand away, pulling the arm from the burned remains of his friend. Before his gaping eyes, she crumbles to dust and from the swirling black plume steps the shrouded corpse with tray in hand.

Vin's beleaguered brain swoons wearily between terror and madness. Something in the depths of his instincts refuses to relent even in the face of so sweet a peace at the point of the thin daggers. Misery and loathing moans from his chest. Over the delirium droning in his head, Billy's voice is shouting, "There! There! There!"

Climbing furiously between the suspended trolls, T. J. clambers desperately under Billy's perched direction.

"Fuck, fuck, fuck!" Billy bleats anxiously as Vin reaches for a knife. His gaze pivots to T. J., who will never reach him in time. Wild with dread, he paces, panning the chamber for means.

Vin watches his own fingers caress the silver lace rim of the tray, drinking in the cold comfort like an aperitif.

A blind and sudden blow to the neck slaps his consciousness. Pain wrings a gasp and prods Vin's heart, the rush of blood and adrenaline clears his head as a wine bottle shatters at his feet and second smashes against the tray of temptation. As the wine bottle crashes onto the flagstone, the shrouded agent of the curse flies angrily into the stygian heights. Before Vin can recover, however, the frenzy is reignited, and he is once again swallowed up.

Caught within the sudden surge and press of the decadent throngs, T. J. taxes his strength and agility to keep his feet in pursuit of his imperiled friend. Pushing through thick and fetid limbs, he wrestles his way deeper into the heart of the carnal vortex. A soul-shattering shrieking rises over the ruckus as if the spiteful curse were giving voice to T. J.'s desperation, and his eyes catch sight of Vin, who stumbles into the terrible eye of the ghoulish hurricane.

His languid eyes sharpen and bulge at the sight that greets him in that hollow, and he bites into his knuckles through an abject scream as the despicable bacchants surrounding him jeer at the gruesome spectacle at the heart of the craven party.

The revenant of a corpse, mottled and diseased, with the face and form of Julia, writhes on the filthy floor, laughing through screams from a gaping and bloody mouth. Her legs are spread, and between them heinous fiends rupture one after the other from a raw and gory cavity as if she had been gutted by some nightmarish ripper. With each atrocious birth, the encompassing ghouls expel a vicious, "Huzzah!"

Vin's sanity breaks from his consciousness, sliding away like an avalanche. His fist pulls at his jet-black mane as crimson dribbles from the fist clenched in his own teeth.

Beside him, the stilettoes sing a promise of final peace on the entreating wings of the black-shrouded corpse.

Reduced to mad and gibbering sobs, the chamber spins on his surrender.

The tortured eyes of the specter, bloodshot and cloudy, mark him in the margins, and the phantasm of Julia lifts a twisting hand on a pleading scream.

"Huzzah!" crashes from the leering sea of ghouls as Vin lunges for the waiting tray.

A force stronger than his despair catches his reckless reach.

The brume of torment clears, and Vin finds himself contending with T. J.'s iron grip.

"Not for me..." Vin sobs, turning a wincing glance to the vile abomination.

T. J.'s reluctant eyes follow his gaze and, as the piteous horror softens his grasp, Vin heaves.

"No!" Billy shouts, breaking through the mocking crowds just as Vin's hand gobbles up one of the three stilettoes.

To their horror the angel's dagger appears on the tray in place of the stiletto.

As fast as reflex, T. J.'s grabs for the golden hilt as Vin flies to the aberration of Julia with the blade poised to vanquish.

Yet as soon as T. J.'s fist lays hold of the golden dagger, the flight of the enchanted stiletto in Vin's desperate grip lunges for a new target, arresting his momentum.

T. J., thrown onto his back by the black explosion of spectral abandon, grips the hilt of the golden dagger as if it the very source of life.

The dagger pulls away from the athlete's grip as a horrified Vin wrestles against the stiletto his helpless hands cannot discard as it burrows through his strength toward his chest.

"Huzzah!"

Billy bolts to T. J.'s side, patting and shaking him triumphantly even as the heinous ghoul of Agnot's corpse coalesces from the darkness around Vin.

Stooping with cruel and mocking fascination, the abomination leans its shrouded face close to his chest as if to relish the piercing. Inches from the trembling fists straining to keep the steel at bay, the fiend cocks its head, eager for the revelation with giddy malevolence.

The point of the spiteful steel pierces Vin's noble breast, and a soft and horrible gasp falls from his lips as it sinks into his chest.

Seized by the stench of fresh blood, the entire host of depraved bacchants recoils as if from a damning contagion and escapes suddenly into the shadows clinging to recesses of the chamber.

The triumph of T. J. and Billy turns to ashes with the gruesome thud of Vin's body, the knife protruding from his blood-sopped breast like a demented calling card. The two descend on him as the dark truth burgeons over their fallow souls with the heavy price of their victory. With forlorn gentleness, T. J. gathers Vin into his arms as Billy takes the handle in hand and pulls the blade from its mortal sheath.

"The mark..." Vin chokes, his eyes lolling horribly. "Before...it's...too...late..."

T. J. nods at Billy, whose tears cannot be repressed, and the symbol of the sixth scapular is quickly etched into the hand of their dying friend.

"Up," he wheezes.

The bereft athlete obeys, propping him gently.

Peering through the darkness clouding his sight, Vin uses the last of his life to confirm the escape of his friends.

The gloom and grime of the rancid bacchanal evaporates, and Vin finds himself standing amid the luminous splendor of the castellated abbey's original glory before it was tainted by Prospero's mad inventions. The priest, who had relegated himself to the office of spectral sentinel, opens his arms in welcome even as Vin's own voice resounds through the high arches over that ill-chimed and brazen clock.

"The hope in life continues."

CHAPTER 17

The Black Chamber

THE BLACK AND FINAL BALLROOM greets Billy and T. J. like the consummation of their anguish, forcing them to their knees with fingers aching to gouge out their own eyes. Howls, squeezed from their stricken bodies, bloat and vein their contorted features as they swoon amid enormous pedestals that line the black walls in hateful derision of the ruined chapel.

Upon those broad marble biers, the ravaged and mocking caricatures of their murdered friends personify the bizarre statues of the devastated sanctuary like grotesque trophies. The garish glare of crimson glass deepens the violent pallette of the compounded hell and casts the scowling face of the great spectral clock in the likeness of a blood moon as it hangs suspended between those ill panes. In the murky depths at the end of the colonnade of horrors, the Masked Death lords over like a calculating empyrean.

A hideous clang from the wicked clock is answered by a shriek that wrenches their attention to the exalted defamation of Julia behind them. Her disease-riddled belly is swollen with nightmarish anticipation as she writhes in the wings of three demonic bacchants impersonating the angels from the chapel desecration. Her face is a contagion-mottled mask of vile agony and dread and rage with eyes bloodshot and seething.

The men's miserable brays are stunned by a discovery that sets them scrambling to their uncertain feet: the gaping threshold to the previous gallery.

Billy and T. J. ogle the portal like desert castaways upon an oasis, desperate for the promise but suspicious of mirage. The lurid tenor of the violet ballroom is faded with ruin and devoid of chimeric revelers. Both men chafe under instinctive restraint in the face of so liberal an escape, for the doors that had sealed them in each of the malevolent ballrooms have long since rotted from their tracks, revealing chamber after chamber into the depths.

T. J. starts with abandon but is seized by Billy, who returns his burnished glare with a nod to the body of Vin lying in a pool of his own blood amid the skeletal vestiges of carnal debris strewn throughout the deep ruins.

The reminder is arresting, and T. J. backs away from the threshold with a furtive and wincing confirmation to the tortured doppelganger of Vin hanging horridly crucified upside down atop a pedestal in the black chamber.

A second hideous *clang!* sets their nerves on edge like Pavlovian minions and lashes their want to flee.

T. J. begins to pace, his harried thoughts flying beyond the boundaries of the curse to Motisha.

Billy gives way warily, bracing for the inevitable and delineating climax.

Exorcising the rending, T. J. disgorges a primal roar that raises the last shred of courage from the tomb of his broken heart.

• • •

A dark and woeful resonance reverberates through Motisha's heart even as gunmetal clouds overshadow the streets and wipes the smile from her features.

"I cannot tell you how happy I am that you called!" Coquette gushes absently as she and Motisha rise from the idling Mercedes to the welcoming facades of Via della Spig. "Meetings, meetings, meetings! J'en ai marre! One would think designers might want to spend their time with color, texture, fabric, and other gorgeous things. But I have had enough of that, as well as you, eh? Oh! What is it, mon amie? You look dreadful!"

Motisha bristles under the observation and shakes off the ominous bane as the entrance to Fendi anticipates them with a wide greeting. "Not a thing," she declares with an untainted grin. "And, as my luggage has yet to return from Monaco, I could do with some shopping."

"How can I believe that you did not break even a heel jumping from the train west!" Coquette trumpets as she ushers Motisha into the emporium.

Motisha's laughter as they enter is subdued by the play of Coquette's fingers on the ruby teardrop that had engendered their friendship. "Is something wrong?"

Catching herself, Coquette replies with a smile of resignation. "With so many deadlines, there is always something wrong. But we shall not allow such things to ruin our afternoon together. I've not much time and have been simply dying to show you this dress!"

• • •

Billy risks assessing T. J., whose reduction finds him bowed on his knees with a fist marking the ebony marble like an anchor. His head is likewise bowed and face shrouded in the darkness.

"You here?"

A tear anoints the paver with a ringlet at the tolling of another terrible *clang!* T. J. rises like a giant against the preternatural chill spreading from the aphotic wings of the Masked Death to permeate the black ballroom in a frigid hush.

Billy checks him with a resolute nod as silence is fractured by an unnerving rustle.

As if to test their newfound resolve, the carcasses of Prospero's thousand dead nobles are resurrected in their damnation from the very flagstone where they fell to the red death. Like devices from a horror movie, they lurch and pivot with baleful intent to set upon the men.

"Shit!" Slapping Billy's shoulder, T. J. bolts to the margins of the threshold and wrestles the great panel door out of its niche. The cragged and dusty panels protest and buck, but their reluctance is no match for the fear-fueled power of the athlete as they are pulled from their enchanted atrophy and dragged shut against the macabre onslaught.

"It'll buy us a few seconds," T. J. sighs with resignation.

Cacophonous shrieks crash against the buttresses of their fortitude as the gruesome avatars of Ravenword in torment answer the third jarring *clang!* of the insidious clock with a harrowing din.

Recovering quickly, Billy starts and shakes the ragged rucksack from his back.

T. J. puts his ear to the ancient wood before turning to find Billy digging a book out of the pack.

"Are you going to read them to death?"

Billy rebukes him with a glare, breaking both the spine of his limited-edition hardbound of *The Castle of Otranto* and his heart. "You're strong, right?" he growls, ripping the back cover from the treasure and handing it to T. J. petulantly. "Fold it—twice if you can!"

T. J.'s stall evaporates as Billy presses the hard binding of the front cover over itself.

"Here!" T. J. barks, forcing the cover into a second fold swiftly and pounding it underneath the panel door.

Billy hands him the other makeshift doorstop and tests the stubborn slider as T. J. wedges the second into the seam.

"They won't budge easy!"

"Yeah, out of the frying pan…" Billy quips darkly as they turn to face the doom of the black ballroom.

Bones clawing against grain play hideously on their ears as the sabotaged panels begin to rumble against the barrage of desperate and desiccated hands.

"Now what?"

Cringing under Julia's labored screeches, the men brace themselves against the stirring of some nebulous form at the heart of the stygian chamber. The oppressive madness of the ensuing wailing from the bloody sacrifices is deflected by a spark in Billy's brain that sends him diving for the ruined and discarded book.

T. J. falls upon him with rapacious hope as Billy's fingers rifle through the harried pages of the archaic novel. Seizing on the creased manuscript fragment from Fichtenberg's novel, Billy sharpens and the two men rise through the swamping screams with new purpose.

All is subdued, however, by a resonant and disembodied voice that evokes a dire recollection from T. J.'s harried memory and a temblor of invidious spite from the monolithic Masked Death.

"Dance with me."

• • •

Flanked by a petite Fendi associate, Coquette leads Motisha past racks of little black dresses to a prominently displayed powder-blue fifties revival sundress accented with a navy sash.

"Now tell me you would not look gorgeous in this!" Coquette challenges playfully.

The charming dress fills Motisha's eyes with delight, but a shimmer of hesitancy provokes Coquette to press her.

"Do not tell me you do not like it?"

Motisha demurs graciously, taking Coquette by the hand. "It's lovely. But I'm not sure that I can justify the expense."

Coquette smirks jovially, waving away her pragmatism. "Don't be ridiculous!" she declares, nodding to the associate. "We are women of means, are we not?"

● ● ●

Riveted to the stirring in the shadows, T. J. hangs on terrible anticipation for the confirmation of his fear as Billy unfolds the composition against the terrible intrigue. The garish crimson light falls upon the parchment in welling hues that cast the text with sinister significance, and Billy curses himself for not salvaging his book light.

T. J.'s chest thunders like an engine as the manifestation reaches fruition.

A withered and maculated cadaver garbed in tattered and moldy rags staggers from the murk and into the garish crimson rays with reaching and grasping claws as if released from the grip of Death.

T. J. gasps!

The exclamation jolts Billy from the pages to focus on the rotted corpse with new understanding. With the designs of fate coalescing in his brain, he looks to T. J. with a face as white and wan and withering as the mask of Death itself.

Like the pummeling of Vin's door on the day the invitations arrived, the panel doors quake and thunder feverishly, as if the dead were desperate to be reunited with the approaching corpse.

The ghoul, mottled and tattered with the festering of centuries, presents itself, sending T. J.'s sanity grappling against a nightmare from which he cannot wake. His tormented eyes find no rest as the agony of his ensnared friends, the slash of crimson in the hemming blackness, and the hideous ghoul dominate his every glance.

"Dance with me."

• • •

Motisha admires the reflection of the blue summer dress flattering her figure as the door of the fitting room closes behind her, and Coquette stands next to her assessing her happily.

"It fits you like couture!" she sings while running the pendant along its gold chain absently.

"I do like it," Motisha beams. "I think it's a justifiable extravagance."

"Of course it is," Coquette retorts, her demeanor clouding.

"What is it?" Motisha presses, her smile fading as she searches Coquette's eyes.

With the pendant cradled in her fingers, the young Frenchwoman takes Motisha's hand and gazes into the mirror. "Life is so beautiful."

A solemnity that seems to dim the very light descends and subdues the looking glass as Coquette continues, "Yet so often people cannot see the principals who make it so."

As she speaks, their reflection fades and the glass is haunted by images of T. J. striding through a narrow street with an elderly maven, a handsome young Italian man, and a ghostly priest in a hall of statues.

"How are you doing this?"

The scene changes to a stark and grim castle as Coquette continues in a low and hypnotic tone. "But there are also agents of fear. Your noble beau and American friends are in the grip of such agents."

Horrified and dumbstruck by the images of Ravenword in torment, Motisha glares at the woman, "What the hell is this? What are you?"

To her surprise, Coquette laughs with unsettling liberty. "I am no spirit, mon amie. I, and many others, work to see that evil things done are undone."

Darkness overtakes the looking glass, and from the recesses, a figure masked with an ancient porcelain face wrought in the very likeness of a crimson-speckled victim of the red death emerges. The apparition turns that horrible countenance on Motisha fully to curdle her blood as it extends its hand.

"You must go to him!"

"You're mad!"

"Motisha—"

"I have no intention of being some Alice in horrorland!" she spurns breathlessly, storming the door.

"Stop!"

The grave and virile tenor of Coquette's command is like an ocean tide drawing unmined courage from the depths of Motisha's soul.

"Without you they will perish there in that damnable castle."

Pursing her lips against her own foolishness, Motisha turns slowly. "What are you talking about? What have I got that can save anybody?"

The vixen gestures to the bidding mirror and then to the blue sash decorating Motisha's waist. "Life, ma cherie, life."

"How? I haven't even told Terrence!" Motisha stammers rashly, an avalanche of suspicions plummeting through her harrowed soul.

Imbued with a sudden luminous grace Coquette takes her hands and, with eyes that peer into the very heart of Motisha, calls to her soul. "It is time to stoke the fire that has kept you strong for so long, ma cherie. Stoke it into a torrent of faith! Nothing can harm you. That is no ghoul, but only your guide. You are the salvation of so many. If you refuse, you will be their ruin and your own. Your heart will shrivel into dry bitterness and torment that will plague your whole life long."

With her heart drumming in her ears, Motisha hesitates. Her fierce and furious intellect thrashes against the overwhelming depths of the spell as if drowning in a cerulean gulf. Yet the fire that was captured and tamed and saved by the love of Terrence Elders flares like a beacon, which points to the appalling specter in the glass. Helpless against the call of her touchstone, Motisha succumbs to the spell and allows the young woman to usher her before the mirror where the figure in the gruesome mask bids. The last thrill of fear rushes through her, and she turns in the dizzying shower for a final draft of grace, only to discover herself swallowed in vast darkness, her hand caught by that of her masked guide.

● ● ●

Transfixed by the entreating cadaver, T. J. is deafened by a profound silence to all but her lure as if suspended in the eye of a curse's horrific hurricane. His mind sinks into a coldness reflective of death's creeping hold until it also lies quiet with only the rhythm of his heart remaining. In that grounding pulse is love, courage, faith, and a guide that ushers him into the arms of the putrid corpse. Without revulsion, he takes her bony waist in hand while clasping the fleshless claw and, as the pulse of a profane and distant melody cankers into a discordant symphony, sweeps her into an enchanted waltz.

As Billy turns to face the horrors of the Masked Death's affectations, the panel doors begin to splinter under the assault of the damned and the ghostly lungs of the hateful clock bray with a clear and abhorrent chime.

Clang!

The hideous imitation of Julia howls as a vile and gaping cavity yawns between her legs like an open sore oozing bile and venom in anticipation of the horror ripping itself from her ravaged form, and Billy taxes all of his discipline to subdue a terrible curiosity. Yet upon her monstrous labor, his eyes cannot avoid the execution of the Ravenword trophies in kind.

Amid a riot of screaming, heads are sliced horridly from shoulders, tumbling off the enormous biers with a sick and heavy clamor. Crude clubs and stones viciously pummel the blood and bone from Parson and Vin's ravaged bodies, and a salvo of hot desert bullets riddles the diseased and broken brawn of Grayson. The wounds explode in a rain of gore and blood that spackle Billy in his tepid advance, permeating the fetid air with the stench of carnage quickly insinuated with burning flesh.

Despite his shrewd and calculating understanding, Billy is helpless against his own instincts as the decapitated bodies of Fichtenberg and Romero fly from their shared pedestal to snare him. To his shame, a pitiful squeal erupts from his throat as the two carnal fountains of blood grab his arms and force him forward. His boots backpedal wildly through the sanguine slick as the remaining Ravenword ghouls sweep through the air to rush upon T. J. and his decayed partner like macabre puppets on the strings of that great and looming masked specter.

● ● ●

Sinking ever deeper into the embrace of her guide, Motisha dances through the void on the ill-set tempo of a distant and unsettling melody. But with the increasing warmth of his embrace, that erroneous symphony grows closer and more harmonious. Even the mask, which had seemed so ghastly, softens with her growing trust. Soon Motisha finds something blooming in her heart, melting away the illusion of inferiority and soothing the stinging wounds of her father's indifference. A smile, artless and genuine, breaks over her countenance to apply a beauty more flawless than any found in the salons of Milan.

• • •

Likewise enchanted, T. J.'s microcosm is unscathed by the legion of the Red Damned pouring in from the breached threshold. As he and the uncanny corpse sail across the floor, the dead surround them like a barricade and defend them from the rush of the Ravenword ghouls.

Tight in the clutches of the duplicitous and headless hosts, Billy evokes memories of his parents to ground and tame the imminent betrayal of the insulating apathy that has served him so well. His stare hardens even as the wings of the aphotic phantom plume beneath the hideous mask to reveal a rough and bloodied wheel, rimmed with eager spikes, awaiting him at the feet of that cold, looming visage. As if to unseat his resolve further, the ghoulish black and shrouded cadaver of Agnot beckons to Billy from beside the abominable Catherine wheel like the immutable voice of fate.

The ranks of the Red Damned overwhelm the Ravenword ghouls and spill deeper into the black chamber until momentum sends them charging the specter of the

Masked Death with brazen fury. With a frigid pulse from the black wings of that hideous strength, the floor beneath the scowling clock collapses to bar the onslaught. As the dead sweep past the headless snatchers, Billy uses their own impetus against them by heaving his substantial weight forward abruptly.

Slipping from the blood-slick grip of the decapitated, he closes his eyes against the unforgiving stone striking his hands and knees. His shuttered sight is impressed indelibly by that terrible mask. Within the death pallor of that vision, the fear and horror of his parents' agony turns back the clock. In the throes of their terrible passing, that mask hangs unseen over his soul to inundate his mind with all the fears of a child facing abandonment.

Billy shudders under the culmination of the haunting. His anguish at their ultimate end screams to a harrowing climax before being wiped away even in the face of such profound loss by the liberation of release and a glimpse of that merciful and wondrous Empyrean.

In that instant, the mask of fear usurping his mind shatters.

Billy lifts steely eyes to glare across the gulf.

Behind him the bloody wraiths grapple after him as the hapless damned hurtle headlong into a great chasm.

On the might of Ravenword's valor, Billy bolts toward the smoldering precipice.

A voice rises in his heart in the tenor of Charlie, as he gauges the swing of the pendulum.

On Parson's cue, he leaps.

The fiery chasm yawns beneath him and the pendulum swings to meet him.

His arms slap around the crushing counterweight, and it is on Agnot's gruff admonition that his grip does not falter.

The pendulum yields to the force of his momentum and delivers him to the other side of the gulf on Julia's happy squeal.

Billy tumbles to the ebony flagstone before the timber of his impending crucifixion and the looming masked specter retreats swiftly into the roiling billows of its stygian wings.

Billy rises, spitting contempt, as the black-shrouded ghoul of Agnot's monstrous imposter rushes upon him.

The golden dagger sings from its makeshift sheath as he turns on the fiend.

As if caught by the luminous rays of morning, the phantom shrinks from the brandishing.

With a blast from within its inky ethereum, the Masked Death strips the craven fiend of the death shroud to force the entirety of the ghoul's fetid gore and rancor against Billy's courage.

Billy deflects the stench and horror of the corpse laid bare with a hand over his gasp, but he does not falter.

The wheel behind him creaks with anticipation.

● ● ●

The symphony carries Motisha to the peaks of harmony as she sweeps through the void in the arms of her strange suitor. Yet with each sway, his elusive familiarity increases his allure until she is convinced that those lovely eyes behind the mask can be set free only by a fairy-tale kiss.

• • •

The truth of T. J.'s vision grows increasingly impotent against the spell of Beauty, leaving his heart blind to the hideousness of her condition. Drawing her withered and exsiccated face into his, he can feel her intent as her bony hand presses against the back of his neck.

• • •

The grotesque carcass presses its advantage until Billy's calves meet the stinging grain of the fetid spikes.

With eyes fixed and calculating, Billy lunges at the ghoul with blade poised.

The corpse dodges before charging him with an unbridled riposte.

Billy pivots abruptly, and the foul puppet of their tormentor careens into the Catherine wheel, and he drives the singing dagger through the neck of ghoulish cadaver, pinning it to its fate. A harrowing thrill rifles through him as his victory brings him face-to-face with the invidious buttresses of the masked villain under the shrieking exorcism of the wraith.

Clang!

The ethereum of pitch and spite churns, but the architect of their torment remains hidden.

Brazen and unflinching, Billy yanks the dagger free and wills the devil forth.

The mask emerges from the ebony veils as if disembodied, setting all its devices against him.

The visage of a stiffened corpse with all the features of the scarlet horror of Poe's avatar challenges the defenses of Billy's courage.

He does not yield.

Matted blood and weeping blisters and cracking burns and breathing tubes resurrected from his madhouse of memories pry at Billy's fortitude.

His eyes sting with tears, but even with his defenses breached, Billy steps forward.

The pallid and blood-speckled Masked Death stares coldly upon his advance.

Billy ascends the steps of the black rampart with the dagger clenched tightly in his trembling hand and a heart pummeling against his ribcage. Trusting the powers that have wrought the means of redemption in the face damnation, he kneels before the great and terrible incubus in submission to his fate.

● ● ●

"It's okay to go," Billy chokes amid the machines and monitors and tubes surrounding the frailty inflicted on his mother.

Hovering over her, he kisses her scarlet forehead. "It's okay to go…"

In answer, the monitors fall silent.

In that moment his world shatters, only to be resurrected like a wreckage with alarms and rushing footfalls.

• • •

The black wings of the Masked Death close around him.

• • •

Surrendering to her guide, Motisha presses her lips against the white lips of the warm porcelain.

• • •

T. J. closes his eyes and presses his lips against the dry and rank and filthy mouth.

• • •

Caught in Billy's ploy, the Masked Death explodes with fury at the kiss, spewing malevolence and terror from those atramentous wings like a deluge of black lightning as the Red Damned succeed in making contact with liberating life!

Martyred Ravenword scream, and the noble damned cower.

Billy springs, thrusting the dagger into the very heart of their stygian nemesis!

Hatred and terror and despair and grief scream on black consumption, only to evaporate in the hemorrhaging power of the curse.

At Death's threshold, Billy straightens and reaches, joining the phantom's scream as he takes the horrible mask in hand.

Repulsed by the rage of the specter, Billy's grasp does not fail, and he rips the mask from the animus of fear as he is cast to the chasm by its final and vengeful strike.

Beneath the shock wave of truth that strips the curse from the surrounding castle, Billy watches the fiery abyss yawn wide to swallow him.

CHAPTER 18

The Eighth Chamber

UNMASKED, THE MERCILESS HOLD OF the spiteful tormentor is broken and the black damnation of the curse lifts like a murder of ravens taking wing.

Falling amid the transformation, Billy's heart swells with bittersweet gratitude. His reluctant descent, however, is interrupted by a sudden strength. Cold stone slaps his back as his confused brain recalls his eyes to duty. To his astonishment, the noble Italian is panting over him.

With an extended hand, Aldo brings Billy to his feet with a warmth and joy that he has never known. Before he can resist, the Italian is crushing him in an embrace.

From over Aldo's shoulder, Billy is astounded to discover Motisha in T. J.'s arms, radiant and imbued with joy.

"You're the woman in blue?"

Motisha's laugh is like music in the open air.

T. J., still stunned by the transformation of his macabre partner into his beloved, interrupts her with a gasp and a rapturous kiss.

Beside them, the Lady in Blue stands flush with the suppleness of youth and loveliness with Prince Prospero at her side. The thousand restored nobles rise into the air around them.

Motisha looks to Beauty and takes her hand.

As their spirits mingled in the moment of translation, each woman knew the other completely and, in that knowing, set the other free. In the radiance of freedom, unbridled joy breaks over the company, redeeming the castellated abbey in cheers and weeping and embraces.

As the pastel pink of the Venus belt blushes the horizon, Prospero and Beauty and the thousand nobles ascend finally into the gossamer brush of those glorious beams and to their rest. With the curtain raised, the spirits of Ravenword are left to their farewell.

The discovery of their liberated friends catches Motisha's breath, and Billy and T. J. join her in sweeping across the gallery. Beside the Ravenword martyrs, Fichtenberg and Romero and Grayson and the chapel priest, who remained true to his vow, follow the imperial translation into the blushing dome.

With countenances beaming with love and gratitude, Julia and Parson and Agnot and Charlie and Vin join hands. Resolution, peace, and warmth crown the celestial company, who in turn impart those healing stars to the grief of their beloved friends. As the belt of the sun's rise deepens to a ruby hue, Ravenword catches sight of that great and merciful Empyrean filling the expansive morning sky. The visage is fleeting, and with her majestic translation, the honored dead of Ravenword are raptured on her grace.

THE END

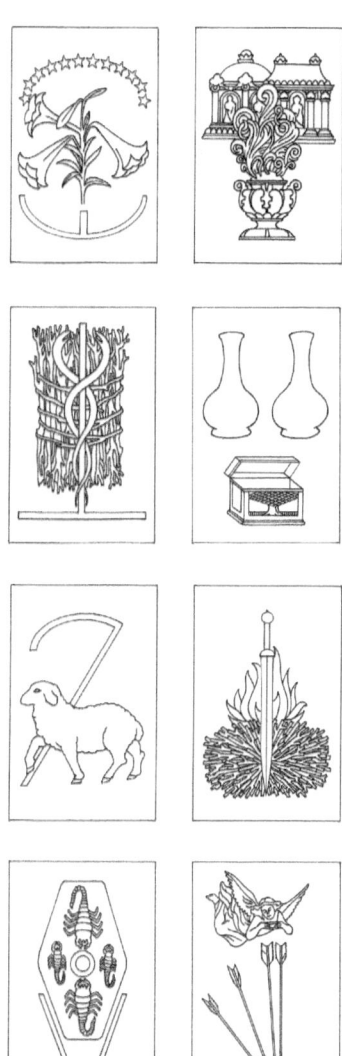

seejane.org

NOH8campaign.com

blacklivesmatter.com

earthjustice.org

GLAAD.org

ABOUT THE AUTHOR

FROM AN EARLY AGE, JUSTIN Greenway displayed surprising creativity and dreamed of pursuing a life as an artist. That aspiration shifted in elementary school after a creative-writing assignment brought his talent for writing to the forefront with accolades. By his early teens, he was a staff writer for the school paper and began his first attempts at writing a novel. After he convinced his mother to type his handwritten manuscript, his motivation to be an author was spurred when he overheard her marvel to his grandmother that he "wrote like a real writer." Soon, however, any literary indulgences were waylaid by the death of his mother when he was fifteen, followed by the death of his father a year later.

At sixteen Justin found himself reluctantly emancipated and thrust into the turmoil of adult life. His only remaining outlet for writing was as editor of his high school newspaper his sophomore and junior years. Traumatized and struggling to navigate premature adulthood without a support system, he wandered in hopes of finding his place in the world. Settling in the Sacramento area in his mid-twenties, he began to gain a foothold and wrote his first novel, a primordial fantasy. Although publishing wasn't a goal, the endeavor solidified his ability to start and finish a project. As his life began to normalize, he began working on a science-fiction novel that became the focus of his aspirations. Soon he was a young thirtysomething homeowner toying with side projects and writing exercises to clean the palate of his muse. One particularly stormy morning, he sat down to capture the ferocity of the inclement weather, and the result was the opening scene of what was to become *Ravenword and The House of the Red Death*. The draft, however, languished on his hard drive in favor of his penchant for science fiction. In 2004 his desire to stretch himself resulted in his writing a screenplay for a sequel to *Star Trek: Nemesis* that garnered an invitation to Paramount Studios. Although optioning the screenplay was not conducive with the plans for the franchise, the sophomore success fired his motivation, and he refocused his efforts on his own science-fiction story. Trying to write while pursuing a career impeded his progress, but he steadily chipped away at the story, insulated by a sense of comfortable stability. The ravaging of the Great Recession, however, changed everything.

In the aftermath, Justin found himself among the millions who had lost everything, and renting his best friend's mother-in-law cottage. It is here that the story that began with the stormy morning years earlier sprouted from his hard drive like a seed after a long winter. With few prospects in Sacramento, he relocated to his childhood home of Portland, Oregon, where he would navigate more years of struggle yet find the means to finish *Ravenword and The House of the Red Death* and the hope to write other projects, including *Ravenword and The House of the Great Empyrean…*

www.ingramcontent.com/pod-product-compliance
Lightning Source LLC
Chambersburg PA
CBHW051541250626
47157CB00001B/135